Victory Colon

Praise for the Book

'I struggled to breathe as I read this novel—the calm beauty of the telling demanded my attention, there was the anxiety of the thriller, of the search for the brother, but what stayed with me long after I'd read it breathlessly was the tremulous but unwavering belief in human dignity. This book about the refugees of Victory Colony is one to be read and remembered.'

—Sumana Roy

'A touching portrayal of the aftermath of the Partition, this book, true to its name, is less about despair and defeat, and more about victory—about the resilience of the human spirit, its ability to rise again after falling. A compelling story, set against a Calcutta that's vividly depicted in the smallest of details.'

—Madhulika Liddle

'Bengal comes alive in all its sensory immediacy in Bhaswati Ghosh's novel. A sensitive love story, redolent of a period, set against a lost page of our history, India's 'other' Partition.'

—Neelum Saran Gour

'This classically structured novel, set in eastern India in the aftermath of partition, brings the past vividly to life, and tells tenderly of tragedy and hope, heartbreak and love, survival and resilience.'

—Namita Gokhale

Victory Colony, 1950

A Novel

BHASWATI GHOSH

YODAPRESS

YODA PRESS
79 Gulmohar Enclave
New Delhi 110 049
www.yodapress.co.in

ISBN: 978-93-82579-66-3

Editors in charge: Arpita Das and Tanya Singh
Typeset by R. Ajith Kumar
Printed at
Published by Arpita Das for YODA PRESS, New Delhi

'Our love is an inherited disease. Countries that grow by tossing us into the unknown.'

— MAHMOUD DARWISH, 'AND WE HAVE COUNTRIES'

For Ma

1

Amala felt nauseated. This wasn't the escape she had imagined when she left her village two days ago. A blast of foul breath mixed with the smell of sweat and urine hit her as she and Kartik got off the train on a sticky April day.

Before landing here, *melas* were the only place where she had seen so many people at once. But Sealdah station was no boisterous fair of her village. None of the loud cackle of her friends' laughter or hawkers bellowing their throats out to attract customers. Instead, there was swirling chaos—people boarding off trains, passengers pushing each other to catch trains, porters elbowing the crowds as they ferried luggage.

Amala's eyes caught a family of three, a couple and their infant, lying on the cold, hard platform, barely a few feet away from a latrine. The sleeping family, all three members wrapped in a single torn blanket, appeared to be oblivious to the fetid smell coming from the toilet. Or to the swarm of flies buzzing around them.

Beggars lurched in soiled loincloth. A few stray dogs scanned the platform for edible scraps. As she stood there clutching her brother's hand, Amala did not want to make sense of anything. If anything, she wished to lose consciousness in that instant. But it was Kartik's turn to faint. Amala could feel his grip slipping off her hand.

The sight of Kartik collapsing shook Amala out of her fogginess. She had to get her little brother something to eat, somehow. Although he wasn't awake, she said to him, 'Just sit here, Shona, I'll bring some food and water, *kaemon*? Don't move. I'll be back in a minute.' She dropped the bundle stuffed with their clothes next to where the boy sat and dashed ahead.

Outside the station, more crowds jostled, more hawkers hollered. Porters pestered potential customers until being told off. Amala saw a woman sitting on her haunches by the roadside, busy cooking a meal on a makeshift oven of three bricks. A few fat automobiles rolled by, and their honking stopped Amala in her tracks.

She had barely moved past the crowd when Amala hit the cart of a banana seller. The man, with a graying beard and *paan* spittle in his mouth, spat out the red-orange juice right next to her before yelling some abuses.

'*Duto kola diben go?* My brother is fainting,' Amala begged, hoping her plea for bananas would soften the man's ire allowing her to get some food for Kartik. But her entreaty only brought forth sharper expletives before the banana seller shoved his cart and stomped ahead.

About half a dozen attempts later, Amala had collected little more than a heap of scorn for daring to ask for food without showing any money first. She couldn't manage even a morsel for her little brother. As she recalled his face, dry and miserable from hunger, her stomach twisted into a knot. She darted back to the station.

When she reached the spot where she had left Kartik, Amala's feet hit against something soft. She looked down and saw her cloth bundle—untouched.

But even with her eyes wide open, she couldn't see Kartik anywhere.

2

Kartik's disappearance made Amala realise how utterly unprepared she had been, despite the unthinkable past two weeks, for this moment. She kicked the cloth bundle and howled. As she kept shouting her brother's name unintelligibly, a few policemen came up to her. The head of the pack banged the stick he held with his right hand to the ground with a thump so loud, it scared away a few of the platform mongrels. Resting his right palm over the stick while tending to the *bidi* in his mouth with the fingers of his left hand he said, '*Ei*, girl! Stop barking or you may have to give us a visit at the police station. Don't mind that, do you?'

The other constables guffawed and voiced their own suggestions: 'Outside the police station, too,' said one of them. Amala's howling transmuted into a whimper even as she scanned herself. Sure enough, her sari's end had loosened, revealing part of her right breast. It didn't matter that it rested under a blouse. The mere suggestion of flesh was meat enough for the policemen. Amala pulled her sari's *anchal* over her shoulder and lowered her glance. This made the cops laugh louder. Their mutterings grew in volume and coarseness.

As another constable stepped forward to join this gang, a group of young men appeared on the scene. One of them had in his hands the cloth bundle Amala had kicked not too long ago. Standing beside Amala, he placed the bundle near her and turned towards the *bidi*-smoking pack of policemen. Before they could ask what he was doing there, he pulled out a folded sheet of paper from his *kurta* pocket. 'My name is Manas Dutta,' he said. 'We are from the Gariahata Refugee Relief Centre. Please see this, sir; it has all the necessary approvals. Kindly allow us to take this lady to our centre; we are here to help you out with the refugees.'

The lead constable snatched the paper from the man's hand and skimmed over it while still gaping at Amala every few seconds. He returned the letter to Manas and hit the ground softly with his stick. 'The letter looks genuine,' he muttered. 'All right, you can take her, but we'll have to keep coming to your centre to check how well you are taking care of her, *hain?*' His belly bulged with laughter, becoming louder with the cackle of his comrades.

Manas only said, 'Of course, please come as you see fit' and turned to speak to Amala. As he picked up her bundle, the mini police brigade started moving to tackle 'more business'. Manas was glad to see their backs, more on behalf of the young woman who stood by his side. Little did he know that the policemen were the easier part of the equation. When he politely requested Amala to join him and his friends to go to the camp, she exploded. '*Kothao zamu na!* I won't go anywhere!'

She grabbed the cloth bundle from Manas's hands, taking care not to touch him. Her yelling, however, invited renewed attention from the policemen. Manas made Amala aware of this with a swift glance towards the constables. Amala quietened and agreed to follow Manas and his group.

A few quick questions helped Manas learn that since landing in Sealdah, Amala hadn't joined the queue that new refugees had to for receiving inoculation. *After all, these people aren't just 'pests' for the government, but also the potential carriers of pests. They need to be immunised against cholera and other deadly diseases before they become immune to the more sinister jokes that await them.* Manas shook his head in an attempt to get away from the gloom coming over him and advised his co-volunteers to look after some of the other refugees they had found. '*Ei je, ei dike ashun,*' he prodded Amala to follow him.

Noticing her hesitation, Manas said, 'It's nothing, we have to get you an injection for some diseases spreading around.'

Amala reluctantly followed him. Half an hour later, once she had been vaccinated against she knew not what, she had another hurdle to cross—the queue in front of the *Relief and Rehabilitation Office*—to receive her official stamping. The label that would mark her 'Refugee' and entitle her to accommodation in a relief centre. As she dragged her frame to join the new queue, Manas could tell she'd had enough for the day.

'This is the last one, I promise,' he said.

To Amala, the station now appeared like the crowded fish market in the town where Baba used to sell his catch. She kept turning her head back, looking for Kartik amidst the multitude of human faces floating about her. Noticing this, Manas said, 'Don't worry, the police won't trouble you. We are here to make sure of that.'

His assurance elicited nods from Subir, Proshanto, and Manik, the other volunteers as Manas introduced them to her. Amala's blank eyes offered no reaction; she just kept following the four young men, halting only when they did, to pick up other refugees.

Soon, the group grew bigger. And louder. More of her current ilk—father-less children dangling in their mothers' arms, widows—old and young, elderly couples and a few young men and women—now walked with Amala. The sound of her native tongue and the spontaneous association brought about by loss did little to break Amala's silence. She kept looking behind and as she turned around to look ahead, her eyes caught Manas glancing at her through the corner of his eyes. Amala immediately looked away.

After gathering about twenty refugees—enough for the small van hired for the purpose—the volunteers were ready to leave the station. Just then, near the exit, Manas saw a child, less than two years old, crawling on the platform floor. The toddler seemed to be without an adult. Manas scooped up the child and struggled to cradle him in his arms.

The little one, evidently in a good mood while crawling, turned belligerent at the stranger's touch. His muffled whimper intensified into loud wails, complete with the flailing of his arms and legs. Unable to manage the bawling bundle, Manas scampered over to Amala and pleaded with her, 'Please, hold this baby. He seems to have no one; we must take him with us. Will you please try to calm him?'

Amala shook her head vigorously to decline the suggestion but Manas still thrust the child into her arms. As she held the baby, Amala gently patted him on the back. She had barely stroked him a few times when a young, scruffy woman came charging, her eyes spewing fire. '*Chor kothakar*! Must have lost your son, *tai na*, so now you steal mine!'

It became clear to Manas that this woman was the toddler's mother. The baby himself was anything but perturbed at her aggression. His mother's scream must have sounded like a lullaby to him, going by the lunge he made to reach her bosom.

All through this chaos, Amala remained quiet. After the young mother dashed off with her son disregarding the volunteers' requests to join their group, Manas walked over to Amala. 'I am really sorry for that, didn't know it will....'

Before he could finish, Amala bolted ahead with the rest of the group. Manas lurched on with his head bent. Only when Subir addressed the refugees in a high-pitched voice asking them to form a line to board the van did Manas realise that they had reached their vehicle. As he saw the refugees boarding the van one by one, his eyes kept looking for a young woman in a pale green sari and a black blouse clutching a cloth bundle, the first member he recruited today.

No sooner had everyone—the refugees and the volunteers—crammed themselves inside the van and the driver was about to start the engine that Amala let out a shriek. A whirlwind swept through her mind. She could see her father cajoling her mother to accompany him on a fishing trip 'just this once'; Kartik laughing at the suggestion only to be rebuked by Amala; Ma finally yielding to Baba's persuasions; Amala taking Kartik to the house of the *bauls*; coming back to find a crowd in front of their house; the bodies of Baba and Ma, lying motionless on the ground.... As the images raced in her mind, a blackout galloped at Amala. Getting up from her seat, she rushed towards the van's door. Manas tried to stop her from attempting to fling open the locked door. Amala pushed the door harder.

'*Ei je*,' Manas called out, 'Don't do that, please. Here, sit down, you'll be fine.'

The words became meaningless in the face of Amala's fist-fight with the door. Subir and Manik came forward but failed to make Amala return to her seat. The scene turned even more melodramatic as some of the other female members of the refugee group tried to reason with the 'mad woman' with shrieking urgency.

When they all failed to calm her down, Manas opened the door lock and motioned for Amala to get down. He stepped out of the van, too, and gestured to his friends to wait. Before he could make another attempt to persuade Amala, a loudspeaker blared out from an open jeep, '*Anyone found loitering in the streets or sleeping on railway platforms without proper identity proof will be taken into police custody.*'

The announcement was in Bangla and although it sounded different from the tongue Amala spoke, its meaning was clear to her.

Manas looked at Amala and said, '*Cholun*,' as he directed her to climb up the vehicle.

She obliged without a word. Or fuss.

3

A soldier is condemned to live a war and a refugee, its aftermath. So while the second big war of the world has been fought, finished and somewhat forgotten, making a handful its financial beneficiaries and another fistful the controllers of its political equations, the soldiers' barracks still remain—vacant, ironclad, mocking their new occupants. Inside these barracks, where soldiers once rested and received orders for combat and attack, refugees will now have to fight their own battles—with no commander to steer them and no empire to honour their feats. And while I am not one of them, thank god for that, I, too, am condemned to witness their endless struggle.

— DIARY ENTRY, MANAS DUTTA, DECEMBER 1949

By the time they reached the camp, Amala had turned into an automaton. She followed the instructions parroted by the volunteers without thinking. The huts in the military barracks were crammed with other refugees. Several makeshift tents had been set up outside the covered area. Amala was asked to stay in a tent that already had an elderly couple. A single wooden table—a plank placed over wobbly legs and a couple of basic hospital stretchers—completed the furniture. Amala crouched with her bundle and sat down on the ground. She hardly noticed the other two people in the tent.

The elderly lady said, 'Ma, don't sit there on the ground, come here, you'll fall sick.'

Amala looked at her with a start and gestured a 'No, thanks' with her hand. As her eyes wandered around the camp, another flash hit Amala—her father's giant fish tank with fish of all different sizes and textures squabbling in water, desperate and powerless. That same scene played out before her now. Only people had replaced the fish—refugees scrambling to receive their daily dole of watery rice-lentil porridge. She felt queasy again.

The lady in Amala's tent, a little older than Ma perhaps, asked her to join them for lunch. She turned down the request with a feeble smile. There was no escaping the ration though; a bunch of volunteers making rounds of the tents urged her to go and eat. They would be in trouble if she didn't. Amala slapped her forehead and got up. This is how long it took for her to become another fish in the dirty tank. A few hours.

Taking the aluminium bowl of porridge doled out to her, Amala went to sit at the end of a line of squatting refugees eating their fill. She had barely gulped the second or third morsel when she began throwing up. Manas, who had been keeping an eye on her from the serving table, came running. Pulling out his handkerchief, he held it out to her. She wiped her face and Manas offered his hand to help her stand up. The defenceless fish obliged.

Ignoring curious glances, Manas gently held Amala's hand and led her to her tent. The beads of sweat trickling down Amala's forehead weren't a good sign. Something was amiss with her. And it wasn't just physical. 'Here, lie down,' he said, adding, 'I will bring you some medicine, you'll be fine.' With that he left the tent.

A few minutes later, he returned with Proshanto, who carried a rumpled bed sheet and a rolled-up straw mat. Manas himself carried a bottle of water, another small bottle of medicine and a spoon. They found Amala lying down, her eyes closed, her body stolid. The elderly couple had returned too.

Manas whispered to the lady, 'Mashi, she needs to drink the medicine.'

Malati only had to stroke Amala's forehead softly to have her open her eyes. 'Here, sit up for a minute, Ma,' she said.

Manas followed with, 'Drink this, it's *joaaner arok*, will make you feel better.' Amala sat up like an obedient child and swallowed the spoonful of bitter liquid that Manas eased into her mouth. The next moment, she grabbed the bottle of water, now in Proshanto's hands, and poured half of it down her gullet. Handing the bottle back to Proshanto, she lay down. Proshanto spread the sheet over her.

On their way out, Manas thanked Malati and her husband, Nimaichand. 'We are trying to get another bed arranged for you. Meanwhile, please use this mat,' he said to them.

The elderly man remained quiet, but his wife said, 'We don't need another bed, Baba. *Benche thako;* may you live long, my sons.'

Most volunteers usually left the camp once lunch was over. A couple of them would stay behind to respond to any emergencies and to prevent the occasional altercations that broke out among the refugees. As a leader, Manas had the privilege of taking most of his afternoons off. He returned in the evenings for a few hours. Right now, though, he thought of remaining at the camp.

Raghu, an eighteen-year-old volunteer seemed to have read Manas's mind. He said, 'Dada, go home. I will make sure the new Didibhai is fine and has no trouble.'

Manas tapped Raghu's head and smiled, 'Okay. *Dekhish*, don't forget all the other didibhais and grandparents, all right?'

'Sure, Dada,' Raghu confirmed with a grin.

Manas was grateful to get rest, brief as it was. More than his body, his mind needed it. The April sun shot through the fabric of his shirt to sear his skin. The city had submitted to its ritual siesta. While walking towards the rickshaw stand, Manas looked at the downed shutters of Mahalakshmi Mishtanna Bhandar, the local sweet shop that had a cloud of flies feasting around its base.

Down a few more shops, a stray dog had curled itself under the shade of the tin roof of Protima Sari Kendra. The cawing of a lone crow broke Manas's meditation, only to add to its melancholy. At a short distance, the rickshaw stand looked bare. The tram station was further ahead and Manas decided if he could walk that far, he might as well drag himself to his house. He regretted not carrying an umbrella to beat the heat; he seldom did when it wasn't raining.

Hunger pangs got the better of him and Manas reached for the small packet of roasted chickpeas in his trouser pocket. The empty streets belied the uncomfortable burden they were bearing of late. Every day, new batches of refugees spilled into the city like sugar falling off a torn sack. Calcutta seemed to be bursting at its seams and its denizens weren't happy about it. The voice of resistance was still mellow like the throaty warnings of a police officer before he launched into an offensive. Manas feared it wouldn't remain suppressed for too long. No matter how much the *bhadralok* class prided itself on its liberal outlook, it couldn't accept the city filling up with street asylums.

Once past the tram station, Manas spotted a rickshaw behind a Krishnachura tree covered in a blaze of crimson clusters. He drew closer and found the driver sleeping on the seat. Manas didn't want to wake up the old man but his limbs were giving way. He waited another minute, then nudged the rickshaw-wallah. The man got up with a start and on seeing Manas, immediately started wiping the seat with his cotton *gamchha*.

'*Ballygunge jabey?*' Manas asked him.

'*Jabo, Babu, jabo toh,*' the driver replied with a quick jerk of his head.

Despite the short distance left to cover, Manas was happy to be transported home. The old man pulled the rickshaw with his bony hands, gnarled veins visible all over it. '*Teen taka lagbey, Babu,*' he said.

'*Achchha,*' Manas said. It wouldn't hurt him to pay an extra rupee. He usually did so anyway; it made the rickshaw-pullers happy and kept his conscience a little less saddled.

It was 3.30 in the afternoon, way past his lunch time. Manas sighed at the thought of facing his mother's court-martial. To his surprise, it went rather smoothly. Her fire melted the moment he narrated his plight of walking almost all the way to home. The light fish curry with *potol*, his favourite summertime vegetable, and the roasted yellow lentil curry restored his energy.

The sun's fury had subsided by the time Manas got down at the tram station in Kalighat to return to the camp. Rickshaws were easy to find this time around; with the end of the siesta hour, the city had hobbled back on its limbs. Manas sat down on a rickshaw and opened the dog-eared page of his latest reading companion, Dostoyevsky's *Crime and Punishment*, borrowed from the home library. The plot was engrossing enough and Manas marvelled at the author's ability to capture a criminal's internal drama. *The action inside one's head is no less power-packed.* Despite its dark undertone, the novel was his antidote to the despondency he experienced on a daily basis.

At the camp, Manas headed straight to the kitchen to oversee the preparation of the evening meal. He had entrusted himself with this responsibility to ensure the gruel served to the refugees was cooked hygienically, even if it tasted like sand.

Raghu and the other volunteers came to say their goodbyes. Manas patted their backs and waited for them to leave the camp before walking towards the tent that had been on his mind since he left in the afternoon. He had timed it carefully; this was the hour when the elderly couple would move inside one of the barracks to spend time with their village folks before dinner.

Manas entered the tent with a lantern. Amala was sitting on her haunches on the stretcher her sickness had allotted to her. Manas placed the lantern on the floor and uttered the words he had practised before coming. '*Kaemon achhen?*'

'I am all right,' Amala said.

'Did you eat anything...I mean, afterwards?'

Amala shook her head to say 'No.'

'Aren't you hungry?'

Amala suggested a 'No,' again with her head.

'Hmm, you need to eat something. If you fall sick, there will be trouble all around. Here, have this,' Manas said and took out a small packet of puffed rice from the handbag he carried. Tearing it open, he held it before her. Amala took a handful and started nibbling, still abstracted.

Glad to see the ice breaking, Manas kept the *muri* packet next to her and said, 'All of this is for you.'

He then poured water in a steel glass from an aluminium can nearby and held it as she continued to chew on the *muri* with the same faraway look.

'*Ek* minute,' Manas sought her permission to be back in a minute. As with most of the conversation, he didn't receive any response.

Manas returned with a chair and placed it so he could face Amala in the flicker of the lantern. Her face remained a profile, even as he sat down and made it clear that he wasn't in a hurry to leave.

'*Ki holo*, why aren't you eating the *muri*?' he asked.

'I'm not hungry.'

'It's only *muri*, won't stuff you up. And it's good for your heartburn too. I'm sure you know that already.'

Amala hugged her raised knees tighter and buried her chin in the hollow of her arms.

'Okay, you don't have to eat. But you can at least speak with me, can't you?'

'What is there to talk,' Amala said.

'Well, I know nothing about you, apart from your name. Malati Mashi, who shares this tent with you, tells me stories about her village, her life there, her....'

'What village, *ha*?' Amala's head automatically turned towards Manas as she snapped. 'Do I have any village, Babu? What stories do you want to hear? Why? To see if my mouth bleeds when I tell them? Or so you can feel happy it's not your story?'

Manas lowered his head and remained silent for a while. Then he said, 'Not stories, Amala. I only want to know about you. I'm here to help, not harm. Just to let you know, my name is Manas. Manas Dutta. And you may ask me anything you like.'

As the darkness grew, so did the menace of mosquitoes. Manas martyred a few between his palms with grunts of 'Uff' and 'Eesh'.

A dull smoke joined the parasites and made the air thicker. A few minutes went by before Amala's voice broke. Not into a shriek this time but a murmur. '*Shob toh chole gaelo*. Everything is lost.'

Welcoming the possibility of a conversation Manas said, 'I really don't have any words to make you feel better. The one thing I can promise you is my friendship.'

A snicker escaped Amala's lips. 'You look like a good man, Babu, but I won't trust anyone that easily. Nah, nah, not anymore.'

Manas swallowed a sigh and said, 'Fine. You don't have to trust me. Or anyone. But we can still talk, can't we?'

'What do you want to know?'

'Well, a little about where you come from, who all are there in your family, where they....'

'Father, mother, and a little brother...all gone,' Amala cut him short.

'Do you want to look for them? We can help....'

This drew a roar of laughter from Amala, more vicious than funny.

'Babu, you'll have to go there,' she said, pointing her finger up, still laughing.

Manas's head unconsciously turned upwards even as he said, 'I am truly sorry, Amala....'

'*Bari* Barisal. Or that's where home used to be.'

'Did any of your village people come with you?'

Amala shook her head. 'No.'

Manas picked up the packet and took out a handful of puffed rice. He passed the packet to Amala. '*Ei je*, have some.'

Between the crunch of *muri*, some more ice melted, a little more weight was unburdened.

'Babu, how many days do we have to stay here? Forever? And after that? Will we get a chance to go home?' Then as if to nix her illusion, she tapped herself on her forehead and said, 'What home, *haan*? What home?'

'I don't have the answers to all of your questions right now, Amala,' Manas said. 'But I do know that you won't have to live here forever. The government is working to make sure of that.'

'They took away all of my family. Why not me? What good is it for me to be here, like a dead stone?'

'So I can pick your brains and you can eat *muri* with me. And see me sending some mosquitoes to heaven.' Manas said, inviting, at last, a light chortle from Amala.

As dinner time drew closer, Manas got up. 'Please eat properly now,' he told Amala. 'You hardly seem to have eaten anything for days. Eat well and don't worry. I'll have more medicine sent.' He folded the chair and said '*Ashi*,' ready to take leave.

Amala packed her fist with some *muri* and said, 'Here, your packet.'

'That's for you. I already ate from your share,' Manas said with a smile before merging into the darkness.

'How many days do we have to stay here? Forever? And after that? Will we get a chance to go home?' When she asked those questions, I put them to rest with a vague reply. Because those are my questions too. And I have no answers. So many people have been left without anywhere to go. God knows how many more are to come. All of them had a home, a patch of land, cows and hens to call their own. Now all they possess are small bundles of clothes and a few utensils if they are lucky. Oh and the flesh and bones on their bodies. That's about it, for they have even lost the dignity of being a human. I don't understand why this was necessary to gain freedom. I won't be with them forever, but misfortune will not leave them any time soon— that I am certain of.

— DIARY ENTRY, MANAS DUTTA, 16 DECEMBER 1949

4

'Wha-t, what is it?' Manas struggled to look beyond the mosquito net encircling him.

'It's time to get up, Maanu,' Mrinmoyee said. Her face remained a blur to Manas.

'I want you to take me to Kalighat today,' she continued.

'Oh, it's you,' Manas said, gulping a yawn. 'You know I have classes....'

'On a Sunday? I didn't know that,' Mrinmoyee said with a chuckle. 'Enough now, get up, take a shower and get dressed to come with me.'

Manas bit his tongue without sticking it out. He needed to think of something else, and quickly. 'I forgot. We have a study circle meeting today. At Jayanta's house. Don't think I have time to eat breakfast. What time is it?' He flung aside the mosquito net and stormed out of the bed without waiting for a response from his mother.

An hour later, Manas was at the camp. It took him twice the usual time as fewer trams plied on Sundays. He ran into Manik at the entrance. When Manik told him he had stopped by their house so they could come together, Manas was mildly alarmed. 'Did you meet Ma?'

'Yes, she said you'd already left,' Manik said.

'And you told her we were coming to the camp?'

'Yes, why? You think....'

'*Na, kichhuna.* Did she say anything?'

'No, just that you had already left. I'm sorry, Manas-da, if I....'

'No worries, brother,' Manas said, patting Manik on the

shoulder. 'Let's get going—lots to do today.' To himself, he said, *Whatever. Good for her. It's time she got used to the fact that my work here is more important than chaperoning her to the temple.*

Manas's eyes travelled to the camp's periphery. The lengthening queue of refugees outside took him back to his school's physical training and march-past drills. For him, someone who didn't care much for athletics, such discipline-enforcing activities were 'unnecessary evils'. Now, as he looked at the serpentine stretch the refugees were coiling into, those school drills suddenly lost their vileness.

The scale of migration told Manas he wasn't going to be done with volunteering at the camp anytime soon. But a long-term commitment wouldn't be possible for his friends; they didn't have the luxury of living off their family fortune. Proshanto had already mentioned his father's retirement, only a few months away.

The surly behaviour of the government officials in charge of dealing with the refugees didn't escape Manas either. One could hardly blame them. As if shrinking space, inadequate food rations, and the lack of clean drinking water weren't hassle enough, they also had to deal with the looming threat of disease and malnutrition. Occasional outbursts from the refugees didn't make their job any easier.

Within the space of a few months, Manas had seen the beast of a split nation turn into a monster with an endless pit for its stomach. He could smell death that had clawed its way into the camp, wearing the garb of cholera and protein malnutrition. It clearly liked children more. Even in death, the refugees were robbed of the dignity of a decent farewell. He and his friends watched mutely when tiny corpses were flung into a nearby forest for wild animals to feast on.

One morning while taking an inventory of items, Manas recalled the face of a young mother who had arrived a few days ago. No older than twenty herself, she had been left with an infant son. Manas had learned from the people she came with that her husband had been killed before her eyes during riots in their village. She made it to this side thanks to fellow villagers who thought of bringing her along. *Otherwise, the young woman would have perished on her own, without anyone having to kill her.* Manas shuddered as her face flashed in his mind.

He remembered being appalled by her hysterical behaviour the very first time he saw her. Her meanderings around the camp made it clear that she had lost her bearings. Perhaps anybody who witnessed her husband's throat being slashed with a dagger would. *If only memories could be slashed, too.* More alarming was the fact that Urmila, the young widow, didn't seem concerned in the least about her toddler. Any time he cried from hunger, she slapped him hard on his cheeks, which only increased the baby's bawling.

Manas and his friends were quick to see the futility of counselling the mother. The raw force of tragedy had left her too wounded for her to heal soon. Her frail child, however, needed immediate attention. Manas struggled to think of a solution. There was no way Urmila could be separated from her son, even if it ensured better care for the little one. He wondered if a more responsible camp member could help with the situation.

The good news was that funds had been sanctioned for a hundred millilitre of milk for every child under the age of nine.

～

Three months without Kartik, each day a shrapnel that singed Amala with restless anger. Finding her brother seemed less and less possible with each passing day. She looked closely at the face of every new male refugee—boys, young and old men—entering the camp. Every day, she thought of new plans to find Kartik—all her imagined missions began and ended at the Sealdah station. Besides the camp, that was the only place she had set foot in, in this crazy, endless city. And she had no idea how to make her way back to the station. It seemed like such a long and winding journey.

Three months were all it had taken for her to get used to the camp routine. Her day started with the morning wake-up call at seven for a daily head count. A refugee officer and a volunteer would conduct the 'roll call'. There wasn't any official provision for breakfast; the government provided one meal a day: the afternoon rice gruel. The volunteers pooled money to arrange for each camp member to have a packet of puffed rice and a few *batashas*, candied half- moons, every morning.

Post-breakfast, all able-bodied refugees had to contribute labour—cleaning the premises, washing utensils, filling up buckets of water from hand pumps and other sundry chores—to keep the camp machine running.

For Amala, this regimen came as a godsend; she felt relieved to find herself useful to do anything at all. *The more to do, the less time to think.* Her readiness to shoulder other camp members' responsibilities didn't translate into that many bonds of friendship. Friendly overtures from other women campers met with her cold, almost ruthless indifference. Even with Malati, with whom she shared a good relationship, she wasn't ready to get past the general courtesies.

Yet, she made the acquaintance of another camp member one afternoon. Amala overheard Minoti, a girl of fifteen, say something to Paban-da, her village brother, which caught her ears. They were in the line for the afternoon gruel, and Amala heard Minoti utter the words 'Sealdah'. As she sat down to eat, she kept her eye on Minoti, engrossed in her conversation with Paban. When she saw Minoti scooping up the last morsel of *khichuri* from her plate, Amala gulped the food off her plate and got up.

In the swirl of people who gathered to wash their hands with the sanctioned half a mug of water that a volunteer poured from a bucket, Amala lost sight of Minoti. But she knew where her tent was. Luckily, she found Minoti alone; the rest of her tent sharers hadn't yet returned from lunch.

'Oh, Sealdah. Nah, it's nothing, Didi. We were just chatting,' Minoti said.

'Please, *Bon*, tell me. I need your help. I...need to get to the station. Can you help me?'

The curves of suspicion Minoti's eyes held only a moment ago dissolved slowly as Amala shared her desperate story to visit the station, even though she replaced Kartik with a 'village uncle' who had accompanied her and got separated before she was brought to the camp.

A kitten interrupted their conversation with its meows and Minoti went deeper inside the tent to fetch a bowl of water. When she returned, a few pieces of crushed *batasha* floated on it. Minoti placed the bowl before the kitten and resumed talking to Amala. A few sips later when the tiny animal meowed again and looked up at her, Minoti picked up 'Mini', a stray they had 'found outside' their tent one morning. They walked over to a clearing behind the tents. A blast of soot and dust hit Amala. She clumped together a part of her *anchal* and covered her nose with it. Minoti patted the kitten and relayed the plan. She was expecting her mother and sister to arrive from Kumilla in a couple of weeks' time. She had only received the news a day earlier and shared it with no one other than Paban who would take her to the station. She wanted to go so they didn't get taken away to a different camp.

'But, Didi, we need to make sure even the wind doesn't get wind of this.'

'Ha, ha, don't worry, *Bon*,' Amala said. 'But your Mini knows.'

Minoti stroked the now-drowsy kitten's head and said, 'She's good with secrets. I've shared a few with her.'

~

As she sat untangling the knotted mess of her hair along with a jumble of thoughts, Amala saw Manas approaching her tent. It was late evening and the stars hid behind a sultry cloud. Manik accompanied Manas. It struck her that she no longer felt agitated at the sight of Manas or his friends. She had learned to distinguish them from the government officials. As they drew closer, both joining their palms to gesture a 'Namaskar', she offered a hint of a smile in return.

'*Ashun*,' she said, inviting them in.

The volunteers entered the tent and sat down on a bench. Amala noticed a file in Manas's hand.

As he browsed through it, rolling up the sleeves of his shirt, Manas asked Amala, 'Can I have some water?'

Amala stopped combing her hair and poured them a glass of water each.

Sipping from his glass, Manik got to the point. 'Amala-di,' he began, 'we came to request a favour from you.'

'Oh,' Amala said without hiding her curiosity.

'You see, in tent number 34, there's this lady called Urmila Debi. I'm not sure if you know her; she arrived only a week ago. Lost her husband in the riots.' Manik stopped speaking, hoping Manas would reveal the rest of the plan. That didn't happen.

'What about her? Does she need any help?' Amala asked.

Catching the drift, Manas said, 'Yes...well...I mean not she herself, but her little baby.'

'She has a child?' Amala asked.

'Yes, a little more than a year old.'

'What does the baby need? And what can *I* do about this?'

'Well, you see,' Manas said, 'Urmila is in a shock because of her loss. She's unable to look after the child, to feed him....'

A chuckle escaped Amala's lips. 'What do you see in my face that makes you thrust babies at me? Remember what happened at the station, Babu?'

Manas hadn't forgotten that unpleasant episode and had come prepared. 'I promise that won't happen here. Trust me, Urmila will be only too happy to see her child being cared for. Right now, she isn't in a state to do that.'

Amala found it hard to imagine herself mothering a baby. Yes, she had been like a parent to Kartik many times but that was different. Despite her maternal petting, they still fought for the better piece of fish and the choicest slices of mangoes. They accused their parents of showering more love on the other sibling and didn't let go of any opportunity to complain against each other.

With her head bent, Amala tried to form a response. 'Umm, I'm not so sure. Trouble, it's just trouble....' A long, dry sigh trailed her words.

'Amala-di,' Manik said, 'don't bother yourself too much. It's totally up to you. If you can't, no worries.'

His sincere manner helped. Amala straightened her chin up and said to him, '*Bhai*, give me at least a day. I will let you know by tomorrow afternoon....'

'Sure, Didi,' he said, adding, 'you can take longer if you wish.'

'*Aaj tawbey ashi*, Amala,' Manas said, asking to take her leave. Amala held up a *namaskar* and said, '*Ashun*.'

∼

As the food rations dwindled, Manas saw malnutrition become an active verb walking around the camp. Frail, near flesh-less human frames, groaned and cursed. Those who couldn't moan or curse just cried. These were mostly children. The curtailed supplies also caused squabbles among camp members. Women scrambled for the last squeeze of the *khichuri* that dropped off the ladles and didn't spare a volunteer if the person standing before them in the queue received even half a spoonful more of the gruel. And yet, despite such bickering over the belly's fire, it amazed Manas to see how admirably civil the camp atmosphere remained.

As he looked at the camp dwellers every evening, chatting away, their banter spilling with laughter, looking after fellow camp members' children, letting the kids play with each other, Manas wondered if like Malnutrition that prowled through the camp, it was actually Hunger that quibbled and screamed during the lunch distribution. He didn't want to make too much of it though. *The behavioural paradox might be a good subject for psychologists.* As for himself, he was glad to collect even scraps of colour and light in the camp's mostly grey-black environment. These scraps kept him buoyed in planning for people who still dared to laugh while possessing nothing. Rehabilitation seemed too distant a goal to Manas at this time, when even relief was failing.

As he took out a flashlight from his bag to make his way out of the camp, Manas smiled at the irony of it all: while the refugees' future remained in his mind like a stray cat refusing to leave the house that fed it milk, the destitute themselves remained fiercely entrenched to their rootless present. Their lives seemed to cloister around their haphazard fates. And that was just right, too. The very fact that these men and women didn't look beyond what each day brought helped them survive what was essentially an unlivable life.

The vapid sameness of the camp mornings exhausted Manas. Cries of children overtook the cawing of crows, waking up the parents to run for their ablutions. Toilet meant a hole dug in the ground that lay about 200 metres from the camp. A makeshift thatched wall surrounded it. Three such toilets had been dug up. The refugees had to bring their own water and take turns to get through this morning routine, an ordeal on the best of days. Manas avoided those spots like the plague; the stench choked him.

Once the adults were back in their tents, the roll call began. Soon after, young mothers scampered to collect milk for their children in the aluminium mugs they had been given. This morning, Manas managed the office while Manik and Subir were busy distributing the milk.

By the time Urmila held out her mug, Subir had run out of milk in the bucket. To refill it, he started cutting open a packet of milk, only to see it slip into the bucket, triggered by Urmila's loud wail. Manas tried to imagine the scene as Manik described it to him minutes later. With bloodshot eyes, Urmila clutched her son and beat her forehead with the aluminium mug. Her outburst caused her son to bawl, turning the routine morning exercise into a spectacle. Manik and some of the refugees tried to calm Urmila down but she screamed even louder, pointing to the pair of scissors in Subir's hand, 'Leave him, Babu, don't kill, don't Babu, I beg....'

The moment he realised the scissors were the source of the trouble, Subir put them aside and held up his empty palms to say, 'See, Didibhai, it's gone. No harm done.'

The assurance arrived a little too late though. Urmila continued hitting her forehead with the mug even as her tears flowed unabated. When all efforts to soothe her failed, Manik gestured to a couple of other women in the queue to give him a hand to help move Urmila. They pulled her aside gently as Manik assured her, 'Everything is fine, don't worry. We are all your brothers here, Didi.'

Manas was anything but surprised. A sound of alarm marked his response, 'Nah, Manik, we can't let this continue. Her child will die of hunger if this goes on.'

As Manas darted out of the office room, Manik asked, 'Shall I come with you?' Manas nodded a 'yes'.

When they stood outside Amala's tent a couple of minutes later, she was nibbling on puffed rice and sugar candy. Manas asked her permission to enter. She gestured them both in but neither of the volunteers bothered to take a seat.

Manas came straight to the point. 'Amala, you have to help us out this one time. Please.'

Putting aside her breakfast bowl, Amala poured some water for herself, then offered the bottle to Manas, '*Jol*, Babu. You're out of breath.'

'Thanks,' Manas said, taking the bottle. 'Urmila isn't quite stable yet. I fear for her child. I couldn't wait until this afternoon for your response.'

'Tczhk,' Amala rubbed her tongue against the roof of her mouth, a sound of frustration. Bending her head, she said in a muted tone, 'If there's no way at all, then....'

Her response, clearly reluctant, relieved Manas. He had to hold back a smile as Manik said to Amala, 'Didibhai, you have saved not only that child, but also our worries. *Onek dhonnobad.* Really, Didibhai.'

'Don't get so excited, Bhai,' Amala cautioned. 'Let's see if I can actually do what you want me to.'

'I know you can, Amala,' Manas said, 'I have faith in you.' On his way out, he gestured a casual salute instead of the usual *namaskar*.

Amala felt like having a little talk with herself. The anticipation of Urmila's reaction frightened her. Accounts of her explosive temper helped little. Amala also wondered what made Manas put little babies in her lap with such confidence. Was it just an impulsive response to the circumstances? Or was there more to it?

She smiled self-consciously as the earliest brush of her motherliness surfaced in her mind. She was just seven when Kartik was born. As her mother recuperated from the anemia that had depleted her body since she became pregnant with Kartik, Amala was thrilled to finally have a living doll—one that moved, licked, raised hell, and dazzled with smiles like a blooming bud— in place of the rag dolls her mother made her.

Amala's joy would spill alongside milk from the pan on the earthen stove as she helped Baba prepare meals and bathe little 'Kaattik'. Slathering the wool-soft baby with mustard oil was the favourite part of her job. Ma did get better in two months, but the seven-year-old big sister refused to relinquish her self-entrusted maternal duties.

'*Aar chinta nai*; no need to worry,' Subimal would say to Sumitra. 'Kaattik is in good hands now.'

When he was a year old, the baby started muttering in a language no one understood but everyone loved to hear. Amala became more and more possessive of this bundle of entertainment. When Kartik was around three and prattled away the funniest of sentences everyone 'understood' but didn't find much meaning in, Amala would take him around the neighbourhood in her arms, only to plonk him down when she couldn't bear his plump little frame any longer. This delighted Kartik more than it offended him. He would start waddling as quickly as his feet allowed him to, only to be reined in by Didi who wouldn't let her grip on him ease for as long as they walked together.

One time, Amala took Kartik to Husna's house, where her

friends gathered for late-afternoon huddles. They were playing *Ghuntikhela* and sat in a circle. Each player had to throw five pebbles on the ground. None of the pebbles were supposed to touch each other upon hitting the ground. The player had to pick one pebble, and while flipping it in the air, pick up another one from the ground; this had to be repeated, with two pebbles at a time and so on. The process would then be reversed and a series of complex challenges had to be completed. Whoever managed to complete the most would be the winner.

Although Amala was a champion pebble thrower and picker, her performance lapsed that afternoon. As she put him down beside her, Kartik's tiny fingers raced to pick up the pebbles the moment Amala dropped them on the ground. Despite repeated censure from his sister and cajoling by her friends, Kartik couldn't keep his fingers off the shiny pebbles. Amala gave up in frustration; her friends broke into peals of laughter.

In summer months, the girls indulged in their favourite treat after the game. One of them would bring a bowl of raw mango slices to be savoured with mustard oil, chili powder and salt. The girls vied with each other to grab the bigger pieces. When the refreshing scent of the tender, green mango mingled with the pungent smell of the mustard oil, Amala forgot all annoyances and forgave everyone, including her devil brother. She would give him tiny bits of the mango, taking care he didn't choke.

The scent of unripe mango lingered in Amala's mind when a government officer doing his rounds of the camp approached her. He had a pudgy build, no more than five feet two, and sported a handlebar mustache that appeared rather incongruous with his overall appearance. His thunderous call, which matched his fleshy fingers twirling one end of his mustache, shook Amala. The man reminded her that she had to get to her chores for the day: filling water from the hand pump and helping cook the day's lunch.

'Hey there, you, we're getting late! Let's get going,' he shouted.

Amala didn't look at him. She kept sitting, looking sideways.

The officer cleared his throat and spoke louder, 'Here, lady, I am talking to you, are you listening?'

Amala moved her head towards him and nodded.

'Don't waste your time sitting here. Get going; there's plenty to do.'

'Can you please relieve me of my morning duty today? I'll be there to cook lunch,' Amala said, wiping a tear at the corner of her eye with her sari's end.

'Look, this is what I don't like about you people. You've been here for so long, the government is providing for you from its own pocket, and you don't like to work.'

'It's not that, Babu,' Amala said, 'I am not feeling too well today.'

'Why? Are your legs breaking?' He said.

'No, *mon kharap*,' Amala said.

'Feeling sad!' The officer roared, 'And that's what you call being unwell? My God, the nerve of these people!'

As he raised his voice, a small crowd, mostly of refugee women, gathered around the officer. He looked at them and said, 'Look, look how your dear sister is behaving. She wants to be off duty today because of sadness. I should expect more of you to feel sad tomorrow, shouldn't I?'

He spared no time in reminding Amala and everyone else that failing to do their duty could lead to them being expelled from the camp.

This set off a whispering stir among the crowd. Soon the voices grew louder. 'Ah, how convenient for her to take time off like that. Is this her father's home that she can just sit and relax while we all work?' said one woman.

'You're right,' said Mokkhoda, an older woman, twisting the *paan* in her mouth. 'Must be her father's precious princess.'

Amala couldn't take it anymore. She stood up and said in a loud voice choked with tears, 'Yes, I said I want the morning off. Why can't I be left alone for a few hours? So you will kick me out, Babu? You think that scares me? Ha, ha, ha,' she laughed viciously. 'What do I have that I will lose?'

Manas heard Amala's protest in the nearby office tent where he sat crunching numbers. Subir sat on a chair next to him, updating him with data. The moment Manas heard Amala scream, he got up to get a closer view of the scene. He returned to his seat almost immediately. *Subir's irreverent style would be more fitting for the officer.*

'Hey, Subir, do you mind checking what's going on there?' He asked.

'What do you want me to do?' Subir asked.

'Just talk to the gentleman and calm the women around him. You can speak to Amala when they're gone.'

Though he didn't go, Manas kept an eye on the scene. The situation had already cooled down a bit when Subir reached the spot. Amala stood quiet yet resolute, her arms folded, looking away from the officer. Some of the refugee women, when they saw Subir, moved away. The officer took out a cigarette from his pocket. After lighting it, he offered a smoke to Subir.

Subir waved his hand to indicate a 'No'.

'Any trouble here, Mr Sen?' He asked the officer.

'Nah, nothing much. This is to be expected when hordes are brought in and fed on government dole, you see.'

'Why, what happened?' Subir asked, feigning total ignorance, looking at Amala from the corner of his eye.

'*Arrey*, this woman here,' he said, pointing to Amala with a move of his head and a pouting face. 'She's asking to be relieved of her day's duty. What for? Because she's feeling saa-ad. Ahh, what a pitiful situation,' he said with such sing-song melodrama that Subir had trouble restraining his laughter.

'Oh, *ei byapaar?* That's easily solved,' said Subir with a swagger that took the officer by surprise.

Subir continued, 'No way can she be relieved just like that. There's something called discipline, after all,' he said, casting a quick wink at Amala, who looked at him with disbelief.

'Here, Didimoni, you'll have to come with me,' Subir said to Amala. He assured Mr Sen that the lady won't be allowed the luxury of wallowing in heartsickness.

'Hmm, are you sure? She looks pretty stubborn to me,' said Mr Sen, as he crushed the butt of the cigarette under his foot.

'Oh, don't you worry, sir. I will make sure she carries out her duties. No free dole here, she must realise.'

His words had the desired impact not only on Mr Sen but also the handful of women still standing, waiting for the spectacle to reach its finale. Turning towards them, Subir said, 'Didimonis, you too must get to work. As you can see, we've already lost half an hour.'

When they had dispersed, Subir looked at Amala and said, '*Ashun.*' She followed him without any argument.

They reached the tent where Manas sat. He was caught unawares by Amala's arrival but didn't show it. 'Please sit,' he said, motioning her to the chair on which Subir had been sitting before.

Subir excused himself as he had to get a fresh batch of medicines for the camp.

'Give me a few minutes,' Manas said to Amala, 'I will finish this and talk to you.'

Amala wrung her hands in silence as if she were a culprit who had been brought to the court. *That Kartik! Always gets me in trouble.*

Manas shook his head as he closed the register. 'Calculations are pure trouble, I tell you. There's nothing I hate more than working with numbers.'

Amala still wore a look of abashment and kept wringing her hands.

'Are you all right? What were you upset about?' Manas asked.

This was just what Amala had feared. Now the court martial would lead to unnecessary complexities. 'I promise this won't happen again. It was a mistake,' she said.

Chuckling at her apology, Manas said, 'Here, look at me. You're not before a headmaster that you have to keep your head bent like that. I just want to know what happened; I won't scold you.'

Amala did indeed feel like a truant student who had received a reprieve from the headmaster. She summarised for Manas her exchange with the government officer, careful not to mention the cause of her melancholic attack.

'Oh, I see,' Manas said, rolling up his shirt sleeves, 'I understand. But you see, in a big camp like this, one person's genuine request can lead to ten fake ones. That becomes a problem for Mr Sen and his colleagues. You get that, don't you?'

The gentleness of Manas's tone made Amala even more miserable. She repeated her promise to behave in the future.

'I trust you. I was just trying to make you see why Mr Sen reacted the way he did. You must not take it personally,' Manas said.

Subir returned to the tent with the stock of medicines and tea in three earthen cups perched on a steel plate. He placed the improvised tray on the table and pulled a stool from inside the tent. Manas smiled at the sight of both the tea and Subir. His presence would perhaps put Amala at ease.

As they sipped the over-boiled, sugary tea, Manas's eyes wandered across the camp to nearby tents. A puddle created by the last two days' rain attracted three toddlers who dipped their little hands into the muddy water and smeared themselves and their pals with the sludge. Their grandfathers, too frail to engage in anything constructive either lay on cots or just sat with an empty look on their faces. *At least their naivete allows the children to be oblivious of their future, no matter how muddled and mired it is.*

Sipping the last of his tea, Manas turned his attention back to Amala. Clearing his throat, he said, 'If it's not too personal, may I ask what kept you busy back home? Besides all your daily chores, of course.'

Amala wasn't expecting the question and took a few seconds to answer. 'Nothing that useful,' she said.

'Still, let's hear it.'

'Well, we girls used to play, pick mangoes during summers, do *bratas* (fasts) and pujas every Monday....'

'For a handsome husband,' Subir said with a slight chortle.

Manas noticed Amala's embarrassment as she started coiling her sari's end around her index finger. 'Ah, Subir, let her speak. Your jokes can wait.' He gestured at Amala to continue.

'I also liked to cook and sew.'

'Sew? What did you sew?'

'*Kanthas* and baby clothes for my bro....'

She stopped at this point, uncomfortable with continuing the conversation.

Judging it best not to end the discussion, Manas said, 'Did you also knit?'

'Yes,' Amala replied unconsciously, 'Yes, I learned a bit from my mother and Manada Mashi, our neighbour.'

'Excellent.'

'Why?'

'Well you are so *guni* for one. I have little talent for any of the things you just talked about, except, maybe, playing with friends.'

Manas's comment brought out ripples of laughter from Subir. Amala joined him too, in softer tones.

'But more seriously,' Manas said, 'You can perhaps teach sewing to some of the younger girls in the camp. What do you think?'

'Me, teach? I only know simple sewing, not any of those beautiful patterns you get in shops.'

'That will be enough. Just look at those kids,' Manas said, pointing towards the puddle-hopping toddlers. 'Won't it be nice if we can have some blankets and clothes for them?'

Amala and Subir nodded in agreement.

'Good. Let me ask Mr Sen and his colleagues how we can get this started,' Manas said and stood up.

'I should get to work,' Amala said and bustled out.

That evening, Manas gave Amala the good news that the authorities had approved the idea for starting a sewing class in the camp. He didn't tell her that Mr Sen had said the government wouldn't sanction any money for this. If the volunteers could manage the resources, he had no problem with the scheme.

'It's very kind of you to think of me,' Amala told Manas.

'Oh, never mind that. I'll have some other news to share with you soon. It might just swing your opinion of me in the opposite direction.'

5

Despite the stress of camp work, Manas remained thankful for a few things in his life. Experiencing mornings at home ranked high among these. As the great grandson of a *zamindar*, he wasn't just born into, but poised to inherit, a huge double-storied mansion. The east-facing balcony extending from Manas's bedroom on the upper floor brought him greetings from the sun every morning. As a translucent film penetrated the half-pulled shutters of his windows, Manas would step off his bed, still rubbing his eyes.

Before starting his day, before even washing his face, Manas felt like daubing some of the morning sun on his skin. He would step over to the balcony, barefoot and with just a vest and pyjama, every sunny morning of the year. Sunlight, not the grating ring of a table clock, became his wake-up alarm. The clock only came in use during the monsoon season when the sun took long leaves of absence. Even on those cloudy days, Manas made it a point to stand in the balcony, if only to drink up the beauty of clouds interlocking in the sky and taste on his skin the tingle of the rain darting into the balcony.

The house, once a symbol of high aristocracy, had long since moved past its prime. A curious intermarriage of Western-style architecture and Eastern necessities, the mansion—Manas had heard as part of family folklore—had brimmed with people and the fanfare of a landlord's lifestyle in its better days. The ground floor dominated businesses of all kinds—the temporal, the sensual and the spiritual.

Manas's grandfather occasionally reminisced about how the *nahabatkahana* had once seen dazzling nautch girls dancing to the strains of light classical music brought alive by trained vocal singers and their accompanying instrumentalists. Haraprasad remembered how the plaintive notes of an ustad's sarangi blended with the smoke swirling off the hookahs of the babus, enmeshing them in a snare they had no desire to escape. Money flowed freely and without much toil, and *zamindars* like Manas's great grandfather felt almost obligated to indulge in whatever their senses led them to.

Manas would also hear the stories of those 'glorious' years from his mother. His father almost never mentioned any of it, probably consciously, Manas would infer later.

Manas's childhood memories, when they visited him now, hovered a lot around the *kutchery* or the courthouse that had long been divested of its official function. With disuse came dereliction, and that was exactly what drew Manas and his brigade of pals there. The moss-laden walls and dusty interiors worked as a perfect hiding place. The boys loved the sense of secrecy the place offered and guarded it as a lion would its territory. The red-tiled brick walls had cracked and lost their sheen to protracted neglect as had the *kutchery's* gate, but the rooms within were still good enough to host the meetings of the boys' club for planning events—*dol,* the springtime festival of colours, the megastar of all occasions, Durga Puja every autumn, and Kali Puja, which followed a month later.

With the abolition of *zamindari,* which followed the country's independence, the *nat-mandir* adjoining the mansion became public property. Although his mother rued having to part with the temple complex, Manas remembered his father saying this was for the best—the home of gods had finally gone back to the true devotees, the people.

Before Manas's train of thoughts drifted too far back into the Dutta mansion's nooks, he reined it back. The memory of his father's words about the nat-mandir nudged him. In the instant that bridged the past and the present, he began thinking about Amala's home. *Home as she knew it is gone forever. But what about her home tomorrow, a week later, a year from now? Where is her home now?* He chided himself for thinking only about her but couldn't help it. On his own, he was too small to work out a solution for all the people caught in the migration juggernaut. But was he too small to help one person? Amala?

Manas began considering options for Amala and other able-bodied single women like her. In every scenario he could imagine, he found himself present in Amala's future. This was partly due to the fact that there weren't many like her, not just in terms of personality, but her peculiar circumstance. There were not too many women in the camp who were young and fit of body and mind yet without a man, a parent, a sibling or a child. For this reason alone, Manas felt compelled not to desert her even if he were to discontinue working at the camp for some reason.

~

Drinking tea was another of Manas's morning rituals. His grandfather had introduced him to the brewed beverage, a tradition he had himself acquired from the British whose sedulity ensured that tea became a thriving industry in India.

As a three-year-old, Manas loved sitting on his Dadu's lap as the then successful lawyer sipped from his large cup of evening tea. The biscuits and cream crackers he enjoyed dunking in the tea had to be shared with the little boy. But this didn't divert Manas's persistent interest in the hot, skin-coloured—for the tea was always whitened with milk—drink itself. Unable to resist his need to indulge, one day Haraprasad fed his grandson a small spoonful of tea he had carefully cooled by blowing over it. That smidgen of tea sparked off a revolution in Manas's taste buds. Growing up, he would work for his cups of tea, which came to him only with some tangible accomplishment and much imploring.

Passing high school turned this privilege into a right. Manas's mother now allowed him a cup of bed-tea every morning, brought to him by Photik, a young servant, only a year older than Manas.

Not too long after that, he convinced his mother of his capacity to handle two cups in the morning. He drank the second cup with his grandfather at the breakfast table.

Manas had noticed how Haraprasad took special care to keep the conversation lighthearted during breakfast. He didn't think Dadu doubted his grandson's penchant for serious discussion; it was his daughter-in-law that he was less sure of, Manas suspected. He seemed to avoid talking about anything that carried as much as a mite of controversy when Mrinmoyee was around. This morning seemed to be an exception as Mrinmoyee had left for the Kalighat temple early in the morning. She hadn't asked Manas this time. He knew she wouldn't return before noon.

Haraprasad started the discussion casually. 'How have you been, Dadubhai? I hardly get to see your face these days.'

'Um, I am fine, Dadu, fine as ever,' Manas said while applying butter to his toast, avoiding eye contact with the elderly man.

'And how is your work?'

'Work is good too,' Manas said, pausing for a nibble before adding in a low tone, 'as good as it can be.'

Haraprasad spooned some wheatgerm porridge into his mouth and nodded. 'I know what you mean. Nobody was prepared for this.'

'But why, Dadu? Why such terrible unpreparedness? Did our leaders not see this coming when they agreed on the Radcliffe Line?'

Haraprasad smiled and said, 'I'm sure they anticipated some upsets on both sides. But the scale....'

'Why?' Manas cut him short. 'They decreed Hindus and Muslims couldn't live together any longer. Did they have no idea how many people of either community lived on the two sides?'

'Difficult to say anyone had any idea that the influx would be this huge. I myself didn't.'

'You should look at the state of the old and the invalid, Dadu— it's almost a miracle they are still surviving.'

'I know, I know—it's pathetic. But if you ask me, I am more

concerned about the children. What future are they walking into?'

Manas took a while as he thought of a response. His grandfather seized the opportunity to divert the course of the conversation. 'What have you planned; will you apply for a job or study more?'

'Right now, I don't know,' Manas said, adding, 'I think I'm more inclined to getting employed.'

Haraprasad took out a vitamin pill from a little glass bottle. 'I understand your choice,' he said, 'given these uncertain times.'

Manas welcomed the frank discussion with Dadu. He had been looking for an opportunity to share the anxiety he'd had trouble suppressing within himself for a while now. And although he couldn't bare it all, he somehow felt his grandfather read his state of mind and wasn't merely feigning empathy.

Dadu makes a good point. The plight of the aging and invalid refugees is hard to contend with, but at the most, they have had a few years of their lives cut short by this tragedy. But the children? Those tiny beings who waddle about the camp in nothing but soiled underpants and the ones even younger, naked, sucking at their mother's empty breasts— what have mornings in store for them other than doled milk?

— DIARY ENTRY, MANAS DUTTA, 27 MARCH 1950

On his afternoon trip to the camp, an incident made Manas more despondent than ever. The rickshaw he was on had barely stopped at a traffic signal in Mudiali when a beggar woman came charging at it. She didn't look too old, only a few strands of gray speckled her dishevelled and muck-covered shock of hair. The moment she approached the rickshaw, arms outstretched and yelping unintelligibly, the rickshaw puller threw the butt of the *bidi* he had been smoking to the ground. Crushing the butt with his slippers, he growled at the woman as if she were a street dog eyeing a morsel. This only made the beggar woman adamant; she yowled louder and shook her head. Her matted hair danced like a crazy wave in the middle of the road. Manas feared the scene would attract a crowd. He lightly tapped on the rickshaw puller's back and whispered to him to stay quiet. By this time, the signal had turned green, but Manas got down, took out his wallet from his *kurta* pocket and offered a two-rupee note to the beggar woman. She snatched it and went off.

At the camp, Manas called for a meeting with Manik and Subir. Proshanto had joined the Calcutta Electricity Supply Corporation as a clerk a week ago. He could only volunteer for a few hours on the weekends. In the meeting, Manas wanted to come up with some concrete plans for organising activities for the camp's women and children.

'We can start an informal school for the children,' Subir said.

'Yes, but it has to be fun and not a place that brings on sleep,' quipped Manik, which drew the empathetic laughter of his mates.

'I've thought about that too—it has to be interesting,' said Manas, 'especially because we have children of all ages and we can't have separate classes in this camp setting.'

Subir proposed designing some educational material using simple artwork and making learning interactive for the children. His younger brother, a school-goer and a budding artist, could be roped in. Manas liked the idea.

For keeping the women in the camp engaged, Manas suggested starting the sewing class he had already discussed with Amala.

'Hmm,' said, Manik, 'that's a good idea, but we'll have to identify suitable instructors. Last time I checked, none of us had as much sewing skill as to attach a button to a shirt.'

Manas chuckled. 'I agree, it won't be easy, but we'll have to find a way.' Even as he spoke, Manas fought hard to brush aside the image of the beggar woman from his mind; her tangled hair and bony face, her whimpering yelp and garbled mutterings.

～

As she helped Malati cook the rice gruel for dinner, Amala got the details of Urmila's morning meltdown. Darkness hid the contours of Malati's face, yet Amala sensed she was wiping a tear with the corner of her sari. Malati had her own bundle of sorrows, which Amala thought she hid remarkably well.

Before moving to India, Malati and her husband lived in their ancestral home in Khulna while Kanai, their only child, worked in a jute factory in Faridpur. Malati and Nimai had got him married a little over a year ago. When the most recent riots broke out in Faridpur and Barisal, they made frantic attempts to contact their son and daughter-in-law, but without much luck.

The best piece of information they got, from a neighbour's son who worked in the same city as Kanai, also happened to be the worst. Kanai and his wife, Lata, had gone missing. The neighbour's son had checked at the factory where Kanai worked and even dared to visit the neighbourhood where he and his wife lived despite the burning and arson. Besides learning that Kanai hadn't reported to work for a couple of days, the neighbour's son wasn't able to find out much. Amala remembered the anguish that had choked Malati's voice when she shared this story of loss with her only a week ago.

'I wonder if it would've been better to know they were....' Amala had stopped Malati from uttering the rest by putting her hand on Malati's mouth. It was a selfish action, seized as she had been by Kartik's thought.

The glow of the firewood stove on which the big *degchi* of *khichuri* was cooking stung Amala's eyes, and her thoughts returned to Urmila. She immediately knew why Urmila had behaved the way she did that morning. *What is just a pair of scissors to the world is a knife for her; the same dagger that finished her husband.* For Amala, it was fire. The embers cooking the evening's meal had a sinister face she had been condemned to live and then relive in her memory. The flames that had seemingly been extinguished to ashes with the cremation of her parents rose again the very next day and changed the entire landscape of their village.

Amala and Kartik were eating their lunch of boiled rice and vegetables, a ritual to be followed by the family of the deceased, when Husna barged in through their door.

'They are going around the village, burning down houses, looting things,' she said, breathless with panic.

'There's nothing to loot here,' said Amala even as she saw Kartik withdrawing from his plate of rice.

'Hey, don't worry,' she told her brother, 'no one will harm us. Everyone knows us here....'

Before she could speak any more, Husna said, 'There's no time to talk, Amu. Just wash your hands, the two of you and come with me.'

'Come with you where?' Kartik asked, his voice trembling with an unknown, primal fear, as if he'd been thrown before a wild boar in a forest.

'To our home. *Chalo*, we'll talk more there. They might be here soon.'

Amala had no idea who 'they' were but she could see her friend and neighbour meant business. She went inside and brought out a light shawl for herself and Kartik's favourite book of children's verses.

The evening carried not the day's dust but its ashes in its folds. Not remnants from the previous evening's pyre where the fishing couple's bodies had burned. But heaps of it, flying all over, blanketing the village in a grey haze. In its fury, the carbonised residue mocked the edifices—houses, belongings, inventories of memories—they once had been. Nothing was distinctive about ash, nothing intimate about its appearance. It effaced all notions of personal history in one blazing flash. House after house belonging to Hindu residents had been torched. The violence did not discriminate; the rich and poor got the same end result: ashes.

That night, Husna's mother, Firdous Chachi to Amala and Kartik, huddled the two siblings on her either side in bed. They had an early dinner as Rahman Chacha, Husna's father, had advised. Late in the evening, the women retreated into the back room. After instructing his wife to bolt the bedroom door, Husna's father took Rafiq, Husna's younger brother, to sit with him in the front room. Husna's mother had made a bed for them on the floor there.

At around three in the morning, a pounding on the front door woke up Amala. As she would later hear from him, Rafiq sprang awake. Husna's father woke up too, and gestured to Rafiq to feign sleep. He then got up, drew in a deep breath and went to answer the door. Four young men, two of them with *laathis*, stood outside. Even at that wee hour, they were drenched in sweat and glared with the hungry look a wild beast had when eyeing its prey.

The door-thumping was loud enough to wake up Husna's mother and Husna. Kartik had been hidden deep inside the blanket and still seemed heavy with sleep. Amala strained her ears to catch the conversation between Rahman Chacha and the men.

'What brings you here?' Rahman asked in a calm voice.

'*Aar Chacha, ki haal-chaal tomaar?* How are you doing?' asked one of the men.

'I'm all right, but you all seem excited. Have some water,' Rahman said.

'We don't need water, Chacha, but tell us if you have any gold or silver hidden in trunks here,' said another man in a voice dripping with malicious laughter. His mates responded with a cackle so loud, it almost woke up Kartik. Amala felt a quick gasp escape her mouth as Firdous Chachi patted him gently on his chest to put him back to sleep.

'What treasures can a poor ironsmith have, baba?' Rahman said, pointing to his son on the floor. 'We can't even get a bed for the growing boy, and you talk of gold and silver.'

The laughter ebbed a bit, but not the probing.

'Ah, Chacha, you didn't understand. We're looking for those Hindu pigs. The village must be made *paak*, cleansed of those swines.'

'Hindus?' Rahman sounded his incredulous best. 'We don't even have enough room for the four of us; where will we keep more people? Can't you see—my son and I have to sleep here in the front room. Rafiq's mother can't lie on the floor with that terrible pain in her lower back. So....'

In the back room, Amala, Firdous and Husna remained alert yet motionless, afraid to break the silence with as much as a sigh.

The voices of the young men sounded a bit muffled, and what they said was no longer audible. They were probably consulting among themselves. That ended when one of them said to Husna's father, 'Well, Chacha, we'll let you sleep now. But make sure you let us know if you spot any of those sons of bitches around here, all right?'

'I will, Baba,' said Rahman, his voice calm and unruffled as before.

That's how Amala and Kartik managed to remain underground that night, huddled to safety by the same community that was trying to butcher them.

~

Looking at the rate at which refugees were pouring in, Manas could tell the influx was going to be a prolonged affair. The dramatic shift in the movement of Hindu refugees started in late February, 1950—a few months after Amala arrived. A targeted attack on Hindus, resulting in indiscriminate killings, torching of houses, rapes, pushed the community in droves towards West Bengal. The victims were mostly poor farmers, artisans or fisherfolk.

It had become clear to Manas that the state administration didn't have a solid plan to tackle the worsening refugee situation. Nor did the central government for that matter. An agreement had recently been signed by the prime ministers of India and Pakistan. It sought to protect the rights of minorities in the two countries. But the ink they stamped on paper failed to arrest the flow of blood on the ground.

The knee-jerk official response being presented baffled Manas even more. After all, this wasn't unexpected or even unheard of. Swarms of refugees had crossed the borders on the country's west too, in the wake of mind-numbing bloodshed, loss of family and property. But on that side, there had at least been an exchange of population and land, which posed its own challenges, sure, but was better than nothing. The victims who had migrated over that border were beginning to be rehabilitated, and there was talk of schemes for helping them set up businesses.

Why then did the the same government not learn from its experiences of handling the situation on the Western border? Why this abject lack of planning when it came to the settlement of the refugees from the East? What prompted feelers being sent to the state government to restrict assisting these hapless people with only relief and not rehabilitation? Some newspaper editorials even indicated that the official expectation was for the refugees to return to where they came from once the embers of communal violence were doused. Manas found the whole idea ridiculous and sordid at once.

And what if the refugees got wind of the fact that the ministers flipping files in Delhi and West Bengal hoped to see them gone? Will they be willing to return to the land both dear and dreaded to them? What if they are coerced to? Will they resist?

                    — DIARY ENTRY, MANAS DUTTA, MAY 1950

The next morning, the discussion with Mr Sen regarding an evening school and a sewing class for the women went more smoothly than Manas had expected. Not only did the officer welcome the ideas, he also gave the young men some practical suggestions like conducting a door-to-door sari and old cloth collection drive and recruiting a few female volunteers to work with the women in the camp. Manik said he could talk to one of his aunts who had expressed her desire to work for refugee women. He knew she was a good seamstress and thought she could also join as a volunteer for the sari-collection drive. Manas jumped at the idea.

For the door-to-door drive, they divided areas in the city

between the four of them. Subir and Manik would tackle the northern part while Manas and Raghu would visit houses in southern Calcutta; Proshanto could join them on weekends.

In the evening, Manik brought with him some good news. Chitra, his mother's cousin, had agreed to work with them. She told him she could teach the camp women embroidery and crocheting as well as other kinds of stitches. The news lit up Manas's eyes. He hadn't felt this hopeful in a long time. The last three months had in particular tested his resolve to remain optimistic. 'Can we meet her before taking her on board?' He asked Manik.

'Sure, that's a good idea,' Manik said, quickly adding, 'we can go to her house for lunch tomorrow. She makes the best kaatla curry I've ever had.'

Raghu seemed to lap up the idea, and seeing him drooling at the imagined taste of curried fish, Manas said, 'We shouldn't bother her with all that. Where does she live?'

The meeting with Manik's aunt at her small house in Dhakuria brought Manas a lot more than hope. A childless widow, Chitra Sen lived by herself with a young servant girl to look after her daily needs. With white yarn draping her medium frame, she appeared like any other widow to Manas. When the three of them, Manas, Manik and Raghu, entered her living room, they found her sitting on an easy chair by the window overlooking the street. She had a book in her hands that she read with a thick pair of glasses wound around her eyes. She welcomed the boys to sit on the sofa across the chair, separated by a table, on which rested a flower vase with three bright yellow dahlias. The vase was placed on a round crocheted mat, Chitra's own handiwork, Manas assumed.

Chitra called for Rani, her young maid, asking her to bring water for the 'dadas'. As Manik's widowed aunt put her book down on the table, Manas noticed the *rudraksha* beads she was wearing around her neck. Her sari, too, looked different from the one his mother wore as her widow's garb. At first glance, Manas couldn't tell the difference. Only after they got talking and Chitra adjusted the *anchal* of her sari a few times did it strike Manas that her white drape looked ordinary in its softness; the ones his mother wore were paper crisp; the family washerman was well instructed to ensure they were starched enough after every wash.

After the customary introductions, Manik came straight to the point. 'Mashi, remember I told you about the sewing classes and the collection drive? We wanted to discuss our plan for that.'

'Sure,' said his aunt.

Manas said, 'Manik must have already told you we want to start a sewing workshop for the women at the camp. If we can get them to make some blankets, they will have some cover for the coming winter months. It also gives them something to do.'

Chitra nodded silently. Manas wasn't sure if that meant her assent or unease. He cleared his throat and asked, 'I hope this is all right with you, Mashima? You won't have to come to the camp every day, two or three days a week should be enough. And one of us will take you there.'

'I am mostly sitting at home, my dear,' Chitra said. 'Rani doesn't even let me enter the kitchen. I'll be more than happy to join you all!'

Manas smiled and said, 'Then we can trouble you some more. Will you join us on our cloth collection drives?'

The widowed lady said yes to that too, and when Rani came to collect the empty glasses, Chitra asked her to make some tea for the boys. 'Sure,' said Rani with a flashbulb of a smile that lit up the room for Manas.

'No need,' Raghu said with apparent diffidence but Chitra dismissed his show of formality, and, as if she had read his innermost wishes, added, 'Not just tea, you all will also have lunch with us today. Simple *dal-bhaat*. This *buri* will get some company too.'

A little later, Rani arrived with a tray holding four cups of tea and a plate of *kucho nimki*, the savoury diamonds Manas looked forward to every year after Durga Puja, when his mother would have them fried in large batches for guests who came to greet them for *Bijoya*. Rani held out three tea cups on a tray with great care and placed them before the volunteers one by one. Moving aside the flower vase, she placed the plate of *nimkis* on the crocheted mat.

Looking at Chitra she said, 'I put ginger in the tea, so you can have it too.'

Manas felt as if he had been to Chitra's house many times, as if he had known that crocheted mat on the table, as if he intimately knew her hearty laughter. It also seemed to him as if he could talk to Chitra about anything, ask her any question without offending her. Not just the widow's own gentleness, but Rani's—who Manas concluded couldn't be more than thirteen or fourteen—loquacious candour with Chitra put him completely at ease.

Manas realised how different it was from when he was with his mother. There, he struggled to find common ground for a two-way conversation. He rarely shared the things he was most passionate about with her; she just wouldn't get it, wrapped as she was in her cosy world of gods, gold, saris and neighbourhood gossip.

The meal was simple and delicious—red lentils, fried potato sticks, and a thin curry of *chara-pona*. Apologising for the size of the fish, Chitra said, 'Had I known you all were coming today, I would have made *kaatla* curry. But you must make do with *chara-pona* now, thanks to Rani.' The small fish was the girl's daily fare, she explained and added, 'Hope you like our Rani's *jhol*, made for her Dadababus.'

Manas felt guilty. '*Ei ma*, you shouldn't have given us your share; the *dal-alubhaja* was enough,' he said to Rani.

'*Arrey*, it's nothing, Baba. You don't know how happy Rani is to see you eat here. She will get more from the market in the evening. But do let me know a day in advance the next time you come. I will cook *kaatla* for you all.'

Her words brought a sheepish smile to Manik's face as he looked at Manas.

Rani broke the silence with her chuckle and Chitra admonished her, '*Ei* Rani, stop your *phik-phik haashi*.'

6

Manas loved the rains in Calcutta. He wasn't alone. The entire city awaited the first drops of rain with the yearning of a lovelorn heart eager for just one glimpse of the beloved. All through early summer, there would be insinuations, the *Kalbaisakhis* which delighted Manas. The tempestuous thunderstorms split people's eardrums and rooftops alike as they blew through the city in mad twists that resembled Shiva's *tandava*. As the sky flashed crimson, fire and violet from one minute to the next, palm and coconut fronds swayed like dervishes in a trance.

The gusts banged doors open and shut, bringing in their wake clouds of dust and petrichor. Sure, the Nor'westers often caused damage, felling trees and uprooting tarpaulins off shacks, but the beauty in the *Kalbaisakhi*'s violence was such that even the great poet Rabindranath had been prompted to say, in one of Manas's favourite songs,

Let your life and death dance
With the Kalbaisakhi's swirl

Whenever he could, Manas would run to his balcony to watch the downpour; the rain seemed to him like a fugitive who couldn't stop running even after arriving at a safe spot. The *Kalbaisakhi*'s Janus-faced dance symbolising both life and death was endlessly intriguing. With the first rumblings, the sky turned a sombre, almost angry grey, only to turn playful the next moment with a light and sound spectacle. Then the dusty winds blew, blanketing one's view and ripping all order apart. Once the wind completed its crazed somersaults, the rains came in torrents that tore through the stratosphere and everything below it, lashing trees, roofs, streets and footpaths.

When the rains returned three months later, now as full-blown monsoon, Manas's alarm-clock season, he rejoiced again. Not only because it brought relief from the blistering summer days, but more for the way it transformed the city. With every splash, the leaves on trees turned into the colour of tropical rainforests, the streets became silver mirrors with upturned reflections of the umbrellas that people held.

Manas felt a lot less excited about this year's monsoon. With the very first drizzle, he dreaded the impending nightmare. For all its verdurous beauty, the rains also made Calcutta a pregnant city with waterlogged streets. At a time when refugees were trying to find shelter in its alleys, the annual downpour posed the looming threat of a miscarriage.

True to his worst fears, anxiety had wiggled its way into the refugee camp. With few government initiatives to rehabilitate them, the camp members were impatient to take charge of their lives. 'You may want to discard us like scrap, but we will be counted,' they appeared to tell the authorities. And so they started turning scraps into a living, by making paper bags using newspapers and selling them to the roadside stalls outside the camp. Some men ventured out on the sly and found work as porters and construction labourers. Manas even heard whispers about some of the camp women looking for work as domestic helpers in nearby houses.

~

Even before his clock rang its alarm, Manas woke up to the sound of rain, tapping softly at his window. He could tell it was a drizzle. As he opened his eyes and sat up, another sound drifted to his ears, the strains of flute playing on the radio. Every morning, his grandfather, whose ears were no longer as sharp as they used to be even until a year ago, would play the All India Radio's broadcast on a high volume soon after waking up. Manas recognised the music of Pannalal Ghosh, the flautist who had stormed the musical scene in the past few years. The notes of his flute, imbued with an ethereal, lenitive essence, mingled with the drip-drop of rain. Manas dashed to the balcony.

It was indeed a light spell. Rain splattered against the balustrade. Manas stood holding the railing, letting his hands moisten. The raindrops, though fragile and short-lived, weren't devoid of persistence. A sudden burst of crepitating thunder diverted his attention to what the clouds portended, a heavier downpour later in the day. He retreated inside. After a quick bath, Manas headed downstairs.

He crossed his grandfather's bedroom, then his mother's and descended the stairs to get to the kitchen. Once at the threshold, he greeted Sharoda, the Brahmin woman who cooked their meals. 'Sharoda Mashi, please make me a quick breakfast, I'm in a hurry today.'

The elderly cook looked up, a bit startled. On the floor where she sat on a mat, a *bonthhi* rested in front of her along with a pile of brinjals, potatoes, and half a cauliflower head, ready to be chopped off into curry-worthy pieces.

Sharoda wasn't the only one to be surprised. Mrinmoyee had rarely seen her son wake up this early. And here he was, bathed and ready for the day. 'What's the hurry, Maanu? Anything special today?' she asked, adjusting her spectacles as she covered her head. The bunch of almirah keys tied to her *anchal* jangled in compliance.

'Did you look at the sky by any chance? I should get going before it starts pouring,' Manas said.

'*Rosho*,' said Mrinmoyee, thrusting her palm forward to tell Manas to take it easy.

To Sharoda she said, '*Ei*, Sharu, fry a few *luchis* for Maanu. And make some *alu-phulkopi chhenchki* with it.' She knew the combination of deep fried flour breads and potato-cauliflower stir-fry made Manas weak in his knees.

'Quick please, Sharoda Mashi,' said Manas.

'Here, you come with me,' Mrinmoyee said to Manas, 'we need to talk.'

'What is it now?' Manas said, a long sigh trailing his words.

They proceeded to the large living room in one corner of which was the dining area—with a low-level teak wood table, surrounded by low *jolchowkis*. On the wall hung Kalighat paintings depicting nava-Durga, the nine avatars of goddess Durga. Manas sat on a stool, his back to the paintings. His mother sat facing him.

Manas tapped on the table, covered with a tablecloth. Its floral embroidery was too ornate for his taste. His mother broke the silence. 'So how's your work at the camp?'

'Usual.'

'And for how long, may I ask?'

Manas could see which way the conversation was headed and had little appetite for it. 'These things don't get sorted in a day, Ma,' he said. 'Nobody knew the situation was going to become such a messy *jhamela*. It's about thousands of lives.'

'And you and your handful of friends are going to change these thousands of wretched lives?' Mrinmoyee asked.

'You know very well that we alone can't do it. But we can't run away from the situation either.'

'Look, I don't understand all that. All I want to know is when will you focus on your own future? You can't fritter your time away doing social work while not bothering about yourself.'

'What do you mean by my future?'

'Well, you'll soon have a college degree and you are old enough to work at a job, aren't you?'

'You don't have to worry about me,' Manas said.

Sharoda appeared on the doorway with a plate containing Manas's breakfast and a glass of water. She put the plate and glass on the table. She stood for a moment and asked Mrinmoyee if anything else was required. When Mrinmoyee gestured in the negative, the cook went back to the kitchen.

'Ma,' Manas said, salivating at the food in front of him, 'can we talk about this some other day?' The fluffy *luchis*, soft enough for a baby's fingers to tear them apart could make Manas forget the world.

Mrinmoyee indulged her Maanu like any other mother. He was, after all, her only child, and since her husband's death twelve years ago, her greatest support. Even as she showered him with material comfort, she also made it clear that he would do well not to rely solely on family wealth. In this, Manas agreed with her as did Haraprasad; sooner or later Manas would have to earn his own living. But he also wanted his mother to know he wasn't going to be the obedient *bhalo-manush* his father was.

Right now, Manas had other things on his mind. In a few hours, he got down at the tram station in Dhakuria and took a rickshaw to go to Chitra's house. Today was supposed to be her first day at the camp. She looked ready in a crisp cotton sari when he arrived at her doorstep and offered Manas a glass of water. Manas drank the water and as he put down the glass on the table, he saw Chitra picking up a wicker basket from the floor.

'What's in that?' he asked.

'Just a few sewing things and some embroidery and crocheting samples.'

Manas couldn't help admiring the senior volunteer's attention to detail.

She sure looked much more composed than he felt. Taking the basket from her hand, he stepped out of the door. The rickshaw he'd come in waited outside. Once they both sat down, Manas asked the rickshaw puller to take them to the nearest taxi stand.

Chitra protested, 'What do we need a taxi for? We can go by tram; it's not that far.'

'Don't worry, Mashima. Taxi only for your first day. Later, you will have to board the tram with us.'

'*Shei bhaalo*, be happy to,' Chitra said with a smile.

Taking the taxi turned out to be a good idea as Manas looked at the sky. It had turned an ominous grey by the time they arrived at the camp. Moisture hung heavy in the air, bringing in clumps of sweat.

The refugees who were in the tents had all been made to huddle in the barrack building, inside hall rooms that now resembled the platform of the Sealdah station, teeming with heads and the smell of stale breath. Nothing could be heard amidst the din that echoed from the rooms. As he stood outside one of the halls with Chitra, Manas shook his head. *What a welcome for Chitra Mashi!* When Manas saw Subir emerge from the next room, he suggested they sit in the office to help Chitra make sense of what was going on.

Due to the inclement weather, the officer-in-charge, Mr Moitra, had decided to bring all the refugees under the roof. His solution, though based on logic and need, exacerbated the camp's chaos. The volunteers and Chitra sat quietly sipping the tea Mr Moitra had arranged for them. After a while, Chitra broke the lull.

'I have a suggestion. May I?'

Mr Moitra looked up from his file and said, 'Of course. Please go ahead.'

'Can't some of the refugee men and women be given the responsibility to manage groups of people?'

Manas and Subir nodded, and even Mr Moitra felt it was a good idea. Seeing their own people in charge would inspire confidence, he said.

Manas's thoughts turned to the task of organising the sewing classes. Now that space was a challenge because of the rain, the initial idea of holding the class in the camp's open area wouldn't work. When Manas mentioned this, Mr Moitra said, 'We have two big storerooms in this building. They need some cleaning but are mostly empty.'

'How do we go about the sewing classes, Mashi?' Manas asked Chitra.

Before she could answer, Mr Moitra said, 'Well, we can invite the women group leaders and discuss it with them first.'

'Exactly what I was thinking,' Chitra said.

Although the emergency precluded the formal inauguration of the sewing class, it helped identify leaders from among the refugees. The names were picked from a register that the officers maintained. It had details such as name, sex, age and date of joining the camp. Next to many of the names were short notes describing the person and their conduct as observed by the officer on duty on a given day. On the basis of this as well as the volunteers' interactions with the refugees, four men and four women were selected for the roles. Each of the man-woman pair would be responsible for a certain number of camp members. It was also decided that they would take turns to supervise different groups every fortnight.

Amala featured among the women leaders. After lunch, Manas and Subir brought the eight chosen group leaders for a meeting to the office room. Manas noticed nervousness tightening their faces. There weren't enough chairs, so Manas, Subir and Manik vacated their seats for the women leaders, while they stood with the men in a crescent around Mr Moitra's desk.

'I'm sorry we don't have enough place for all of us to sit,' Mr Moitra said. He stood up, as if embarrassed to hold on to his seat.

'Dada, *aapni boshun*, please sit down,' Manas said. The refugee leaders endorsed his suggestion, and Mr Moitra reluctantly sat down.

Once everyone looked comfortable in their spots, Mr Moitra relayed to the refugees the news of their selection as group volunteer leaders. 'It's better if you are directly involved. As you can probably tell, there are no quick solutions to the problems we have here.'

Manas noted the relaxation Mr Moitra's words brought to the leaders' faces. Some of them even started nodding. Amala, however, retained the stolid look Manas had lately seen her mastering.

'Mr Moitra is right. I think this will also help the camp

members to open up more. It's always easier to talk about problems with one of your own people, isn't it?' Manas said.

Bhola, one of the chosen refugee volunteers, had a question, one that probably buzzed in the minds of all his just-appointed colleagues. 'What do we have to do, Babu?'

'That's what we're going to discuss right now,' Subir said as he introduced them to Chitra. 'Here is Chitra Mashi, she will also help us at the camp.'

Chitra smiled as she looked at the women refugees seated next to her, then turned around and acknowledged the male refugees and volunteers.

One of the female volunteers coughed. Manas recognised it as Amala's and tensed up. Clearing his throat, he said, 'Do you want to say something, Amala?'

'Umm, I don't know how I can help. I've never done this kind of work,' Amala said without looking at Manas. Her words received the support of the other three female volunteers, who too started muttering about their lack of experience.

'Nothing to fear,' Manas said, 'we only want you to join our team. The more of us, the better, no?'

'We need your help in organising some of the activities here,' said Mr Moitra. Then, pointing at Manas and the volunteers, he said, 'If you face any problem, these boys are always there to help.'

'And look, we have Mashima here too,' quipped Manik, 'in case you want to complain against Manas-da, Subir-da or Proshanto-da. Of course, saying anything against me won't work as I'm Mashi's favourite nephew.'

'Don't be so sure,' Chitra said with a pursed smile.

Her comment invited giggles from the women. Amala released a shy chuckle. Manas seized this opportunity to tell the women volunteers about the sewing workshop and urged Chitra to give them the details.

'Sure,' she said, turning towards the young women. 'We are thinking of starting some sewing activity with the women and girls here. I'm sure most of you know how to make *kanthas*, and we'll need those in the coming months. I can also teach you some embroidery and decorative patterns if you are interested.'

The women's faces beamed at the idea; Manas noticed even Amala's face had a flicker of a smile.

'So what do you think, can we start this tomorrow?' Manas asked, his question aimed at both the senior volunteer and the refugee women.

'I don't see why we can't if you can organise everything for us,' Chitra said with a wink, meant more to draw the solidarity of the women leaders than to challenge the male volunteers.

'We sure will,' said Manik. Looking at the male refugees around him, he said in a mock rebuttal, 'What do you say, brothers?'

His question received emphatic nods and a chorus of 'Yes, sure' from the male refugee volunteers.

∼

As the refugee volunteers filed out of the office, Manas raised his right index finger to beckon Amala to wait a bit. She stood outside the office.

Chitra came out of the office after the others had left. Manas took her and Amala to a section of the corridor that overlooked an open ground in the centre of the barrack building. The rain continued its incessant patter. Water gathered in stray pieces of junk littered on the ground: torn clothes, old newspapers with blotting ink splattering on the ground, a perforated aluminum plate that sang stridently as the rain hit its base.

'Do you mind helping introduce Chitra Mashi to Urmila?' Manas asked Amala in a soft voice. He knew any meeting with Urmila could be difficult to predict.

When the trio reached her, Urmila appeared calmer than usual. Her hair was a mass of matted mesh, her sari dirty, her breath heavy with the smell of roasted nuts. She sat in a corner, munching on roasted chickpeas from a paper cone. Her son lay next to her, sleeping.

Manas motioned Chitra and Amala to sit down. Then, closing his palms, he bent down and said to Urmila, 'How are you?'

Urmila looked at him but didn't answer. She picked a few more chickpeas from the paper cone and popped them into her mouth. Manas bent further down and asked her if he could sit next to her.

This time, Urmila responded with 'Haw', a brief utterance indicating consent.

Manas slowly sat down and introduced Urmila to Chitra. 'And you already know Amala, don't you?'

Urmila looked sideways, her eyes moving from Chitra to Amala without offering any answer. She resumed snacking on the chickpeas.

'We haven't met before but I have seen you many times,' said Amala, attempting to break the ice.

'Amala is here to help you; if you need anything or if anybody troubles you,' Manas said. Amala nodded in agreement.

Urmila kept munching on her snack, and as the paper cone became almost empty, she furiously scoured it to ferret the last two or three peas out of it. She seemed so absorbed in the act that Manas doubted if she had listened to any of what he had just said.

When Urmila had finished or rather been forced to stop eating, Amala said with a chuckle, '*Chhola bhaja* is delicious, isn't it? Ma used to put it in *muri makha*.'

Suddenly, Urmila looked at Amala, intently, without uttering as much as a word. Her gaze didn't seem intimidating, it was more quizzical. Her look brought to Manas's mind stories of patients in semi-conscious or comatose states, responding in momentary flashes, to particular stimuli believed to stir their brains. He let that moment of quiet interaction linger; his fellow volunteers took the cue.

When it finally evanesced and Urmila looked away, Chitra said to her, 'Both you and Amala can think of me as your aunt.

I also make a good *muri-makha*, you know.' With a playful smile on her lips, Chitra went on to detail the ingredients that made her puffed rice snack irresistible: chopped coconut, green chillies, *chanachur*, finely-diced onions, roasted chickpeas, cucumber pieces, and extra-pungent mustard oil.

This, too, drew Urmila's attention. This time she even allowed herself a half-hearted, inchoate laugh. Amala joined her with a hearty chuckle and said, 'You're funny, Mashima. Now I'm so hungry, I want a big bowl of *muri*. Plain *muri* will do, too.'

'Why plain, I will bring you my special *muri-makha* tomorrow. Until then, you two must promise to be good girls,' Chitra said, directing her eyes toward Urmila. Her son woke up, aroused by the cheerful sounds around him. To Manas's surprise, he didn't cry or evince the slightest irritation. If anything, he looked to be greedily taking in the company of the people around him, as if he understood every word being spoken.

Manas marvelled at the wind that blew through the words, smiles, and even the awkwardness these women exchanged. He smiled, delighted at the progress Amala had made. She spoke with such ease with Chitra Mashi.

Manas felt a touch of envy—a warm, comforting envy. The manner in which the three women bonded gave him a sense of the miracle the camaraderie of women could be, regardless of their husbands and histories.

~

As she counted the days, two more to go, for her secret trip to Sealdah station, Amala was grateful for the distraction the sewing class brought. It made her happy to see how in only a couple of days the class had become popular with the camp women. The first day went by mostly in introductions and getting the women organised. Chitra noted down the names of those participating in a register and divided them into groups based on their preferences for stitching, crocheting, embroidery and knitting. A lot of the women wanted to be in all four and were thus accommodated on a rotational basis.

The next day Chitra introduced the class to basic patterns like straight and running stitches. At a time, she gave ten women small pieces of cloth to stitch on. These would then be passed around to the others in the group. The four groups had almost a hundred members each, so Chitra further divided the groups into four more clusters and had them sit in circles. She would spend about half an hour with each group, while one of the women refugee volunteers remained with the three other groups and maintained order. Most of the women seemed happy with the class; they were delighted at the opportunity to do something they were already familiar with and to add to their repertoire.

Amala left for her secret mission shortly after lunch that afternoon. She and Minoti joined Paban separately; he waited for them under a Neem tree outside the camp they had identified as the meeting point. The women had veiled their heads with the ends of their saris. Paban asked them to 'hurry up', as he led them towards the nearest bus stop, a good kilometre and a half away. It hadn't rained since the morning and the cloud-now, sun-now weather made the walk easier. The road looked like a noisy field to Amala on which vehicles of all shapes and sizes kept appearing like mushrooms in the rainy season. A man pulling a bullock cart heaped with bales of who-knows-what walked right next to them. Buses, cars and lorries yelped past them with fearsome speed. The memory of the day she had landed in Sealdah came zipping back to Amala like a sour belch. She tried to remember the spot where she had left Kartik on the platform but knew it was like trying to locate a *ghunti* pebble amid a barrel of rice. She had seen but a slice of that huge station and that too, briefly, before Manas had rescued her from the policemen and the station's labyrinth.

That's exactly where she found herself more than an hour and two bus rides later. The same maze of a station, jammed and grimy, mercilessly confounding. Paban stood in line at the enquiry counter and asked Minoti and Amala to wait nearby. He needed to find the arrival times for all the trains coming from the Kumilla route; Minoti had no specific information. Amala began her investigation at once. Her legs remained stationary, but her eyes moved wildly, pinning themselves on the faces of boys of Kartik's age. She tried to convince herself that she would find him at the station; he must surely be looking for his Didi too.

Paban returned with a chit carrying the arrival times for three trains. The earliest one would enter Sealdah in the next hour or so. The other two trains were to arrive after three hours. Amala wrung her hands and started pacing. She couldn't just stand there and hope for Kartik to appear.

'*Chalo*, let's look for your uncle. Then you and Paban-da can return to the camp. I will wait here,' Minoti said.

'Wait here? Alone?' Amala was alarmed.

'Yes, why not? There are so many people here, Didi. Don't worry; I will remain close to the *enkoy-ree* babu's window. It's a safe spot.'

Paban agreed and said he could return later and take Minoti back to the camp. It wasn't a good idea for all three of them to be missing for too long.

For the next three quarters of an hour, Paban took them around the station, through its three sections and countless platforms connecting hundreds of train lines. Amala saw everything she had seen on her first day here—the lurching beggars, the urchins caked in grime, the porters in red shirts balancing the load of the world on their heads, the flies hovering around dog shit, and the crowds of people rushing into and out of platforms. She relived the horror of the first day with each step. But she didn't see the face she had come looking for. Her sandal had almost come undone and she sagged against a wall before picking herself up and walking again.

She returned with Paban to the camp, empty-handed. How could a single visit to the station help her with her search mission? She needed to go there daily, preferably twice a day. An idea so impossible, Amala felt locked in a windowless room.

The next day at the sewing class, as their teacher showed the girls how to hold the hook and pull the yarn from the fingers, Subir darted into the room and went straight to Chitra. He whispered something into her ears. Amala noticed how he kept wiping his forehead with a sweat-drenched handkerchief.

A moment later, Chitra said to her students, 'I'll be back soon. Please keep working on what you started yesterday.' Turning to Amala, she asked her to manage the class until she returned. As she got up, Chitra put her crochet needle and yarn on the chair and tapped Amala on the shoulder, motioning her to take the seat. A wan smile floated on the corners of Amala's lips. After Chitra left, she sat down on the ground and tried engaging the other women by getting them to work on the projects they had started the previous day. It wasn't easy. The women took out the pieces of cloth they had started sewing but the sudden departure of their teacher set in motion a confabulation of semi-alarmed whispers.

'Shh,' Amala tried to calm them down. 'Please let's wait till Mashi is back. I want to know what happened as badly as you.'

The buzz eased a bit and the women resumed their needlework. Amala stole a glance at the open window to the south. A drizzle created a blurry curtain, eclipsing a line of trees lining the backyard of someone's house. She surmised a cluster of areca nuts clumped around the topmost branches of a betel tree. Close to it stood several banana trees, laden with fresh green bunches of the fruit. A goat whose tether had come loose lolled about, chewing on fallen leaves. A couple of home mynas joined the goat to scrounge for breakfast.

The amplifying hum from the women jolted Amala out of her reverie. She felt embarrassed for being abstracted when she was supposed to manage the class. Striking her forehead with a soft, admonishing tap, she said, 'Dear sisters of mine, when Chitra Mashi returns, she will ask to see the work we have done. Let's hurry up.'

'How much have *you* sewed, Didi?' a young woman asked with

a pursed smile, pointing to the peach-coloured cloth Amala held, a future pillowcase. Amala had barely moved the needle. Looking at the cloth, she bit her tongue and said, 'See, that's exactly what I mean. Now what will I show Chitra Mashi?'

The girl pressed her lips with her hand as though to hide her laughter, but her inflated cheeks gave it all away.

Amala smiled bashfully, then said to the girl with a wink, 'Think we can exchange our pieces?' The girl laughed aloud now, joined by her classmates in a chorus of mirth the sound of which was as alien to Amala in the refugee camp as the possibility of returning to her village.

Yet, here they were, forging a sisterhood of limping back, most likely not to normalcy, but at least to the mundane. The camp had even started looking like a village to Amala, complete with raillery, suspicion, gossip and geniality. *For now, this will have to do*, she thought, hastily running her needle through the pillowcase-to-be, a mud-coloured thread dotting it like pebbles on the dirt roads of her village.

More than half an hour had passed before Chitra returned to the room. As she walked in, Amala caught her wiping the corner of her eye with a handkerchief. By the time she reached her chair, she seemed her normal self, ready to get on with the class. Taking her seat, she asked Amala, 'Was everything all right?'

'Yes, Mashi,' Amala said. 'We worked on what we started yesterday.'

'Oh, good, good,' said Chitra. But only her voice seemed to be present in the room, not her whole self.

Gouri, the girl who had teased Amala over her tardy needlework said to Chitra, 'Mashi, would you like some water?'

'*Na, na*, leave it. Already half your class time is over. I'll be home in another hour anyway.'

'But it's right here, Mashima,' the girl persisted, pointing at the *kunjo*, a small earthen pitcher with a craning neck for easier decantation. She brought Chitra a glass of water.

Although she couldn't put a finger to it, Amala knew something was amiss. Serious enough that even Gouri had smelled its stink in Chitra's demeanour.

In the evening, Manas and the boys came calling on Amala and the other refugee volunteers for an emergency meeting. The news froze Amala. Minoti had been raped the previous evening. The incident occurred 'somewhere outside the camp'. Not too many details were known, but Minoti had managed to make her way back to the camp in the morning and remained in a delicate state.

When Manas approached her with a new request a little later, Amala only heard the word 'Minoti' before a black cloud clasped her. She felt her eardrums splitting with the harsh whistle of a train, its wheels clanking the tracks in Sealdah; Minoti's self-assured voice 'Why not, there are so many people here...' 'Let's look for your uncle...'; the train schedules blaring out of the PA system. A surge of bile gagged her. Manas kept saying something but Amala heard nothing and spoke with an abruptness that startled Manas.

'Where is Minoti? Can I see her right now? Please, I need to.'

So it comes to this. A girl who could be my little sister, violated by some ravenous rogue. I guess this was waiting to happen. A woman is the best piece of meat for all hungry men—rioters, criminals, political leaders. And you and me. For her to lose her home, hearth, family, is never enough. She must lose her final, and sometimes, her only belonging—the freedom of her body. Little sister of mine, I am guilty of your crime for I could not save you from this indignity. The purgatory you were spared even as your house was torched on the other side of the fence, you must burn in now.

— DIARY ENTRY, MANAS DUTTA, SEPTEMBER 1950

7

The last spells of rain meant soon there would be no trace of nimbus as globs of fluffy, rainless clouds sailed across clear sapphire skies. To most city dwellers, and Manas was one of them, these tufts of cotton wool were the portents of celebration, a time when the mother goddess would arrive in homes and neighbourhoods, when music and mantra wafted in the autumnal breeze, and little children flaunted the only new clothes they got for the entire year.

Crisp afternoons were bathed in a balmy sunshine. At times a soft zephyr blew carrying the scent of *shiuli*, the small white flowers with mandarin stems that blossomed in and defined the season for Manas.

This year, the goddess's face appeared as anything but that of Annapurna's, the avatar in which she provided bountiful food. If the faces Manas met daily at the camp were any indication, the goddess seemed to have acquired an incarnation of emaciation that failed to invoke even pity. And this avatar of the *devi* seemed intent to stay put.

Manas noticed a change in the attitude of most of the refugee volunteers, particularly the men. They weren't as forthcoming in suggesting steps to prevent incidents such as the one that scarred Minoti. In one meeting, he tried to push them by specifically addressing the men. 'Dada-ra, please don't be so quiet. We need to hear from you.'

The men remained quiet.

Taking the baton from Manas, Subir asked one of them, 'Paban-da, what do you think we should do?'

No matter how sincerely they tried to take it forward, the

conversation seemed stuck like a jar of coconut oil in winter to Manas.

Amala suddenly spoke. 'What solution can we offer, Babu? We were all happy in our homes; we had no wish to come to Hindustan. For the poor like us, how does it matter where we live? We will earn the same pennies everywhere.'

Some more throats started clearing. Paban said, 'Yes, and so we stayed on. For as long as we could. Even when the rich ran away, we didn't. Until they came after us.'

'Homes burnt, property looted, all we were left with was this life,' Amala said, 'and what happens here? Minoti...' the name left her mouth as a gasp, a wail crushing it.

Manas decided not to drag the discussion any further. Minoti's wound had become like the mangle that stuck to one's fingers when a tender jackfruit was cut open, stubbornly resisting even furious hand-washing. 'Piriti kathhaler athha,' sang the baul friar, likening the jackfruit's glue to love for the divine, which, once it took hold of a human heart, was unlikely to leave. But to Manas it now resembled nothing but an abcess.

The refugee volunteers slowly left the room. Raghu, always the mood lifter in such situations, offered to bring tea for his dadas. This brought a smile on Manas's face. He succumbed to Raghu's suggestion.

Amala took Minoti's violation personally. It was like losing Kartik all over again, only worse. She felt responsible for Minoti's condition. How could she have returned to the camp with Paban leaving Minoti in that clamouring den with monsters lurking in every corner? Had she forgotten her brush with the policemen on her first day? Minoti had sounded confident and capable but what did she know? She was a little girl. When she went to see her after hearing about the horror from Manas, Minoti looked calm but that was because she was asleep. The doctor attending to her suggested that for the first few hours no one apart from him and the nurse be there; seeing familiar faces could re-trigger the trauma that had seared her. Amala felt like the big sister who had

failed her sibling twice. And failed irreversibly. First she left him
behind; then she left her to be....

After lunch at the camp, Manas went to see Dr Bose, the
doctor attending to Minoti. They met in the corridor outside the
makeshift ward for Minoti. The doctor said she was improving
physically but cautioned against rushing to have her resume
routine life anytime soon. Minoti trembled at the sight of a man,
any man. This made Dr Bose's task challenging, and he kept his
meetings with her as short as possible. Given the patient's delicate
psychological state, the doctor advised that only women should
be with her. 'Be careful with that, too. Any female attendant must
not probe her. Their purpose should be to solely give her company.'

Manas took it all in quietly. He found it difficult to look the
doctor in the eye, as if he were a culprit on the run who had
suddenly bumped into a cop. The doctor handed him a list of
medicines for Minoti and said he would return in a couple of
days. Until then the nurse working with him, a trained girl
from Jalpaiguri, would be in charge. Nandini, the young nurse,
appeared no more than of seventeen to Manas. Her soft smile and
the doctor's confidence in her gave Manas some relief.

Must speak to Chitra Mashi about this, Manas told himself as he
and the doctor went their ways. The maternal kinship of Chitra
made Manas see her as a confidant. Until now his only options
were to have a chat with his co-volunteers or seek Amala's help to
deal with a crisis, despite knowing she herself needed as much, if
not more, support as those she was expected to comfort.

～

Manas left the camp earlier than usual and headed towards
College Street. Whenever thoughts mildewed his mind, a walk in
the *boi para*, the Mecca of books, worked as a cheap and likeable
cure. Usually, he went there with a list of books to purchase. His
list mostly included titles based on book reviews he'd read in *The
Statesman* or *Basumati*.

These trips demanded a fair amount of walking and Manas enjoyed the expedition precisely for this reason. Books piled on footpaths in stark cubbyholes were merchandised by scrawny booksellers who knew their stock no less than diligent bookworms working away in libraries.

College Street also boasted a couple of brick and mortar shops. On the rare occasion when Manas couldn't find one of his wishlist titles in the roadside stalls, he stepped into one of these shops. Though the prices here were a notch higher than what the footpath vendors offered, availability was almost always certain.

Manas scanned the book piles for Ivan Turgenev's *A Sportsman's Sketches*. A recent review in *The Statesman* had piqued his interest in the book, not so much because of the reviewer's assessment of Turgenev's writing, as for the human subjects of his stories. The lives of the marginal had always stayed in the margins for him—Sharoda Mashi, who cooked in their house; Menoka, the married young woman who washed their dirty utensils; and the water-bearing *bhistis* and the rickshaw-pullers around the house; they all existed, but only in the periphery of his life's map. Over the past few months, this had changed as he found himself amidst a sea of refugees and witnessed how the 'little people' walked the daily tightrope of their lives.

Manas ambled along, hands inside his *panjabi* pockets, eyes searching for something, until he stopped at one of the stalls. The shopkeeper knew him well and greeted him with '*Aajke ki boi, Dada?*'

Manas retrieved a scrap of paper from his pocket and handed it to the shopkeeper.

'*Dekhchhi*, I'll look for it,' the man said, asking his assistant, a boy of thirteen to manage the counter as he went inside the stall. He returned after a good ten minutes with a tattered copy. The cover, a binding with glossy floral paper, couldn't have been original. Part of it was already gone, probably towards a rat's lunch.

The shopkeeper dusted the book with his *gamchha* before handing it to Manas.

'How much for this?' Manas asked as he flipped the book's pages.

'*Aggey*, two rupees,' the shopkeeper said, flicking off a *bidi* from behind his left ear.

'Hmm,' Manas said as he stumbled upon a half-eaten page. His gaze remained stuck there as he tried hard to decipher a sentence the torn part had left incomplete.

'Okay, you can pay a rupee for it,' the shopkeeper said, worried that the book's condition might cost him a sale.

'Oh, that's all right,' Manas replied, still distracted. He pulled out a two-rupee note from his wallet.

As the bookseller started fishing for a coin in his pocket, Manas said, 'Nah, nah, you keep it. I needed this book badly. Thank you.'

8

When Manas landed at Chitra's door unannounced, she welcomed him like she had been expecting him. Rani brought tea and *muri-makha*.

Manas didn't speak much; seeing his demeanour, Chitra said to Rani, '*Jaa*, take your *muri* and go play with Kamala.'

Rani sprang from her quilted mat on the floor and dashed across the front door to catch up with her friend. Kamala was her age and worked as a house help in the neighbourhood.

'*Kichhu bolbe?*' Chitra asked him in a voice Manas had come to identify as that of a friend. His father had the same tone when a vulnerable Manas approached him.

Manas seized the opportunity. 'I have lots to tell, Mashima. Will you feed me dinner?'

'Do you need to ask?'

Manas sighed and put down his empty glass on a hexagonal stool next to the sofa. The intricate design on the stool caught his attention.

'Meenakari, isn't it, Mashima?'

'Oh, that one. Yes, you are right. One of my brothers-in-law, my elder sister's husband, brought it from Jaipur on our anniversary.'

'Jaipur? What took him there? Or were they just visiting?'

'Nah, nah, my Didi didn't go. Jamaibabu was a senior officer with the government and had gone there for audit work.'

'Ah, I see,' Manas said, removing his glasses to wipe the sweat from his face with a handkerchief.

'Would you like some more *cha*? Or *muri*?' Chitra asked.

'Not *muri*, but tea yes,' Manas said, adding as he saw her get up, 'only if you want it too.'

'Don't you worry, I'll have one more cup as well,' she said with a wink and took the glass from the stool on her way to the kitchen. Manas picked up *A Sportsman's Sketches* from the centre table where he had put it down. Within seconds, he had been swept over to the Russian countryside. He didn't think of himself as an escapist, but there were times when Manas felt grateful for the power of books to create a curtain of oblivion better than soporifics.

Chitra returned with a teapot in one hand and a steel plate with some edibles in the other.

'Just fried some *beguni*. You must be hungry,' she passed the plate of hot eggplant fritters to him.

'*Arrey*, Mashima,' Manas said, 'there was no need for this.'

'It's not just for you, Baba. I also get an excuse to have some,' Chitra said with a chuckle. 'Otherwise, it's just dry muri for Rani and me every day. Now, let me call her.'

Rani returned with a bunch of assorted flowers, jasmine, *karabi*, *dopati*, stuffed inside a *thhonga*. '*Ei nao*, your puja flowers,' she handed Chitra the paper bag. Chitra wasn't amused.

'Hee, hee, not them, *Jethhi*,' Rani said with the grin of a consummate snitcher. 'This time, we went by the garden of the Mitras. These were just lying outside. You don't worry, no one saw us.'

'You won't think that way when Mittir ginni comes complaining tomorrow morning. How many times have I told you not to steal flowers from other people's gardens?'

'Ooh, *beguni*!' Rani's eyes suddenly rolled over to the plate on which the eggplant fritters were getting cold.

'Yes, *beguni* it is, but you won't get even one, you *dosshi meye*. And if you continue to steal flowers, I won't even let you play with Kamala anymore,' said Chitra with mock contempt while winking at Manas.

Still eyeing the *beguni*, Rani now turned to Manas for defence. She didn't address him directly but looked at him and said, '*Bah rey*, it wasn't I who wanted to pick the flowers. Kamala only insisted as she wanted some for her hair.'

'*Ei nao*, have a *beguni*,' Manas said, holding the plate of fritters to her. The moment she tried to take one, Manas moved the plate and said, 'Nah. First you must promise you'll follow what Mashima just told you, okay?'

'All right, I will. I only brought them for her puja. Won't bring any more,' Rani said as she grabbed a deflated *beguni*. Manas held the plate out to her with an encouraging glance for her to take more. The young girl responded with a wide grin, not caring to hide her mouthful of minced *beguni*.

Chitra asked Rani to clear the table once she was done and chop some vegetables in the kitchen, for Dadababu was to have dinner with them. Turning to Manas she said, 'Come I will show you something,' leading him inside. Manas followed her to a small room packed with books, on a frail wooden shelf, on a study table, even on the floor in vertical columns.

'This used to be your Meshomoshai's study,' Chitra said.

Manas took a few minutes to absorb the sight. This wasn't the library in his house that his grandfather was so proud of, a good-sized hall adorned with mahogany bookcases, varnished every two years, with the books dusted and stacked in their places by a dedicated servant of the Dutta household. The library boasted an eclectic collection—19th-century European literature, ancient and medieval Sanskrit texts, books on history and philosophy, poetry from Persia and Turkey and other prized titles. Every book had its own place in the cabinets, catalogued and shelved to precision. And here was this library, if one could even call it that. Shorn of any sophistication or order, this room of Chitra's husband looked more like a congested literary warehouse. Two wooden chairs completed the furniture in the room.

'You sit here, Baba,' Chitra said, 'I'll go and show Rani a few things and join you here. You can pick up any book you want to.'

'Thank you, Mashima. Don't take too long.'

'I'll be right back.'

Manas skimmed over the books engulfing him; a lot of them were on physics, textbooks and the like. He pulled a chair and after looking at a few titles concerning thermal physics, optics, and mathematical methods for physics, he decided to sink his eyes into the Turgenev book he had bought. He took it out of his *panjabi* pocket. Paying attention to the words was another thing though, for in the back of his mind wiggled the question of how he would articulate what he wanted to share with Chitra. He had barely read two or three pages when she reappeared, wiping the sweat off her face and neck with her *anchal*. She closed the door behind her and bolted it.

Pulling over the other chair, Chitra said, 'So, what is it that you wanted to share, Baba? Is it something serious?'

'A few things, Mashima. You know Minoti, the girl at the camp who....'

'Yes, yes, that terrible incident. How is she now?'

'Difficult to tell, Mashima. Physically her condition remains stable, but...' Manas ran his fingers through his hair as a sigh escaped him.

Chitra drew closer to him, 'But what? Is she having panic attacks?'

'Well, not exactly, but the sight of men terrifies her. The doctor suggested only women should attend to her. Now, the question is who do I ask? The only two people I can turn to are you and Amala. And I don't want to burden the two of you with every problem at the camp.'

'Amala *ke*, that tall girl, no?'

'Yes, she works with you as a volunteer in the sewing class, Mashima.'

'Hmm, she is nice. Mature for her age. Speaks little but is intelligent and helpful.'

Manas smiled at how Chitra's impressions matched his. 'See, you think so too. Maybe I saw the same qualities in her when I requested her help for a few issues we've had to deal with before you joined us.'

Only minutes ago, the dilemma of how to talk about Amala had vexed Manas. Now, even as he spoke, he noticed how she had flowed into the conversation like a tributary joining a river—inevitably, if not willingly.

'You leave it to me, Baba. The girls are quite free with me. I think I can persuade a couple of them for this job. You won't have to ask Amala.'

Her words brought a smile on Manas's face. 'You're a lifesaver, Mashima.'

'So this was bothering you? I thought there was a new crisis at the camp. Don't burden yourself so much, Baba. Sure, this refugee problem is a big one. But you have a life beyond the camp too.'

'I know what you mean, Mashima. But it's becoming difficult for me to separate my two lives. When I sit down to eat at home, with the choicest dishes my mother gets prepared by our cook, sometimes the fly-infested *khichuri* flashes before my eyes.'

'But Baba....'

'You know, Mashima, I even considered leaving all this, finding a job and leading a good life. But I don't know why I want to return to the camp every morning.'

Chitra remained quiet. Manas appreciated that she didn't try to dissuade him from the relief work. Nor did she cheer him up with fake consolation. *This is more validation than words can ever express.*

'You were talking of a crisis, weren't you, Mashima? Well, there is one. Not at the camp, but...but in my life.'

'Oh, what is it?'

'Nothing alarming. It's a personal issue. I'm not sure if I should even bother you with it.'

'Bother or trust? Are you uncomfortable sharing it with me?'

'Not at all. I would trust you more than I would myself. It's just that....'

'Let's do one thing. You sit and think of a way to frame your question; I will put the water to boil and check on that wicked girl.'

Manas still couldn't think of the right words to present his quandary to her. Not even after a quarter of hour when she returned with two cups of golden-milky tea, neatly balanced on two small saucers, which also carried two arrowroot biscuits each. Chitra closed the door behind her.

'So, my son, what troubles you?' Chitra asked as she settled on the chair facing Manas.

'It's about Amala, Mashima,' was all Manas said, taking a sip of the hot tea.

'What about her? I thought you wanted to discuss something about yourself.'

'Yes, about me. And...and her.'

'Aha, I see. I think I understand what you mean,' Chitra said, putting her cup and saucer on the table piled with books. She took off her glasses, which had gathered steam from her visit to the kitchen. As she wiped them, she said in an undertone, 'Does she know?' She didn't look at him while asking this, and Manas took that as her way to spare him the embarrassment.

'No, Mashima. That's part of the problem. I don't know how to tell her. And I don't know how she'd take this.'

Chitra picked up her tea cup and said, 'So you have feelings for her. Or is this more serious?'

'Yes to both, Mashima,' Manas said, his eyes fixed at the teacup in his hand. 'I...want to marry her.'

'Oh!' Now Chitra looked at Manas directly. 'Well, how she'll react depends on your intent. Do you know why you want to marry her?'

'I wish I could give you a clear answer to that, Mashima, but truth be told...' Manas finally looked up to meet Chitra's eyes, 'I myself don't know. I just know I want to share my life with her.'

'That is all very well, Baba, but what draws you to her? Do you feel obligated to rescue her from the pits?'

'No, Mashima, no.' Manas's voice suddenly found the strength and conviction he felt when faced with a stiff challenge. 'It's not pity; that I am certain of. It's anything but pity.'

'Please don't mind my words, Baba; I'm only trying to put myself in that girl's position, trying to think what she would.'

'You go on, Mashima. Better your court martial than hers,' Manas couldn't help a sheepish grin.

'Good, good. So you're sure it's not pity. But can you honestly admit you are not driven by the urge to give her dignity?'

Chitra's persistence with that question made Manas pause. He never thought of it that way, as if Amala needed his deliverance. The quiet strength that sparkled in her eyes, her measured speech, the weight of her conviction—these were the things that drew him to her.

Manas simply said, 'Dignity? Nah, Mashima, she has enough of that—she can possibly give me some if she wanted to. I think of her as a friend. Not sure if she feels that way too, but....'

'That's better. Because, Baba, I guess you know women are a sensitive lot. No matter how strong we are, it takes very little to cause us heartbreaks. So you have to tread carefully on this path.'

'I know, Mashima. I'm not sure why I am even talking to you about all this—it feels so unreal and impossible to share with someone what I've been feeling for months. I hardly know how to approach her, or...if I even have the courage to do so.'

'All that will happen when the time comes. Don't rush. But before that, I must ask, would you have your family's support in this?'

Manas sipped the last of the tea left in his cup—cold and bitter. 'No, Mashima,' he sighed. 'I don't think that will be possible.'

'*Maaney*? What do you mean by that? How will you proceed if that's not possible?'

'Well, I have thought about it but it's not the biggest of my concerns. My mother and grandfather are dear to me, and I understand my obligations towards them. But since this is about my life, I still get to make the decisions.'

'And what if your dear mother and grandfather don't agree with your decision?'

'It's very likely they won't. But I will still go ahead.'

'*Orey baba*, Amala has cast a spell on you, I see,' Chitra said, leaning forward, her eyes glinting with a puckish light that reflected off the thick lens of her spectacles.

If Manas was embarrassed, he didn't show it. He knew if he were to make any progress with the life he envisioned with Amala, he could certainly do with some sage advice. So he apprised Chitra of the vehement opposition that he would almost certainly face from his mother and grandfather. He told her he might even be disinherited from the family property. But that he didn't care. As he babbled on, beads of sweat arched his brow, his throat went dry and his hands moved fast. At the end of it all, he was exhausted. And thirsty.

Night had crept in with cricket calls and the faint shimmer of halogen lights streaming in through the lone window in the study. Chitra got up and switched on a table lamp. Walking up to Manas, she softly placed her hand on his shoulder. 'Let's eat now, Baba. You have to go home too.'

Manas got up. As he started walking towards the door, Chitra said, 'All will be well. I'm there for you. If you find no other place, know that you have a home here.'

'I know, Mashima,' Manas said, looking back at her with a smile.

Dinner came in steel plates and bowls—*mushurir dal, maachher jhol* and *begun bhaja*. The modest three-course meal of red lentils, fish curry, and fried eggplants suited Manas well. The food was delicious and much more manageable than his mother's elaborate five-to-seven-course spreads. It wasn't as if he didn't like the food; on the contrary, as the only child of a rich family, he had come to appreciate a well-cooked fish, mutton or prawn curry; the choicest of sweets like rosogolla, ledikeni, and chawm-chawm; the different types of fried vegetables that gave company to lentils tempered just right. But lately, he found these indulgences obscene; particularly when he saw the refugees eating nothing but brackish rice gruel day after day at the camp.

Manas returned home a lot lighter and very late. As he closed the gate and moved towards the door, a bolt of brightness hit his eyes. The silhouette of his grandfather sitting on the porch with a flashlight startled him. Manas scuttled over to him and asked why he was sitting there, suffering mosquitoes and other creatures of the dark.

Haraprasad simply said, 'It's late, Dadubhai. Let's get inside. Your mother is worried.'

When he entered the dining room led by his grandfather, Manas felt sorry for his mother. Her head was bent on the table. She had fallen asleep, apparently waiting for him. Before quietly stepping out of the room, Haraprasad motioned him to wake her up.

Manas softly patted Mrinmoyee on the shoulder. She woke up with a start, and on seeing her son, tried hard to focus on him. Then, gathering herself she said, 'Come, food is ready. Wash your hands and eat.'

Manas didn't have the heart to tell her that he had a stuffed stomach. For once, he obeyed her and joined her at the table. Not only had she been waiting for him, she hadn't eaten a morsel herself.

'But why did you not eat, Ma? I don't understand,' he asked as she put rice, cold and hard, on his plate.

'It's late, Maanu. We can talk about this tomorrow,' she said as she forwarded him the plate and took some rice and daal in a small bowl for herself.

While nibbling on a piece of fried fish, stringy and tasteless, Manas's thoughts turned to the evening's exchange at Chitra's house. For the first time, the thought of Amala evoked in him a strange mix of trepidation and delight. Although in reality he hadn't moved any closer in his relationship with her, the very act of letting his heart's floodgates open, relaxed him.

I found the book I was looking for. It's rat-eaten and shabby. The paper is cheap and so is the ink, now fading in many places. A few pages are torn. How symptomatic is that of the lives of the people whose stories these pages contain. Lives gnawed and spat out, stories erased without

*remorse, memories shredded with disdain. If there's any consolation,
it is that at least these stories were told. For the people I am working
with, even that possibility seems remote. Who is going to write their
stories when no one even cares whether they exist or not?*

— MANAS DUTTA, DIARY ENTRY, SEPTEMBER 1950

That night, Manas slept like a stuffed log.

~

A different wind had started blowing in the camp. The mornings
still began with children and mothers with infants lining up for
milk, the afternoons were selfsame with the doling out of the
rice-lentil gruel, and the evenings sank into the same depths
of darkness. In between were the sewing classes and the night
school for children. Yet, something wasn't the same anymore.
Manas noticed that the able-bodied refugees, especially the men,
weren't subservient like before. They now walked with their heads
held high, spoke with confidence and seemed to care less and less
about ruffling the feathers of those in authority, especially from
the government's side.

Manas couldn't quite put his finger on what had led to this
change. Minoti's violation must have been the major trigger but
could it also be that the sewing classes and the night school had
filled these drifting, hopeless people with the conviction that they
were useful after all? While their newfound confidence inspired
Manas, something about it also alarmed him. Where would this
dynamism take them? *Energy, by its very nature, has to be channelled
in some way or it could implode.*

Chitra, meanwhile, had come up with a novel idea to help
Minoti heal through her trauma. She now came to the camp
four days a week, and on most of her visits, Rani accompanied
her. Amala had been keeping her company since the traumatic
incident but during the sewing and craft classes, Rani stayed
with Minoti. She would bring toys—broken utensils, a bob of

wool crafted with multi-coloured strands, a piece of lace, a roll of golden *zari* thread, even a rag doll she had made herself with instructions from Chitra.

The idea worked. Initially reluctant to have a conversation at all, even if it were with a chatterbox like Rani, Minoti eventually opened up to this forced friend of hers. Over the next few weeks, they became playmates and then confidantes.

One afternoon when Rani told Chitra and Manas how excited she was that Minoti and her cat Mini were coming to stay with them, she didn't find them reciprocating her enthusiasm. Apparently, the idea was Minoti's. She had received a letter from her village informing her of the postponement of her mother's and sister's journey to India, as the situation had improved there. Rani saw no problem in the proposition and didn't think Chitra would object.

'Who asked you to say yes to her?' Chitra chided her when Rani told them.

'How could I say no? If she came here, wouldn't it be easier for you?' the teenager, who Manas thought was going on forty-three, retorted.

'Oh, *thhandidi*, you don't have to worry about me. You didn't even think of asking me once?'

Rani was about to say something when Manas intervened. 'Ah, Mashi, let her be. She's only a little girl.'

Chitra asked Rani to sort out vegetables in the kitchen; she wanted to discuss the matter with Manas. Her finances were tight as it were, she confided in him. 'Adding another member to the household....'

It took some convincing but Manas could make Chitra see the value of letting Minoti stay with her for a few days. The change of environment would do her well, they both agreed. Spending time away from the camp might help her heal faster.

'Please don't worry about the finances, Mashima,' Manas said. 'We have a fund set up for emergencies like these. We'll work this out together.'

9

Manas's house geared up for the annual autumnal frenzy of Durga Puja. Like most Bengali children, young Manas looked forward to this time of the year, not just for the month-long celebrations but also the indulgences the festival brought—no school for an entire week, new clothes, fewer restrictions on play time, and almost no stress on studies. He even received some cash from his grandfather and a few other relatives who seemed to appear from the void only for this occasion.

Such latitude was mostly courtesy Manas's father. Part of this was because as an agricultural scientist, Jyotirmoy had to be frequently away on field trips and laboratory tests. He made sure to dedicate most of his time at home to young Maanu, taking him to the Birla Planetarium and the Alipore zoo during the winter months. In summer, they would spend entire days walking through the Shibpur botanical gardens, a place dear to both of them for their own reasons. They went to other interesting places, too, like the National Library, and the National Museum, where Manas saw a mummy for the first time. But after his father's death, it was the trips to the botanical gardens that Manas missed the most. Despite the camaraderie he felt with a few trees from his years of association with them, he couldn't bring himself to visit the gardens without Baba.

Jyotirmoy had allowed, even encouraged, his son to do things that weren't seen in a favourable light by his wife or father. But neither of them objected overtly to any of his decisions. So Manas could invite friends, both from the neighbourhood and his school, to the Durga Puja celebrations at their house. On the evening of *navami*, barely hours before the goddess's immersion, Jyotirmoy took the boys around the town in his car to the *sarbojonin* Durga Pujas that had started coming up in various Calcutta localities. The dynamism of the youth organising these pujas inspired him and he wanted Manas to cross the confines of family and home to experience the community spirit of the festival. The evenings spilled over to nights as Jyotirmoy and his young squad stayed up to listen to singers and artists performing in *jalshas* across different pandals.

If the Manas of the future were anything to go by, he had certainly grown up to be his father's son. Even though he couldn't break away from the family tradition completely to organise a Durga Puja with his friends, he still went to see the various community pujas with them. For the past couple of years, the boys took a group of slum children from Ultadanga with them. For Manas, this wasn't so much about altruism as about reliving his boyhood days—when his pals used to fill up the absence of a sibling.

For the upcoming puja, he thought of including Chitra and a few kids from the Gariahata camp in that group.

~

Though a bigger unit of their family once used to live in the Dutta mansion, soon after Manas's parents got married, his grandfather's only brother, older than him, moved out along with his side of the family. Manas didn't know too many details about the estrangement. Whatever he gathered from snatches of conversations between his parents and grandfather amounted to the fact that financial dealings had caused fissures between the two senior Duttas.

Manas didn't remember any exchange between the two branches of his paternal family. During Durga Puja, relatives did appear though, from his mother's side. Her brothers and older sister, his mamas and Bawromashi, would visit them from time to time. Whereas the uncles, his mother's cousins, only came during special occasions like Durga Puja and *bhai phonta*, his aunt often came without occasion and stayed with them for extended periods. As someone who had been widowed at a young age without bearing a child, his aunt seemed to find in her sister's house the solace and company that had eluded her in her in-laws' home. Manas liked her a lot; her unencumbered presence was wrapped in a serene smile that had almost glued itself to her face. Her voice, though soft, sounded resolute to Manas. He also admired another trait in her: she never whispered. No matter how intimate the discussion, she held the same even timbre in a conversation.

Some of Manas's cherished childhood memories were of listening to Bawromashi telling him stories, of which she seemed to be an endless repository. Her enactment of the stories with hand movements and lively expressions made Manas ask her to repeat the same three or four stories that had become his favourites.

Even as he grew up, their relationship remained the same, only the stories changed. Every visit of hers made Manas happy, although, of late, these had become infrequent on account of her poor health. There had been times when Manas ached to see her and even considered visiting her in her village in the 24 Parganas.

Today, as he remembered her, sadness engulfed him. She won't be here for this year's puja.

～

When she arrived at Chitra's house a few days later clutching Mini to her chest, Minoti still looked weak to Manas. The boys had organised a cot for her, which they placed in the room next to the kitchen, where Rani slept. The room no longer served its original purpose as the *bhnarar ghor*, a storeroom meant for stocking grains and produce. Chitra now used the space to keep some of her husband's belongings she had shown Manas during one of his visits—clothes and a few special utensils, a wooden desk with a drawer, and a teak armchair on which he would spend hours reading.

Over the next two months, it seemed to Manas that Minoti shed her resentment of men like a garment she didn't find use for any longer. The comings and goings of Manas and his friends at Chitra's house didn't bother her at all. Although she never joined Rani in serving them tea or water, she would sometimes stand by the door, clutching the curtain drapes, allowing Mini to lick her feet, listening to the conversations that took place between her Chitra Mashimoni, and the dadas.

Gradually, she started coming into the room and sitting quietly beside Rani. They made an endearing contrast—Rani the unstoppable chatterbox, and Minoti, her tongue-tied follower. The most one would hear of her would be short chuckles, diffident and abrupt. Nobody tried to get her to speak; it was as if they had signed an unwritten, unspoken pact to let her be. Even Rani, otherwise given to goading people to yield to her ways, didn't ever bother her new friend.

Minoti has become a part of this house like the ancient smells and the cobwebs that hang in its air—hard to pinpoint yet unmistakably present.

10

On afternoons when they went around the village wading from one pond to the next, splashing water on each other and smearing their legs and saris with mud, Amala sometimes took a moment to admire the *shapla*, the slender water lily she and her friends picked from the ponds in which they abounded. How bright and peaceful the flower looked as sunlight dappled its petals, its reflection floating softly on the water. The *shapla* itself had an element of resigned calm to it; as one plucked the flower, its root submerged in water, it offered little resistance.

For a snack as delicious as the *shapla* stems, the kids didn't mind getting wet, especially given how easy it was to procure the delicacy—the flick of a thumb and two fingers, and they snapped right off. Kartik found it fun to break the flowers with a few inches of the stem. On some days they would gather a whole bunch and bring them home, demanding of their mother to make them *shapla boras*, fritters she made by chopping the stems into matchsticks, which were then stitched together using a bamboo stick, soaked in salt water, dipped into batter and deep fried. It wasn't often that Amala's mother had to go through this tedious process because mostly the kids liked to munch on the freshly-plucked stems raw.

And just like that, I have become the shapla *myself*, Amala thought as she got ready to start her morning chores at the camp.

The morning air carried an early winter chill. Amala pulled on her only shawl, green and thinning with perforations. She took out the straw broom from under her cot and began sweeping.

Lately, the camp folks had started making a few items for their everyday needs. The brooms were among these, as were wicker baskets, clay pots, and now, thanks to Chitra's sewing classes, *kanthas* and small baby clothes. This didn't take them anywhere near self-sufficiency, but Amala felt it added to their confidence. Of taking things into their own hands and claiming what was rightfully theirs—a life beyond tents for roofs and doles for existence.

As the winter months started creeping up on them, the patience of the camp dwellers ran thin. Amala felt strangely buoyed by this combination of crushing despondency and defiant hope. Taking charge was good, even necessary. The more she aligned herself to this line of thinking, the more determined she became in her mission of finding Kartik, even if a dark cloud edged that resolve.

And just like that, it occurred to Amala that she hadn't seen much of Manas lately. He looked busy whenever he was around, particularly because of the festival season that had recently passed. Amala recalled the reaction of many refugee parents, mostly mothers, when Manas suggested taking their children to Durga Puja celebrations across the city. They were hesitant, even scared after what had happened to Minoti.

Most of the parents remained reluctant to let their children step outside the camp. The few who had initially liked the prospect of their children frolicking for a couple of days later felt discouraged by the reactions of the others. The idea had been dropped in the end.

It struck Amala that Manas hadn't approached her to help reassure the refugee parents. She found this a bit odd; in the past, he had sought her help for even the smallest of emergencies.

It was good he was moving on, Amala thought, leaving her to her own resources. Given how the force mustered in the camp, Amala felt purposeful, not helpless. As she blew a whiff of dust off the ground with the broom, she smiled with a shrug. *Why am I even thinking of Manas Babu? What is he to me?*

Even as she wrestled with that thought, mildly unsettling,

Amala's mind turned to her village. To how Kartik had given her and Ma such a hard time on an oppressive, jackfruit-roasting, mango-bursting Baishakh day. Their school had closed for the summer holidays and the kids had planned to spend it as purposelessly as was fit for any day of the month-long vacation.

That morning, they had gathered in the school playground, left open and unmonitored during the holidays, for a game of *ha-du-du*. Two groups of boys and girls faced each other in their respective combat zones, divided by a line drawn in the middle. One player from each team would dare to infiltrate the opponent's zone. If the brave boy or girl could evade the touch of all the opponents as they pounced on their potential victim, he or she would be a victor. The team with more victors won the game.

After they were done with a couple of rounds, Amala left for home. Not that the game tired her out; she loved the challenge of it. Her slender, lanky frame and nimble movements made her difficult to catch, and for this reason, she and Kartik were never placed in the same team. Kartik, though short, was slim, too, and while not as agile as his sister, was a good dodger. He distracted his opponents by making funny faces.

But today Amala needed to help her mother make *boris*. She had a vested interest in this; she ate the maximum number of those sun-dried lentil nuggets her mother put in fish curries and in fresh greens cooked into a warm mush. Kartik would have to fight for some *bori* on his plate so Sumitra always kept a few pieces hidden for him in her sari *anchal* and dropped them onto his plate as he started mixing the rice and curry.

But where was he, even as the morning rolled into a sweltering afternoon? The sun was intense enough to dry a fresh batch of *boris*, and once lunch had been cooked, Sumitra sent Amala to bring her brother back. She went but grudgingly, for she could hardly wait to relish the fish curry her mother had made that day—with a big *rui* her father hadn't been able to sell in the market. Such treats were rare for the Manna family; usually they had to do with small fish that Sumitra caught from the pond daily.

The school field stood starkly empty when Amala got there.
It echoed none of the hollering of a couple of hours ago. The
sun pounded its blazing fury on Amala. She went around and
knocked on the doors of all their friends. Curiously, none of the
boys had returned.

Tired and exasperated, Amala went to Saleha's house. She
needed a drink of water or she would faint. That was where she
learned that the boys had headed off to Kirtankhola to see a
steamer launch. One of the boys had a relative coming aboard the
huge boat and he took his pals to receive the guest.

Kartik had never seen a steamer, nor had Amala. They had
only heard about their roomy decks, much wider than the boats
they sailed on, of how the boat ran on a steam engine and didn't
have to be propelled using oars. Of how passengers were treated to
meals prepared with freshly-caught fish, of luxuries they couldn't
dream of in the village. Boarding one of those remained a dream
for them; the opportunity to see one couldn't be missed at any cost.

Amala had no energy left to walk to the river. She retreated
towards home. She was mad at Kartik but also relieved he wasn't
alone. By the time she reached home, the rice had become stone
cold; the *boris* in the curry were more like pebbles than moist
nuggets. Amala didn't feel like eating, but upon her mother's
insistence, had a small bowl of cold rice and lentils. Sumitra herself
wouldn't eat until her son returned, though. Amala didn't press her;
she knew her mother would never eat before feeding her children.

～

Amala and her sewing class sisters got a surprise at the next
class. Chitra entered the classroom along with Manik, who
carried a heavy-looking object wrapped with a soft *kantha*. The
girls recognised the *kantha* at once, the work of Bimala, one of
them. She had gifted it to Chitra; this was the teacher's way of
honouring her student's work. The women's surprise doubled
when Manik lifted the cover and placed the object, a sewing

machine, on the table. This would be the first time most of the women had seen such a machine. They were eager to touch it, feel its different parts—the spool pin where the thread reel was wound, the stitch regulator, the needle bar, the flywheel—as if it weren't a tool but a toy.

'One by one, please. You may hurt yourself otherwise,' Chitra cautioned.

The women stepped back a little, allowing her to take over. Manik left the room but not before promising to send tea for everyone.

Chitra started describing to the girls the functions of the machine's parts. 'I wish we had a few more of these so you all could practise. For now we'll have to manage with just one.'

The women had a thousand questions. *Can you make kanthas on this? Is it possible to make designs the way one can by embroidering by hand? What do you do when the thread runs out of the spool pin? How long does it take to master the machine?*

Chitra patiently answered every query and assured her students that she would teach them the nuts and bolts of the machine no matter how long it took.

By the time tea arrived, the ladies had already started testing their new training equipment; they were trying out fixing the needle to the needle bar, putting in place a thread reel and the happy act of spinning the flywheel. Seeing their enthusiasm, Chitra told them she would bring the machine twice a week. But the focus, she reminded them, had to be on knitting, not sewing, given the cold weather creeping up on them.

The weather, coupled with malnutrition had already claimed six lives, all infants, at the camp. Surely the dole milk hadn't been enough to make the children resistant to the germs that infested their surroundings. Amala knew that knitting a few woollens couldn't save them. Nothing could. Except escaping this putrid, breath-snuffing squalor.

~

Manas didn't arrive at the camp before noon. Manik was already there. Subir and Raghu had gone to buy some sewing materials requested by Chitra and her students. A few young boys, having got hold of a flat bicycle tire from somewhere, were making it 'run' with a stick. Manas made his way towards the sewing class. Seeing Amala working at the machine, with Chitra guiding her, made his heart swell, not exactly with pride but with a warm happiness. He nodded at them and at the other women in the room with a smile, then waved and quietly left.

For the next ten days, Manas remained tied to his bed at home. A body-burning, bone-aching fever had seized him. Dr Dasgupta, who had treated members of the Dutta family for more than three decades, prescribed for Manas the necessary antibiotics and an extended period of time away from the 'germ-infested refugee camp'.

Even as he slipped in and out of a state of semi-consciousness, Manas heard his mother speak to her father-in-law about sending an urgent telegram to Sreemoyee, Manas's beloved Bawromashi.

When Sreemoyee arrived from her village two days later, Manas was better, but only slightly. The fever receded during the day but came charging back in the evening.

Manas's aunt had come armed with divine remedy: *sindoor*-smeared flowers from the Dakshineshwar Kali temple where she had made a stop on her way to her sister's house. As she rubbed the flowers on Manas's forehead, he smiled wanly. Bawromashi's arrival seemed to have instantly buoyed the patient's disposition if not his physical health.

'Maanu will be fine in no time, you'll see,' Sreemoyee said to a downcast Mrinmoyee.

'*Hain*, he will. His favourite Mashi is here,' Mrinmoyee said.

As Manas would later learn from Subir, although his co-volunteers understood how badly he needed the rest, this was the time when they needed him at the camp more than ever before.

Even though it was mostly brewing in the background, the camp members' disquiet had begun to show up in more ways than one. The male volunteers were seldom available to help with the tasks entrusted to them. At times they even stepped out of the camp for an entire day without offering any explanation. But that wasn't all. What appeared worrying to Manas's friends was the dwindling attendance in Chitra's sewing class. Not all the women had stopped coming to her classes. But some did and remained consistently absent.

Amala was one of them.

11

When Manas returned to the camp, his friends were worried he might suffer a relapse of his illness. Not because of the germs that floated around but the mental shock awaiting him. The camp had a deserted look save for a few old and infirm refugees who still hobbled around.

Over tea at the camp office, Subir broke the bombshell to Manas. The missing camp members weren't coming back. They had set up a new colony by occupying a large tract of unused land some twenty kilometres away, near Shibpur. The land reportedly belonged to Niranjan Chowdhury, a local zamindar.

Manas wasn't the only volunteer to learn about this uprising second hand. His co-volunteers had heard the story from Chitra, who, in turn had been informed by Minoti.

～

For Amala, the decision to join the agitation had been an easy one. From all the talk in the camp, it had become clear to her that the government wasn't in a mood to provide dole to the refugees for much longer. Moreover, what happened to Minoti had shaken Amala to the core. When Paban-da revealed to the refugee volunteers the plan he had hatched with the help of a local left front leader, Amala voiced her support from day one.

At odd moments like when she wiped her wet hair after a bath or as she sat down to mend a torn blouse, she would think of Manas and all his kind gestures. Kindness, yes. That she was alone had possibly heightened that instinct in him. More than these thoughts, what caught Amala by surprise was that she was thinking of Manas and so often at that. It was as if he had become privy to her secrets despite remaining absent from the camp for days.

For now, Amala had to be more pragmatic than anything else. If she were to find Kartik, she needed to get out of the camp prison. She volunteered to lead a batch of women and children, one of the three refugee contingents preparing to occupy the zamindar's land. The story she would later hear from Ganesh, a member of the men's contingent, about what went on inside Nirajanan Chowdhury's house that night would become part of Amala's post-camp folklore.

On the evening of Kali Puja, the zamindar and his coterie gambled over card games as they sipped fine Scotch whiskey and inhaled tobacco from a *hookah* in turns. Nautch girls, hired especially for the occasion, kept them hooked throughout the evening. Servants scurried about the house, doing the bidding of the womenfolk who focused their attention on the actual puja of goddess Kali, and of the children, who didn't want the moonless night, dazzling with sparklers, crackers and other assorted fireworks, to end.

A special batch of *thakurs*, Brahmin cooks, had been hired to prepare the *bhog* offered to the goddess. Inside another kitchen, detached from the main part of the mansion, a team of Muslim *khansamas* slogged away to please their masters with the most succulent *biryani* and goat curry they could conjure.

Early that afternoon, Amala and her fellow refugees began a journey from the Gariahata camp—partly by tram, then by foot— towards the mansion's east. That's where a vast empty stretch of the zamindar's land lay. Upon reaching the school nearest to the vacant land, they divided themselves into three groups and reached the destination from three directions until they all stood at the spot that would shape their destiny.

The squatting refugees wasted no time in clearing up the dense vegetation of tamarind and *shimul* trees that flanked the disused plot of land. Having scanned the area in advance a few times, they had come prepared with axes, shovels and other implements. Within a few hours of arriving at the spot, they had installed nearly a hundred makeshift tent-like dwellings with *hogla* leaves and bamboo poles. To cover the occupied area, they erected a fence with banana tree trunks and thorny branches, also part of their ammunition for this mission.

When Manas returned to the Gariahata camp, cured of his fever but still weak from it, there was thus little left for him to do. The few old and infirm men and women left in the camp had no family to speak of. They were now at the mercy of government doles and private philanthropy.

From his conversations with the government camp officials, Manas knew the camp's existence itself had come into question. Encumbered by a growing number of camps and without a composite plan for integrating the refugees into the mainstream society and economy, the authorities couldn't keep a camp with only a few refugees running. The people in this camp would eventually have to leave, either with someone they knew or to other camps. Some of them were so feeble they didn't have the faintest idea about the latest insurrection and remained secured to their beds, indifferent to anything that went on in the world, to the dole money, the meal rations, the change of seasons, to life itself.

～

Manas found in Minoti, now Minu and a little sister to him, a bridge between his world and the one the squatting refugees had created for themselves. Minoti had visited the new colony, unnamed and devoid of any official legitimacy as yet, only once. To Manas, she represented the last flicker of hope for reconnecting with Amala. *We sure have a lot of unfinished business*, Manas told himself, unable to not see a hint of betrayal in Amala's departure. He supported her decision to move to the squatter's colony wholeheartedly. But the fact that she didn't even think of letting him or Chitra know saddened Manas. He felt the ground beneath him slipping away.

The absence of Amala—the face that had shone for him like a beacon, its radiance surpassing even *Bawromashi's* —hit Manas hard. Not even the memory of his candid conversation with Chitra or her reassurances filled the pit he felt he was sinking into. Nothing could help, he knew, but the sight of Amala's face. He had to meet her.

~

When the news of the occupation of his land reached the landlord's ears the morning after Kalipuja, his head, still heavy with the alcohol that had been offered to the goddess and then to him as *prasad*, reeled with a pounding ache. Any kind of stress triggered headaches for him; the pain would sometimes last days. The last time he had been assailed by one of these unbearable headaches was nearly six months ago, when a boat carrying jute produced in his fields had capsized. A thunderstorm had caused the accident, drowning the entire produce, a hundred kilos of jute bales, being ferried to the nearby Kamarhatty jute mills.

Niranjan Chowdhury disliked *ingreji oshudh*; it made him nauseous and sick. But when his headache entered its third unrelenting day, he had to submit to the powers of the foreign-brewed allopathic medicine prescribed by Madan *daktar*, the physician who was summoned to check on Chowdhury only in extreme situations.

What could be more alarming than these scrounging refugees squatting on his land? Before collapsing on the bed placed especially for him in the sitting room, he commanded his best goons to 'hound the scoundrels out!'

~

As she didn't have any family of her own, Amala shared her new 'home' with Malati and Nimai. This worked out well for both sides; Amala had developed an easy, informal relationship with the senior couple and they in turn were happy to have her support, especially now that they were on their own. It comforted Malati to have another woman around.

Dried *hogla* leaves and bamboo poles had been distributed to each 'family' unit to help them mark the boundaries of their dwelling. Amala began fixing those in the area designated to her new, made-up family. She wanted to finish the fencing before the sun became too strong. She'd barely covered half the area when she saw a group of armed men charging towards the squatters, mouthing vulgar expletives. Amala dropped the leaves and rushed to a semi-constructed primary school building close to her plot of land.

As the only building in the occupied area, the unfinished 'school' served as the refugees' community centre. Amala saw Paban-da and his friends engrossed in a conversation with Dibyendu Gupta, a local communist leader. The politician had come with a few of his party comrades to extend support and organisational help to the refugees. Amala knew there was no time to waste. 'A group of men are coming this way, they have *laathis*,' she said, her voice quavering even as her eyes zoomed beyond the small window in the room.

The men picked up the spears, sticks, and even a few hand grenades they had kept handy for such eventualities. When they came out of the school building, they saw a muddle of destruction—earthen stoves and pots broken to pieces, clothes torn to shreds, fences levelled. Niranjan Chowdhury's men spared no time in going about their business; they attacked every visible sign of settlement.

Two mongrels, one black, the other brown, who had become members of the refugee group while they were still at the camp got up from their slumber under the umbrella of a massive banyan tree and charged towards the refugee men. The brown dog, older and suffering from a recent limp, took longer than his black friend.

Before he could join the group, a stone hit him and he lurched to the ground with a groan.

Women and children were asked to rush inside the school as most of the men went out to face the zamindar's goons. Not that the so-called school, little more than a few walls and a window, provided any more safety than the outside. There were no doors and anybody could walk into it at any time. Amala stood close to the window to keep an eye on the conflict.

Bhola, who was only a couple of years older than Kartik received the first blow of a *laathi* from the zamindar's men. The squatters responded by hurling stones at their opponents. The fight turned ugly. Two refugee men were hit in their eyes. Bhola, whose left arm bled from a rough *laathi* blow, ran to escort them back to the school building.

The weapons were more or less the same on both sides with the exception of the hand grenades, which only the refugees and their communist friends had. These were their last line of defence, to be used only if all else failed. As more of their boys and men received menacing blows from the zamindar's henchmen, trained *lathhiyals* all of them, the refugees struck with their first hand grenade. This thwarted the advance of the zamindar's men. They were stronger for sure, but fewer in number compared to their opposition, ten against sixty odd. Three of them had already been badly injured; the grenade injured a fourth man in his right leg and he collapsed to the ground. The henchmen began retreating, vowing to come back 'soon enough'.

The refugees, more emboldened than ever, accepted the challenge with, 'Sure. See you then.'

Manas learned about this bloody clash when it had already entered its third day. Minoti brought the news when she visited Chitra's house with Bhola. Subir, Manik, and Manas were in the colony the next day to join the refugee group. Proshanto took leave from work to take care of the Gariahata camp's duties along with Raghu and Chitra.

The clashes continued for another day. On the fifth morning, the police arrested eleven men, eight of them refugees, one, a communist party member, and two of the zamindar's men. Four critically-injured refugee men had to be hospitalised.

Despite these setbacks, the squatting refugees, not the zamindar, emerged the winners.

As the local left-wing politicians threw their hats into the ring, the state government intervened and settled the matter by promising monetary compensation to the zamindar. For now, the refugees would stay in their new colony. Partly, they had the broken school building to thank for this, which they had begun using as a school for their children on the very next day of squatting. According to a government rule, if refugees had an educational institution that children attended, they couldn't be displaced. They would eventually need to get the colony, christened *Bijoy Nagar* (Victory Colony), registered for it to be entitled to the same legal and administrative facilities as were granted to other areas under the city's civic corporation.

Manas had little chance to interact with Amala over the past two days as the women were still holed up inside the school. The morning after the clashes ended, Manas and his friends took a tour of the freshly-seized squatter colony. Manas could see the enormousness of the task that lay ahead for the space to become truly habitable. There was no clean water supply or electricity. Nor did the residents have any sewage or waste collection system in place.

As they walked through the area, Subir thought aloud the need for setting up a few hand pumps at the very least. Manas nodded, saying they needed a new fundraising drive to get the basics in place in Bijoy Nagar.

'We'll also need more volunteers, Manas-da,' Manik said.

Manas agreed as he thought of the added effort needed to manage the camp and work with the squatting refugees.

They landed close to Amala's shack. The landlord's goons had razed the incomplete fencing Amala had earlier put up. Manas saw Amala resurrecting the fence with a fresh batch of *hogla* leaves. She seemed engrossed in what she was doing. Manas noticed her lips moving with the hint of a sweet smile.

As the boys came closer, Manas said softly so as not to break Amala's reverie, '*Ei je*, how goes?'

He thought he had caught a fragment of a song in her voice before it faded away as she looked at him and smiled. A tiny hurricane swept through Manas's heart.

'How are you all?' Amala asked.

'We are well, Didi,' Manik said, 'though we could do with some *cha-muri*.'

'Why sure, Bhai,' Amala said as she invited them in for tea.

Manas hesitated. 'Nah, nah, please don't bother. We have to visit the rest of your neighbours anyway.'

'You surely have time for tea, Manas Babu,' Amala said.

Her voice, courteous yet firm, surprised Manas. As did her calling his name for the first time ever. He quietly entered the tenement; Subir and Manik followed suit. Manas took in the scent of freshly-plastered mud on the walls. At the far end of the room, Malati swept with a broom. The moment she saw the boys, she covered her head with her *anchal* and beamed a smile, flashing her *paan*-reddened teeth.

Putting the broom in a corner, Malati said to the boys, '*Esho, baba, esho.* Come sit,' pointing to the lone handwoven rug spread on the floor.

The volunteers took their seats on the ground. Manas couldn't help but notice how spotless the small, unventilated room looked. A long-necked earthen pitcher rested on a stool in a corner. In another corner, a few jerry cans stood on the floor like soldiers on alert.

Amala followed the men into the room and said to Malati, 'Mashi, I will get some water for the tea. Please give them water to drink for now.' She reached for the jerry cans and picked up a couple.

'Where will you get the water from?' Manas asked Amala.

'From the pond we have here,' she said, '*ei jaabo aar ashbo*. Be back in a minute.'

'May I join you?' Manas asked, even as he got up. He couldn't miss this chance.

'Nah, nah, please don't bother. It's not too far away. You talk with Mashi here; I'll be right back,' Amala said.

'Let me see where the pond is,' Manas said and offered to carry one of the jerry cans.

Amala, clearly embarrassed, handed it to him and said, '*Ashun*, let's go.'

They followed the ridge path the refugees had roughly carved out after clearing the land of shrubs and weeds. Amala remained quiet except when she greeted a passing neighbour or other women walking to the pond to fetch water or with piles of unwashed laundry. Manas was glad he had worn covered shoes. Pebbles, twigs and shards of glass filled the earth beneath his feet. He lifted his *dhuti*, not because he didn't want it to get dusty but because he couldn't afford to trip on this uneven terrain.

Manas broke the silence gathering between Amala and him. 'So, how have you been?'

'How do you find me to be?' Amala said, her gaze still averted.

'You seem to be doing fine,' Manas said, adding with a chuckle, 'now that you don't have to listen to my odd requests.'

Amala laughed lightly. A few quiet moments followed.

'So...so you ran away without saying goodbye to...' Manas clipped back the last word, a pronoun for self. Amala heard it anyway.

'You took so long to get well, Manas Babu,' Amala said with a sigh. 'How could I not join our people here, you tell me.'

'Hey, I was only teasing you. Of course, you did the right thing. I am happy for you. In fact, I am...I'm proud of you.'

Amala remained quiet. They were just a few steps from the pond when she said, 'Are you feeling better now?'

'I am as well as you see me. And how is that?'

'You look weak and thin. I hope you're eating well.'

'Oh yes, don't worry about me,' Manas said even as their conversation came to an abrupt end when they reached the pond. Groups of women had scattered across the bank. Boys and girls of all ages were plunging into the pond's cool, algae-green water for an afternoon dip. From the trees on the banks, crows and mynas created an odd sort of symphony as the birdcall blended with the women's and kids' giggles. Manas looked around and saw three or four men on the other side of the pond. They had a couple of fishing rods in the water, evidently in search of fresh catch for lunch. A mini village scene had taken shape, and it soothed Manas's nerves.

'It is good, Babu, our coming here,' Amala's words cut through Manas's reverie.

'Hmm, I see that,' Manas said. 'Better than that sickly camp for sure.'

'Better than living on handouts,' said Amala as she dipped a jerry can into the pond. Manas followed suit, if a bit reluctantly when he saw how mucky the water was. With the help of what Manas considered the sixth sense women were born with, Amala seemed to have read his mind.

'Don't worry,' she said with a smile, 'I will boil the water and strain it well for your tea. You won't fall sick again, not because of me.'

Manas managed a faint smile, not enough to hide his embarrassment.

As they turned around to return to the hut, Mokkhoda, an elderly refugee woman Manas remembered for the sharpness of her tongue, faced them. She had a brass pitcher tucked around her waist and betel leaf juice swirling inside her mouth. On catching the sight of Manas, she quickly covered her head with her *anchal*. Swallowing the juice in a single gulp she said, '*Arrey, bhawlentyaar Babu jey!* What brings you here?'

Before Manas could answer, Amala snapped, 'Why, Mashi, don't you know Manas Babu and his friends have been here for three days, fighting with the zamindar's men? And if you will, we're in a hurry.' Looking at Manas she said, '*Cholen*, Babu. Malati Mashi is waiting.'

Manas dithered for a second; he had half a mind to talk to Mokkhoda. But Amala had already marched ahead and all he could do was to mumble an '*ashi*' to the inquisitive woman before picking up pace to join Amala. He had to nearly run but when he finally caught up with her, huffing, he couldn't let go of the opportunity to ask her. 'I wanted to talk to you about something, Amala.'

'I am listening. *Bolun.*'

'Umm, not here. Can we meet somewhere else? Only if you don't mind.'

'Meet where? What's on your mind, Manas Babu?'

Her tone, not wary or suspicious, but steady and sincere, reassured him.

'Can we meet at Chitra Mashi's house?' *Please...say yes.* Manas realised he must have sounded desperate but considering how brief his time with Amala was going to be, he had no choice. Seeing her surprised-bordering-on-shocked look, he said, 'No, I mean Chitra Mashi wants to see you, too. She misses you.'

Without probing him any deeper, Amala agreed to visit Chitra on Saturday, two days later. Manas thanked her with a face as inflated as a football.

Tea turned into lunch, which Malati insisted the boys stay for. Manas tried his best to resist the idea; he could see their hosts' resources were stretched. But Malati would have none of that and made them an elaborate meal: mashed pumpkin served with a dash of mustard oil, fried pumpkin peels, and khesari dal, grass peas cooked in a thin, runny soup, and thick grains of rice, malodorous with age.

~

On their way back from Bijoy Nagar, Manas could barely contain his excitement about the new colony: 'Finally a home they can call their own.' Sure, there were problems, he conceded, especially for the women with no earning members in the family. Yet, this could only lead to good tidings for the squatters and provide their nameless, faceless lives an identity. He also saw the establishment of this colony as the heralding of a new dawn for the refugee children; they would have a chance at education, the same as other kids.

The next two days were the longest in Manas's life.

~

If there was one thing that weighed on Amala's mind as much as looking for Kartik, it was Urmila's future, especially following the occupation of the zamindar's land. Amala had heard stories of women being forcibly dragged out of refugee camps and thrown into prostitution. Malati reassured her that the camp was a safer place for Urmila, especially as she had never ventured outside.

Amala had considered including Urmila in their household, the one in which she now found herself. But she doubted that would work. This three-member family had no earning member. Amala knew she had to take up a job sooner or later; she had heard of refugees from other camps getting jobs as *bidi* rollers and *thhonga* makers. Some others were making pickles and *bori*, which the babus bought. The good thing about these jobs was that one could do them from home for the most part. You only needed to go out once in a while to purchase materials and sell the finished products.

Malati's husband, Nimai had been having trouble walking lately. His knee joints were stiff in the morning and even a short walk caused him pain. He'd been thinking of finding work in one of the jute mills in the city. But as his pain worsened, Amala and Malati's pleas for him to stay at home prevailed.

Malati had an ache in her lower back, too, but not bad enough to stop her from carrying out everyday chores. She had asked Amala if they could get a sewing machine like the one 'Chitra Didi' had; that way, they could stitch a few clothes and sell those

in the market. Amala, in turn, told her about the pickle- and
thhonga-making opportunities.

'If we can gather a bit of money selling those, Mashi,' Amala
said, 'maybe we can buy our own sewing machine. Not right away,
but maybe in a year's time?'

The idea appealed to Malati. 'How do we get started?'

Amala assured her she would find a way. In her mind, she
knew individual efforts would yield little result. She envisioned
a collective of Bijoy Nagar women creating products and
establishing a future for their children. She planned to discuss
this at Chitra's house the next day, hoping for some practical
advice from the sewing teacher.

Now, more than ever, Amala felt hopeful of finding Kartik. She
hadn't found any new information that gave her this confidence.
But the fact they had taken control of ther lives had made her feel
optimistic. And although she knew little of Kolkata's big roads or
narrow alleys, Amala felt ready to venture out and explore. She
was certain Kartik was there somewhere, alive and well.

When Manas came to pick up Amala the next day, she was
surprised to find his co-volunteers, usually by his side like shadows,
missing. Instead, two teenage girls walked next to him. As she
spread out a bunch of wet clothes on a clothesline in the slice of
open space they had in front of their house, Amala recognised
one of them as Minoti. The other girl, chattering animatedly,
didn't look familiar.

A few kids from the colony surrounded Manas as he held open
before them what looked like a box of sweets. The children, all
boys, kept following him towards Amala's quarters. She couldn't
help but notice Manas's indulgent smile as he shared the sweets
with them. When he finally appeared within her immediate
view, he didn't say anything, only handed the opened and much-
depleted box of sweets to her. Amala fumbled in her bid to grasp
the box.

A little boy greeted her. '*Kolketar mishti*, Didi. *Khey dyakho*, it's
really nice!'

Amala smiled and made her way inside and asked Manas and the girls to come in. Manas motioned the girls to go in first; Minoti stepped forward and lightly hugged Amala. She then introduced Rani to her. Given her not-so-shy disposition, Rani didn't take too long to make herself comfortable as she stepped inside.

Malati put the sweets on a small enamel plate for Amala to serve to the guests along with water. As he sipped from a glass, Malati asked Manas the question nagging Amala. Where were his friends?

'At the camp,' Manas said, unwilling to say more.

Amala made as if to say something but didn't. Malati urged her guests to have the sweets and offered to make tea.

'Nah, nah, Mashi,' Manas said, 'We should get going. And please take those sweets away; they are for you. I am giving you a half-empty box anyway.'

'You should have brought two boxes of sweets any...' chirped Rani. Amala noticed Minoti cut Rani short with a slight tap on her wrist.

'I should have, no? Will make sure I check with you next time, Grandma,' Manas said with a light guffaw. The laughter echoed through the room as the others joined in a chorus. The sound roused Nimaichand, who had been lying on a cot in the inside room. He slowly walked to the outer room. The girls muted their laughter. Manas got up from the floor and greeted the old man with a namaskar. Picking up the plate of sweets, he requested Nimaichand to have some.

'*Arrey*, what is all this, Baba,' Nimaichand said with a faint smile. Malati brought a stool for him to sit.

'Just some sweets, Meshomoshai. To celebrate your arrival in Bijoy Nagar.'

Nimaichand picked a sandesh and bit into it abstractedly.

'You will see how this colony grows, Meshomoshai. The young men and women here give me a lot of hope,' Manas said.

Malati nodded in agreement. Nimaichand muttered under his breath, 'May you be right, Baba.'

Soon, Amala appeared with two cups of tea, for the two men
in the room. Manas hadn't noticed her slipping into the room
inside to make tea on the stove.

'Why this special treatment for men?' Manas asked.

'Mashi and I just had some tea. I can make some for Minoti
and Rani,' Amala said.

'No, no, we don't drink tea that much,' Rani said.

As Manas took a sip of the milk-deprived tea reeking of
kerosene, he noticed Amala had taken care to ready herself for
the visit to Chitra's house. Her hair, smelling of Jabakusum oil,
had been rolled up into a neat bun. She wore a printed white
cotton sari with light green petals dotting it. Her preparedness
made Manas more nervous about their impending meeting. For
now, he just kept looking at her.

Green looks good on you—verdant and fresh.

12

Standing by the window of his room, Manas looked at a pair of sparrows on the betel nut tree outside. The avian couple had busied itself foraging for a late-morning breakfast. Their task had been made easier by the scarps of leftovers Manas's mother had had her maid distribute for the larger fraternity of the neighbourhood birds. As he witnessed their frisky movements, Manas recalled the afternoon he had brought Amala to Chitra's house. Now, a week later, it amused him to think of the embarrassment he'd caused himself that day.

Amala had kept her curiosity in check. Her lack of inquisitiveness only added to Manas's frustration. *Why doesn't she ask me what it is? That would make things simpler, wouldn't it?* Instead he babbled—how delicious the fish curry was; the taxi driver had turned out to be such an interesting character what with his Bihari accent; that he should indeed have taken two boxes of sweets as Rani suggested, 'That girl is way smarter than me....'

Twenty minutes later when Chitra entered the room with *paan* for them, she found Manas browsing through a magazine and Amala staring at a wall. When Manas looked at Chitra, she winked at him. He shook his head hopelessly.

Chitra smiled and turned to Amala to offer her a *paan*. As she put it into her mouth, Chitra asked her, 'How did you like the food?'

'*Bhalo*,' Amala said, 'nice it was.'

'I know a *Bangaal* girl like you would probably not relish the food us *Ghotis* make. But what to do, Ma? I know no better.'

'Why? It was nice, Mashi. A bit different, but still delicious.'

'You have a *shona mukh*, you like everything. But tell me something; will you cook for me some day?'

'Why not, Mashi? For you, I will cook the things my mother used to make. But you will have to eat even if you don't like them, *haan?*'

The mischief in Amala's tone relieved Manas; as if she had just given him grace marks for his pathetic attempt at a conversation.

'Why would I ask you to cook if I wouldn't eat?' Chitra said. Then, turning to Manas she asked him, '*Ki*, Manas Baba, you will eat too, won't you?'

Manas said yes with a nod even as a shy smile escaped his lips.

'So, did you tell Amala what you meant to?' Chitra asked.

'Uh, no, I mean, *maane...*' Sweat eclipsed Manas's brows and made him fumble. He kept wiping his face, even though the handkerchief had turned into a wet ball.

Amala looked quizzically, at Chitra first, then at Manas. Finally, she said, 'Yes, please tell me why you brought me here? I thought you wanted to share some information. What is it?'

Manas tensed in his seat. There was no escaping now. Whatever the consequence, he had to get his act together. 'Well, Amala' he said, lowering his gaze, for he could take Amala's 'No' for an answer, but not the glare of her disdain, 'I want to marry you.' A sigh followed that sentence, a captive bird finally released.

The silence of the next few minutes threatened to swallow Manas up. When he finally lifted his eyes, he saw Chitra looking at Amala with loving indulgence as she chewed her *paan*. Amala's face had reddened with incredulous horror.

Amala turned towards Chitra to make sense of what was happening. She surmised this wasn't entirely a joke or meant to harass her. Yet Manas's directness and the absurdity of what he just said puzzled her. *Is he in his right mind?*

After what must have been only minutes although it seemed like an eternity to Manas, Amala cleared her throat and said, 'Is that all?'

'Yes,' Manas said, this time facing her. After all, they were both still sitting there and the earth hadn't cracked open and swallowed him whole.

'Well, I don't know what to say, Manas Babu...' Amala's voice trembled.

'You can drop the Babu for a start,' Manas said, 'no matter what your decision; I will still be your friend.'

'It hardly matters what I call you or if you consider me a friend. Your request makes no sense to me. I don't know why you would waste your time thinking all this.'

Chitra intervened. 'Aha, why don't you take some time to think about what Manas says, Ma? You don't have to make a decision right now.' Her tone calmed Amala. She picked up her tote bag from the floor and took out a few pieces of embroidered and crocheted covers, which she placed before Chitra.

'*Bah*, such a fine hand you have. These look lovely,' Chitra said. 'I hope you're making more of these? We can arrange to sell them in the market. I'll be your first customer, right now. Will you sell these to me?'

'What are you saying, Mashi? I will sell, to you? These I brought for you, my little gift.'

But Chitra would have none of that. She certified Amala's work fit to be taken to the market and insisted she make the first sale right away. Her teacher's reaction emboldened Amala to ask about the cooperative of Bijoy Nagar women she had in mind. Chitra agreed it was a good idea.

'Sure, you all can get started with whatever skills you have, but to earn better, you'll need to train better.' Turning to Manas she asked, 'Baba, I've heard of vocational training centres for women across the city. Can you find out more about them?'

'Sure, Mashima... I will find out right away.' Chitra's request gave Manas a fresh lease of life. She had made him relevant to the conversation again.

'Mashi,' Amala continued, 'Malati Mashi and I were also

thinking if we could start making paper packets and pickles. I
hear women in some camps are doing that.'

'Why not? I see no reason you can't, although...' she paused
briefly to add, 'you will need some initial capital for buying raw
material.'

Amala hadn't thought about this and felt disappointed. Before
she could dwell in that state for too long, Manas quipped, 'I think
that too can be arranged, at least the initial part. I will see what
we can do to get these smart ladies started.'

~

Manas shuddered to recall the awkward exchange between Amala
and him that afternoon. He felt as if both he and Amala wanted
to speak to each other but couldn't after Manas's utterance.

In the end, Amala had left a more hopeful person, or at least
that was what Manas thought. He had requested Chitra to join
them on the taxi ride back to Bijoy Nagar; he knew Amala would
be uncomfortable. Chitra agreed without hesitation, she was
eager to meet her students in their new surroundings.

After tea at Amala and Malati's house, Chitra asked Amala if
she could take her on a tour of the colony. The school impressed
her the most. The residents had already enlisted a few volunteers to
teach the colony's children with some help from local politicians.
Another thing charmed Chitra: she saw three or four women around
an open fire on which *khichuri* was cooking in a large cauldron.

As he walked with them, Manas guessed this communal
cooking was as much about camaraderie as about economic
prudence. It was only practical for the colony residents to share
their food.

~

The flavour of that afternoon, a mix of chili peppers and sugar
crystals, lingered in Manas's mind. Amala's response to his

proposal, though distressing at first, seemed like a veiled blessing now. For one, it had given him more time to bring up the matter with his mother and grandfather. Not that the extra time would make the conversation any easier; it just allowed him to plan better. One obvious solution seemed to be Bawromashi; he had seen her ability to convince Mrinmoyee. Manas's other hope, though a lot fainter than his aunt, was his grandfather.

Amala's response reassured Manas for another reason. Inflamed as it was, her reaction hadn't ended in a rejection. His rational side inferred Amala's response to be just short of a decline, but for now Manas would hang on to every tendril of hope that swung his way.

〜

Much as the creation of Bijoy Nagar inspired hope in Manas, the Gariahata camp left him despairing. With the migration of the able-bodied refugees, the camp bore its new status like a yoke placed between the two words that now qualified it: 'Permanent Liability'. The words, shortened to *PL* in official parlance, less pathetic and without any obvious connotation, denoted camps exclusively sheltering the old, infirm and 'unattached' women. In the absence of family or friends to support them, they continued to subsist on the scant and uncertain government dole.

On each of his visits to the camp since the establishment of Bijoy Nagar, Manas found the PL camp members to be less and less spirited. This wasn't suicidal but worse—a complete apathy for the very idea of existence. He saw no spark in their eyes. They didn't complain about the gravel in their food, the rat-chewed blankets, or the stench of the squalor piling up around them like dead fish on a shore. Already invisible to the world, they weren't alive even in their own eyes.

〜

Since her visit to Chitra's house two weeks ago, Amala's mind was a tangled web of thoughts. She couldn't shake off the shock of those five words from Manas, 'I want to marry you.' His mental state had become a riddle for her. Despite her limited knowledge of his personal life, she could clearly tell he belonged to a different world—the clothes he wore, the language he spoke, why even the way he combed his hair—all pointed to that fact.

Why did Mashi ask him to speak his mind to me? She knew. And the obvious question that followed was that if Chitra already knew, could Amala be mistaken in thinking that Manas was out of his mind? Surely, he had already discussed it with Chitra and had her consent. *So Mashi wants this, too. But why?*

As one thread knotted itself into another, Amala couldn't decide what to make of Manas's words. She concluded he hadn't uttered those words on mere impulse. Although she hadn't accepted his proposal, the very fact of its occurrence rattled the fragile sense of stability she had recently started feeling. She thought of discussing the matter with Malati but rejected the idea immediately. There was no way she could risk this news spreading among their neighbours. What a scandal that would be! She had to deal with this herself.

What if she spoke with Chitra, just the two of them? An intimate conversation might help Amala better understand Manas's intentions. Not that she suspected him of having any ulterior motive; what could it mean anyway for him to marry a refugee woman?

Her mind raced to when she first met Manas, that muggy April day when she lost Kartik. As she recollected the various times they had spoken with each other, Amala now viewed their interactions through a new lens. The time he implored her to get into the van when she resisted being brought to the camp; the way he had entrusted her with the care of neglected little children; the evening when he brought her *muri* and wanted to hear the story of her life....

At the time they had occurred, each of these episodes had

made Amala think of Manas as a kind-hearted man. Yet, even now, she couldn't fathom why he would want to share the rest of his life with her. His kindness, ultimately, seemed the only explanation. But there were other candidates, young refugee women far prettier *and* gentler than her....

No, it couldn't be compassion alone. Amala had to speak to Chitra to get to the bottom of this. And do that soon if she were to remain sane. Amala felt grateful to have Minoti as a conduit to take her request to Chitra. The poised shoulders the young girl carried on her head impressed Amala to no end. She could trust her with a secret.

~

Amala was keenly aware of Bijoy Nagar's progress in acquiring its unique character. The colony's residents were determined to stamp its imprint on the city's expanding cartography. They already boasted a functioning school, even if it was limited to primary education.

As word of this *jabar-dakhal*, occupied colony spread, outsiders, both the good and the bad kind, were attracted to it. Dr Majumdar, a general physician at one of the city's major hospitals, came visiting one day. He had been so impressed with the 'enterprise of the refugees, especially the womenfolk', as Amala heard him say to Paban-da, that he had decided to set up a weekly clinic in the colony.

'Daktarbabu' to the residents, Dr Majumdar quickly became popular in Bijoy Nagar. Malati's husband became one of his very first patients. Amala, now virtually a daughter to the couple, accompanied him on his visits to the doctor. The doctor made a definite impression on her, mainly because of his no-nonsense way of doing business—sharp questions, direct eye contact, and firm directions to patients. Amala liked how he treated medical conditions with a combination of medicines and tips for everyday changes to one's routine.

For Nimaichand, the doctor prescribed a battery of easy-to-do stretching exercises to relax his muscles and help with his joint mobility. He would ask Amala on every return visit how diligently the elderly man followed the regimen. On the slightest indication of any laxity, Nimaichand would receive a mild dressing down from the doctor. Amala had to tread this slope cautiously. She felt guilty whenever the doctor reprimanded her new guardian. But she also saw how Daktarbabu's words seemed to work as well as his pills and bitter liquids, sometimes even better.

Dr Majumdar didn't charge his patients in Bijoy Nagar but had a cash box placed somewhat inconspicuously in a corner of his small, windowless clinic. The box was for voluntary donations, but going by the fact that hardly anyone ever dropped anything into it, Amala inferred the doctor kept the box to provide his refugee patients with a sense of dignity, so as not to let them feel he was doing them a favour. *When I start earning a little money, I will put something there.*

The clinic room came up as yet another one of the many irregular structures in the refugee colony. Constructed with makeshift materials, it betrayed a sparse look. Besides a table and a couple of chairs, one of which was the doctor's, and the cash box, it had a wash pitcher on a stool next to the small table the doctor used for writing prescriptions and keeping his bag. The bag worked as his mobile dispensary, containing not only his stethoscope and other tools but also sample medicines that he distributed free of cost.

~

One morning, as Amala returned from the pond, she found her beloved Chitra Mashi waiting for her. Amala's new routine included a trip to the pond every morning for her shower as well as to fetch some of the greens the residents had planted close to the pond. On most days, a quick stir fry of these in mustard oil with a hint of nigella seeds, along with rice, would be their lunch and dinner. On the rare occasion when the resident fishermen had a particularly good catch, they would get a handful of small fish, which, when fried, would turn a meal into a feast.

Amala could see that today's meal would be a feast, even though she hadn't got any fish. Why, it would be a grand feast, thanks to the parcel of edible treats Chitra had brought with her. As the items, all neatly packed in small steel boxes, tumbled out of her bag, an explosion of smells—of *chalta* pickle, shrimp cooked with fresh coconut and mustard paste, *narkel naaru*, coconut balls drenched in melted jaggery—hurled Amala into ecstasy.

When a slightly-embarrassed but mostly-delighted Malati tried to resist the gifts, Chitra said, 'I will think you hate my cooking if you don't take it. It isn't much, Didi.' Chitra went on to tell them how the two girls who governed her house these days wouldn't let her visit Malati and Amala without some of those goodies, which they had helped Chitra prepare.

'Go, Ma, take these inside,' Chitra said to Amala. 'Keep them in a cool place.'

As Amala picked up the boxes, the taste of *chalta* pickle as her mother made it tickled her tongue's memory. Every autumn, Firdous Chachi would give them a bunch of these tart fruits, enough for Sumitra to make several weeks' worth of chutney and pickle that would last them a few months. Amala could see why Rani and Minoti had lent Chitra Mashi a hand in preparing the pickle. She used to assist her mother in cutting and peeling the fruit, which would then be boiled in water with salt and turmeric. As her mother poured mustard oil in a hot wok, in which the five-spice mix of *paanchphoron* spluttered moments later, the aroma filled Amala with a heady anticipation. She could barely wait to taste the final product as she dumped the slices of elephant apple into the wok. Soon, blocks of jaggery would melt into the mix, enveloping the entire kitchen with the sweet, earthy scent of spiced, melted jaggery.

Amala smiled at that sticky memory as she stepped out of the inside room. She could hear Chitra saying to Malati, 'I am going to the Dakshineshwar Kalibari today. Hope you don't mind if I take Amala along?'

'*Bah*, that would be so nice, Didi. Why should I mind?' Malati said, opening a knot in her sari's *anchal* and taking out a few coins. 'Please offer some puja for him,' she said, handing Chitra the coins and gesturing towards her husband who sat in a corner on a stool.

'You keep the money, Didi, I had it in my mind to offer a puja for Dada,' Chitra said, but Malati wouldn't agree and shoved the coins into Chitra's palm.

Chitra's ingenuousness impressed Amala yet again. How effortless she had made it for them to have a private, one-on-one conversation.

Amala had no more than a sketchy idea of the Dakshineshwar temple, renowned because of Ramakrishna Thakur, a crazed Kali devotee who spent his days and nights talking to, humouring, and getting angry with the mother goddess. It had become a coveted pilgrimage for Bengalis everywhere, and Amala could scarcely believe her luck in being able to visit the site in this manner. She was headed to a place where people went to sort out the trickiest problems of their lives. Maybe it had the answer to the riddle that puzzled her, too.

As they came out, Amala and Chitra saw three young women, regulars at Chitra's sewing class at the camp, standing at the door. They had brought something for their *shelai mashi*, 'sewing aunt', as some of her former students called Chitra. Gouri, the young girl who enjoyed teasing Amala in the class, was among them. She carried two enamel boxes, a big one containing *khichuri* and a smaller one with brinjal and potato fries, a portion of the communal lunch cooked that day.

'*Arrey*, why all this?' Chitra said. 'I didn't bring anything for you beauties.'

'So you can taste our cooking, Mashi, and tell us if we pass or fail,' Gouri said, her lips puckering into an impish grin Chitra was only too familiar with. Amala gave Gouri a light snap on her shoulder.

'Nothing you create can ever fail, Gouri, that I'm certain of,' Chitra said with a broad smile. 'I can't wait to taste this.' Then lowering her pitch she said, 'To be honest, when you were cooking *khichuri* the other day, I felt a bit greedy. Maybe you read my mind, *haan*?'

Gouri laughed loudly even as her two friends contained their chuckles by pressing sari *anchals* to their lips.

'Another day I will come and have lunch with you all here, *kyamon*?' Chitra said as she pinched Gouri's cheek. Turning to Amala she said, 'We should get going now, Ma.' On their way out, Amala filled in Chitra with the latest developments in Bijoy Nagar. The news of Daktarbabu and his clinic was, of course, there but they also had their own hand pump in the colony now. Some of the colony's young men had begun working at odd jobs, as helpers at roadside tea stalls, shoeshine boys, daily wage labourers, whatever they could find that didn't require formal education or specialised skills. And then, on an impulse, Amala said, 'You know, Mashi, I have...had a brother, too....' She stopped as abruptly as she had started.

'Oh, I didn't know that,' Chitra said, putting her hand on Amala's shoulder.

An awkward silence filled the space that had only moments ago buzzed with Amala's updates. Amala was glad they were now on the road where a few rickshaw pullers stood with their rickshaws.

'They are regulars here, Mashi,' Amala said.

Chitra smiled and told Amala this was a sign that Bijoy Nagar had come to be recognised as a locality of its own. She walked up to a rickshaw and asked the puller if he could take them to the nearest taxi stand. The man, wiry and hunched said he could, but as the nearest taxi stand was no less than five kilometres away, the fare would be six rupees.

'*Ta besh*. Let's go,' Chitra said and as soon as the man wiped the seat pulling a *gamchha* from his shoulder, she climbed onto the rickshaw. Amala sat down beside her. The world around them teemed with activity—a fruit seller hawking his produce, a group of young women cackling with chatter and laughter on their way to work as maids, an odd cow mooing in the middle of the road. They were noises that reassured Amala even as they left her a bit anxious. How long before she could add her pitch to this city's cacophony, before she became someone who would be heard?

A single row of automobiles announced their arrival at the taxi stand. Chitra paid a ten-rupee note to the rickshaw driver. He shoved it in the pocket of his faded *fatua* but apologised saying he couldn't return the change as the two ladies happened to be his *bouni*, first passengers of the day. Noticing Chitra's readiness to give it away, Amala told the man he needed to adjust the amount against their fare on the way back. He indicated his agreement with a jerk of his head.

Chitra fixed a taxi and asked Amala to step in. The driver held the door open, and as she got in, a stab of pain cut through the happiness Amala felt. Sitting inside a motorcar never figured in any future she'd ever imagined for herself. Before coming to Kolkata, she had only ever seen them on a picture postcard one of their rich village neighbours, a jute businessman, had brought from the city. Amala remembered how much the image of the vehicle attracted Kartik, whose endless questions left the neighbour so exhausted that he promised to take the young boy to Kolkata to give him 'a taste of a motor ride'. Kartik couldn't wait for that day to arrive....

The taxi wound its way through the city's thoroughfares, places Amala saw for the first time, her eyes greedily taking it all in. It helped that Chitra instructed the taxi driver to keep a steady pace. Amala noticed a tall, regal building overlooking a river.

'That's Babughat,' Chitra said, 'and that's the Hooghly River.' She went on to tell Amala that Rani Rashmoni, the zamindar everyone in Bengal revered for her benevolence and mettle, had built the *ghat* in her late husband's memory. The flurry of activity on the steps descending to the river reminded Amala of the ferry port back in her village. Except, this place seemed twice as big and busy. Even as their vehicle continued to move, Amala could see a few women taking a dip in the river; there were no men in that section of the *ghat*.

All along the route to Dakshineshwar, Chitra served as Amala's tour guide, telling her anecdotes about this temple and that tree; the cranky middle-aged man who sold utensils in Bara Bazaar; and the times she persuaded her husband to make a shopping detour to Shyambazaar on their way back from the Kali temple. Amala listened intently. The ease with which Chitra shared her personal stories filled her with a warm sense of intimacy.

It was an intimacy that allowed Amala to ask a question she hadn't intended. 'Mashi, how do you find a lost person in this city?'

Chitra was taken aback at first, but when she realised Amala was serious, she asked her for more details. Amala gave her the same 'uncle' story she had made up for Minoti. It amazed her that she didn't fumble even once while telling the lie.

'Hmm, that's a tough one to answer, Ma,' Chitra said. 'The only good way I know of is to file a missing person's report with the police. But even with that...you know how things are right now. So many people....'

Amala knew. She knew that people like her were not a priority for the police, Kartik even less so; he probably didn't even have the 'refugee card' Manas had helped her get on her first day. And would she ever approach the police after how they made her feel when she had just lost Kartik at the station? The memory still made her queasy.

Chitra had piqued Amala's curiosity about her husband. From what little she had heard of him during their conversation in the taxi, 'Mesho', as Amala called him in her mind, seemed to have been a nice man. In a flash, scenes involving her parents swirled in her mind.

Three years ago, Amala and Kartik had joined their parents and some neighbours to attend the *charak mela* in their village. Amala looked forward to this end-of-the-year fair; it wasn't merely a feast for her senses, what with her favourite foods and toys flooding the place but a hub for her girl gang and their unbridled frolicking.

That year, as soon as she spotted a few of her friends, Amala had left her parents and brother to join them. She had been allowed this independence only a year ago and knew how to enjoy it responsibly. Subimal liked to give the children a little token money to spend at the fair. Amala always aimed to save some of that.

After a quick snack of pumpkin fritters and *jilipi*, Amala strolled around with her friends. The trace of incense mixed with the smell of smoky oil in which the fritters were being fried mildly nauseated her. At one stall, she picked up a small clay Ganesha for her mother. She had wanted to get it the year before as she knew Ganesha was missing among the deities on Sumitra's modest altar. She couldn't buy it then as her allowance money had nearly finished by the time she had spotted it at the Mela.

The stall owner, who returned to the fair every year, had endeared himself to Amala because of his gentle manner and hearty smile, both of which remained unfazed even after he started losing his vision a few years ago. Ratan Das, 'Ratan kaka' to the village kids, offered Amala a discount on the figurine; he knew how much she prized it and how disappointed she had been when she couldn't buy it the previous year. Back then, he had even asked her to take it and pay him at the next fair but Amala had refused.

Three years later, Amala still resisted taking handouts and found living in Bijoy Nagar better than at the camp, even if it meant going hungry every now and then.

Back at the fair, Amala and the girls had been drawn towards a troupe of *gajan* singers and *shaungs* or jesters, dressed in bright costumes and heavy, colourful make-up. They were regulars at the event, enthralling crowds with their enactment of scenes from Shiva's life. Shiva's headstrong ways—wandering about in his rag-tag tiger skin, smoking pot, even dancing in crematoriums—made this seemingly hot-headed god oddly adorable for Amala.

The *gajan* songs held Amala in a spell. The troupe usually wandered through villages; the more places they performed in, the better their earnings. Even as her girlfriends started going home, Amala kept following the troupe as if in a trance. It wasn't until they were on the outskirts of her village that Amala realised how far she had come.

A faint glow of the setting sun hung in the air like a limp kite. Amala's heart skipped a beat as she thought of how long it would take her to return home; she wasn't even sure if she knew her way back. This was the farthest she'd ever come.

Amala knew every nook and alley in her village; there was scarcely a spot within the perimeters of Madhabpasa that Amala and her friends hadn't explored. But outside its limits, every place was a foreign country. An inky blanket swallowed the last of the sun's light as Amala retraced her steps. On her lips, parched dry, quivered the name of Ma Tara, the goddess her family remembered in distress. But as the blanket grew thicker, Amala, despite her constant invocation of the mother goddess, started crying. She had lost her way.

Amala picked up her pace only to land in a puddle. She could tell she had come across a swamp. She froze at the sight of fireflies flickering in the marsh. The glow of the insects reminded her of *aleya*, the strange light fishermen sometimes saw when passing through wetlands. The light either snuffed the life out of them or left them unable to make sense of the world around them, insane and useless. *A light worse than the darkest of nights.* As she lifted her sari to her waist to avoid tripping, Amala began wailing.

She walked another fifty metres like that, crying and desolate, even after she had landed on dry ground. Another source of light approached her and she nearly fainted. It took a familiar voice to bring her out of the chasm Amala felt herself sinking into. She saw the face of her friend Meenu who accompanied Ma. Meenu was one of the girls Amala was with earlier in the evening. Grabbing Amala in a mad embrace, Sumitra told her how she had almost died of panic when she learned Amala was missing. Amala's torrent of tears wet her mother's bosom.

'Never go anywhere alone again, you understand?' Sumitra rebuked her daughter as she and Meenu walked Amala back home.

'*Ei*, careful, Ma.' Chitra's words yanked Amala out of her trance. She had almost tripped over a puddle as they made their way inside the Dakshineshwar temple. Amala stepped over to the side and gazed around her; the vastness of the temple courtyard awed her. The biggest temple she had seen before this was the Sugandha Shaktipeeth, a four-roof structure in Barisal dedicated to the goddess Sugandha. *Sati's* nose had supposedly fallen there when Shiva had danced in rage with her body after she had immolated heself to express her anger at the humiliation of her consort. But this place was far grander. Amala didn't know where to start. She silently thanked Chitra for helping her navigate the nine-spired temple.

They stepped forward to reach the *garbhagriha*, the sanctum sanctorum housing Bhabatarini, the idol of goddess Kali that Ramakrishna worshipped in turns as a mother and a daughter. As they joined the long queue to the shrine, Amala let herself be distracted by a flock of pigeons pecking on grains of rice and wheat offered by devotees.

Even though she stood in a queue at a temple and not a refugee camp, Amala felt restive. Manas appeared in her thoughts out of nowhere and his words kept vibrating in her ears. Unable to push him out of her mind, she looked at the temple walls intently.

'Once we're done with offering puja to Ma, we'll go to the shrines behind, near the river,' Chitra said.

'River?' Amala's face lit up.

Chitra told her about the twelve shrines dedicated to Shiva along Ganga's riverfront, the one dedicated to Krishna and Radharani, as well as about the *nahabatkhana*, the quarters where the 'Paramhansa, Ramkrishnadeb himself lived'.

Amala could scarcely believe she was going to see all this for herself. Much as she wanted to offer her prayers to Bhabatarini, she was more keen to see the spot where the Paramhansa had lived and met his devotees. She'd heard so many stories, each more astonishing than the other.

Upon reaching the sanctum sanctorum where Bhabatarini faced them standing atop Shiva, Amala wondered why the innermost retreats of temples were always so constricted. Necks of other devotees craned over and around her for a single glimpse of the goddess. Amala could barely keep up with all the pushing and shoving and dispatched a silent prayer to Bhabatarini before quickly stepping out of the room. She knocked her forehead as it struck her how her prayer was about two men, one absent, the other whose presence had left her anxious.

From a relatively quiet corner outside the *garbhagriha's* gate, Amala peeped inside to check if Chitra was still there. Amid the jostle of devotees, the two of them had got separated from each other. To her relief, Amala saw Chitra walking out with her *puja* basket, her face drenched in sweat.

'Mashi, here,' Amala called out to her with a wave of her hand.

Chitra responded with a gleaming smile as she trotted over. Before handing the plate with her *puja* offering to Amala, she put a dot of *sindoor* on Amala's forehead. The vermillion mixed with oil was the same one that adorned the Goddess's head and formed part of the tangible blessings the temple priest provided to devotees. He also put flowers from Bhabatarini's feet and a few *batashas* into each devotee's basket before offering their sweets and money to the Mother.

Amala followed Chitra as they next made their way towards the riverside. Clearing her throat Amala asked, 'Mashi, what do you think?'

'About what, Ma?'

'Umm, about...what Manas Babu said the other day...?'

'Oh I see, is that why you wanted to meet me?' Chitra said, a smile edging her lips.

Amala remained quiet.

'Well, what is there to think, Ma? He told you what was in his heart; that is all.'

'But you knew about it, didn't you, Mashi?'

'Yes.'

A few moments of silence followed. Chitra suggested they sit down on a bench under a tree that didn't seem to attract too many people. 'See, Ma,' she said, putting her hand on Amala's shoulder, 'Manas is a good boy. Honest.'

'I'm sure he is, Mashi, but why would he...' Amala shook her head, still unable to solve the puzzle.

'Why not, Ma?' Chitra said, leaning closer to Amala. 'Why can't a man want to marry the woman he loves?'

Amala burst out laughing. 'Loves?'

'Yes. Manas loves you, he truly does. Don't think this is a joke.'

The purpose in Chitra's tone struck Amala. *Mashi isn't just saying these words. She means the very last one of them.* Which left Amala more, not less, perplexed.

'*Achchha*, Amala Ma, do you trust me? Be honest, you have nothing to fear.'

Amala knew where Chitra was taking her with this question. She felt surprised and embarrassed at once. 'Why else would I talk to you about this, Mashi? It's not that, it's just that....'

'I understand,' Chitra said as she handed Amala a *batasha* from her basket. 'I would be just as confused had I been in your place. It's natural to feel that way.'

These words calmed the pounding of Amala's heart. It helped to know she wasn't going crazy. She popped the *batasha* into her mouth and looked at Chitra with a thank-you smile.

'Look, Amala,' Chitra said. 'Why would I allow Manas to say what he did to you in my house if I wasn't sure of his intentions?'

Chitra went on to tell Amala, how she, too, had had her doubts about Manas's desire. How she had asked him all the tough questions to unearth his real intent. And how he had come out clean and resolute. 'His heart has no trace of malice, Amala. He does not pity you if that's what you're thinking. In fact, he doesn't pity any...' Chitra held herself back before uttering the next word.

'Any what, Mashi? Tell me,' Amala asked, her voice betraying more firmness than curiosity.

'Re...refugee. Manas has great respect for all refugees.'

'Respect? For us? He respects me?'

'He does,' Chitra said, making her way up. 'Let's get going, Ma, before someone asks us to vacate the bench.'

Chitra led Amala closer to the riverfront so they could continue talking. She seemed to have read Amala's mind. 'I may be Mashi to you,' she said, 'but remember, I'm a woman, too. The questions that are troubling you also occurred to me.'

This revelation startled Amala and left her wondering about how little time it had taken for this silver-haired woman to turn into her aunt and, now, a close confidante.

'Manas began respecting you long before he had any feelings for you, Ma. Your courage gives him strength.'

Amala remained quiet. She didn't know what to make of qualifiers like strength and courage for herself. As far as she knew, she had only been living her life. She had to, for Kartik, if for nothing else.

'But I don't know what to do, Mashi.' Amala's admission was as much to herself as to Chitra. The knowledge that Manas wanted to spend his life with her made her dilemma more complex. She couldn't scoff at him anymore or be dismissive of his 'outrageous idea'.

'I would feel exactly the same way if I were you. Let me give you a secret tip. Your mind will give you a hundred reasons to say no. But if your heart says "Yes" even for an instant, hold on to that and nurture the feeling some more. You will get your answer.'

'You make it sound so easy, Mashi,' Amala said with a chuckle. 'Come, let's do our rounds of the shrines now.'

'*Chalo*. Who knows, the gods might be listening to us and preparing a solution for you,' Chitra said with a wink.

And there they were, facing not one or two but a dozen Shiva shrines, neatly laid along the riverfront in traditional *aatchaala* style. Amala could barely hide a grin as a sly thought crossed her mind. Girls in her village fasted in Shiva's name every Monday to get a husband like him. And here she stood, with the prospect of a potential husband she didn't know what to do with. She knuckled her forehead, this time in sheer amusement. The cool breeze blowing across the Ganga danced in her hair. It also steadied her mind, if only temporarily.

She asked Shiva to clear her head some more, in case he planned to bring along a husband for her.

13

Ever since he began volunteering for the refugees, Manas hadn't had too many opportunities to sit down for tea and have a leisurely chat with Dadu. Despite the differences in Haraprasad's and Manas's father's personalities and outlooks, Manas enjoyed talking with his grandfather. For all his elitism and, what to Manas appeared a smooth transition from feudalism to capitalism, Haraprasad welcomed contrarian viewpoints. Whether he agreed with his son, and now his grandson, on their ideas of social responsibility, was a different matter altogether. In his own way, he tried to persuade them, but without imposing his will. Manas also felt that since Jyotirmoy's death, his grandfather had become more indulgent towards his 'idealistic luxuries'.

For as long as he could remember, Manas had seen his grandfather have a cup of mid-morning tea, usually with a handful of cashews and raisins as a snack. He sat on the south-facing balcony attached to his room with a book and soft classical music playing on the gramophone in his room. A servant would bring him a plate of nuts and raisins and tea steeped just enough to lend the liquid the colour of a setting sun.

A tender smile suffused Haraprasad's face when he saw Manas approaching the empty chair across him this morning. Manas returned the smile and took his seat. As a little boy, he shared at least one Sunday every month with his grandfather, joining him at this very spot. That was, after all, how he had acquired his taste for tea. Haraprasad would always have a gift ready for him—a book or a sketchbook, pencils, colours, prints of famous paintings....

Another thing drew Manas to this part of the house. He enjoyed watching the activities below, the scene of all action, from the corridor's vantage point. The public areas of the house were on the ground floor. The kitchen, Mrinmoyee's empire, saw a stream of human traffic on most days. Late on Sunday mornings, Nando, their long-time manservant brought a big basket of fresh vegetables from the market, followed by Manas's father Jyotirmoy who returned with a bag of goat meat for the must-have Sunday special of succulent meat curry cooked with chunky potatoes.

Today, however, Manas had a different focus as he sat across Dadu.

Haraprasad greeted him with, 'So, Dadubhai, did you lose your way again?'

Manas knew his grandfather didn't say this to embarrass him so much as to put him at ease.

'I hope to be more regular, Dadu. You know I miss talking to you.'

'Don't worry, Dadubhai. That chair has your name written on it, you can take your seat whenever you feel like it. So how are things? Oh, I forgot to ask, would you like some tea?'

'Not a bad idea, actually.' Manas knew he would spend a while with his grandfather today.

Haraprasad walked over to his room and brought a small brass bell and rang it to call Photik, who came running within minutes. He used the *gamchha* on his shoulder to wipe his face shining with sweat and said, '*Aggey kawttababu*, did you need something?'

Haraprasad asked him to bring a cup of Manas's favourite ginger tea along with some *gurer sandesh*, sweets Mrinmoyee made at home especially for her son.

After completing his routine stock-taking of Dadu's health, mainly the knee pain that had lately limited Haraprasad's movement, Manas asked him about his business. The news on that front wasn't too positive. Given that the bulk of raw jute came from East Bengal, Partition had hurt his business. Manas could see why his mother prodded him to seek employment. With his grandfather's deteriorating health and declining business, they couldn't sit back and take it easy any longer. They were still doing well, with rent coming from Haraprasad's four *kothhabaris* in Calcutta. But that couldn't be an excuse for Manas not earning his keep.

'Can we sit inside, Dadu?' Manas asked somewhat abruptly. He realised the balcony didn't make for the most private of surroundings.

'Why, Dadubhai, *ei toh besh*. Is the sun bothering you?'

'Na, na, it's not the sun...and I know how much your knees must like that,' Manas said, a little shamefaced, adding quickly in a soft pitch, 'I need to tell you something...ask too. It won't be too long....' He had to cut the sentence short as his eyes caught Photik climbing up the stairs with his tea and sweets. He felt relieved when Haraprasad told the servant boy to bring the refreshments to his room where he and Dadababu would spend some time talking about books. Photik followed the command with a nod. As he stepped out, Haraprasad told him that no one was to disturb Manas and him.

'*Je aggey*,' Photik said and left. Haraprasad shut the door.

Manas saw the most recent issue of *Masik Basumati*, a monthly journal on Haraprasad's study table. He sat down and flipped its pages while sipping tea.

'Is something bothering you, Dadubhai?' Haraprasad sat down on a chair across Manas's, the table lending them some distance.

'I don't know how to share this with you, Dadu,' Manas said, 'but I must.'

'What is it?'

'What if I were to tell you...' Manas got up from the chair and went over to one of the bookshelves behind Haraprasad. He picked up a book, then immediately put it back on top of the other books.

'Tell me what, Dadubhai?' Haraprasad asked, his voice firm yet patient. He hadn't turned back, as if to spare Manas the discomfiture of being caught fidgeting.

'That...that I were getting married, Dadu?' The words flew off Manas's mouth in a hurried jumble.

This time Haraprasad turned. Not just his head but his entire body as he rose up to move closer to Manas. Gently grabbing his shoulder, he said, 'Come, sit down, Dadubhai. Would you like some water?'

Manas followed Dadu's advice. He still couldn't look his grandfather in the eye.

Haraprasad poured him water in a tumbler from a jug sitting on a bedside stool.

Manas gulped the water and kept staring at his cup on the table. It still had half a cup of tea in it.

'What you just told me ought to make me happy, no? But you look troubled, Dadubhai,' Haraprasad said. 'And wait, have you shared this with your mother yet?' He looked straight at Manas.

Manas shook his head to say no. With the most difficult part of the conversation behind him, he felt relieved. He got up to refill his glass and said, 'It's a long story, Dadu, if you have the time for it.'

'I sure do. More than for any other story you will tell me, Dadubhai.'

And so Manas told him everything. About Amala and the circumstances in which he had met her, about how much he had grown to admire her. At the end of it, he admitted he didn't even know if she wanted to marry him but sincerely hoped she did. Haraprasad lent him a patient ear without flinching or showing any expression that Manas could construe as judgement.

A brief pause followed Manas's 'confession'. Dadu's silence worried him and he looked at Haraprasad with an imploring look.

Finally, his grandfather spoke. 'What about her family, Dadubhai? What do you know about them?'

'I told you, Dadu. They are no more. She has no....'

'Ah, yes, you told me they aren't alive,' Haraprasad said, a tinge of impatience betraying his voice, 'but what did they do? What was their social condition?'

Manas could see where this was going. Short of asking about Amala's caste, his grandfather had posed every question that would help him determine her background and social status. This wasn't unexpected. Yet Manas felt uneasy.

'Well, her father was a fisherman. I don't know too much about her past and am not interested. I'm interested in who *she* is, Dadu.'

'I see,' Haraprasad said, his face a stolid wall.

Manas could tell his grandfather wasn't impressed. But he wasn't going to give up so easily and tried to steer the conversation in a different direction. 'Dadu, I don't know how to speak with Ma on this. Will you help me?'

'Well, you will have to figure that out,' Haraprasad said without any trace of uncertainty. 'Sorry, I won't be able to help you. I reject your idea.'

Manas had expected his grandfather to have some reservations, especially as selecting one's own partner wasn't such a welcome exception. But the cold surety with which Haraprasad used the word 'reject' shocked Manas. Dadu's tone implied there would be no room for negotiation on this.

If Manas felt cornered, he wouldn't show it. He had to keep trying, for whatever it was worth. An hour had already passed and he couldn't make Haraprasad wait any longer for his afternoon meal. Before taking his leave, Manas asked his grandfather if he could meet with him once more at a later date. Haraprasad gave him a silent nod. Manas suppressed a sigh. As he opened the door to leave the room, Manas requested Haraprasad to keep the conversation to himself.

'No worries, Dadubhai,' Haraprasad said, adding, 'I suggest you rethink the matter. Don't take hasty decisions based on emotions.'

Manas left without replying. He felt unburdened and exhausted at once. Though hungry, he had no desire to eat at home that afternoon. He wanted to rush to Chitra or Amala but resisted the urge. He wanted to face Amala only with something concrete for her. Since their last meeting, he had been able to obtain a few odd leads about potential training and employment opportunities

for her and other Bijoy Nagar residents. He decided to spend the
afternoon further investigating those. Once downstairs, he made
sure Mrinmoyee wasn't in the vicinity and quietly left the house
using the side entrance.

On his rickshaw ride, the early March sun became Manas's
mellow companion. A few minutes later, he was in Subir's
neighbourhood in Naktala.

The prospect of visiting the now-PL camp depressed Manas.
His sadness stemmed not so much from the abject condition of
the refugees themselves as from the government's increasing lack
of concern for them. The camp's residents weren't allowed to seek
any work outside. There were several women without any family,
widows and young girls, who had the willingness to work for a
living. But in the absence of a safe shelter, they simply couldn't
think of leaving the camp.

At the camp, Manas approached a tent with the packet of
sweets he and Subir had picked up on the way. About a dozen
women were huddled there. They sat in clusters of twos and threes,
and Urmila was among them. Manas moved closer to the tent and
saw a few of the women briskly rolling *bidis*, while Urmila and the
two women sitting next to her were making *thhongas* or paper
bags. Manas caught her toddler's outline on a tattered blanket
right behind her. The soft rays of the setting sun curtained the
tent and the women appeared to be in haste, going by the speed
with which their hands and fingers moved. On seeing Manas,
one of the women rolling *bidis* got up from the floor, desperately
gathering the disheveled folds of her sari. She greeted Manas and
Subir with a namaskar, a gesture they reciprocated.

As the other women saw the volunteers, some of them stopped
working. Manas caught them trying to hide the *bidis* under the
blankets on which they sat. He felt guilty for invading their privacy.

'How are you, Urmila-di?' He asked, looking at her.

'*Bhalo*,' she said, lowering her face to hide a grin.

Manas wound his steps delicately around the squatting women
to get closer to Urmila.

He held the packet of sweets before her and said, 'This is for you and your friends here.'

Urmila looked up to meet Manas's eyes but didn't accept his gift. Her face betrayed suspicion. She turned to look at the other women in the tent.

Basanti, the older woman who had first greeted the volunteers encouraged Urmila. 'Take it, Urmi. Babu is so kind.'

Urmila reluctantly took the packet from Manas's hand. The next minute, she thrust it into Basanti's hands, saying, '*Ei nao*, eat sweets!'

Basanti and the other women burst out laughing as did Subir and Manas. By this time, another woman had brought them stools, inviting them to join the sweet-eating party. The men sat down and Subir picked up a single piece of sandesh for himself and Manas, explaining how stuffed they both were.

'So, what were you up to, Urmila-di?' Manas asked, encouraged by her mostly-friendly response. 'What were you making when we came?'

'*Thhonga*,' Urmila said, but before she could say any more, the women around silenced her with 'Shhs'.

Manas understood their hesitation. 'You can tell us, sisters. We aren't from the government, you know.'

That's when Basanti told them about their opportunity to earn a little money on the side. A young boy, himself a refugee, came once every ten days to collect the *thhongas* and *bidis* and paid cash to the women. The boy got his supply from various refugee camps in Calcutta. The work had to be done on the sly, though, because the government could stop the dole the moment it found out the refugees were 'gainfully employed'.

Manas responded to Basanti with an admiring salute. 'This does call for another *sandesh*,' he said, spontaneously picking up a piece of sweetmeat from the packet in Basanti's hands.

'We are with you, dear sisters,' Subir said. 'Let us know if we can help you in any way.'

*On trams and buses, in marketplaces, why even in my own house, I
keep hearing about the refugees' lack of industry, about how lethargic
and sterile they are, burdening the city and the state. It's easy to accept
that as the truth, especially going by the newspaper photos from the
Sealdah station. But get to know them a little more closely and they
smack a slap on your face. The ones who grabbed land and built entire
colonies surely didn't lack industry? And those women in the PL
camp? Father-less, husband-less, without anybody to call their own.
Who would have thought they could take charge of their future?*

*It is me who lacks industry, not them. I have the luxury to feel
helpless about their situation. They have neither hope nor hopelessness;
they merely have their own lives and those of their children. And this
life they live with a zeal and dignity that doesn't just amaze me, it
stimulates and challenges me. Why, even my nutcase sister, Urmila,
isn't sitting idle waiting for a messiah to fix her life. Bravo, dear
ladies, bravo!*

— MANAS DUTTA, DIARY ENTRY, MARCH 1951

Two days later, Manas met Chitra at her house. He had exciting
news. 'Mashi, let's have some tea,' he said. 'This is surely going to
make you happy.'

Manas's unusually chirpy voice brought Rani out of the kitchen
in an instant. 'Let's hear what the good news is, Dadababu!'

'*Ei, paka meye*, what does this have to do with you?' Chitra
scolded Rani. 'You bring Dadababu water. I will make some tea.'

'Oh, as if I can't make tea,' Rani said, making a face. 'But you'll
have to tell me what you tell Jethhi,' she said to Manas.

'OK, OK, I will, my big sister,' Manas said with a laugh. 'Now,
can I have a glass of water, please?'

Rani bit her tongue and sprinted to the kitchen.

Manas first relayed the news of the Gariahata PL camp to
Chitra; he simply had to share his joy with her. She reciprocated
his hope but felt that a lot more needed to be done to bring the
camp residents out of poverty.

There was a knock on the door; Rani rushed to open it. Minoti stood at the door but Manas's heart nearly shot through the ceiling when he saw Amala behind her.

An awkward moment followed even as Chitra welcomed Amala. 'Come, Ma, come in.' Turning to Manas she said, 'Manas Baba, I forgot to tell you I had invited Amala for lunch today. Why don't you join us, too?'

A spasm of uncertainty agitated Manas. 'Umm, nah, Mashima, don't worry about me,' he said. 'I will come another time. You all enjoy lunch.' He didn't want to intrude into the space Amala and Chitra shared.

Rani proceeded in the direction of the kitchen, ostensibly with the intent of getting water for the guests. Amala and Minoti joined her. Grateful for the breather, Manas got up to take his leave but Chitra stopped him. 'Weren't you going to share some news?'

'Yes, but maybe another day. Amala might find it odd to have me around. I wouldn't want to ruin your time together.'

Chitra gently patted Manas on the shoulder to make him sit down. 'Don't worry, she'll be fine. I have invited her to spend the night here, so we will have ample time for *adda* once you leave.'

Though Manas still felt ill at ease, he plonked down on the chair.

Rani reappeared with tea for everyone, followed by Minoti who held a plate of sweets. Amala emerged from behind the curtain next, sipping from a glass of water. She stood next to where Chitra sat, close to the door leading to the kitchen and the inner rooms. Chitra motioned for her to sit on the sofa next to her, right across from Manas, the familiar table separating them. Amala obliged.

Chitra's glance moved to the plate of sweets and she said in mock reprove, 'Look at this girl. Who asked you to buy sweets now?'

'Take a bite, Mashi. Tell me how is it?'

'Of course, I will. Manas Baba, you have some, too,' Chitra said. 'And you, too, dear ladies.' One couldn't ignore Queen Rani and Minoti, her fast friend.

Rani chuckled and said, 'We will have, no worries. You all have some first.'

Manas gingerly picked one up and could immediately tell this wasn't a regular, run-of-the mill *sandesh*. As soon as it touched his tongue, it melted. The freshness of the *chhena* hypnotised him enough to reach the plate for seconds.

'I made these,' Amala said, her face flushed with the satisfaction she remembered seeing in her Ma's eyes whenever her father relished something she had made. Realising she might have expressed more emotion than she would have liked to, Amala quickly turned to Chitra. 'Did you like it, Mashi?'

'Look at you—sinking, sinking drinking water. You never told me you make such delicious *sandesh*!'

Amala cast a shy smile and told them how one of their neighbours had got some fresh *nolen gur*, the palm jaggery that intoxicated taste buds across Bengal every winter. The neighbour, Balai, had a distant cousin who had been living in Kolkata with his family since before Partition. They had a few palm trees and would have the liquid *gur* extracted every winter. This time Balai received a big pot to share with Bijoy Nagar residents.

'I hope you didn't mind that I've already gulped a couple of these,' Manas said, purportedly to Chitra, but also as an apology to Amala.

'What are you saying, Baba? Do you think Amala would mind your eating the sweets?' Chitra winked.

'I am glad you enjoyed them,' Amala said softly. It wasn't clear to whom, as her gaze remained fixed on the floor.

'I do have some good news for Amala, Mashi.' Manas considered it safe to communicate to Amala via Chitra and shared the information he had gathered over the last few days. *Refugee Arts and Crafts* helped weavers and crafts persons from East Bengal by buying their work and selling these in the market. They also trained refugees in tailoring, carpentry and pottery. Chitra's students could produce embroidered textiles for home and decorative uses and sell this to the organisation perhaps?

This wasn't all. Manas also brought the news of a new tailoring shop in Ultadanga that employed mostly refugees. The shop had been set up by one Jogen Babu who had himself been displaced from East Bengal in the wake of communal riots.

Both pieces of news sounded like music to Amala's ears. She wanted to ask Manas a hundred questions about how and when she could get started but remained quiet.

The glow on her face didn't escape Manas, and he felt encouraged to continue talking. 'Do you know,' he said, looking at her, 'I met Urmila and her little boy the other day.'

This worked like a charm. Amala looked at him and asked, 'How is she doing? How is Mona?' Her voice trilled with delight. For the little time she had cared for him, Amala had grown attached to the child.

'Quite well, quite well. You'll be happy to know she looks a lot better and has even made some friends at the camp. The little boy seems to be doing well, too! I can't tell if he misses you, though,' Manas said with a twinkle in his eyes.

Amala's face inflated into a broad grin.

For Manas, the afternoon at Chitra's house rolled into a giant cotton ball of mirth, banter and the happy burps off a lazy lunch. He felt a lot more at ease compared to the last time he had sat across Amala there. More importantly, he found Amala to be just as relaxed and engaged in the jokes, repartee and discussions. None of the earlier stiffness, as if someone had wiped a curtain of thick glaze off her horizon.

Manas tried to ascertain the reason behind this carefree Amala. Was it the hopeful news he had brought? Or was it the appreciation Amala had received for her sweet-making? Nah, Amala wasn't flippant enough to lap up cursory praise.

During the tram ride on his way back home, Manas couldn't help remembering Amala's face. Every time she smiled, her complexion shone with a radiance that reminded Manas of the earthen lamps during Kali puja. Her eyes had fire as always but it wasn't a blazing fire, rather one that illumined his whole being.

He hadn't come any closer in terms of the deadlock over his 'proposal'. But strangely, he felt no anxiety. Her peals of laughter echoed in his ears.

The state government had only recently taken over the rights of the Tramways after entering into an agreement with the Calcutta Tramways Company and passing the Calcutta Tramways Act. The tram swerved its way through the busy roads of Chowringhee and Bhowanipore before taking Manas through some less busy areas.

Manas pondered on the next steps for him and his volunteer friends. They certainly needed more manpower. The official response to the crisis had deteriorated from being lukewarm to semi-hostile. Even as he thought about this, Manas saw from the window a long line of rickshaws stacked together. Almost every one of them had a rickshaw puller enjoying a late afternoon siesta. One or two of them had *gamchhas* over their faces to keep the sun away. And the pestering flies that thrived in this season.

~

Manas and Mrinmoyee were caught in a cold war. Since Manas's 'escape' from the house without eating lunch the previous Sunday, his mother had stopped talking to him. To his mundane questions such as 'Where's my towel?' and if she had seen the book he had left on his bed, she responded with no more than 'Yes' or 'No'. She didn't enquire after him when he returned home late, nor did she coax him into having an elaborate meal.

Finally, he could take it no more and tiptoed into her room to find her reclining on her bed with the latest issue of *Masik Basumati*. Mrinmoyee had been subscribing to the magazine almost since the start of its publication. Manas enjoyed reading it too. He didn't always agree with the opinion pieces but still looked forward to its thought-provoking content. *Masik Basumati* also featured the writing of the day's literary heavyweights, and for Manas's mother, the short stories and serialised novels were of the greatest interest.

'Ma?' Manas's voice jolted Mrinmoyee out of the latest novel by Gajendra Kumar Mitra she had sunk her eyes into.

'Yes?' She said simply, not making any effort to sit up, her bespectacled eyes glued to the magazine.

'Do you have a minute?'

'Hmm,' Mrinmoyee muttered glancing at Manas once, then immediately shifted her focus back to the magazine.

Manas sat on the corner of the bed by her feet. 'I know you're upset with me for leaving without telling you on Sunday. I'm sorry but I had to....'

'Please stop it, Maanu. This apology business.'

'I mean it, Ma. You see, I suddenly remembered I had to meet Subir.' By now, Manas had become adept at telling white lies. They seldom weighed him down with guilt but sometimes held the power to assuage her wounded sentiments.

'Why are you telling me all this? You're grown up now. I am sure you can decide what is good for you.'

Taking out a small paper bag from his *kurta* pocket, Manas thrust the packet in Mrinmoyee's hand. 'Something for my sweet Ma.'

Susceptibility to flattery was Mrinmoyee's weakness. Manas had seen his father take advantage of this many a time when he got late returning home from work or forgot to bring the key item on his wife's Sunday list because he'd misplaced the list while chatting up a fellow shopper.

The *nolen gurer* sandesh surprised his mother even more than Manas had anticipated.

'Where did you find this? These aren't from a shop.'

Manas knew he couldn't fault his mother's food instincts and had come prepared with another half-truth. 'Chitra Mashi sent these for you. Along with her regards.'

Mrinmoyee knew Chitra only through the snapshots Manas shared from time to time. Although she wasn't too happy with her son's involvement with the 'lost cause' of the refugees, Mrinmoyee respected Chitra. The *sandesh* had a dramatic effect on her mood.

'She has a good hand, that Mashi of yours,' she said.

14

Dol, the spring festival of colours and irreverent bonhomie had come and gone a week ago. Amala shared a love-hate relationship with *dol*. She enjoyed the part in which she and her gang of friends painted the village in all the colours of the rainbow. And the part in which her mother made delicacies for their family to enjoy. What she liked a lot less was the effort required to wash all that colour off her long hair. It drove her crazy to extricate the powdered *abir* congealed in the knots of her hair during the post-play dip in the pond with her girlfriends.

This year's *dol*, her first since landing in India, was a lot kinder on Amala's hair. She had no desire to play without Kartik. When Minoti and Gouri insisted she join them, Amala agreed on the condition that no one would put *abir* in her hair. After putting colour on Malati and Nimai's feet and the photo of Lord Krishna Chitra had given her during her last visit to her house, Amala went out with the girls. She returned within half an hour to give Malati a hand with cooking lunch.

Ever since Manas had proposed to her, Amala saw herself in a new light. Now she wore the drape of her sari more carefully, taking care to cover her chest and midriff. She also began noticing the heaving and resting of her breasts, the blossoming and withdrawing of her nipples, the subtle changes during her monthly lunar cycles. In these moments, she missed her mother unbearably; Sumitra had been her closest confidant.

Dol having come and gone meant that the pleasant days of spring were fast giving way to the suffocating humidity that Amala had had to cope with the previous summer. There would be no respite this year; she remembered the misery last year's monsoon had brought upon their camp. But now they were in their own houses, even if makeshift. Most neighbours had planted some vegetables in the small patches of land they had next to their living quarters. The produce—bottle gourd, pumpkin, cucumber, potato, radish—mostly served personal consumption needs, but a few residents had been lucky enough to grow some extra to sell at the local market.

Nitai, one of the refugee volunteers at the camp was among those who received a bigger patch of land in Bijoy Nagar. A farmer's son, he didn't take too long to work his magic on it; he started with sweet potatoes. A fortnight after *dol* when Amala took Nimai to the doctor's clinic, she met Nitai there. He had come to get medicines for his youngest brother who had had a bad case of cough.

The clinic also served as a community centre with Daktarbabu acting as the glue binding the colony's residents. It made Amala happy that the visits to the clinic helped Nimai stay connected with colony life. Nimai asked Nitai how things were. The young man was excited to share the success of his small-scale farming efforts. He said he looked forward to the approaching hot months for the tubes to grow plump underground. The lush green vines on his patch of land had raised his hopes.

Originally from Khulna, Nitai had lost his mother as a teenager. Back in the camp, Amala had learned how Nitai had little chance at education. He joined his father in tilling the land, making sure his two younger brothers attended school. The middle brother was thirteen and the youngest, nine. After migrating to India, Nitai, at twenty, had already become the unofficial family head.

Amala knew that Nitai's father was keen to see him get married. He had spread the word as he was worried that his younger sons would go astray without a mother figure to keep them in line. He didn't seek anything special in his potential daughter-in-law. A girl who could manage basic household tasks and had a pleasant temperament was all he asked for. A few residents visited

Nitai's father and suggested Tara, who, too, had volunteered at the refugee camp.

Nitai's father liked the suggestion; he had hoped all his sons would marry women from *desh*, the eastern part they had left behind. Things had moved all too soon, Nitai said. His father went with Putu, his middle brother, to meet Tara's parents and the match was accepted.

~

Bijoy Nagar bustled with wedding planning and preparations. It amused Amala to see how everyone in the colony wanted to do something or the other for the event. The bride and groom were strictly kept out of the discussions.

Thanks to Dr Majumdar, a priest had also been arranged. Ashok Bhattacharjee was in his thirties and had only recently inherited his father's *purohit-giri* after the older priest's untimely demise a year ago.

The colony's menfolk collected donations to buy the items on the list *Bhottchaaj bamun*, the moniker by which the colony residents called the priest, gave them. The women got busy organising the items for a host of wedding rituals—turmeric for *gaye-holud*, *alta*, the blood-red paint that would bleed deep around the bride's palms and feet, and some basic utensils. Malati presided over this part, being among the few senior women who had the status of being married.

The role was both easy and difficult for her, Malati told Amala. She had done it all before for her son and his '*mishti bou*', their petite bride, Lata. Amala noticed that every so often as she gave instructions to the men entrusted with the shopping, Malati would tear up just enough that it didn't show through her steady voice.

Thanks to Minoti, the news of this exciting Bijoy Nagar event didn't take long to reach Chitra. In return, she sent word that the bride's and groom's costumes were on her.

Some of the colony folks resisted the idea. This wedding had to be shouldered by Bijoy Nagar residents and them alone, they argued. Taking help from the government or other well-wishers belonged to their past. Amala concurred with this viewpoint. She also knew Chitra meant well and would be hurt if her offer was turned down.

When Chitra came to see them, Malati broached the subject of the wedding attires. 'Please don't bother with those, Didi. You have already done so much for us. How will we ever repay...?'

As Amala handed Chitra a glass of water, she spotted a glint of hurt in her eyes. 'Oh, I didn't know I was giving you a debt,' she said.

Amala sat down next to Chitra and said, 'Mashi, don't misunderstand. Please. You know how much we all love you. You never forgot us.'

'But I'm not one of you, am I? Not that I'm asking you to think of me as family,' Chitra said, taking a sip of water.

Amala felt nervous. She had never seen Chitra lose her calm. Putting her hand in Chitra's she said, 'All right, it will be as you say. Now tell us what we need to do.'

'You can decide well for yourselves, Shona,' Chitra's tone softened. 'But I've already prepared Tara's wedding trousseau. I hope it's not too much for you to accept it.'

Malati said it would be Tara's good fortune to wear the sari Chitra chose for her.

'I can't wait to see it!' said Amala. The fog of stiffness was clearing. Malati requested Chitra to have lunch with them. Amala clinched the deal by describing how, as part of the wedding preparations, the colony people were eating together in the school premises. Later that afternoon, Chitra couldn't stop raving about the meal she had eaten with them, of *bhuni khichuri*, a scrumptious combination of rice and roasted lentils with vegetables and a side of *begun bhaja*, fat chunks of deep-fried eggplant.

As he stood among the small group of wedding invitees along with Manik, Raghu, Proshanto, and Subir, Manas's eyes were on a woman other than the bride. Everyone commented on how pretty Tara looked in the onion-pink *Benarasi* sari Chitra got for her. Yet Manas couldn't help following every movement of Amala's. She wore a sea green cotton sari. The frills of her white-bordered red blouse brought out a delicate beauty Manas hadn't yet noticed in Amala. The small dot on her forehead and her sharp eyes, kohled for the occasion, made her face radiate with irresistible sensuality. It was a pity, Manas thought, to only catch fleeting glimpses of her, a lock of her curly hair that remained aloof from the loose bun hanging down the nape of her neck, her *alta*-bordered feet scurrying to bring an item for Malati or the priest, the green glass bangles on her wrists....

'*Ei je*, Manas-da,' Raghu shook him out of his trance. As 'brothers', they were required to lift the *piri*, the wooden seat on which Tara sat, and take it around Nitai seven times to bind the bride and the groom in a secure marriage. The women and girls standing on the other side, Amala among them, kept up the pressure with their loud cackles and ululations.

'Careful! It's our sister you're carrying on your shoulders,' one of them screamed, and the others joined the chorus.

At the end of it, Manas thanked Tara in his heart for being such a lightweight. This was his first time lifting a bride atop her wedding *piri*, and despite it being a team effort, he wasn't sure if he wanted to sign up for any more.

~

Every communal celebration left Amala more bereft than before. She missed her family in these times, but more than that, she felt like a failure for not having been able to trace Kartik in more than a year. Part of the difficulty lay in her remaining tight-lipped about it. She couldn't tell why she had kept this a secret from everyone in her new world. Maybe Kartik remained her last hope of returning to her known universe? Revealing his existence would mean corrupting the very idea of that universe. She also saw this search as her personal responsibility. She hated to take help beyond what her circumstances had forced her to.

Navigating the city, going to the nearby markets on foot, to Chitra's house in trams and buses, visiting relations of neighbours, raised Amala's hopes. Although none of these trips were solo, they increased her confidence. Bus and tram conductors were helpful and would tell you how to get to your destination. Amala was positive she would soon be able to ride on trams and buses on her own. Who knew, maybe she would even find Kartik somewhere in this mad, messy city?

Amala prepared to make a visit to Chitra's house. She hadn't been invited but decided to surprise Chitra by taking Malati with her. Malati was reluctant at first; she didn't want to leave Nimaichand alone. Amala assured her it wouldn't be a problem; she had already arranged for Bhola to spend the afternoon with Mesho.

The two women woke up at five in the morning, an hour earlier than usual, to finish cooking and other chores. Malati was nervous and excited; this would be her first tram ride. Amala told her about other refugee women, some of them Bijoy Nagar residents, who were out on the streets on their own. Most of these women were elderly widows who had found jobs as cooks or maids in nearby houses. To Amala, they typified how one claimed a city with hard labour and love.

The sun's ferocity compelled Amala to open the big black umbrella she carried, another gift from Chitra. The searing *Chaitra* heat scorched them. Luckily, the tram station was only a short walk away. Malati would tell Amala later, how, throughout the journey, she had been impressed with the poise with which Amala managed the trip—from reading the tram number to negotiating with rickshaw pullers. Amala smiled and told her it wasn't too difficult once you had done it a few times.

Amala had a vested interest in visiting Chitra. She had become restless about finding work. Recent reports of young refugee girls being sexually abused or trafficked to brothels frightened her. Bijoy Nagar had lately seen more than a few outsiders. Some of these people like the local politicians who worked with the residents to demand better rights for refugees were well-wishers. But Amala knew beyond doubt that a few unscrupulous elements had infiltrated the colony, too. These men mostly appeared with 'business' interests but from conversations she'd been part of or overheard, Amala could tell they were part of something more sinister.

Chitra sprang from her sofa at the sight of Amala and Malati. Surprise and joy, accentuated by something Amala read as a proud smile, suffused her face. She stepped forward to embrace Malati, who looked tired, yet at ease. Amala gave Chitra a quick hug and darted to the kitchen to get water for herself and Malati. When she returned, she was surprised to see a new face in the room. In her haste, Amala hadn't noticed a lady who sat on the far side of the sofa.

'Meet my new neighbour, Snehalata-di,' Chitra introduced the plump woman, about her own age.

'Should we go inside, Mashi?' Amala asked, unsure if they had chosen the right moment to come.

'Why? Do I bite?' Snehalata said, a row of paan-stained teeth flickering through her grin. Amid the roar of laughter, Amala felt silly at her stiffness.

The wife of a retired accountant, Snehalata was a school teacher herself. The couple had two daughters, and after getting their younger daughter married off a month ago, they had sold their house and were renting the ground floor of the house right next to Chitra's.

'This girl Amala is like a daughter to me, Didi,' Chitra said to Snehalata. 'She has a fine eye and a lovely pair of hands when it comes to stitching and embroidering.'

'Let me see what Rani is up to in the kitchen,' Amala said as she dashed off to hide her blush.

Along with tea, Amala also brought an empty plate from the

kitchen to serve the banana fritters Malati had packed as a gift
for Chitra. 'Mashi made these this morning,' Amala said, even as
Malati resisted taking the credit by saying, 'Amu helped me with
them....'

Snehalata continued to be as direct as ever. 'I don't care which
one of you made it. I am hungry and I really like *kawlar bora*,' she
said, picking up a big fritter off the plate.

Laughter filled the room again and Amala realised she liked
this new mashi already. Snehalata had no pretensions. She
seemed to possess the ability to strip anyone she met of their
awkwardness. A little later when Snehalata made as if to leave,
Amala was the first one to protest, her remonstrance finding vocal
support from Chitra and Malati.

'Not today, young lady,' Snehalata said as she put her sandals
on. 'I will see you another day, that's a promise.'

Over lunch, Chitra shared with Amala and Malati more
facts about Snehalata's life. A teacher of Bengali literature, she
also doubled as the students' arts and crafts mentor. On hearing
about the school in Bijoy Nagar, she wanted to lend her time to
the colony's children on weekends. Chitra's face gleamed as she
talked about the innovative ideas 'Sneha-di' had shared with her.

Amala was even more delighted than she had expected to be
on this visit; her joy wasn't just for the future of Bijoy Nagar, she
felt happy for Chitra too, who seemed to have found a friend to
join her volunteer work.

After lunch, Chitra invited Malati and Amala to her bedroom
to stretch their limbs as they chatted away. She brought her box
of *paan* and listened to Amala's and Malati's concerns about
women's safety in refugee colonies. The good news, she said, was
that Manas and the boys had found some solid leads, which could
help at least some Bijoy Nagar women get trained in different
areas and also find long-term employment.

Amala could scarcely wait to hear about that.

~

Bijoy Nagar Prathomik Bidyaloy. The school. The vein that carries the pulse of this emerging refugee colony. The one emblem of brightness that lights up the residents' hearts amid all the gloom that surrounds them. A hub where young minds, boys and girls, play, chatter, study. The broken edifice of bricks and peeling paint the children's parents love to send their children to so they don't have to scavenge for scraps of opportunities to make their destinies. The dilapidated structure whose roofs are sure to leak come monsoon, the structure that genteel folk love to deride.

— MANAS DUTTA, DIARY ENTRY, APRIL 1951

As part of the combined volunteering efforts for Bijoy Nagar as well as the Gariahata PL camp, Manas had identified a fresh initiative for collecting clothes for the camp and books, stationery, and toys for the children of Bijoy Nagar. The good news was that a lot of the donations could come from the volunteers' personal collections. Manas couldn't wait to pull out books off his shelves and from inside tin trunks, most of them gifts from his father. He knew donating these books, signposts of his father's conversations with him, would make Baba happy. He almost felt Jyotirmoy patting him on the shoulder when he opened a trunk packed with the dust and smells of his childhood.

A flood of memories swept over Manas as he sorted the pile of books he'd spread on the floor—everything from mystery novels to adventure series books to science fiction and collections of folktales from all over the world. The pages of some of the older books had started peeling off the spine; Manas made a mental note to mend those before giving them to the children. He began putting the ones that were in good condition in a big cloth bag. Next, he extracted a pile of children's magazines, *Sandesh* and *Suktara* forming the biggest chunk of these fun monthly reads.

These magazines had bonded Manas to Subir more closely. Over the years, Manas had exchanged dozens of issues of *Sandesh* with Subir in exchange for the sandesh and other sweet treats Subir's mother made at home. Manas smiled as he remembered that unwritten pact between him and Subir. He would lend new issues of the magazines to Subir before he'd even read them, only to get a taste of the latest batch of *labangalatika* Mashima, Subir's Ma, had made.

~

With a reduced camp size in Gariahata, Manas and his friends took turns to volunteer there on alternate days. The extra time allowed Manas to take up a couple of home tutoring jobs. This would bring him some income, something he desperately needed if he were to continue on the path of refugee rehabilitation work. Three times a week, he spent an hour in the evening with each of his students. The jobs came his way through his grandfather's contacts and gave him a sense of fulfilment he had long been seeking. As a bonus, it made his mother happy to see him finally make good use of his time.

~

Mrinmoyee's loud wailing stopped Manas in his tracks as he approached the door on his way to Bijoy Nagar. He dropped the large bag of books by the door and ran up to her in the kitchen. Rarely had he seen his mother like this. Not even after her husband's death had anyone seen Mrinmoyee display the typical sorrow of a widow lamenting her cursed fate. She had held herself remarkably then, a poise thirteen-year-old Manas had failed to emulate when Jyotirmoy's body was brought home from the hospital.

This morning, Mrinmoyee didn't seem to gather herself as well; her bulbous teardrops soaked the piece of paper, evidently a letter, in her hand. Manas gently put his arm around her and asked her what the matter was. Mrinmoyee responded with louder sobs, handing Manas the letter. Some of the ink had splattered across the page but Manas extracted the gist. The letter was from his Bawromashi and carried grim news: she had been battling high fever and vomiting for nearly a week now.

The news filled Manas with a stinging sadness. A part of him wanted to rush to his dear aunt who had cured him of his illness only a few months ago. But with his final-year examinations a week away, Manas couldn't leave the city now. In fact, he planned to take the next few days off his volunteering duties. Right now, he needed to help Mrinmoyee.

'Here, calm down, Ma. Your crying won't help Bawromashi. Let me see what I can do,' Manas thought aloud. After he'd helped Mrinmoyee sit on a marble bench close to the kitchen, he said, 'How about I go to Biren Mama's house and request him to take you to Bawromashi?' He thought of his mother's first cousin who lived in Konnagar and visited Mrinmoyee during Durga Puja and Poila Boishakh every year.

Manas's suggestion brought Mrinmoyee some respite. She gulped a sob. Sharoda, who had just entered the kitchen to make breakfast, sensed something was amiss and brought a glass of water for Mrinmoyee. Once his mother looked a bit more composed, Manas set out at once.

Manas looked at his watch and realised he needed to take a taxi to make it to Biren Mama's house in time. At the door, he didn't forget to pick up the bag of books. He was glad he had started out early. Had it been even an hour later, he would have missed his uncle who took a train every morning to reach the bank in Bandel where he worked as a senior clerk.

Biren and his wife, Anita, were surprised to see Manas at such an early hour. When he revealed the reason behind his sudden appearance, Biren put his briefcase down. They decided it was best for Biren to take Mrinmoyee to the village the next day. That way he wouldn't have to miss work without informing *Bawro Babu*. Manas knew how much his uncle dreaded the head clerk.

Manas took out an envelope containing some cash from his pocket. His grandfather had sent it through Photik after overhearing Manas's conversation with Mrinmoyee. When Biren refused to accept the money, Manas explained it was meant for the train tickets. Biren would have none of it, but Anita reasoned,

'Where will you find all this money in a day? It's still two weeks until your next salary.'

'Maima is right, Mama,' Manas said. 'Time is of essence. Ma would be relieved if you went with her.' The thought of his Bawromashi's face, as she lay helpless and groaning in pain, agonised Manas. He softly pushed the envelope into his uncle's hand. On his part, Biren said he would try to take an early leave in the afternoon and visit Mrinmoyee. He thought it best to spend the night at their house so they could catch the early morning train.

His aunt stopped him when Manas got up to make his way to the college. She insisted he needed to have some breakfast. Manas feared he would miss a crucial lecture on *Marxist concepts of democracy and revolution*. As she rushed to the kitchen, Manas had no choice but to settle on their aging benteak sofa covered with an embroidered cloth. He picked up the *Jugantar* lying on a side table next to him. The newspaper smelled fresh.

A recent inrush of refugees to the city and the burden that posed on the state exchequer occupied a fair bit of the paper's real estate. Manas gave it a cursory read before moving on to other news—municipal developments, local crime and editorial columns punctuated with advertisements for hair oils and strength-boosting tonics. Just before he flipped over to the sports page, a single-column report caught his attention. It mentioned deadly diseases, including the dreaded smallpox, spreading in refugee camps in and around Calcutta.

Manas put the paper back on the table and began wringing his hands. The news made him realise it had been almost a month since he and Subir visited the PL camp in Gariahata. His face gathered sweat. He had to visit the camp sooner than later.

As he had feared, Manas missed the morning lecture thanks to his aunt's 'quick' breakfast of *parota* and *dimer jhuri*, eggs, scrambled and fried to the point of no return. As he copied from his classmates' notes, Bipin, who could accurately recall whatever he heard without using any mnemonics, provided a digest of the professor's lecture. He also invited Manas to a study group at the college canteen once their classes were over.

The study group upset Manas's plans to make a quick visit to Bijoy Nagar. He hated missing the opportunity to meet Amala but decided to drop off the books with Chitra for the time being.

When Rani opened the door, Manas saw a new face in the room. Chitra had apparently stepped out to pick up her homeopathic medicines. Rani introduced Manas to Snehalata. The woman, only slightly younger than Chitra Mashi to Manas's eyes, put him at ease with her broad grin. Rani told Manas that Sneha Mashima would soon start working with the 'refugee didis' in Bijoy Nagar. Manas rued not having enough time to get to know her but had to take her leave immediately. Snehalata assured him she would let Chitra know about taking the books to Bijoy Nagar.

Manas must have walked less than ten steps when he ran into Chitra. She told him he had timed his visit well as she and Snehalata planned to visit Bijoy Nagar in the next few days. She also conveyed her best wishes for Manas's aunt and asked him not to worry.

'I'm here while your Ma is away—don't forget that, Baba,' Chitra said. Manas smiled in acknowledgement and made his way towards the bus stop.

～

Kartik and Baba are at the river to catch fish. Baba holds a big net. A bidi softly burns between his fingers. He shows Kartik how to cast the net. 'Make sure there aren't any tangles,' he tells his son. Kartik watches in awe as his father takes the folds of the net into the crook of his arm, each fold sliding over him like a wave lapping a boat's frame. The moment Subimal throws the net into the river, its clear, sweet water turns muddy and viscous. Kartik is appalled at the sight and lowers his hand to clear the water, only to get pulled by a whirling current. He fights the current, swimming as best as he can in the dirty water. When he finally looks up, he can't see his father anywhere on the

bank. He sees Karim Chacha, his Baba's fellow fisherman, walking in
the distance and calls out to him. The bearded man looks back at the
river but doesn't respond. Karim keeps walking away from the river.
The sludge thickens as Kartik struggles to swim through it....

A throbbing headache awoke Amala from the nightmare. For
most of the night, she'd tossed and turned in the bed: a tatty
cotton mattress covered by a thin *kantha* that she and Malati
shared.

Amala couldn't bring herself to eat anything for breakfast. By
the time Chitra arrived with Snehalata a little later, her headache
had turned into a pounding. The two women were here as part of a
plan. They would accompany Amala and three other women from
Bijoy Nagar to *Refugee Arts and Crafts*. Amala quickly washed up
and got dressed. They picked up Tara as well as Bakul and Gouri.

Nearly an hour later, the four of them entered a modest building
in Gariahata and walked towards a small office room. Two women,
one of them about Chitra's age, the other probably in her forties,
sat behind a desk. By the look on their faces, Amala could tell they
were a bit stunned to see this small all-woman army.

'How can I help you?' The older woman asked.

As Chitra explained to her the intent of their visit, Amala's
eyes travelled to the curtains draping the small window behind the
ladies. They were the colour of wheat stalks but the embroidery
intrigued Amala—it showed a row of identical women carrying
baskets. The figures were all embroidered in geometrical shapes
though, triangles as the women's dresses, matchstick rectangles
for their hands, circles for their faces and half-moons for the
baskets on their heads. Amala thought of reproducing the pattern
on a piece of cloth. When her focus shifted back to the table, she
found Gouri adding voice to Chitra's request to please enrol them
at the centre for vocational training.

The Bijoy Nagar group had a partial win. Mrs Ganguly, the
elderly lady who happened to be the secretary to the centre's
director, told them they could take only one of the four women,
given the limited number of seats at the training centre. After

a little discussion among themselves, Chitra, Snehalata and the
girls nominated Gouri for the spot.

'No problem,' said Mrs Ganguly, with a namaskar. To Gouri
she said, 'You can start from tomorrow—don't be late, we open at
10 am sharp.'

'Sure thing!' Gouri said. Amala could tell from the spark in
her eyes that she could hardly wait to get started. Considering
the sun's glare, Chitra looked into her tote bag and mumbled to
Snehalata, 'See? I forgot the umbrella today. In this heat....'

Before she could curse herself anymore, Amala interrupted
her. 'Mashi, I need to eat something.'

'Oh my, look at you; I guess you haven't had anything this
morning?' Even as Chitra reproached Amala, she scanned the
surroundings and spotted a cucumber seller right across the street.
For four annas, they got a cucumber each in *sal*-leaf packets.
Amala bit into the fresh cucumber spiked with rock salt and lime
juice and cast a pallid smile at Chitra.

'Finish this, then we'll find some place to have lunch,' Chitra
said. When Amala resisted, she simply said, 'Well, I'm hungry
and so are Sneha-di and Bakul, Tara and Gouri. You're free to
watch us eat.'

Gouri's peals of laughter mortified Amala. Inwardly, she felt
relieved, now that hunger was getting the better of her. Still, she
cringed at the idea of Chitra paying for their food.

Snehalata seemed to read her mind. 'Why worry?' She said.
'Once you start working, we will eat at your expense. Just you see.'

Amala didn't say anything. Tears welled in her eyes.

As they walked up to the rickshaw stand, a familiar scent
enticed Amala. Despite the hot asphalt of Kolkata on this May
afternoon, the heady waft of mango blossoms along the avenues
transported her to her village.

The delicious lunch at *Supti Cabin*—rice with lentils, a fry, a
vegetable side dish and runny fish curry—left the women drowsy.
Chitra wasn't in a mood to return home, though. 'Let's go to the
shop Manas had told us about, err, what was the gentleman's

name?' she muttered while rummaging through her tote. Pulling out a folded piece of paper, she exclaimed, '*Ei je*! Found it. Jogen Babu, that's what his name is.'

The bus from *Supti Cabin* to Ultadanga, their destination, was packed. A rally had blocked the road in another part of the city, diverting the traffic. Only Chitra and Snehalata were able to find seats in deference to their silvering shock of hair. Even so, Amala could tell Chitra Mashi didn't have much of a relaxed ride.

A portly bald man, most likely between the ages of fifty-five and sixty, sat at the window of Chitra's seat. As he napped contentedly all through the jerky bus ride, his head bobbed over to Chitra's shoulder more often than it stood still. An overly-used *jhola* bag that must have been green once slung from his left shoulder. His right hand clasped the handle of a tall black umbrella that briefly woke him up every time the driver slammed on the brake. The off-white *kurta* he wore did little to hide his well-nourished paunch.

Amala couldn't help but chuckle even as she sensed Chitra's harried state. She had on her lap all their handbags plus her own tote, all of which she managed remarkably well while negotiating the pudgy man's tumbling assaults. Snehalata, who sat right behind Chitra, silently echoed Amala's chuckles. When the bus stopped at Ultadanga, Amala found Chitra heaving with relief. She scoured her bag once more to fish out Jogen Babu's address.

Looking at the street addresses of the houses next to the bus stop, she exclaimed, '*Arrey*! We are in the right neighbourhood!' Apparently, their destination lay just a few houses away. The actual address, once they arrived at it, confused Amala. It looked like any other house in the neighbourhood—no board announced its commercial nature, nor was there any indication of people working inside. Chitra seemed to share her befuddlement and hesitated to open the gate.

As they lingered outside, an elderly man walked towards them. The face seemed familiar and the umbrella was a dead giveaway. The man walked over and stopped right in front of them, '*Ki byapaar*? Are you all looking for someone?' he asked.

Chitra made almost as if to run; it was the paunchy man who
had given her a hard time in the bus. Amala clutched her hand as
she responded to the man, '*Aggey*, we're looking for Jogen Babu's
house. Is this the one?'

The man looked at Amala with a squint, then at her teammates,
before answering. 'Hmm, that it is. But I'm afraid, I can't recognise
you.'

Chitra tried to unclasp her hand off Amala. She wanted to
have no more of this overbearing gabby man, who stepped ahead
to open the gate and began walking in. Amala winked at Gouri
to keep talking to the man.

'Sir, we are here to meet Jogen Babu,' Gouri said, her voice
quavering with the thrill of someone whose lottery ticket was on
the verge of matching the very last digit of the winning number
being announced.

'So I understand,' the man said, even as he proceeded to unlock
the door, taking out a key from his *kurta* pocket. 'But truth be
told, I don't even know you ladies.'

The man's thick East Bengali accent shot an electric wave
to Amala's brain. She scampered ahead, sidestepping Chitra,
Snehalata and her girlfriends. Before the man could walk inside,
Amala blurted, 'Jogen Babumohashoi, we are here to find out
about the tailoring institute....'

The man turned around and flashed a smile. '*O, ei byapaar*, why
didn't you say so before,' he said, as if the purpose of their visit had
elevated his stature.

Which, apparently it did, for even Chitra moved forward and
joined her palms to greet the supposed Jogen Babu.

'We are so lucky to be able to meet you,' Chitra said, in a voice
that belied any disdain she might have been feeling minutes ago.

'*Ashun, ashun*, please come in,' he said, wiping the sweat on his
forehead with the sleeve of his kurta.

As drops of his sweat dripped onto Chitra's arm, Amala pulled
back before she stepped forward.

15

The room they stepped into looked rather bare to Amala. But for a desk and a couple of chairs, it carried little by way of furniture or the usual trappings of a wealthy man. The lone window to the west was closed, shrouding the room in a cool, mysterious darkness.

Somewhat embarrassed at having more visitors than he had furniture for, Jogen Babu bit his tongue and said, 'Truth be told, I need to buy some more chairs, you know. Please sit, sit....'

Turning towards the inside of his house, he called out to someone called Poltu. Within minutes, a boy Amala thought to be of Kartik's age, appeared.

'*Ei je*, call your Mashima and get some *moras* for these ladies.'

Jogen Babu's peppering of his sentences with '*Shottyi kawtha bolte ki*' or 'Truth be told' amused Amala no end. She suppressed a chuckle while also appreciating how that phrase complemented Jogen Babu's different moods.

The appearance of a woman she guessed to be a little older than her mother brought Amala back to the room. The lady wore a light *dhanekhali* sari and her short stature made her appear plumper, an image completed by her chubby face. She pulled the *anchal* over her head and greeted the visitors with a broad smile that unveiled her *paan*-stained teeth.

Soon Poltu came, balancing five *moras* on his hands and arms. He plopped them down with a soft thud and disappeared inside in a flash. The purpose of the women's visit made Jogen Babu and his wife very happy. Amala could tell that after looking at their faces as they intently listened to Chitra. Jogen Babu's wife kept moving her glance from Chitra and Snehalata, who added weight to Chitra's words, to the four young women sitting next to them. Her eyes perked up when she learned 'the girls' had been trained by Chitra and already knew a few stitching types and embroidery patterns. Amala felt lucky to be sitting there.

Jogen Babu, despite his comical entry into her life, seemed like a good-natured man to Amala. His wife seemed equally convivial, a *my-dear* sort of person you could open your heart to. They must be from the village Amala thought, for in the city she hadn't yet come across a trader so shorn of streetwise smoothness.

Chitra cleared her throat and asked for some water. Mrs Haldar, whom Jogen Babu introduced as Purnima, got up and flitted inside. She returned with a tray holding steel tumblers.

'We're so happy you came here,' Purnima said. She related how they had only started their tailoring establishment six months ago. Currently they had five girls, all refugees, working with them but they could easily take five more into their fold. This was the best news Amala had heard in a long time.

She noticed smiles on Bakul and Tara's faces too even as Snehalata said, '*Bah*, that's good to know. Hopefully, you would consider these girls of ours.'

'Yes, of course,' said Purnima as she assured Chitra's students that they didn't need to worry about the work. She would train them herself.

Like Amala, Tara, and Bakul, the couple had been forced to flee East Pakistan more than a year ago because of rioting. Luckily, a neighbour had looked after their property, which Jogen Haldar later sold off to a friend. The transaction took place in his absence, and although he didn't get the price he had expected, Jogen Haldar counted himself among the fortunate few who had got anything at all off their ancestral property.

The couple didn't have any children, seemingly a curse, but one that now worked as a strange blessing, Amala thought. Setting up the tailoring shop was Purnima's idea as was training and recruiting refugees, predominantly young women, but also men. The results had been surprisingly good. Being located in a residential area had its own advantages. Women from the neighbourhood could approach them directly without having to board a bus or tram to visit the more established markets. As word spread, *Jogajog Tailors*, as Jogen and Purnima named their shop, even started bagging orders from the neighbours' relatives and acquaintances.

Purnima brought tea and biscuits for everyone. Poltu followed her with a plate of *alur chop*.

'You didn't have to, Didi,' Chitra said, to which Purnima said she knew tea and fried snacks were never a bad idea, no matter the season or the hour of the day.

Jogen Babu added his voice to that. '*Shottyi kawtha bolte ki*, she is absolutely right.'

'I agree,' Snehalata said with a chortle.

A soft chuckle was heard from Poltu who stood in a corner of the room. Purnima asked the boy to come and partake of the *chops*, but he hesitated. 'They are just like your Dimoni,' Purnima said.

Amala couldn't tell if Poltu was a servant boy or someone known to the Haldars. Purnima solved the mystery when she told them Poltu happened to be the younger brother of a girl training with them, possibly seventeen herself. They had been separated from their parents in the chaos that followed when they crossed over to India. Jogen and Purnima sheltered the siblings who came to them from a refugee camp in Baguiati.

On their way back, Amala thought about the strangeness of it all. The man who had annoyed them on the bus turned out to be their benefactor. In the past one year, life had repeatedly compelled her to look beyond the obvious. Often what was in plain view didn't make for real seeing.

Over the next week, as they rode on the buses that took them from Bijoy Nagar to Ultadanga, the hour-long trip didn't seem all that difficult to Amala. Having Tara and Bakul with her made the journey anything but dull. Sure, there were days when they encountered passengers who were way more annoying than poor

Jogen Babu had been when they first saw him in the bus. But what was that compared to the surge of independence Amala now felt? On more than one day, she thanked Manas in her heart for this job.

Amala didn't realise how a month flew by after she, Bakul, and Tara first started going to Purnima Mashimoni's, as the trainee girls and boys called her, shop-factory at the edge of the city. Purnima taught them a few commercial tailoring tricks: distinguishing between different types of fabrics as well as threads and their properties, making piping, and creating patterns on cloths and hand-sewn and machine hems.

The interest Chitra had kindled in Amala with her threadbare resources at the camp found its real purpose in this Ultadanga house that was now her school and workplace. *Jogajog* also helped her escape the grimy trap of Bijoy Nagar. Lack of regular water supply and proper sanitation made their surroundings a breeding ground for diseases. The intrusion of property dealers, petty criminals and possibly even some pimps disguised as well-meaning people with 'business interests' made Amala fear her neighbourhood at times. She had invested a lot of hopes in this colony, this brick-and-mortar manifestation of the refugees' handiwork and determination. It would break her to see it crumble....

On her way to work one morning, Amala saw Mintu, a young boy, talking to two strangers at the colony's newly-opened tea shack. The boy had endeared himself to Amala partly because of his innocence—his mind didn't seem to have developed as fast as his body—but also due to the fact that he had lost his father on the train that had brought him and his mother to India. His father belonged to the same nameless heap of humans that had been created by hacking people in the name of religion. Mintu escaped the killers' wrath as he and his mother were in a different cabin at the time and he was wearing a skull cap given to him by Masud, his friend from their village in Khulna.

Moyna, Mintu's mother, came to know about the horror only after they boarded off the train in India. But a sliver of hope waited for them across the border. Ganesh, her husband's younger brother, had already moved to Calcutta with his wife a month ago and had found place in the Gariahata refugee camp. Following the riots, Ganesh had sent a message to his brother via a village acquaintance asking them to cross over as soon as they could.

When Mintu and Moyna finally reunited with Ganesh and his wife, Mintu was mostly in the care of Mamata, Ganesh's wife. Ganesh had been a volunteer leader at the camp and a key strategist in the founding of Bijoy Nagar. His high school education also got him a part-time job as an apprentice at a printing press. Mamata remained at home and made pickles, chutneys and other edible items ordered by the office babus Ganesh worked with.

Moyna rarely came out of the house, preferring to help with the cooking and cleaning when her body allowed it. Amala learned from Mamata that the thought of her husband's slashed body drenched in blood still caused Moyna seizures, though these had become rarer. With time, her horror slowly morphed into grief. Her loud wails turned into sobs no one heard, until those too evaporated, leaving her a dry bed where no stream ran. She became severely anemic and lost her appetite.

Back at the camp, Amala had seen how Mamata attempted more than once to make Moyna socialise with the other women. On one occasion she even dragged her to Chitra's sewing class. She gave up when Ganesh suggested leaving 'Boudi alone' until she felt like it, considering the amount of coaxing it took to even get her to comb her hair for attending the class.

Because of this history, Mintu had become something of a collective responsibility for Bijoy Nagar's residents. The boy enjoyed the attention showered on him. As she found him talking to the two strangers when he should have been in school, Amala asked Tara and Bakul to wait and skittered over to the tea shack.

Ignoring the men, she asked Mintu, '*Ki re*, what are you doing here? Shouldn't you be in school?'

The boy, startled at Amala's sudden appearance, mumbled, 'I was going there, Amu Mashi, but these gentlemen....'

Amala scanned the smoker and his associate, a lanky youngster sporting a shirt with printed flowers and drainpipe trousers, his oiled hair neatly combed.

Turning back to Mintu, Amala said, 'I will talk to them. You walk to your class. Come on, hurry up now.'

Mintu rapidly walked towards the school building.

'Is there anything I can help you with?' Amala asked the two men.

'Nah, nah, Madam, don't you worry. We were just chatting with that boy, er, what did you call him? Mintu isn't it, yes, yes, Mintu,' said one of them.

Something about him made Amala uncomfortable. She couldn't pinpoint if it was his tone or the way he called her 'Madam'.

'Nomoskar, Madam,' he said and turned to face the tea stall owner to ask if their tea was ready.

His voice reminded Amala of raspy frogs croaking in rain. Not in a mood to waste any more time, Amala walked back to Tara and Bakul. The encounter left a bitter taste in her mouth.

At work that day, Amala couldn't focus; she hurt her finger more than once as it came under the machine's needle. She kept repeating the same mistake. Purnima noticed and took her inside for a glass of water. When she asked what the matter was, Amala narrated the morning's episode, her voice quaking with anxiety. She apologised for being behind on her project that had to be delivered in a couple of days.

'Don't worry. I will work on it this afternoon,' Purnima said, adding, 'Why don't you go out for a bit? Take Tara along if you want.'

On any other day Amala would have turned down this suggestion. Once immersed in her world of needles, threads, and the machine's rolling motion, she didn't take any unnecessary breaks. But as the faces of those men at the tea shack repeatedly flashed in her mind, Purnima's idea comforted her. Tara was delighted at the opportunity to discover what lay beyond the bus stop.

Before they could step out, a jangling sound stopped Amala in her tracks. Purnima, who always had the keys of the safe tied to her sari's end, came up to her and Tara. She took out a two-rupee note from a thin roll of cash folded inside the sari's end and shoved it into Tara's hand, and before either Tara or Amala could murmur a protest, Purnima gently pushed them out of the door. 'Come, get going now, have some *jhalmuri*. Or you girls might like the spicy *phuchka*. Try it, try it,' Purnima whispered with a wink.

Amala and Tara had barely made it as far as the bus stop when when the sight of two men getting off a bus startled them. Two warm faces this time. Nitai and Ganesh were just as stunned as their eyes met the two women walking in their direction. Tara tugged at her sari's corner, squeezing it hard; Amala could tell she felt awkward. From whatever she had shared with Amala, Tara and Nitai were in a happy relationship. But for him to see his wife on the road instead of behind a sewing machine must be a surprise. The bright smiles on the men's faces relieved Amala, although she still had to drag Tara to help her face her husband.

Ganesh was the first to speak. '*Arrey*, how did you know we were coming, Boudi and Amu-di?'

'You came to visit us?' Amala asked.

Nitai held a big earthen pot covered with paper before her and said, 'I just got a job and thought of sharing some sweets with you and your work friends.'

Amala's heart flooded with love. She stole a glance at Tara and found her face flushed with a happiness she knew to be rare. She decided to let the couple have a moment to themselves lest the magic slipped away. '*Ne bhai, tora aego*, you two carry on,' she said to Tara, adding, 'I want to have a word with Ganesh-da. We'll follow you.'

A week later, long after the syrup-drowned rosogollas in that earthen pot had been polished off by everyone at *Jogajog*, the memory of that afternoon still brought sweetness to Amala's lips. She remembered how, as Tara and Nitai walked ahead of Ganesh and her, their steps matched and their voices filled the summer air with the lightness of a spring breeze.

Like a bolt of lightning striking a tree, the desire to see Manas seized Amala. They hadn't met in nearly a month; was he ignoring her? Or had she, with her knee-jerk reaction, turned him away? What about *her*? Had her response to his proposal changed? She didn't know. All she knew was that the day she had started working at *Jogajog*, she thought of Manas. Not as her benefactor, but as an equal, an accomplice even, in the mystery she had set out to solve.

~

The drill of examinations and its ancillary devices—staying up late, missing meals, gulping far too many cups of tea, scrawling notes on endless scraps of paper—enslaved Manas for two weeks. Between volunteering and tutoring kids, he had little time to focus on his own course. Thankfully, being a nerd had its own benefits. He often read textbooks for pleasure.

Within a couple of days of Mrinmoyee's departure, Biren returned with an eyewitness report on Bawromashi's condition. The village doctor attending to her had written a prescription but the medicines weren't available in the village. 'Send these medicines as soon as you hear from Biren,' a note from Mrinmoyee said.

Manas was able to have the medicines delivered within the next two days by paying for express mail delivery and showing a note to the postmaster from his grandfather.

The medicines worked their charm as Sreemoyee got better in a week's time. In a letter to Manas, his mother sent him her and Sreemoyee's blessings. Manas thought of visiting his aunt after his examinations, but within a week, another postcard arrived. The two sisters were joining a group of pilgrims headed to Puri. Considering how Sreemoyee had come back from the brink, they wanted to thank the almighty. 'Don't be disheartened,' read the letter, 'for I will bring your Bawromashi home with me when we return from Puri.'

Manas smiled. How well his Ma knew him in some respects,

yet how unmindful she remained of his feelings about other things.

Manas decided to spend the first week after his examinations alone. He hadn't felt this need in a long time; if anything, he found his greatest release in working in a group. The personal time he now craved stemmed from a need to bring his mind, scattered all over like spring pollen, together. Bawromashi's health weighed on him as did the question of his career and the future of the refugees in the Gariahata camp. The guilt of not visiting Urmila nagged him. And then there was Amala. Not so much a worry as an enigma, a mystery that kept deepening.

Late one evening, after spending the entire day sifting through the books in the home library and reading newspapers, Manas ventured out. Reading the news—police firing on farmers; ministers living lavishly and talking big on welfare spending; a blind widow's eviction from her house by her zamindar landlord—didn't help his anxiety. He needed some quiet time; not necessarily a secluded spot, just somewhere where he didn't matter to those around him.

A blazing mandarin sun descended down the Hooghly River when Manas reached Babughat. The crowds were thinning out. The muggy summer air made him scoot towards the riverbank. He sat down on one of the cemented steps, taking in the flow of the evening river. The darkening horizon suited him well. He thanked himself for not choosing to come to the *ghat* in the morning when the place buzzed with bathers, masseurs, *champi malish wallahs* who, in their zeal to apply oil for great hair and a cool mind, drummed customers' skulls like percussion instruments.

Though Manas could have done with a calm head at that moment, he didn't miss the flurry of the morning hours. His eyes travelled to the spot where four ferry boats stood anchored. The song, *Ke tumi boshi nodi kule aekela* by Atulprasad came to his mind, causing a slight ripple in his thought stream. He recalled the second line, *Kaar laagi aeto utawlaa:* 'Who do you pine for, thus?' Manas shrugged at the thought, lightly tapping his forehead with his knuckle. He instantly recognised that to be Amala's influence. Didn't she slap her forehead whenever she felt frustrated or sad?

Manas sat watching the Hooghly flow by for a long time before an army of mosquitoes swooped upon him. He walked over to the bus stop, his head abuzz with cricket calls and noisy thoughts. *This alone thing isn't working. Maybe I do need a champi after all!*

All Manas's ideas of a quiet week were turned upside down the very next morning when Manik literally yanked him out of his sleep.

'*Ki re*, what's the matter?' Manas said with a wide grin, pushing back the tousled shock of hair clouding his forehead.

'Your exams are over, aren't they?' Manik demanded.

'Erm, yes, why?'

'Why are you not showing up, *haan*? You forgot us?'

'*Arrey nah*, I meant to....'

'Okay, okay, you don't have to make things up now. Chitra Mashi wants you to visit her.' Seeing the alert look that replaced Manas's grin, he quickly added, '*Arrey*, nothing serious. We haven't had an *adda* in a while so she suggested we join her for breakfast and lunch today.'

'Breakfast *and* lunch?'

'Well, Mashimoni had said lunch, but when I mentioned *luchi*....'

Manas jumped off his bed and twisted Manik's ear in mock reproach. 'Sit here,' he motioned Manik to his chair. 'I'll have some tea sent for you.'

~

After the scrumptious breakfast of *luchis* puffed up to perfection along with *alur dom, begun bhaja, sandesh* and tea, Manas wondered if he or his buddies had any room left for the promised lunch. If anything, he needed a walk to digest the nine *luchis* he had just eaten. When he thought that aloud, Chitra lapped up the idea. 'Wait. I will come with you. I need to get my glasses from the

optician,' she said. 'It's just round the corner. I hope you don't
mind my company?'

'Why, it's my pleasure, Mashi! Let's go.'

On their way back from the optician, Manas couldn't contain
the grin his face kept relaxing into. He wondered how he had
missed reading Chitra's ruse of picking up her glasses. The real
cause of her accompanying him brought his adrift mind right
back on track. Just like that, a drab week had turned into the most
intoxicating one he had known yet.

The news Chitra gave Manas involved Amala. And him. Amala
had accepted his proposal. Manas tried to imagine Amala's face as
she had said this to Chitra. The revelation apparently came only a
couple of days ago, when Chitra and Snehalata visited Bijoy Nagar
to deliver the books and art supplies for the kids. Amala had pulled
Chitra away on the pretext of introducing her to Daktarbabu and
had spoken her mind. Chitra asked Amala if she'd thought her
decision through or needed more time. Amala had reportedly
whispered it was final. She had to cross over to the other shore;
she couldn't just keep swimming between the river's ends.

Manas couldn't help a guffaw when he heard this. *Silly girl.
Didn't you see me swimming in the same choppy river? Only I wasn't
wavering, not with your current pulling me in.*

Manas's head whirled with a thousand questions. Did Amala
ask to see him? Did she have a date in mind for tying the knot?
Was it Tara's wedding that made her change her mind? He didn't
know about her but all he wanted to do was to drop everything
and run to Bijoy Nagar to see her face. Once. Talk to her. Laugh
silly with her. Maybe hold her hand and understand her touch.

As he fidgeted, Chitra shared more good news. 'I've asked
Amala to come for tea in the evening. She plans to come straight
from work. Maybe you can take her to New Market or some other
place?'

'Oh, I see. Yes, yes...' Manas hoped to appear as casual as his
happy-as-a-five-year-old-getting-a-new toy face would let him be.

Chitra tapped him lightly on the head and hastening her step said, 'Now let's get back home quickly. Can't trust that Rani with all the cooking.'

Manas could have reached the house in a single leap.

The amber light of the street lamps fused with the sun's fainting rays when Amala arrived at Chitra's house. The other boys had left; Chitra had held Manas back on the pretext of 'helping sort through old clothes people had donated to her for the PL camp'. Amala looked surprised to see Manas when he opened the door for her. She didn't see Chitra around.

Putting her *jhola* bag down, she said, 'Water,' and proceeded to the kitchen.

'Wait,' Manas said. 'I'll get some water and let Mashi know you're here.'

His tone, affectionate yet firm, caught Amala unawares. She plopped down on the sofa, wiping sweat off her forehead.

Chitra appeared with a bag of clothes. '*Ei dyakho,* this is what we've have been doing all day,' she said with a huff as she sat across Amala. Handing over the bag to Amala, she said, 'I found some good blouses and frocks and thought of showing them to you in case you wanted to take them for the ladies and girls in Bijoy Nagar.'

Amala gave the contents of the bag a cursory look and said, 'I think these will be very useful, Mashi. I myself could use a blouse or two. I have only two blouses I can wear to work; the ones that don't have doors and windows yet.'

Her loud laughter ceased when Manas appeared with glasses of water and a plate of sweets. Amala quickly covered her shoulder with her *anchal.*

Manas held the tray, first before Chitra, then to Amala and said with a hint of apology, 'Sorry, it took a bit longer to get the water. I was looking for sweets...you must be hungry.'

'*Ei dyakho*...you could have just called me, Baba,' Chitra said.

'Oh, Mashi, please don't start treating me like some important guest now,' Amala said, her rebuke directed as much at Manas as Chitra.

Her soft laugh spread across the room, absorbing everything in its ripples. Manas wanted to keep floating in that wavelet.

'Do you see how neatly this boy has arranged the sweets for you, Amala?' Chitra made sure she didn't lose any opportunity to tease Manas.

'And since I did arrange them so neatly for *you*, Amala, I hope you wouldn't mind having one?' Manas said with an impish smile, surprised at the liberty he suddenly took with the woman he loved.

'Thank you,' Amala said, picking up a sweet from the plate before passing it to Chitra. 'I think we can safely say you're good at placing sweets on a plate. Hope you're not too bad at other tasks?'

Amala's repartee elicited a roaring laugh of solidarity from Chitra.

They have ganged up to pull my leg. All the same, Manas felt relieved that Rani had stepped out with Minoti to join a few of their neighbourhood friends for their occasional evening *addas* at a nearby park. Had Rani been present, the attack would have been merciless, like a sparrow getting cornered after accidentally landing in a flock of crows. But now that the opposition didn't appear all that daunting, he wasn't ready to give up without a fight.

'Well, you can find that out for yourself,' Manas said. 'Mashi suggested we visit New Market. You can assess my skills as a shopping assistant this evening.'

'Mashi!' Amala shot a glare at Chitra for setting her up like this.

'What's wrong with that, Ma?' Chitra asked. 'All you see of Kolkata is the route your bus takes every day. Go and see some other spots. Who knows, you might actually start liking this place?'

Amala finished the sweet she had been nibbling on, took a sip of water, then went inside to wash up. Minutes later, she joined Manas and Chitra for a quick cup of tea before setting out.

She could hear her heart pounding as she stepped out. This was her first time alone with Manas since that awkward afternoon when he visited Bijoy Nagar a couple of months ago.

So much had changed since then; she no longer flinched on seeing him and could tease him with frank ease. And yet her chest heaved with an unknown agitation. Manas walked a little ahead of her, still within talking range as they approached the local taxi stand.

Amala protested. 'We can take a bus. I'm sure there will be quite a few going to New Market.'

It was too late. Manas had already begun talking to a taxi driver and booked the vehicle for the entire evening. 'Don't worry,' he whispered. 'It's from my own earning. Will tell you more later. Let's go.'

Amala spoke little, busy soaking up the sights and sounds that drifted past the taxi's open window. Manas sat at the other end of the seat, a gap separating them. He kept stealing occasional glances at Amala, happy to see a smile spread on her tired face every now and then. She wore a dust-coloured sari with a light copper border, its sheen the shade of Amala's personality.

When the taxi stopped in New Market, a sensory storm swept over Amala. Smells of fried food vied with those of freshly-cut papaya, banana, and watermelon. Hawkers with everything from spatulas to giant cauldrons were in a constant screeching contest even as the onlookers elbowed each other to get to the next stall. Amala saw an old man pull a cart piled with onions and potatoes and thought of the *haats* of her village: the weekly markets she and her father used to visit to buy fresh produce and other things of utility. This market appeared at least five times in size going by the number of people it accommodated. She must have stood transfixed for a few minutes before she heard Manas's voice. 'This way, Amala. Let's go inside. Our Hogg *shaheber bajaar*.'

As they waded through the swelling crowd, Manas gave Amala a backgrounder of the market, a mix of stories he'd picked up from his father during their monthly excursions to the market as well as from Manas's own impressions of the place. He told her how this market, once the exclusive domain of *Ingrej shahebs* had gone on to become the best-loved bazaar for ordinary Calcuttans.

He led her past the flower sellers; the heady fragrance of jasmine and *rajanigandha*, blending with the scents of marigolds and roses that lingered on Amala's skin. Inside the market, Manas took her to some of his favourite shops: Nahoum's where he bought fruitcakes and cookies which he insisted Amala take for the children back home; a wall clock and watch shop he used to spend hours in as a young boy, fascinated by the work of the clockmakers taking apart the minutiae of wristwatches and making them tick perfectly again; the fishmongers and the butchers at the market's rear, clanging their knives and blades on fat cutting stones. The smell of raw meat nauseated Amala, forcing her to cover her nose with the end of her sari. When Manas showed her the way to the garments section, she heaved a sigh of relief.

Amala browsed through the clothes section for a long time before Manas gently led her to Ghanashyam, the sari shop his mother patronised. Despite his limited knowledge of saris, Manas knew this shop stocked drapes from different Indian states. He quite liked the temple-bordered saris from Orissa and some of the southern states. With Amala standing next to him, he asked one of the salesmen to show them a few silk saris. The man, who looked about the same age as Manas to Amala, swiftly spread saris of different colours and styles on the bed-like platform on which he and other the salesmen sat.

Looking at Amala, Manas said, 'Do you mind helping me select a sari?' The request perplexed Amala, a reaction she couldn't hide.

'You see, it's for my aunt's daughter-in-law...I want to gift her something with my first salary,' Manas said.

'Oh. But how would I know which colour she likes?'

'Don't worry about that. At least you can tell one colour from the other. I can't see beyond three or four,' Manas said with a chuckle.

His comment brought a flicker of laughter from the salesman
who had, by now, started draping the saris on his shoulder and
posed like a model to give Amala a better view of the *anchal* as
well as the body of the sari.

Mortified, Amala wanted this drama to be over with and
pointed to a bright sari, the colour of ripe mango, a forest green
band bordering it. 'That one looks nice,' she said, shuffling her
handbag as if to leave the shop.

'Thank you! You made my task a lot easier,' Manas said.

The salesman folded the sari neatly and passed it on to the
shop owner, a bespectacled, pot-bellied Marwari man who
squinted through his thick eyeglasses and reminded Amala a bit
of Jogen Meshomoshai.

The amount of money Manas paid for the sari was almost
twice Amala's salary for a month. She wondered about his source
of income. It also bothered her that he didn't bargain with the
salesman and the price asked for. Amala saw customers haggling
all around her.

'You paid more for the sari than you should have, I think,' she
said as they stepped out of the shop.

'Ha, ha,' Manas broke into a hearty laughter. 'What do I know
of that, Amala? I don't shop for saris every day. Or for anything
much.'

'Hmm, so much for your skills as a shopping assistant. Do you
plan to buy anything else? Maybe *I* can help you.'

'No, that's all for today...unless you want to buy something.
Oh, you must see the spice section of the market before we leave.'

The spice area mesmerised Amala even more than the flowers.
She had never seen such a sea of spices; some she knew from
her mother's and Malati's kitchen and yet many more she saw
and smelled for the very first time. As she curiously peered over
the giant wooden boxes containing some unfamiliar spices and
condiments, the shopkeeper, a goateed Muslim man, introduced
her to them, telling her their uses and the dishes they went into.

Amala couldn't resist the urge to try out some of these new finds and took out a five-rupee note from her wallet to buy *shahjeera*, a darker and slimmer variety of cumin the shop owner told her to use in rich meat dishes and *kababchini;* small black globules that looked exactly like whole black pepper but apparently had a different aroma, stronger and warmer. A minute later, Amala and Manas joined the crowds drifting out of the market area.

'There's a special place I want to show you today,' Manas said as he approached a taxi.

Amala's heart trembled at the suggestion. If it was where she thought, she wasn't yet ready for it. 'Er, where?'

'Come, you will know.'

'Nah, Manas Ba...I can't visit your house today. I don't mean to sound rude, but I need more preparation for that.'

'My home? Who's going there? I mean we can if you wish to, but that wasn't the place I was talking about. My house can get pretty boring if you have to live there every day!' Manas guffawed, not entirely unmindful of his forewarning to Amala.

Amala reciprocated with a broad smile and didn't hesitate before the taxi ride this time around. It had been a long day after all, the bus ride to work and then to Chitra's house, then the hour-long gallivanting through the every-item-under-the-sun stalls of New Market.

'*Bhai*, Dhakuria lake *cholun*,' Manas said to the taxi driver.

All through the ride to the lake, Amala spoke animatedly about how, though exhausting, the market visit had delighted her and how she wanted to return there with some of her work friends. She also wanted to bring Malati. The idea of taking unknown spices to Malati thrilled her like a little girl. The fact that Amala could find joy in matters of everyday domesticity gladdened Manas. Not because he had decided to make her part of his family but because it suggested she had found at least some measure of normalcy back in her life.

The lake's blue-green expanse soothed Amala's limbs. Manas led her to the shade of a peepul tree that had unfurled its branches in all directions. The evening breeze carried the moistness of the lake and made a few loose strands of hair ruffle against Amala's cheeks. She pushed the hair back and went closer to the water, drinking in its liquid serenity with her eyes. She hadn't been so close to water since the time she visited the Dakshineshwar temple with Chitra.

Amala looked at Manas and said '*Dhonnobad,*' softly. He probably had no idea how badly she missed water. Before coming to India, water permeated her like the air she inhaled. Back then, she didn't have any good reason to imagine that there could be a time when she would have to *seek* water, when it wouldn't pervade every pore of her skin like paddy soaking in perpetual wetness.

Manas sat down on the cool grass under the tree, carefully placing the paper bag containing the new sari beside him. Amala joined him momentarily, her eyes still drawn to the lake. She placed her handbag and purchases carefully to create a little island between her and Manas. For a few minutes, the only sounds around them were the rustle of tree leaves, the croaking of frogs, and the odd human voice wafting from afar.

Manas took the liberty of intruding on Amala's reverie. 'You like this place,' he said, not by way of suggestion but a solid knowing.

'It's so beautiful here. Who knew your Kolkata has such a spot, too?'

'Ha, ha. Our Kolkata isn't all that bad, you know. Give it some time and you'll fall in love with this city.'

Amala said nothing to confirm or deny that prediction. Her gaze now focused on the strands of grass, which she started plucking and chewing on lightly.

'So,' Manas said, clearing his throat. 'Thank *you*, Amala.'

The emphasis on 'you' seemed to be in response to the gratitude Amala had shown for being brought to the water a while ago.

'You have taken such a weight off my chest,' Manas continued. 'I'll probably have the best sleep of my life tonight.' Then, without blinking, he said, 'Wait a minute. I don't think I'd even be able to close my eyelids tonight!'

A sheepish grin covered Amala's face. 'I have added to your burdens, not made them lighter,' she said.

'*Taai shoi*, so be it. This is a load I'll be happy to bear for the rest of my life.'

A sudden quack from a duck that had sauntered close enough to Manas shattered the brief period of silence that followed Manas's heavy-lifting claims.

'Can I ask you something, Amala? You may choose not to answer.'

'Hmm.'

'Why did you agree to, er…marry me?'

Manas's directness made Amala go red in the face. She wished they could go back to the insinuations of a moment ago. But she knew there was no escaping the raw, uncoated intent of his question.

'Who knows?' Amala said. If she had thought that such a response would bring an end to Manas's curiosity, she was mistaken. The ambiguity of her words only stirred him more.

'Hey, that's not fair. You don't want me to believe you decided on a whim? No one can say that about Amala Manna.'

Amala kept plucking at the grass stems. A little later she said softly, 'Why do you care? Isn't my agreement enough to you?'

Manas felt checkmated. She had nailed it. *Do we know the answers to all the whys in our lives?* Seeing Amala preoccupied and distracted he looked for ways to lighten the atmosphere. Luckily, he had just the thing. Manas fished out a *thhonga* from his *panjabi* pocket. It contained chocolate-covered macaroons, his secret purchase from Nahoum's for celebrating this moment with Amala.

Some of the macaroons had broken but he picked one out that hadn't and held it out for Amala. 'See if you like it?'

Amala accepted the treat and began nibbling at its rocky surface that softened as soon as it touched her tongue. As the chocolate melted in her mouth, the twinkle in her eyes conveyed her endorsement. Manas took out a broken piece for himself

and extended the entire packet to Amala. She placed it in the
island, on top of her bags. This quiet act of sharing, typical of
Amala's understated affection, permeated Manas like a beam of
moonlight. It was as if she were saying to him, *'Neither you provide
for me, nor I for you. We merely partake of what's available to us both.'*
Manas was happy with that arrangement.

Manas's frankness allowed Amala the liberty to begin her own
interrogation. 'So, tell me more about your job?'

It was his turn to be taken aback. Amala's tone demanded a
clear, factual answer.

'Oh, that. No job, Amala, you see I'm still studying. I took up
a couple of home tuition jobs. You know, giving private lessons to
children to help with their school studies?'

Amala knew about tuitions and coaching. Some of the kids
in Bijoy Nagar went for group tuitions to a nearby house. 'Good,
good,' she said, a bit abstracted. 'Teaching is good, a good thing.
If only my Kartik were around, he would be studying in a school
here.'

'Kartik—who's that?' Manas asked.

The sudden slip of tongue shocked Amala, and yet oddly
reassured her, too. As she finally revealed to him the fact of her
brother's disappearance, an invisible boulder she'd been lugging
around seemed to dissolve into dust.

Manas brought himself closer to her and said, 'I wish I'd known
earlier—we could have found him by now....But you know what?
I'm glad you finally trust me enough to share this. I'll be on the
job; don't worry, Amu.'

The sun quietly slipped behind the trees, leaving Manas and
Amala with the croaking frogs and quacking ducks. A host of
chirping crickets joined them, enveloping the hour of dusk with
a curious aural wrapping. Amala absorbed the sensations as best
as the mosquitoes invading her skin allowed her to. She made
quite a few of them pay with their lives. In any case, their attack
paled before the peace this evening brought her. She could have
sat there for hours, sheathed in the silence punctuated by the

evensong of ducks and crickets. Suddenly, the sound of Manas clearing his throat alerted her.

'Please take this, Amala. This is for you,' he said, extending a paper bag to her. Amala felt a softness leading up to her hand. She couldn't see the bag in the dark but as she opened it, a flicker of orange peered at her, it was the sari Manas had bought. For his sister-in-law.

'No!' Amala nearly screamed.

Manas knew he had to tackle this delicately. 'Look, Amala, it's a gift from me. Can't I even give you a sari?'

'Why would you gift me such an expensive sari? I'm nothing to you,' she prattled, adding softly, 'yet.'

'Why, you are. You have been since the day I met you. Don't you remember I called you a friend long ago, at the Gariahata camp?'

'Na, Manas Babu, there's no way I can accept such an expensive gift from you. The sweets you gave I didn't say no to.'

'Please, Amala. *Lokkhi meye*. I'll be hurt if you didn't take it. Why, it's with my own money even!'

'Do they pay you so much for the tuitions?' Amala couldn't hide her incredulity any longer.

'Well, I also saved some money from my monthly *haat-khorcha* allowance my grandfather gives me. But...most of it is with my own income. Please, Amala...' His voice had such an honest entreaty, Amala felt it would be cruel to reject the gift.

'Okay,' she said, picking up the bag lounging in the 'island'. 'I will take it. Please don't ask me to wear it until....'

'It's yours and you get to decide when to wear it. I will wait for the day, though.'

Quietness draped them again before Amala decided it was getting late and Malati would worry.

'Yes, let's go.' Manas said, getting up and dusting his *panjabi* of grass straws. 'We'll take a taxi so you can get down first.'

'Hmm,' Amala said plainly.

16

Amala requested Manas to remain inside the taxi as she got down. She hadn't yet told Malati and Nimai about Manas and herself.

'It's quite dark—*ektu egiye diyi*, can I come part of the way?' Manas asked.

Amala reassured him that she could sleepwalk through Bijoy Nagar and still reach home.

Manas waited until he couldn't see Amala's frame any longer.

Being a stepchild of the city as Amala called it, Bijoy Nagar still hadn't received electricity. Darkness clasped the surroundings, dispelled only by the faint light of kerosene lanterns at the tea shack. Amala quickened her pace to get home, barely a few metres from the tea stall. The place looked uncharacteristically busy for this time of the evening. Usually by closing time, no more than one or two customers could be spotted, mostly residents who wanted a cup of tea before heading home.

From the corner of her eye, Amala saw the same strangers she had caught speaking to Mintu a few days ago. She looked away immediately, hoping they hadn't seen her. On reaching the edge of their home, she saw Malati waiting at the door with a lantern.

Amala rushed to her and said, 'Let's go in, why are you standing in the dark like this. With the mosquitoes....'

~

I've never experienced such a strange sensation. As the clear light of the day fills the room, the dream of last evening is beginning to sink

in. I'm not someone to latch on to passing moments and experiences.
Yet, I can't remember anything quite as magical as the time spent with
Amala yesterday. To think there may be more such....

— MANAS DUTTA, DIARY ENTRY, JUNE 1951

Manas placed his diary on the nightstand next to his bed. Choppy sleep had left him drowsy. He needed a cracking cup of tea. During his examinations, he'd had the first cup of tea delivered to him in bed, but in the holidays that followed, he had begun enjoying morning tea with his grandfather in the corridor outside the latter's bedroom.

When he joined Haraprasad for tea and a light breakfast, Manas couldn't focus on the news items his grandfather read aloud from the newspaper. He managed occasional 'Hmms', and 'Oh-I- sees', but didn't engage in any discussion that could potentially turn into a debate. Luckily for him, Haraprasad remained engrossed in the newspaper and didn't seem to notice Manas's lack of attention.

Manas had been planning a visit to the PL camp and decided to pick up Subir and Raghu on his way there. Subir had gone to the market when Manas reached his place but returned within minutes, drenched in sweat. Seeing Manas chatting with his father in the living room, he exclaimed, 'Here you are! Good thing I brought hot *shingara* from the corner sweetshop. I hope you haven't had tea without me?'

Post tea and *shingara*, Manas and Subir went out to get a rickshaw to go to Raghu's house. As they walked towards the stand, Manas uttered in a sotto voice, '*Ei* Subir, there's some news.' Before Subir could react, Manas said, 'I'm getting married.'

'Wha...?'

Even without looking at him, Manas could imagine Subir's eyeballs dilating into miniature *rosogollas*.

'I'm sorry it had to come this way...but please keep it to yourself. You're the second person to know. Not even Ma does.'

Subir gave Manas a congratulatory hug. He couldn't keep his

surprise from showing, though. 'What do you mean, Mashima doesn't know? Then who is the other person? Oh wait, that would be your fiancée, right?'

'Hey, calm down my friend. You will know all. Just promise this won't leave your lips....'

'You know it won't. Tell me more, buddy, don't kill me with the suspense.'

Manas summarised the story as best as he could, editing out the initial hiccups as also the most recent moments of intimacy. Subir's gawking made him mischievously proud of himself; he'd been successful in hiding his feelings all this while.

'If only I had known I would have grabbed some sweets from the market,' Subir said. 'But hey, it's you who should be buying me sweets. *Hain*, you delivered the news like this, *shukno mukhe?*'

'*Hawbe, hawbe*, my friend. Whatever *mishti* you want.'

They picked up Raghu and decided to take the same rickshaw to the camp. The rickshaw puller asked for three rupees extra to go the distance and the boys readily agreed. None of them wanted to go through the bus-tram hell in the sweltering heat. Except for a stray dog here or a *bidi*-smoking labourer there, the roads were bare.

A part of the road had a steep climb. Manas and his friends stepped down to let the rickshaw puller, aged before his time, pull the rickshaw forward. When they finally reached the camp, Manas paid him two rupees on top of the fare he'd bargained for. Raghu tried to stop him but Manas indicated with a wave of his hand that it was all right. The rickshaw puller looked at them with dazed delight.

∼

The news at the camp was grim. Urmila's son, along with a few other children, had taken ill after consuming the milk distributed at the camp. What the camp dwellers had initially taken to be a stomach bug turned into a week-long ordeal of dysentery and vomiting for the little ones. They had been left untreated all this while. The government-appointed camp doctor visited only once in two weeks, sometimes three, and wouldn't be there before another seven days. Manas learned from some of the camp women that Urmila had practically stopped eating. She took nothing other than a few sips of water and occasionally a little *panta bhaat*.

A middle-aged woman led the volunteers inside the barrack where Urmila was lodged. Outside the barrack, six children, all below the age of five, lay on a single cot. Their bodies, shrivelled as much with malnutrition as with disease, horrified Manas. The place reeked of urine and human excrement. Flies swarmed over the children, two of them asleep, one writhing in pain, another two with dazed, ashen faces. A woman sat on a stool next to the cot waving a palm leaf fan over the sick children. Manas recognised her as Basanti, whom he and Subir had met when they had caught the women making *bidi*s and paper bags.

Manas touched the forehead of each child, four boys and two girls, to check them for fever. He couldn't feel anything. He was about to pry open the eyelid of Urmila's sleeping son to check for further signs of infection when Raghu tapped him on the shoulder and pointed to Urmila sitting in a corner. Her head had caved into the hollow of her arms around her knees.

Manas walked over to her. 'How are you, Urmila-di?'

She looked up; a film of dried tears cased her face.

'Don't worry, we're here. Daktarbabu will be here soon,' Manas said, making up the promise of getting a doctor on the spot. Raghu stepped ahead and echoed Manas.

'Yes, your son will be well, Didi. Come, eat something now. Your face looks so dry.' Urmila said nothing but shook her head to indicate a firm 'No'.

Subir took recourse to an old ploy. 'If you fall ill, who will look after your little one, Urmila-di? Come, eat something.'

One of the camp women brought a bowl of puffed rice mixed with yogurt and mango. Manas took the bowl and crouched next to Urmila. 'Here, be a good sister now. Have a bite,' he said lifting a spoonful of the cereal. To his surprise, Urmila acceded without any resistance. Manas gently handed her the bowl and said, 'Finish this like a *lokkhi meye* now. We're around.'

As Urmila continued to eat little spoonfuls, Manas spoke in whispers to Raghu about his plan for the sick kids. Subir stayed back at the camp while Manas and Raghu headed for Bijoy Nagar. Manas knew finding a doctor to visit a refugee camp on a Sunday wouldn't be easy. He thought of Dr Dasgupta, their family physician but was doubtful of his availability on a Sunday.

'Dr Majumdar is our only hope,' Manas muttered as he and Raghu got into a taxi.

Manas knew the doctor didn't run the clinic in Bijoy Nagar every day but he had to try.

As he paid the taxi fare, Manas asked Raghu to run to Malati's house and check with her or Amala about the doctor. He joined Malati and Raghu a moment later at the porch, his eyes searching for Amala.

'Wait, my dears. Amu just went to the hand pump to get some drinking water. She can take you to the clinic,' Malati said and brought out a rolled-up straw mat, which she spread on the ground. She asked the boys to sit.

'Will Amala be long, Mashi?' Manas asked impatiently. 'Maybe you can show us the way to the clinic. It's important we see Daktarbabu immediately.'

'Amu should be here any time now. She left a while ago,' Malati muttered.

Raghu suggested he and Manas go ahead anyway. The tea shack was closed but they could perhaps ask a colony resident to show them the way to the clinic.

Halfway through, they ran into Amala. She was walking towards the house with two large jerry cans of water. Raghu and Manas darted to take the cans from her.

Amala declined the help and said with a smile, 'I see we have guests today. What's up?'

Raghu looked at Manas, who took a jerry can gently from

Amala's hand and said, 'We actually came for Daktarbabu. A few children at the Gariahata camp have fallen ill.'

'Oh,' Amala said, worry lining her face. 'Daktarbabu isn't here on Sundays. He comes twice a week now, but not on Sundays....'

'But,' she added, 'Ganesh-da knows where he lives. It's not too far from here.'

Manas thought it would be odd to trouble him on a Sunday but Amala insisted they visit him. She knew him well enough to know he wouldn't mind. They left the cans with Malati on the porch and headed straight to Ganesh's house.

Within five minutes, the four of them, astride two rickshaws, had arrived at the doctor's house. An elderly woman answered the door and when asked about Dr Majumdar, she said, 'He's having lunch right now.'

Manas politely asked if they could wait. The woman nodded and made as if to go in, when the doctor, clad in a vest and a *lungi*, came out. Grains of rice mixed with curry stuck to his fingers. 'Oh, Ganesh is here,' he said adjusting the frame of his eyeglasses with his left hand, untouched by food. 'And Amala Ma is here, too. *Ki byapaar?*'

As Dr Majumdar finished the rest of his meal in quick scoops, Manas narrated the purpose of their visit. The doctor didn't say much but listened intently, responding with occasional nods.

While he washed up and got ready, the doctor addressed his visitors from inside. 'We will go in my car, no need to waste time looking for transport.'

All five of them got into Dr Majumdar's spacious Hindustan Landmaster. Thanks to the almost empty roads, they arrived at the camp in less than an hour. Manas led the doctor to the sick children. As the doctor began examining them, Manas went to check on Urmila. He found Subir sitting on a *piri* next to her, trying to reassure her about Daktarbabu's visit. Urmila didn't say anything, nor did she try to stop the tears streaming down her face in quiet rivulets.

When she spotted Amala, however, Urmila lunged at her,

bawling and heaving as she held on to her. Amala let her sari soak the torrent of tears and snot flowing down Urmila's face. She wrapped her arms around Urmila. 'You're fine,' Amala whispered. 'And *Mona* will be fine, too. Daktarbabu is here. *Chol*, let's go outside.'

Amala helped Urmila get on her feet and wiped her face with a hanky. Manas and Subir followed them to see the doctor. Manas couldn't see Raghu so he approached Dr Majumdar directly. 'What do you think, Daktarbabu?' He made sure Amala and Urmila were not within hearing range.

The doctor shook his head with a sigh. 'Ganesh and Raghu have gone to bring some medicines from the clinic. I've also asked one of the women here to prepare a saline-sugar solution for the children.'

Manas gauged the severity of the situation from Dr Majumdar's tone. Pulling him over to the side, Manas asked, 'Will they survive, Daktarbabu?'

'Oh, survive they will, most of them at least. But for how long? You see, the illness isn't the real malady. Medicines can control the symptoms, but how will these fragile bodies develop disease resistance if they don't get enough nutrition? Then there's the constant threat of infection....'

Manas listened to everything the doctor said but registered only the news that the children would survive. His mind blotted out the 'most of them' afterthought the doctor had added.

A woman came with a bowl containing the oral solution the doctor had asked her to prepare.

'What's your name?' Dr Majumdar asked as he moved with the woman towards the sick kids.

'*Aggey*, Molina,' the woman murmured.

The doctor lifted one of the babies and asked Molina to gently put a couple of spoons of the solution into her mouth.

'Good,' he said. 'Do this once every hour, for all of them.'

Manas struggled to combat the stifling humidity as he waited for Raghu and Ganesh. His vest was already drenched in sweat and soon his shirt would be too. He began pacing in the narrow verandah to get some air and came closer to where Amala and Urmila were.

'I have a question,' Amala whispered to Manas.

Since accepting Manas's proposal, she had deliberately avoided saying 'you', still uncomfortable using the more informal *'tumi'* in place of the formal *'aapni'*. She now framed her sentences in such a way that they didn't need the second-person pronoun.

'Yes?' Manas said, leading Amala away from Urmila, whose gaze remained pinned to her son on the cot.

Amala told Manas she wanted to take Urmila and her son home. She worried for the child, and even more for the mother. Manas understood Amala's concern but couldn't help wondering about the impracticality of it.

'Will there be enough room for two more there?' he asked.

'I have thought about that,' Amala said. 'We'll have to make some adjustments, but that's all right. I don't think Malati Mashi will mind it.'

'I'd say don't rush. Discuss it with Malati Mashi and Mesho first. You know it's not going to be easy with Urmila.'

'Shhh,' Amala turned her head to look at Urmila.

'I'm not talking about taking her right away' Amala whispered. 'I will speak with Mashi and Mesho, yes. But I think this is the only option we have. Otherwise, both these lives....'

Their conversation was cut short; Ganesh and Raghu arrived with the box of medicines Dr Majumdar had sent for. As the doctor explained to Manas the frequency and dosage of the medicines, Raghu also volunteered for the job. The children needed to be administered the medication every morning and evening, so Manas and Raghu divided their hours. Raghu picked the evenings as he had college in the daytime.

Three hours later, the doctor drove the volunteers back. The light breeze blowing through the car's windows soothed Amala as she made plans for Urmila and her son. A mattress was necessary but that could be arranged. More importantly, she needed Manas to teach her the child's medicine regimen.

Dr Majumdar dropped them all at Bijoy Nagar as Manas had requested. When Manas suggested they go to a nearby eating place for lunch, Ganesh laughed. 'Which place would be open on a Sunday afternoon, Manas-da?' He invited them to have lunch at his house.

'Nah, Ganesh-da, you carry on,' Amala said. 'Let's go to our house. I will boil some rice and lentils real quick.'

Manas felt uneasy. 'Nah, I'm not all that hungry. We'll just say hello to Malati Mashi and have some water. In any case, Raghu has to return to the camp soon.'

They found Malati waiting on the mat she had earlier spread for Manas and his friends. The folds of a *kantha* she was stitching covered her splayed legs. The vines of cucumber they had planted just outside the house offered her a cool shade as well as some privacy. When Amala saw her yawning, she scurried up to her and said, 'Why are you sitting in this heat? You don't want to fall ill, do you? *Chalo*, let's get inside.'

Over the late afternoon meal of *khichuri*, which Amala insisted Manas, Subir and Raghu should share, Amala told Malati and Nimai about the situation in the camp. She also thought aloud about her idea of bringing Urmila and her baby over. Manas noticed that though Malati didn't speak much, she kept nodding to indicate her agreement.

Nimai expressed his doubts. 'Where will they sleep...the three of us are hardly able to spread our legs....'

'I will manage it all, Mesho,' Amala said, her voice carrying both affection and authority. 'Leave it to me. I promise you and Mashi won't have to worry about this. And as soon as the baby gets well, Urmila can return....'

The last part of her statement didn't sound all that convincing to Manas. It came across almost as an afterthought from Amala to reassure her foster parents. And that was the part that worried him.

Amala turned to Raghu and said, 'Bhai, I will come with you to the camp this evening. I can bring Urmila with me in the bus.'

Her words pinched Manas, if only a bit. He wouldn't have

minded an invitation, given all the free time he had these days. 'It would be better if you took a taxi, Amala,' he said. 'I don't think it's a good idea to bring the baby in a bus.'

Subir caught on to Manas's cue and said, 'Manas is right. In fact, one of us should be with you when you bring Urmila back. We need to buy the baby's medicines from the chemist.' Turning to Manas, he said, '*Ei*, Maanu, can you go with Amala-di? I would have come, but Ma needs me to take her to her sister's house in the evening....'

Manas said, 'Yes, of course,' before Amala could react.

'*Shei bhalo*, sounds good to me,' Malati said. 'I would worry if Amu had to return with Urmila and the sick child so late in the evening.'

'We better get going, Mashi,' Manas said, taking care not to speak directly to Amala. It was his repartee to Amala for ignoring him a moment ago.

'Just give me a minute. I'll be right back,' Amala said, taking the plates inside.

~

Flickering lantern glow had replaced sunlight in Bijoy Nagar by the time Urmila and her son Hablu, the name by which his mother now called him, came to stay with Malati, Nimai and Amala. Manas had explained the child's nursing schedule to Amala. He wrote down the names of medicines in Bengali on small chits and pasted them on their wrappers.

Amala had no trouble getting a grip on the schedule; the timetable was fairly easy—twice a day. She gave Hablu his first dose after his daily morning milk and the other one after dinner every evening.

To create a separate space for the mother and the child in the front room, Amala used a wooden partition that Chitra had provided. Chitra and her husband had got it during a trip to Kashmir. The three-panel partition had beautiful carving and could be folded when not in use. It made a nice wall for Urmila's 'room'. A small table from Manas covered the remaining open area. Urmila also used the partition as a hanger, flinging her saris over it, while the table mostly held Hablu's medicines and clothes.

The space lacked a cot, but Manas, Subir and Proshanto pitched in to get a new mattress, bed sheets and a couple of pillows. Manas visited them occasionally, directing most of his energy to the camp.

Surprisingly, Urmila didn't pose any major challenge other than her habit of going for random strolls in the middle of the afternoon. She had told Amala how much she enjoyed a trip to the pond where she would be found sitting even on the most scorching of days. At first, Urmila's jaunts concerned Amala, but Malati reassured her that Urmila never went beyond the colony's periphery. Whenever she seemed to wander, one or the other neighbour would bring her back.

The new surroundings and constant care from a mother, an aunt and a grandma, along with occasional visits from Dr Majumdar, helped Hablu get his health back over time. As he got better, he found his way around the house and determined the kitchen to be his favourite area, followed closely by the front porch. Still weak from his illness, he wobbled and stumbled through his crawling often enough to need help to get back on his feet. Words that sounded meaningful had only just found their way to his throat; he expressed himself mostly with hand movements and a sprinkling of gibberish.

What delighted Amala the most was the meaning the toddler had brought to Nimaichand's life. While Malati, Amala, and Urmila took care of the child's eating, bathing and toilet needs, Malati entrusted her husband with managing him around the house. Nimai stood up to the responsibility better than Malati or Amala could ever expect him to. There were even times when Malati would leave Hablu in Nimai's care and step out to buy vegetables from street vendors who had recently set up shop near Bijoy Nagar.

The little boy had taken to Nimai like a trapped fledgling would to its rescuer; the trust was complete and unshakeable. Nimai could make him do things others couldn't. These included drinking his milk and eating his food as well as not hopping over to the kitchen and dismantling the tumblers and plates stacked on the shelf. Nimai indulged him for every good-boy act with candies Amala brought for Hablu.

Amala took Urmila and Hablu to Ganesh's house one day. She wanted to introduce Urmila to Moyna with the hope of bringing both women a friend. The idea worked well; Urmila's volatile disposition found a sanctuary in Moyna's sedate, unhurried manner. Since that first meeting, Urmila's mid-day wanderings often culminated at Moyna's doorstep. Sometimes she even took Hablu with her.

One day, Amala returned from work to find Urmila hadn't yet returned from her afternoon stroll. When Amala reached Moyna's house, what she saw left her speechless. Moyna was frying *soru chakli*, thin rice-lentil crepes, and serving them to Urmila and Mintu, who had Hablu in his lap. Unlike back home where Amala's Ma would serve *soru chakli* with a dry potato *tawrkari*, Moyna served them with some freshly-made mango pickle.

All Amala's plans to take Urmila to task were razed to the ground. She watched in utter glee how Mintu fed little Hablu tiny bits of the *chakli*, taking care not to put any of the spicy pickle in his mouth, despite the toddler's unwavering interest in that item. Mintu saw Amala before his mother or Urmila did.

'Amu mashi *je!*' he shrieked even as Hablu looked up and said, 'Amu ma, Amu ma!'

Urmila, eating devotedly, looked up. She grabbed the last big piece of *chakli* from her plate and stuffed it into her mouth.

'Easy, easy, you will choke!' Moyna said. She quickly picked a tumbler of water and passed it to Urmila. Then, turning to Amala she said, 'Come, Amala. Have some *chakli*. You must be so tired.'

The sight of the crepes made Amala's mouth water but she did her best to resist. 'Nah, Moyna-di. I will have some other time.

Mashi is waiting, she sent me to check what was taking Urmi so long.'

'Here, take some for Mashi and Mesho,' Moyna said, stuffing a few *chaklis* in a small *thhonga*. 'Look, Urmi taught me how to make these paper bags,' she said with a soft smile.

'O Ma! She's a sneaky one, that Urmi, isn't she?' Amala said.

Urmila didn't react; she had already stood up, ready to leave. Hablu rocked gently in her arms.

His mother's latest letter informed Manas that Mrinmoyee and her sister would get even more delayed in their return. The festival of Rath was only a week away and the sisters had been coaxed by the members of their religious entourage not to miss the holy event in its most revered headquarters of Jagannath Puri. Manas was glad to learn that Bawromashi felt well enough to be on a prolonged pilgrimage. What surprised him more was the loosening of his mother's umbilical attachment to domesticity, even if only temporarily. He didn't mind her extended absence from the house. *She should just leave Bawromashi here, then go on more pilgrimages herself. I could get used to this.*

On his way to the camp the next morning, Manas looked out of the bus window and saw a group of boys playing cricket in Triangular Park. The bus stopped at the traffic lights and Manas focused on the game. The boys must have been between ten and fourteen. They used sticks for wickets but had decent enough bats and balls. Some of the players even sported caps to beat the harsh sun. Manas saw this scene every day; the game would continue even when he returned in the afternoon. He felt like sprinting across to join the boys. Who knew in which dusty corner of the house his own bat now lay hidden?

When he made his way to Bijoy Nagar that evening, he felt a lot less buoyant. He had spent the entire day at the camp and left only when Raghu came for his shift. Tired and hungry, he decided to have some tea and toast in the colony's tea stall as he waited for Amala.

On one of their previous visits, Amala had taken Manas and Chitra to the stall and introduced them to the owner, Santu. At 17, he still carried some of his boyish innocence even as he negotiated the tough world of earning a living, dealing with difficult customers, and taking care of his widowed mother, the only family he had left. He had done more than well for himself, Manas thought. Sure, the tea stall attracted outsiders, some unsavoury ones among them, but that couldn't be avoided in a city like Calcutta. As he pottered over to the stall, Manas recalled how Amala had praised Santu's enterprise.

Manas sat down on an empty bench inside the stall with his plate of two slices of bread that Santu had toasted to perfection on his griddle and buttered generously. Manas ate his meal in silence while waiting for the tea. He had scarfed down the toast almost entirely when Santu brought tea in an earthen mug.

'Shall I make you some more toast, Dadababu?' he asked.

'Yes,' Manas nodded.

The toast didn't just satiate Manas's empty stomach, it also helped numb, at least partially, the pain stabbing him. Not a physical pain like what the rickshaw pullers endured but a gash tearing at him from within. He took hungry gulps of the hot tea and asked Santu if he could have some more.

Midway through his second set of toast, Manas heard the voices of Amala, Tara and Bakul. He had his back to them but their chatter and unabashed laughter floated to his ears. Sounds that always made him happy failed to soothe him right now. He took his time to finish the food before paying Santu and staggered towards Amala's house, hoping Amala and the girls wouldn't turn around and see him. They didn't, too eager probably to reach home and catch some rest before evening chores demanded their attention.

'*Arrey*, Maanu Babu is here!' Nimai's expression startled Manas when he reached their house. He had never heard the man call him by his pet name, nor with such excitement.

The exclamation had the desired effect; Malati emerged from the back room-kitchen. A smile spread across her summer-tanned face as she said, 'Good, good. Amu just came back. I was making some *muri-makha* for her. Wait, I will get you some, too. And *cha*....'

'Don't make anything for me, Mashi,' Manas said. 'I'm full.' He didn't mention the tea and toast at Santu's stall.

When Amala came into the room wiping her face with a *gamchha*, the happiness in her eyes didn't escape Manas. He couldn't reciprocate the emotion.

Manas had taken his spot on a stool next to Nimai and it occurred to him he hadn't looked at Urmila and Hablu's corner. He regretted not getting a treat for the toddler, but when he looked over to that part of the room, the mother-son duo was missing.

Amala noticed his curious eyes and said, 'She has gone over to Moyna-di's house. Ganesh-da's boudi.'

'Oh,' Manas said as distractedly as his faraway glance at the cucumber vines and their abundant yellow flowers, pregnant with the promise of life.

'What happened?' Amala asked, sitting down on the mat in front of Manas and Nimai. 'You don't appear all right.'

Manas hid his face within the hollow of his crook and tousled his hair with his fingers, hiding his tears. After a deep sigh, he lifted his face and said, 'One of the children at the camp...I...I helped bury her. Right there, in the woods next to the camp.'

'What?' Amala stopped with that one-word question. Many more whirled in her head but she couldn't utter anything as a giant ball of grief clutched at her throat. The face she had just wiped was sodden wet with tears. A loud sigh finally rose up her throat and came out as a groaning wail.

The hurricane lamps they used had long been doused but the night stretched on forever for Amala. She lost sleep thinking about the dead child at the camp, about the fate of the ones who still survived, about Urmila, about Hablu and their imminent return to

the camp...what would happen once she got married? How would
Malati and Nimai manage? They had come to depend so much on
her. How selfish of her to think only of her own well-being. The
very people who took her under their wing would be left alone
when they needed her most. *No, no, I can't let Urmila leave.*

Amala knew it was too late to go back on her decision regarding
Manas. But for the benefit of everyone, it would be best if Urmila
and Hablu continued living with Malati and Nimai. She would
have to ensure the financial viability of that, of course. A second
job in the evening would certainly help.

The night left Amala heavy and dry. In the morning, no sooner
than Malati woke up, Amala requested her to accompany her to
the hand pump to get drinking water for the day. She occasionally
asked Malati to come with her. Especially during her periods, she
appreciated Malati's help with lifting the jerry cans. That wasn't
the reason today.

'Mashi, I need to tell you something. Please don't get angry,'
Amala said as they walked in the direction of the hand pump.

'Yes, Ma?'

'We can't send Urmi and Hablu back to the camp. You heard
what happened there, right?'

Malati nodded. The evening's revelations from Manas had left
her weary. No one had touched the tea Malati had made and the
muri-makha had lain there till it became stale and inedible.

'And, Mashi,' Amala continued, her voice discreetly low, 'there's
one more thing I want to tell you. I am...umm...getting married.'

To her surprise, the abruptness of Amala's disclosure didn't
startle Malati. As Amala searched her face, she didn't see a display
of *I-knew-it* smugness; what she found was more of a *this-had-to-
happen-sooner-or-later* surety.

'Hmm, *bhalo.*' Malati said. 'Someone at work?'

Amala felt both relieved and guilty that the obvious had
escaped Malati.

'Na, Mashi. It is Mana... your Maanu Babu.'

'Oh!' This astonished Malati.

'I know it sounds crazy, Mashi. And I think I am going a bit crazy to jump into this fire, but....'

'No, no, why should you be crazy? That is wonderful, dear girl, wonderful!' Malati turned around and clutched Amala in a tight embrace.

'But this is what I want you to know, Mashi. That I'll be your good old Amu, no matter what.'

'*Paagli*, you crazy girl. Do you think I will have it any other way? Or your Mesho?'

'And...and I also want you to know that Urmila and Hablu will continue to be my responsibility.'

'Hmm,' Malati said with a nod.

'No, really, Mashi. I will provide for my family here, and that includes all four of you.'

'Don't worry so much, Amu. The one who has provided for us so far will not desert us. You think of your journey. This time won't come back, Ma.'

Amala's eyes welled up. Time and her life's more-coiled-than-straight alleys had hardened her. Yet she couldn't help tearing up every now and then, couldn't help letting those drops of rain wet the arid patch she thought her heart had become. Everything about what Malati just said to her, from the tone of her voice, her words, down to her gestures, carried for Amala an imprint of her own mother.

Amala was grateful for this residual wetness within her.

~

Manas felt vacant. He hadn't felt this gnawing sense of hollowness since the incident involving Minoti. The death of the child at the camp, mainly a result of her battered immune system, which couldn't resist the most minor of infections, devastated him. Even a good doctor and constant medication couldn't save the little girl. As with Minoti, Manas took this as a personal failure.

Unable to put his mind to reading anything—it all seemed so meaningless—Manas visited Bijoy Nagar more frequently to fill his evenings. He didn't always head straight to Amala's place, though he never left the colony without meeting her, but would visit other residents, many now his friends, or just spend time in Santu's tea stall, where he inevitably met a lot of folks. The days on which Dr Majumdar came to the colony, Manas dropped by to help with the clinic's operations and chat with the doctor. The doctor had had a deep impact on Manas; in moments of utter desolation, he thought of Chitra and Daktarbabu to continue on his journey as a social worker.

One evening when he went to Ganesh's house, Manas found Moyna and Urmila furiously making paper bags, the same kind he had seen Urmila make at the camp. Outside, Mintu played with Hablu, while Ganesh's wife cooked the evening meal in the kitchen. Manas had become a regular at their house and often chatted with the womenfolk until Ganesh returned from work. They all enjoyed his company, including Urmila.

'What's with these *thhongas*, Moyna-di?' Manas asked.

'Oh, didn't *Thakurpo* tell you?'

'Ganesh-da? Why, no! Tell me, what's up?'

With a shrug of her shoulder, her way of downplaying anything she did, Moyna said Ganesh had recently befriended a ragtag man, himself a refugee. When he learned that Ganesh's sister-in-law had started making *thhongas*, he offered to give old newspapers he dealt in; he would even help sell the paper bags in the Bara bazaar market as he knew quite a few paper suppliers.

'*Bah*, isn't that lovely news! This calls for some sweets. Wait, I'll be right back!'

No amount of persuasion by the women could stop Manas from heading out. He hadn't had too many reasons to celebrate in the past week and couldn't let go of one that came his way. As he scampered towards the rickshaw stand, he saw the trio of Amala, Bakul, and Tara returning from work.

'Is something the matter, Manas-da?' Bakul asked.

'Oh, nothing. I'll be right back, just need to get something from the market,' Manas said.

'Are you sure everything's okay?' Amala called out to him when he had already walked further away from them.

'Yes, yes, no worries. Be back in a minute,' Manas said and darted off.

If Manas took longer than expected, it was only because he couldn't keep himself from buying the *telebhaja* being fried right next to the sweet shop. A queue had lined up for the fritters and Manas had to wait a while for his rather large order.

He bought enough sweets and *telebhaja* to feed the entire colony. After delivering a big chunk to Moyna and Urmila, he brought the rest to Amala and Malati. They had been waiting for him. As soon as he entered with the giant bags and boxes, Amala went to make tea. Manas handed the packages to Malati.

'What is all this, Baba? What's the occasion?' She asked and Manas wasn't sure if he saw a twinkle in her eyes.

'*Bolchhi*. I need some water first.'

As he took his seat on the stool marked for him next to Nimai, Malati poured him water from the earthen pot and urged him again to reveal the cause of the celebration. Manas sensed she knew something that she wanted Manas to confirm. He decided to checkmate her. When he mentioned the news of Moyna and Urmila finding a source of income by using their skills, Malati's enthusiasm for teasing seemed to have dampened.

'Oh, I didn't know that!' Amala exclaimed from inside, adding, 'see, Mashi, that Urmi is a sneaky one. Never told us, *haan*?'

'Let her return,' Malati said. 'We won't let her have a single sweet. How's that?'

Manas laughed out loud and said, 'Hard luck, Mashi. She's already had a couple. That's where I went first.'

'Hmph! And Amu thought Urmi was the sneaky one,' Malati said.

Amala brought tea and a big plate for the sweets and snacks. She hadn't paid much attention to the size of the bags before; doing so now shocked her.

'What have you done?' She said, turning to Manas. 'Who's going to eat all this?'

'Why not distribute these right now?' Malati said. 'All one has to do is to go to the school and ring the bell and the kids come running.'

The plan worked like a dream. Malati's suggestion came from the practice of ringing the school bell for emergency school closures, mostly because of heavy rains, in the monsoon season. Since the school was already closed for summer vacations, the bell caught the children by surprise. They all came rushing as Malati had predicted, and some of them feared the school might have opened sooner than scheduled.

When Amala, Manas and Nimai, having teamed up with Ganesh and Nitai, pulled out the bags of sweet they had hidden under a table, the kids erupted in cheers. Most of them were just happy to be indulged, but some did ask what prompted this sudden celebration. No reason was offered, which then made some of the kids wonder in whispers if this were to become a regular feature at the school.

Manas overheard the kids and made a mental note to turn surprise celebrations into a recurring feature at Bijoy Nagar.

17

The opportunity to earn supplemental income came to Amala like a windfall. As Jogen Babu's business flourished, he applied for a new loan and purchased five more sewing machines—all second-hand but in good condition. At *Jogajog*, he had space to set up no more than three more machines. Purnima had heard from Amala how other women in Bijoy Nagar were eager to have a job like hers.

'How about this…' Purnima approached Amala as she put the finishing touches to a blouse that had to be delivered that evening. 'You take the two remaining machines from us and train other women in your colony. That way, we can take more orders.'

As part of the deal, the women undertaking assignments would be paid by the hour, and Amala and Tara were entrusted with the responsibility to track that. As a bonus, both women would be paid commissions on each batch of order they were given. If all went well, more machines could be purchased and the business expanded.

Amala knew how earnest Jogen and his wife were in wanting to help refugees from East Bengal. She herself had an income because of them. Despite building their business by employing rootless, penniless refugees, they had taken it to a point, and not without struggles and challenges, of earning a profit. Amala felt a special kinship with Jogen and Purnima, raw and heart-tugging, like she felt with Malati and Nimai. And Urmila and Hablu.

Amala also had a selfish interest in making this social experiment, of providing earning potential to Bijoy Nagar women, a success. The uncertainty of Malati and Nimai's financial future, as well as Urmila's affairs vexed her. With this scheme, both Malati and Urmila would have something to do with their time and get paid as well.

Amala was happy to see Urmila making *thhongas* but knew it wouldn't bring more than pennies. If Urmi could have a steadier stream of income like what Jogen and Purnima were offering, it would only bode well for Hablu's future. Amala thought of roping Chitra into the training team. Chitra and Snehalata were already conducting arts and crafts classes for the colony's children on weekends. Amala knew Chitra would be more than willing to resume her role as the *shelai didimoni*.

One evening, when Amala, Tara and Bakul returned from work in a taxi that Purnima had paid for to carry the machines as well as the first batch of order, Amala saw the same stranger she had seen with Mintu at Santu's tea stall. He walked on the pavement close to the colony, smoking a cigarette, four rings screaming for attention on as many of his fat fingers. Sweat trickled down Amala's neck. She hadn't mentioned the man to anyone except Ganesh in passing after the incident with Mintu. But his recurring appearance in the neighbourhood made her more than a little nervous.

Amala tried to occupy herself with happier thoughts. Of the women's cooperative in Bijoy Nagar, of Hablu growing up to be a bright boy, of Urmila and Moyna curing each other of their sadness. And of walking these roads with Kartik one day.

The taxi driver, Naruda, was known to Jogen Babu. He got out to help with offloading the sewing machine and delivered it to Tara's doorstep, where Tara and Bakul disembarked. He did the same when Amala got down a minute later. The sky was an intense peach mingled with streaks of ash, portending imminent rain. Amala thanked Naruda and took out a one-rupee coin in appreciation of his help but he refused to accept it.

Malati had come out to the porch on hearing Amala's voice. As the taxi driver left, she helped lift the machine to take it inside. Amala returned to the porch to pick up the bag of the cloth pieces to be stitched as part of her share of order.

'What is all this, Amu? Will you work from home now on?' Malati asked Amala.

'Nah, nah, Mashi. I'll tell you about it. First, I need to freshen up.' As she shuffled to go inside, she noticed Nimai wasn't around.

'Mesho *kothay*,' Amala asked while splashing water on her face.

'Oh. Urmi wanted a few things for the child. So your Mesho took them to the market.'

'Hmm. What did Hablu need so urgently that Urmi couldn't wait for me?'

Being closer to her than to Malati or Nimai, Urmila usually shared her concerns with Amala.

'Nothing much,' Malati said. 'She was talking about getting a new bowl and spoon for Hablu. For his milk and *muri*.'

'I see. So the bowl he currently drinks from isn't good enough. And where did she get the money?'

Malati swallowed a chuckle along with some of the juice of the betel nut she had in her mouth. 'She got her first payment, a full five rupees, from her *thhonga*-making.'

'And you let her go to spend that money? Oh, Mashi, I know Urmi can't decide her own good, but we must guide her, no?'

'Ha, you talk as if you were here! Did I not try to stop her until you were back? Why, even your Mesho did. But does that girl listen to anyone?'

'You're right,' Amala said biting her tongue. 'It's so difficult to make Urmi understand. Uff.'

After a slight pause, Amala said, 'I'm glad Mesho went with them. You can't be sure where she'd lose herself....'

'It wasn't that easy. She kept saying how Mesho would have trouble walking that far, his pain would flare up. I forced her to take him along.' Malati went on to describe how Hablu tugging at Nimaichand's *lungi* helped.

Malati and Amala sat down on the outer room floor with their evening refreshment of *muri* and cucumber.

Clouds rumbled and the patch of sky peering through their door turned darker. Amala ran to the porch to pick up the clothes

Malati had hung out to dry on their two strings of clothesline. Fat drops of rain squirted on her face. By the time she sprinted inside, the rumble had turned into ear-splitting thunder and the drops had transformed into a downpour that blanketed everything, even the cucumber vine and the *kuchcha* street outside. Darkness swallowed the room, forcing Malati to light a lantern.

Amala picked up her cup of tea and stood by the door, her eyes searching the fuzzy street. She worried more for Hablu than for Urmila or Nimai. The kid had only just begun to get better and still couldn't walk. This pouring rain could end up giving him a cold he surely didn't need. The entire household had only one umbrella, which Amala carried to work.

Wet gusts splattered Amala's face as she drank her tepid tea. The rain showed no sign of letting up. Amala couldn't see too far into the distance. She heard a familiar voice, though, emitting joyful squeals. As it drew closer, she recognised it to be Hablu's. She now saw him, wrapped in something in Urmila's arms. The rain had drenched both Urmila and Nimai as it had the bag in Nimai's hand.

'Uff, look at you all! Get inside fast,' Amala stepped onto the porch to urge them in. She helped lift the blanket from Urmila's arm and took little Hablu, dry for the most part, into her arms.

'*Ne*, you change without delay,' Amala said to Urmila. 'And you, too, Mesho,' she said to Nimai.

Malati picked up the damp blanket, in reality a white sari with small blue flower prints on its border and anchal. '*Ei daekho*, it looks like a new sari!' She couldn't help yelping on seeing a new garment meeting with such a fate on its day of purchase.

'*Haw*, I bought that one for you,' Urmila hollered from inside while wiping her hair. 'But what could I do, it started to rain. Mesho covered Hablu with it.'

Malati took off her glasses to wipe a tear. For once Urmila had left her speechless. What could she say to her? Scold her for buying a piece of cloth for her that ultimately protected their precious Hablu? How could that ever count as waste?

'I will put on some tea for the two of you. Amu, do you want some? Ah, let me first heat up some milk for Hablu Babu,' Malati said.

Amala caught in the quivering of Malati's voice a hint of happiness on having a full house that had become a family, however odd. And maybe a trill of fear that she could lose it all over again?

'You will find some ginger in the vegetable basket, Mashi. Put some in the tea for Urmi and Mesho,' Amala said, patting Hablu on the back. The boy, delighting until a moment ago in the victorious escape from the rain he'd been made to accomplish, had fallen into a lull in the cosiness of Amala's arms. She kept murmuring affectionate sounds to keep him awake so he could drink the milk Malati prepared for him.

When Urmila returned after changing into dry clothes, Amala said to Urmila in a tone that while being reproving didn't insult.

'*Ei je, meye.*' She exercised extra discretion while talking to Urmila in Hablu's presence. The boy loved his Ma to bits. Now that he was growing up, Amala wanted to ensure he saw his mother receiving not only love but also respect.

'What was the pressing need to go to the market that you couldn't wait until Sunday?'

'*Haw*, you only scold me.' Urmila said. Before Amala could admonish her again, she said, 'Did I know it was going to rain?'

'But you knew we need to be careful with Hablu, didn't you?' Urmila looked at the toddler who was now sipping turmeric-infused milk from a bowl that Amala held to his mouth. 'What do you say, Hablu Moshai? Isn't Amu Ma right?'

Without understanding much of what was being deliberated, Hablu nodded a severe yes.

'*Haw*. That's what damaged Mashi's sari,' Urmila said, hungrily slurping the hot ginger tea Malati brought her.

Despite her determination to keep a straight face and a steady voice, Amala couldn't help laughing. After all that Hablu had gone through back at the camp and his delayed recovery, Urmila's overwhelming concern at the moment happened to be the sari she bought for Malati.

'Don't scold her, Amu. *Bechara*, I'm worried she might get a fever now. Look at that lock of wet hair.' Malati said.

'So you see, Mashi, is it without reason that I scold her? Now, if only she would listen to me.'

'I will from now on. Mashi, give me some more *muri*. I'm so hungry,' Urmila said, all in the same breath.

Malati knew Urmila loved plain puffed rice the most without any flavouring or condiments. She brought along the tin of *muri* and dished out some into Urmila's bowl.

'Tell me now, why did you buy that sari? You told me you're going to get a bowl and a spoon for Hablu.' Malati asked Urmila.

'Didn't I get that? *Oi toh*, ask Mesho!'

Nimai narrated the story of the sari. As soon as they came out of the utensil store after buying Hablu's things, Urmila spotted a vendor with saris spread on his cart. She wanted to get a sari for Malati as she had noticed the two saris she wore at home were both torn. Nimai helped count the money she carried and told her they didn't have enough to buy the sari. Urmila had already picked up the white sari with the blue flowers and started unfolding it to scan it better. The hawker told her she could pay the amount in instalments as he happened to be a regular at that spot.

'Now, I will scold you, Urmi,' Malati said. 'Shouldn't you be saving those pennies for your son? What if he needed more medicines?'

'And how could you let her spend that money on this, *haan*?' Malati charged her husband. 'What do I need a new sari for, tell me?'

From the look on his face and his muted voice, Amala detected Nimaichand had seen this coming. According to him, despite him trying to stop her from purchasing the sari, Urmila remained adamant and accepted the vendor's offer.

'Besides, that sari helped us save Hablu from rain,' Nimai contended, only to receive an endorsing 'Haw' from Urmila.

'Yes, that's what saved you today, girl,' Amala said, putting Hablu down on his mattress bed. The boy had fallen half asleep even as he drank the milk and eased into a comfortable slumber, his smiling eyes oblivious to the tiny bit of grown-up fracas around him.

To end the argument and prove that she was remorseful, Urmila promised to hand over any money she earned to Amala and Malati. To this, Amala responded, 'I have a better idea. We will keep all our money in a box,' she said. 'Mashi and I will keep the keys. Whenever you need money, tell one of us. But not for needless expenses, okay?'

'*Haw*,' Urmila said, her eyes flooding with relief.

'And you'll also have to learn to sew again. That way you can earn more money and save for Hablu's needs. Maybe we can buy him a cot?'

Turning her face to where Hablu lay, Urmila simply nodded in acquiescence.

Rain pelted down all night long, seeping in through the hogla walls of the colony's houses. It soaked the floor beds on which all four and a half members of Malati-Amala's household slept. Malati got up in the middle of the night to light the stove and dry the damp sheet on which she and Nimai lay. She decided to pull the sheets from beneath Amala and Urmila, too. The tugging woke Amala up, and when she smelled kerosene, she rushed to the inside room. Malati held Urmila and Hablu's bed sheet, folded, above the fire. Next to her were the two other sheets.

'Did I wake you up? Look, these are so moist, I thought....' Malati said.

'You did the right thing, Mashi. Give it to me, I will do it,' Amala said supressing a yawn.

'You go and spread this under Urmi and Hablu as gently as you can. I will start the other two.'

Urmila and her son remained asleep as Amala changed the sheets. Amala tiptoed back to Malati and the two of them soon returned to the outer room with the dry sheets reeking of kerosene. For the rest of the night, Amala's sleep had to contend with sticky humidity and the mosquitoes it brought along.

A delicious, petrichor-laden breeze awoke Amala. The sun hadn't risen yet, but she got up from the bed, still heavy with dampness. An idea flashed in her mind and she thought of ways to execute it. The quiet of the clear dawn helped her plan it out. It would have to be after work. *Manas? No, let me try on my own first. I can always trouble him later.* She washed up and unlatched the front door without making any noise. Closing the door behind her just as quietly, she stepped onto the porch.

The rain had abated, but the sky, spitting fuzzy mist was as pregnant with nimbus as yesterday. Except for a hint of breeze, the air remained still and blurry. A croak poked at Amala's grogginess and as she focused harder, she heard frogs clearing their throats on this wet and wispy morning. And though she couldn't see the singing frogs, they reminded her of rivers back in her village swelling up with rain and soaked cormorants shaking water off their wings. Groups of them would sometimes sit on the trunk of a tree that had fallen off in a storm and partly landed in water. Amala would envy them this monsoon-watching leisure even as she had to focus on school and a hundred household chores.

From the bus window on her way to work, Amala saw a group of crows crowding over a pile of garbage strewn asunder in a part of the city that had not yet filled up to its waist with water. The stench of the open garbage, mingled with sewage water, stormed through the bus's open windows. Amala crinkled her nose and covered it with her sari but couldn't take her eyes off the crows. Notwithstanding the trouble caused by the lashing rains, they were having a feast, complete with a cawing ruckus.

The crows seemed to make the most of the city's waste while the opportunity lasted. What did it matter that they didn't receive it on a platter? They would grab any leftovers trashed by those who had little need for it. And they were together in their scavenging. So what if the world chased them away? By flocking together, they had foregone the need for legitimacy; theirs was a society of comradeship. And so neither the stench nor those whom the stench bothered were of any value to these feisty birds. Bit by bit, they gathered the scraps, each crow its own, but while helping another if she didn't get a fair share.

Not for the crows the luxury of the cormorants enjoying rain and village scenes. Or diving into the water to catch shallow-swimming small fish, the *mouralas* and the *putis* as they pleased. Here, in this exacting city, you had to focus on your target sharply and without wasting time. The key was not to *become* the *mourala* or *puti*.

Amala's thoughts went back to her plan. The fact that it would be after work hours irked her. *But if not now, when?* She looked out of the window again, taking in the grey day and the strange smells it brought.

At work, Amala kept her eyes pinned to the sewing machine, her hand and feet swiftly obeying the commands of her habit-trained mind. She didn't take the usual ten-minute break for a walk outside with Tara. The work helped calm her anxiety. While cutting a new piece of silk cloth for a young girl's frock, she felt grateful for her job yet again. Not only did it keep her grounded, it also provided respite from the oppressive heat and invincible mosquito brigade at home.

The day rolled by quickly. As time for returning home drew closer, Amala realised she hadn't informed Malati about getting delayed. She asked Tara to tell Malati that she had to meet Chitra in the evening and would get late. She had practised the ruse in her head before saying it to Tara so she wouldn't stammer or get caught.

When Tara simply said, 'All right', Amala returned to her machine, relieved. She wrapped up the day's work, cleared the sewing area of cloth scraps and shreds of thread. Then, taking her leave of Purnima, she joined Tara and Bakul to walk to the bus stop.

Amala waited for the girls to board their regular bus even though that meant missing the one she had to take. She didn't want them to suspect anything. Luckily, the very next bus that came after Tara and Bakul had left also plied to Amala's destination. The jam-packed bus disappointed Amala, but she didn't want to get more delayed.

The humidity, coupled with the absence of her friends, made the ride anything but enjoyable. To find a seat during office-closing time on a busy route was next to impossible. An elderly man offered to vacate the ladies' seat he was occupying but Amala gestured for him to remain seated. The bus swerved continuously, forcing Amala to tightly clasp the overhead rod.

The half-hour journey felt a lot shorter to Amala as the Sealdah bus stop appeared in view. She got down and leapt forward. The station looked no different from the way it had appeared to her on the previous two occasions. The same mass of people, porters shoving past each other, passengers shouting for and at porters, family members arguing...the same disquieting chaos that had snatched Kartik away from her, the terrible memory of leaving Minoti behind....

Caught in the swirl of people entering the station, Amala applied the only strategy she knew—zoom her eyes in on the men, then the boys of Kartik's age. Everything else blurred out of her vision as she sharpened her focus to spot her brother amid the gigantic puzzle of human heads floating about her.

Amala ambled from one platform to the next and felt the same dizzy suffocation she had experienced the day she had first set foot on the station. A pang of hunger rose in her throat and she realised she badly needed a sip of water. The deja vu of looking for water made her even more nauseous. She wobbled over to one side where she saw a tap. Amala lowered her face to drink from it and had barely taken a sip when someone tapped her on the shoulder from behind. Startled, Amala looked up. Her feet froze when she turned around. It was the man she had encountered at Santu's tea stall, the same man she had noticed in and around Bijoy Nagar at least twice since their first meeting.

'Hello. Are you looking for someone? May I help?' He asked her while lighting a cigarette.

'Who? Wha…what is it that you want?' Amala said, barely suppressing a scream.

'Eh, nothing, just want to help you, lady, may I?' the man said, pushing his arm on the wall next to the tap, cornering Amala with a menacing laugh. He seemed to have no inhibitions about closing in on her like that in a crowded railway station. Before she could react, his hand had crept up to touch her neck as he let out a coughing sneer.

He has been following me. Terror grabbed Amala's throat as she bent and ducked his clutches to run, ramming her way through the swell of people. The strap of her right footwear came loose; she paused only for a second to pick it up. She didn't bother to look behind to see if the man was still following her, nor did she stop to pay attention to the bruise in her bare right foot as it jagged on a shard of glass.

Only when she spotted a taxi did Amala stop, catching her breath to tell the driver to take her to Dhakuria. She couldn't help looking out of the window to check if the stranger was around but the vehicle took off and she had no way of confirming his presence. She kept mumbling 'Tara Ma, Ma Tara' to herself, trying hard to hide her trepidation.

As daylight faded around her, Amala couldn't tell the way leading to Chitra's house. The taxi driver, a short man whose greasy face stared at her in the rearview mirror, didn't mind Amala's confusion at first. But as the lanes kept getting narrower, he became frustrated. Amala wished Manas would show up and lead them to Chitra's house; she knew it was in the vicinity. The sight of an elderly man walking with a tall umbrella for a walking stick reassured her. She leaned out of the taxi's window to call out to him.

'Meshomoshai, can you please tell me the way to Chitra Sen's house?'

The gentleman pointed to a young man and the house he was walking towards. 'That's where Chitra-di lives,' he said, raising a namaskar to Amala before walking away.

Amala requested the taxi driver to stop. Even after getting down, she couldn't help looking over her shoulder. No one. Hastening regardless, she almost bumped into Manik.

'*Ei je*, Bhai,' she called to him.

Manik exclaimed, '*Arrey*, Didi *je!*' darting over to her, offering to take her things.

Amala gave him the tote bag but not the torn shoe. As they walked towards Chitra's house, Manik didn't ask Amala anything about her distraught state. She appreciated his discretion. The sun had sunk by the time they reached Chitra's house. Rani opened the door. Once inside, Amala dropped her slipper, took the one off her left foot and dashed to the bathroom. When she emerged a few minutes later, she saw Manik leafing through a magazine in the drawing room.

'Come, di, sit here,' Manik stood up and invited Amala. 'Mashimoni is with Snehalata Mashi next door. Rani just went to call her.'

Amala sat down under the cool air of the ceiling fan. Manik got up and brought her a glass of water. She returned a wan smile and gulped the water.

The man's face kept haunting her but Amala felt safe in a very definite way, as if no harm could approach her here. When Chitra arrived, accompanied by Rani, Amala flung herself on Chitra's shoulder. A floodgate of tears burst out of her and she made no effort to stop it.

Chitra let her cry without asking any questions.

When Amala's weeping let up a bit, she wiped her face with her sari *anchal* and said to Chitra, her voice still trembling, 'Mashi, I need to talk to you.'

'Yes, let's go inside,' Chitra said, her hand firmly on Amala's shoulder.

Chitra took Amala to her bedroom. She instructed Rani to take care of things and not disturb them until they were finished. Rani nodded in a comically vainglorious way that made Amala chuckle despite the circumstances.

In the privacy of the bedroom, Amala revealed the details of
her latest encounter with the stranger she had come to dread.
She also told Chitra how she had confronted the man earlier and
saw him reappear around their colony a few times. Then, on an
impulse, she told Chitra about Kartik.

'Oh dear,' Chitra said. 'The same brother you'd mentioned
when we were going to Dakshineshwar?'

'Yes.'

'Dear girl. Why didn't you tell me about him before? Why
does this have to be your search alone?' Chitra took out a fresh
handkerchief from the steel almirah next to her bed and wiped
Amala's tear-sodden face.

'Does Manas know about your brother?'

'Yes….'

'Worry no more, Ma. You did the right thing by coming here.
Sit, I'll be right back. You need to eat something; let me get Rani
to make some tea.'

Tea arrived in a few minutes along with a huge bowl of *muri-
makha*. Amala, who had returned to the living room with Chitra,
patted Rani on the head when she held out the bowl of muri.
'*Lokkhi meye*,' she said to Chitra's sprightly assistant.

Rani flashed a big smile and said, 'You have to stay for dinner
tonight.'

Amala smiled as it occurred to her how this had become a
pattern in Chitra's house. Depending on the hour of the day, she
would be asked to stay over for lunch or dinner. Chitra herself
started it and Rani added her voice to the suggestion every time.

Chitra made certain Rani was safely out of hearing range
before asking Manik to bring Manas over. 'Go to his house first.
If he isn't there, check at the camp,' she said.

'Why Mashi…' Amala began, but Chitra said she knew what
she was doing.

If Manik was curious, Amala thought he did a remarkable
job of not showing it. He mostly talked about the insufferable
humidity and water-logged roads and the resulting traffic jams.

Taking some of the flavoured puffed-rice mix in a paper bag as a snack for himself and Manas, he got up and left. Chitra gave him money for the taxi and asked him to return as soon as possible, without waiting for buses.

'What happened, Mashi?' Manas said as Chitra opened the door for him and Manik half an hour later. 'Manik said Amala seems to be in some difficulty? *Ki hoyechhe?*'

'Calm down, son. Come in,' Chitra said.

Sparing Amala the anguish of recounting her ordeal all over again, Chitra summarised the episode for Manas. She also told him about Amala's past experience with the stranger.

'But why did you go to Sealdah station? Were you expecting somebody?' Manas's concern was laced with bewilderment.

Amala didn't say anything, nor did her blank look allow Manas to decipher an answer. Chitra looked at Amala and asked softly, 'Can I tell them?'

'Yes,' Amala nodded. She saw no reason to hide Kartik from Manik.

A wave of sadness swept over Manas. He tried to wrap his head around the trauma Amala must be going through after this evening's incident. A part of him wanted to reproach her for her solo search mission, but he didn't think this was the best time to do that.

'I think you should spend the night here, Amala,' Manas said. 'Don't worry about Malati Mashi. I will go and let her know.'

Amala remained quiet. Manas began pacing along the room's edge as he combed his hair with his fingers. He looked at his wrist watch once, then at Chitra and asked if he could have a word with her alone. They walked inside to the study Manas knew only too well by now. A few moments later when they came out, Manas asked Amala if she felt like going to the market with him.

'Or you can wait here while Manik and I get a few things,' Manas said.

'I will come,' Amala said. Maybe a little excursion would help calm her mind. Also being with Manas, it always did.

Chitra brought a pair of slippers from her shoe rack and said to Amala, 'Here, wear these for now. Manas can get you new ones from the market.'

Manas smiled and uttered a 'thank-you' to Chitra for giving him money for the evening's expenses. '*Ei* Manik, why don't you come, too?' he said. Manik was only too happy to tag along.

As they stepped out, Manas mentioned they would take a rickshaw to the local market. Amala guessed they were going to bring provisions for Chitra.

When they arrived closer to the market, Manas surprised Amala by steering the rickshaw puller toward a narrow alley that had small shops selling items of clothing like blouses and *fatuas* as well as a couple of *dashakarma bhandars*, stocked to the hilt with provisions for Hindu ceremonies, from birth to death and everything in between.

To the absolute befuddlement of Amala, Manas started walking towards *Adi Dashakarma Bhandar*. 'Does Mashi need anything from here?' She asked, unable to contain her wonder. She had seen a small altar at Chitra's house but hadn't found her to be particularly devout. What could she need from here that was so urgent?

'She doesn't. These are for you and me,' Manas said, showing her a list. 'This is the list the priest had given for Tara's wedding. Chitra Mashi kept it safely.'

This time, Manik's voice, not Amala's, leapt forth. 'Am I missing something, Manas-da? Can you explain to me in plain Bangla what's going on here?'

'I'm getting married, that's what's going on, Manik,' Manas said. After a second's pause, he added, 'Amala will be your Boudi soon.'

'Whaa?' Manik's face lit up like a Kalipuja *tubri*. 'This isn't a joke I hope? Amala-di?'

'Na, Bhai,' Amala said shyly. 'But I myself didn't know it was happening today!' She gave Manas a shocked look bordering on outrage.

'Not today but tomorrow. I'm sorry it had to be in this

fashion, Amala. But I spoke to Chitra Mashi and she agrees this is the best thing. It won't be safe for you to return to Bijoy Nagar anytime soon.'

'But that would be cowering down...' Amala said. 'You want me to run away?'

'No. I want you to fight. Can't I join your fight? Besides, we were going to do this anyhow, weren't we?'

Manas said all of this with such urgency and conviction that Amala couldn't think of a way to refute it.

'Anyway, let's get the things. We can talk about this when we reach home,' Manas said, moving towards the shop.

'Give it to me,' Manik nearly snatched the list off Manas's hand. 'You'd better look for a sweet shop. Don't think I'm going to let you get away with feeding me this news just like that.'

'But what about Malati Mashi,' Amala muttered, still not able to fathom the speed at which things were unfolding.

'Don't worry. I will explain it all to her. I'm sure she will understand.'

Amala felt relieved that she had at least told Malati about her wedding plans. Like with everything that had happened to her since coming to this city, she didn't seem to have any control over this latest development. A hot flush coursed through her body, a mix of intense ecstasy and unspeakable melancholy. In this moment of disoriented emotions, she simply gave in to the current that pulled her along.

When Manas said to her softly, 'Come, let's get the puja items now,' her footsteps matched his, willingly even.

Manas took out a two-rupee note from his pocket and gave it to Manik.

'Here, Manik. If you can go to the sweetshop around the corner, we can wrap this up fast. You and I have a lot to do tonight and tomorrow morning, brother.'

'Hey, Manas-da, I was just kidding about the sweets,' Manik said, scratching his head.

'But I'm not. Go on, get some sweets. Oh, wait,' he took out

another two-rupee note. 'Get two separate boxes. We'll take one
for Malati Mashi.'

'Good idea,' Manik said, his eyes smiling, as he took the money
from Manas. 'I will meet you two right here in a few minutes,' he
said to Amala.

'Sounds good, Bhai,' she said, managing a smile at last.

'Yes, Bou...er, Didi!' Manik didn't wait to catch Amala's
reaction to his audacious quip.

'He's a wicked one,' Manas said with a chortle that Amala
echoed. He still had a lot on his mind but was glad for the comic
relief that Manik offered.

Manas also thanked Manik in his heart for demanding sweets.
That allowed Manas to have a moment with Amala as he asked
her to pick the *shankha* and *pawla*, the white and red bangles
defining nuptial auspiciousness for a woman. The shopkeeper
opened a large wooden box filled with the bangles in different
designs for Amala to look through even as Manas busied himself
with getting the rest of the items on the list.

'Please pick a pair you really like. It's from me,' Manas
whispered to Amala.

'I don't want us to spend too much on this,' Amala said
abstractedly. The next moment panic gripped her. 'What about
your family? When will you tell them? No, no, we shouldn't hurry
like this.'

'Calm down, Amu,' Manas stunned himself by calling Amala
by her nickname even as he noticed her amazement. Gathering
his wits, Manas continued, 'I have thought about it all. It won't be
a problem. You trust me, don't you?'

She didn't say anything but when Manas saw her fiddling with
a thin pair of *shankha-pawla*, he said, 'Here, let me help you. You
can put that one back. Please.'

He picked a different pair from the box, thicker and with more
intricate carving on the *shankha* than what Amala had chosen.

The cramped box of a shop had only a single dim bulb hanging
by an overhead wire but the shopkeeper could locate every item

on the list in no time, despite the thick glasses he wore. Looking at Amala, who argued with Manas on the selection of the *shankha-pawla*, he said, 'Take it, Didibhai. Dadababu's choice is good. I will give you a fair price.'

'New to this neighbourhood?' He asked Manas, who simply said, 'No' with a look that didn't encourage the shopkeeper to probe any more. His intervention did put an end to the argument though, and he produced a bunch of thin metallic bangles tied together with a string.

'You must get the *loha*, too, no wedding is complete without it,' the shopkeeper said to Manas.

Manas accepted the piece of jewellery reluctantly as he thought of the thick gold-plated iron bangle his mother used to wear while his father was alive. As a child, Manas would be bewitched by its glint as it shone between the *shankha* and *pawla* on his mother's left wrist. When she took him in her lap to feed him or tell him a story, he wouldn't stop playing with her red, white and golden bangles.

For Amala, he could only afford the thin bangle, though, all iron, no gold. *Some day*, he made a promise to himself. He had decided not to borrow any money from his mother and grandfather for the wedding.

The shopkeeper had to keep other customers waiting as he got through this big order. He hurried to put the items into bags when Manik returned with the sweet boxes.

'I will go get a rickshaw while you pay up,' Manik said.

Manas nodded and said to Amala, 'Why don't you go along, too? Here, you can carry a couple of these bags.'

Amala picked up the bags as Manas waited to receive change from the shopkeeper. She smiled at how Manas had already begun sharing the labour.

Once back at Chitra's house, Manik and Manas kept the puja items in the study. It struck Chitra they still needed a *piri*. 'I think I have one,' she said. 'Must be in the loft.'

Manas took out the money Chitra had given him earlier.

'Everything got covered with the money I had, Mashi. You keep this.'

Chitra suggested he keep the money for expenses that could come up on the wedding day. 'You might want to host a small feast in Bijoy Nagar. In fact, you should.'

'I have some reserves, Mashi,' Manas said, insisting that Chitra take the money back so not everyone spent all at the same time. 'We are a collective, remember?'

Chitra took back the small bundle of notes without any more fuss. They all came out to the living room. As Manas and Manik made to leave for Bijoy Nagar, Amala mentioned her employers also needed to be informed about her absence.

'Good you thought of that!' Chitra said. 'We need to invite them, too.' She had Jogen Babu's address written in a diary and scribbled it on a piece of paper for Manas. She also wrote down her own address and asked Manas to extend a personal invitation on behalf of Chitra, Malati and Nimai to Jogen and Purnima Haldar.

'Please tell them to bring along Poltu, too,' Amala said.

'Sure, Ma'am,' Manas said waving a *salaam* in her direction before he and Manik stepped out.

~

The long evening, hectic and tiring as it was, helped divert Manas's attention from the anxiety that pricked him. His mother and aunt were to return in two days and Manas shuddered to think of the scene that would transpire in his house then. He worried about his grandfather's reaction too, but it seemed less scary to him.

Once they had informed and invited all the necessary people, Manas sent Manik back to Chitra's house while he left for home. He couldn't determine if he needed to tell Dadu or not. In the end, he decided not to, not at such short notice. The evening's developments were overwhelming enough for him to get into an argument on the eve of his wedding.

Right now, he needed to eat something. He went to the
kitchen where Sharoda sat, her eyes teary from the stove's smoke.
A pot of boiling rice made Manas hungry.

'Ki Maanu Babu?' Sharoda asked, wiping the steam off her
face. 'Are you hungry?'

'Dying of hunger, Mashi.'

'Oh dear. Just give me two minutes, the rice is almost done. I
don't want to give you stale rice from the afternoon.'

Manas didn't mind the short wait. Sharoda gave him a *piri* to
sit at the edge of the kitchen where it wasn't too smoky. 'You look
tired. Eat and then go to bed early,' she said while draining the
starch off the rice pot.

'Come, let's go to the dining room,' Sharoda said, lifting
Manas's large brass plate she had heaped with rice in the middle
and surrounded with bowls of lentils, vegetables and fish curry.

'Can I eat here, Mashi? I'm too tired.'

Sharoda put the plate down and Manas caught her eyes
smiling. This was like a secret pact between them. Every once
in a while, Manas would eat in the kitchen if Mrinmoyee wasn't
around. It gave him a chance to hear Sharoda's stories about her
village where her son lived with his wife and their five-year-old
daughter, Munia. Although she got to visit them only once every
six months, the child meant the world to Sharoda. She couldn't
tire of talking about her exploits and achievements.

Sharoda also spoke a lot about Jaba, her daughter-in-law. To
her, Jaba embodied goddess Lakshmi because of the efficiency
with which she ran her household on the meagre earnings of
her sharecropper husband. Sharoda often lamented Haru's lack
of material wisdom, a result of his predilection for singing in
devotional choirs. Manas took that as a hint for himself to earn a
stable income.

He listened somewhat absent-mindedly to Sharoda's latest
examples of how Munia seemed to have inherited her mother's
intelligence as well as her father's singing talent.

Suddenly, while stuffing his mouth with a large morsel of rice mixed with fish curry, Manas blurted, 'Mashi, will you still love me if I did something you didn't like?'

Sharoda had been in the Dutta household since before Manas's birth. His question surprised her. 'Why, Maanu? I know you will never do such a thing. And if I can love my Haru despite all his silliness, is that even a question?'

Manas finished the rest of his meal in silence. In his mind swirled things to be done before the red-letter day of his life. He handed the empty plate to Sharoda and made his way to the bathroom to wash up. Next, he went to the library to use the telephone. The grandfather clock there showed it was almost quarter to nine.

Shutting the door behind him, Manas dialled Proshanto's number. The phone on the other end rang a couple of times before Proshanto's father answered it. Manas asked him how he was enjoying his retirement and they exchanged a few pleasantries before Proshanto came on the line. Manas almost whispered the news to him and requested him not to show any surprise. Proshanto played along, answering mostly in yays and nays and promised to attend the event at the appointed venue. Before hanging up, Manas asked him to inform Subir and Raghu.

Manas went to bed and sank his face into the softness of his pillow. His mind was caught in a tempest. The thrill of sharing his space with Amala electrified him.

Despite the extreme fatigue, Manas couldn't fall asleep. Instead of fidgeting and fighting the insomnia, he got up from the bed and walked over to the desk next to the window. Turning on the table lamp, he sat down and opened a small notebook to jot down a to-do list. The number of things that needed to be done the next day kept increasing; for instance, he realised he had forgotten to get Amala's footwear. He would need to pick up her old pair for the size and buy a new one; he didn't want to drag her to the shop on the day of her wedding.

Manas kept adding to the list: buy a new sari for Amala, his own costume and, money permitting, a sari each for Chitra, Urmila and Malati and a *dhuti* for Nimai.

Luckily for Manas and Raghu, their nursing duties at the PL camp were now over as most of the sick children were getting better. The two volunteers, as also Subir and Manik, still dropped by often to check on the camp dwellers.

The dim light of the lamp calmed Manas's nerves as did making the list. Writing down what he could actually do made him feel less vulnerable. It was like practising lessons by writing them down from memory before examinations, a trick his father had taught him.

If there was ever a time Manas truly missed his father, it was now. Given how he had always had his son's back, Manas knew Baba would support his choice of a life partner.

Manas turned off the light and went back to his bed, lulled to sleep by his father's memory. He had a short but deep sleep and dreamt of being in a fish market. A woman accompanied him; Manas couldn't recall if it was Amala. Considering the rather domestic nature of their purchase, half a kilogram of pabda fish and four or five small bata fish, he concluded it had to be her.

18

Manas replayed the dream in his mind while taking a shower. He went to the kitchen for a quick bite but didn't find Sharoda there. He helped himself to a bowl of muri and added some milk and a banana to it. From a heap of washed utensils next to the tap, he picked up a spoon and quietly slunk out before anybody saw him.

Back in his room, Manas gulped down his breakfast. He looked at his wrist watch, 7:30, a bit too early to step out. The shops wouldn't open until 9 or 9:30. But Manas didn't want to be at home today, not even for a couple of hours. He fidgeted along the small passage in his room, then rammed down. Before he could enter the kitchen, he almost walked into Proshanto.

'*Arrey*, you're here?' Manas had barely registered his presence when he saw Subir's head bobbing from behind Proshanto's shoulder.

'Yes, brother,' Proshanto said even as he held Manas in a warm embrace. 'I have to go to work in an hour, but will return in the afternoon. Let me know if I can pick up something for you? Oh, and we need to inform Raghu.'

'Thanks, mate,' Manas said. 'I need to buy a few things, but we'll need to organise some food for the evening. The plan is to have a small reception in Bijoy Nagar after the ceremony.'

'Worry not, we have already thought about that. I know someone who can do the job,' Proshanto said as he mentioned a pice hotel near his office. If he placed his order early enough in the day, they could get packets of food that Proshanto would bring on his way back. Manas liked the idea but wanted to know how much it would cost.

'You don't worry about that,' Subir said. 'This is from your friends. In place of a better gift.'

Manas resisted the offer with all his might; he couldn't let his friends, most of them yet to find employment, carry this load. He had to relent when Proshanto said, 'Relax, my friend. It's not a huge cost. And you aren't getting married every day.'

'*Chalo, chalo*, there's no time to waste. We'll pick up Raghu, have some breakfast at my place, then head to the market,' Subir said.

Manas suggested they wait for him at the main door while he kept his empty bowl back in the kitchen. He finally saw Sharoda there and let her know he wouldn't be back for lunch. He then requested her to get up from her *piri* and touched her feet.

'*Eki, eki!*' Sharoda nearly jumped at Manas's act of reverence. Her right hand shook as she placed it on Manas's head and mumbled a blessing.

'*Ashi*, Mashi. Please tell Dadu not to worry if I'm a little late this evening,' Manas said and took her leave.

Subir's mother made *luchi-alur dom* as well as some creamy rice pudding with palm jaggery for all of them. The discussion at the breakfast was mostly about the war in Korea and the food scarcity in several Indian states. As a moderate, Subir's father made for Manas a great companion to chat with and gain insights from. That neither of Subir's parents probed into the nature of their visit to the market relieved Manas. Subir's mother only said they were to return by lunch time; she would wait for them.

'But we might be late, Mashima,' Manas protested.

'That's fine, Baba but I will keep lunch ready for you all. Come back hungry,' Subir's Ma said.

Before heading to the market, Manas and the boys went to Chitra's house. Manas waited in the taxi while Raghu and Subir went in to fetch Amala's broken sandals. They returned carrying not just the broken pair of footwear, but also some news. Apparently, Chitra had sent word through Manik for Bhottchaaj bamun to carry out the wedding ceremony, but the priest was already booked for the evening for a couple of *upanayan* ceremonies. Chitra discussed the matter with Amala and the only alternative they could think of was to request Dr Majumdar. Reciting the mantras wouldn't be a problem as Chitra had had Manik buy the book from the same *dashakarma bhandar* Manas had visited last evening. Amala also gave Subir a handwritten note, a personal request from her to the doctor to help with her wedding.

Subir suggested they split the tasks: Manas and Raghu could do the shopping while he went to Dr Majumdar's house. 'Here, keep this,' Manas said to Subir, pulling out a ten-rupee note from his wallet. He wanted Subir to take a taxi. Subir refused the money, saying even if he were to take the bus both ways, he would be done in good time for lunch.

Manas asked the taxi driver to take Raghu and him to New Market. He had booked the taxi for the day. The driver, a jovial Sikh man, appeared to be in his thirties and was given to easy conversation. Manas spoke slowly, unsure if the driver would understand Bengali. Harbans Singh, as the man identified himself, surprised Manas. Not only did he understand Bengali, he spoke it fluently. He had come to Calcutta fifteen years ago in search of work and liked the city so much that he never left. His steady hands at the wheel impressed Manas.

The shopping didn't take too long; Manas knew exactly which shops to target. Gladly for him, everything fell within his budget, even Amala's deep ochre Benarasi sari. Manas chose a relatively lightweight drape with a paisley motif and delicate leaf embroidery in fine golden thread. They took the items to Chitra's house and Manas waited in the taxi as Raghu dropped them off.

They had a lot of time on their hands; Manas had half a mind to invite Biren Mama, but then decided otherwise. He didn't want any drama before his mother's return. His heart said Biren would receive the news with happiness, but he couldn't take a chance. So they returned to Subir's house.

'What did Daktarbabu say?' On seeing Subir, Manas got to the heart of the matter.

'Well, he was a bit hesitant in the beginning, but when I explained the situation to him, he agreed. He sends you his warmest wishes. They...both do, actually.' Subir had even offered to pick up the doctor and his wife, but Dr Majumdar had said there was no need for that.

The boys chatted in whispers, lest their voice travelled beyond the room. A delicious aroma wafted in as Subir's Ma began organising lunch. Three types of fish, goat meat curry, several types of fritters, lentils and curries made with cauliflower and pointed gourd, a feast that would put a wedding menu to shame. 'Mashima, will we be able to stand back up after eating all this?' Manas said. 'I don't know where to begin.'

'Don't worry, son,' Subir's mother said with a chuckle. 'I will make you another cup of tea, and you'll be on your way.'

When all the food was eaten, washed down with that cracking cup of tea, Manas and his mates got ready to go to Chitra's house. At the door, Subir's mother edged closer to Manas and shoved a small parcel of coloured paper into his hands. Before Manas could say anything, she said, 'I know but your Meshomoshai doesn't. We won't tell him unless you want us to. This is for *her*. Please don't say no, Maanu.'

Manas gently opened the parcel, a pair of gold earrings. He bent down to touch Subir's mother's feet even as she lifted him to a warm hug. At that instant Manas realised Mashima had just fed him *aiburo-bhat*—his last meal as a bachelor.

~

Ay sab sakhigan
cala jai Srivrindaban
eka kunje Radha Syam sajai,
tulsi tuliye chandanti ghasiye
Radha Krishner pran padma
sajai fulti tuliye malati gathiye
Radha Krishner galete parai

The song rang in Amala's ears. She had heard and even sung it at several weddings in her village. A ditty invoking Radha and Krishna and about decorating the couple and their abode of love with *tulsi* and sandalwood paste, flowers and garlands. Nobody sang it right now as she got dressed in Chitra's bedroom and her groom in the study-turned-storeroom, where Proshanto helped him.

'Ooh, Mashi, that hurts!' Amala yelped as Chitra tightened her petticoat string. Amala still felt bloated from the heavy and never-ending lunch Chitra had made her eat as the last meal of her unmarried life.

'No gain without some pain, Amu,' Chitra said. Amala's heart sank even as she returned a wan smile. She knew Chitra meant nothing serious but a cloud floated before her, overcoming her with a moment's worry.

'Mashi, when will Malati Mashi and Mesho come?'

'*Rosho*, patience, my child. They will be here soon,' Chitra said, as she picked up the packet of earrings Manas had handed her when he came back. 'Subir and Raghu have gone to pick them up.'

Amala knew she had no reason to worry. Chitra had organised everything like a machine. Snehalata and her husband were already there to receive the guests, while Rani and Minoti would help with tea and snacks. Manik remained in the house too, for any last-minute shopping needs.

Proshanto had arranged for the food packets to be delivered to Santu's tea stall at 7.30 pm, by which time the wedding ceremony was expected to conclude. Jogen, Purnima and Poltu had been invited to Bijoy Nagar as guests from the 'bride's side'.

'*Bah*, see how pretty you look.' Chitra held a mirror in front of Amala. 'Manas has taste, I must say.'

Amala hid her face immediately.

～

For Manas, the rest of the evening was a reverie he didn't want to come out of. In the rush of getting everything ready, he'd forgotten to buy his *topor* and Amala's *mukut*. He had casually mentioned the slip to Subir and couldn't have imagined he would return with those, along with Malati and Nimai. Subir didn't have to buy new headgear. When Tara, who was already at Malati's house, heard about it, she brought out her and Nitai's *mukut* and *topor*.

Manas nearly gasped when Amala came to the living room, an ochre goddess with the *mukut* on her head. Her face, which Chitra had decorated with sandalwood paste had a glow that Manas wanted to frame as a keepsake.

The similarity with Tara and Nitai's wedding ended with the *mukut* and *topor*. At the appointed hour, despite being presented with the book of mantras, Dr Majumdar decided not to read from it. 'I know nothing about that book or those tough-to-pronounce mantras, so I brought my own. I hope you don't mind?' He asked Manas.

Though intrigued, Manas smiled and shook his head. Dr Majumdar looked at Amala and repeated the question.

'Whatever you do is good, Daktarbabu,' Amala said, a statement echoed by all present.

And so the wedding took place with the doctor reading verses and excerpts from literature he had selected for the purpose. There was no holy fire or blinding smoke, no mantra-chanting and ritual-wielding priest. Despite her liking for rituals, being wed this way elated Amala. She and Manas sat across each other on two chairs, a pot of fresh Rajanigandha on the table separating them. As Daktarbabu read the excerpts, the scent of incense and flowers floated across happy faces.

When he had finished reading, the doctor asked Nimaichand to put Amala's hand into Manas's. Amala's hand trembled as it landed on Manas's clammy palm. They exchanged *jaimalas* that Proshanto had brought along. Chitra picked up a small silver container filled with *sindoor* and motioned Manas to smear Amala's parting with the powdered vermillion. Sweets were exchanged and the ceremony ended within an hour.

To compensate, the celebrations at Bijoy Nagar ran for longer than expected. The residents cooked up a feast and refused to let the new couple off without stuffing them full. The children of the colony presented an impromptu show with songs and poems they had learned in school. Hastily organised by some of the residents who volunteered at the school, this included everything from patriotic and folk songs to nonsense rhymes. They then took turns to distribute the food packets from the pice hotel to everyone present.

Everyone looked happy; even Urmila's face beamed with a smile instead of the usual frown it wore. It only left her when Amala was about to leave. Urmila ran to her de facto sister and bawled her lungs out as she held her. Malati rushed to pull Urmila away but Amala gestured her not to.

'Hey, *pagli*,' Amala said to Urmila, 'I'm not running away, am I? I will keep coming back to check on you. And how can I stay away from my Hablu shona for long?' Her throat warbled before tears streamed down her eyes.

Letting go of Urmila gently, she took turns to say goodbye to the others, Malati Mashi, Nimai Mesho, whom she reminded to keep walking every day; Moyna, Tara, Bakul, the other women....

The Bijoy Nagar residents walked over to see off the newly-weds right down to the spot where Harbans had parked the taxi. They kept waving for as long as Amala and Manas remained in their line of vision.

As the taxi rolled out into the distance, Manas caught a reflection of Harbans in the rear-view mirror. Manas smiled back and the two men shared a moment even as Amala kept looking out of the window.

They arrived at Manas's house half an hour later. Amala looked at the mansion with wide eyes, unable to fathom the reality of it all. Even as she gawked, she pulled her sari's *anchal* over her head.

Harbans opened the car's trunk and helped Manas carry the bags to the porch, shimmering with a bright bulb. Manas thanked him and paid him fifteen rupees over and above the days' fare.

19

Manas hastened to enter the house but couldn't help smiling when he saw Amala agape as she took in her new surroundings. Her head bobbed left and right to absorb it all. Manas had to knock on the main door twice before someone opened it. It was Photik. '*Ashun*,' he said to Manas, turning back to go in.

'*Ei* Photik,' Manas called him. 'Can you ask Sharoda Mashi to come to the door?'

'*Bole dichchi*, I will go tell her,' Photik said without looking back, wiping his face with his pet *gamchha*. Manas never understood why he was always in such a hurry.

Sharoda appeared momentarily. 'What happened, Baba Maanu? Is everything all right?'

'Mashi, look who I brought.' Turning to Amala Manas said, 'Come. Sharoda Mashi has been with us since before I was born.'

Amala stepped ahead and touched Sharoda's feet. The cook put her wobbling hand on Amala's head and said, 'Bless you,' in a shaky voice.

Without further ado, Manas said, 'Mashi, I got married to Amala today. She is the Dutta family's bride.'

Sharoda stood motionless for a moment before saying, 'Wait, wait, don't step right in. Let me bring something to welcome the new bride. Wait a minute, both of you.' She scampered inside and returned with a deep dish filled with milk and *alta*. Placing the dish on the floor, she asked Amala to step on it. Amala obeyed, stamping the inner courtyard with her scarlet footprints. Manas took off his *topor* and tiptoed behind her. When they arrived in the middle of the courtyard, Manas saw Photik scurrying by. He held a plate filled with food that Manas recognised as Haraprasad's dinner. He called Photik again, who nearly tumbled at the sight of a fully-decked new bride.

'Can you ask Dadu to come down for a second so your Boudi can receive his blessings?'

'*Je aggey,*' Photik said, trying desperately to balance the plate in his hands. Manas laughed as he said to Amala, 'Don't mind him, he's a bit odd.'

Amala's chuckle was cut short when Haraprasad appeared at the railing outside his room moments later. Taking off his glasses, he wiped them with the stole on his shoulder and put them back on. He looked below and saw Manas waving at him.

'Wait, I'm coming,' he said and made his way to the staircase leading down.

'What's the matter, Dadubhai?' Haraprasad asked Manas. 'That Photik, he mumbled something I couldn't make sense of.'

'Your granddaughter-in-law is here, Dadu,' Manas said.

Amala moved in his direction hiding her hesitation as best as she could.

'*Thaak, thaak,* let it be' Haraprasad said as Amala touched his feet. His tone was dispassionate yet gentle. He blessed Amala by lightly placing his palm on her head.

'You should eat dinner now, Dadu,' Manas said. 'It must be getting cold. We should, er, going, too.'

'Right, right,' Haraprasad said as everyone assembled started moving towards their own spaces in what still looked to Amala like a big maze. Her tired body followed Manas even as she tried to make sense of the new reality that confronted her like a stern examiner. A clod of disquiet grabbed at her throat as she landed on the stairs; she almost reached over to Manas to hold him for balance but clutched the railing instead.

Manas led Amala to his room. Once they had put down the bags in a corner, he showed her the bathroom. Malati had given Amala a small tin trunk with all her clothes so she wouldn't have too much trouble changing.

'I can use the bathroom while you change here,' Manas said. 'I think the room will be better for you.'

Amala nodded as she suppressed a yawn. While Manas was in the bathroom, she changed into a much-faded soft cotton sari and blouse. She went out and tapped on the bathroom door.

'One minute,' Manas said, his voice blending with splashing water. He emerged soon, wiping his wet hair with a towel. He had a light vest and a pyjama on. 'Here, take my slippers, the floor is wet,' Manas said.

Amala gladly accepted the footwear; it would take her too long to fish out her pair of slippers from their many bags that lay in the corner of the room. She used water from a bucket to wash her face. A mirror mounted on the wall reflected her forehead—greasy with *sindoor* smudge. She picked up the bar of soap on a wooden shelf next to the mirror and started rubbing it across her face, taking care to leave a red dot on her forehead.

The soap's jasmine scent held Amala in a heady spell even as the cool splash of water tingled her skin. She saw only one towel on a handlebar attached to the other wall, probably the one Manas had used minutes ago. Amala grabbed the towel gingerly, then put it right back on the bar, wiping her face with her sari *anchal* instead. When she returned to the room, Manas looked at her, a tired-yet-relieved smile on his face, from his desk chair; he had a book open before him.

Amala sat down at the edge of the neatly-made bed and blurted out the question that had been bothering her since she stepped into the house. 'Where is your mother?'

'I have to tell you all about it. Don't worry, you will meet her. She'll be here tomorrow.' Manas's cryptic response tensed up Amala more than it reassured her.

'Do you want to lie down? I'm dead tired.' Manas said.

Amala acquiesced if only to find out the reason behind her mother-in-law's absence. Pushing the lone pillow on the bed to one side, she sat up on the bed and unfolded the flower-patterned bed sheet lying at her feet. Drawing it to cover herself, she lay down. Manas came forward and offered her the pillow.

'Nah, I don't need it. You can have it,' she said.

'What a worthless man you got for a husband. He can't even give you a new pillow on your wedding night.'

'You're right,' Amala said turning to the other side, hiding her smile from Manas.

Manas used the bed switch to turn off the light. As they lay beside each other, Amala felt a surge pull her closer to Manas. Manas remained where he was but extended his hand towards Amala's. She shivered at the electric contact and moved closer to Manas. He turned over and held her, a warm, relaxing touch Amala could trust. A slither of fear still lurked in her mind, and she whispered to ask Manas if he had any expectations of her.

Manas suppressed what began as a guffaw in his throat. 'Only that you trust me, Amu.'

'Do you want me to, er...?'

'I want nothing unless you want it, too.'

'Can we wait? Just a few days? You must think I'm crazy, but....'

'We'll wait until you're ready. To be honest, I'd rather sleep right now. Oh, I have to tell you about Ma first.'

Manas lay down on his back once more; Amala turned and held him as he told her about Mrinmoyee's and Bawromashi's impending arrival. He gave her enough indication of his mother's temperament and outlook. Amala took the hints the way any daughter-in-law was supposed to, as a part and parcel of her married life. Nothing in what Manas said alarmed her about Mrinmoyee. He also told her a lot about Sreemoyee and how close he felt to her. Amala couldn't wait to meet her aunt-in-law.

Manas expressed another concern. In her last letter, his mother hadn't specified their time or mode of arrival. Manas didn't have enough information to go and bring them from the railway station but told Amala he would go to the Howrah station early in the morning to see which trains were scheduled to arrive from Puri so he could receive his mother and aunt.

'Can I come with you?' Amala asked.

'Maybe not. Let's get some sleep now.'

Manas had his first good sleep in many nights. When his eyes opened, Amala's arm rested on his chest. Manas looked at her; she appeared to be in deep sleep. Manas had no mind to disturb her. He guessed it was around 6:30 am, his usual wake-up time. He didn't have a lot of time to go to the station and shuffled a little, hoping Amala's arm would drop off his chest. As he'd feared, the movement woke her up instead.

'O Ma, the sun's up already,' Amala said, her half-opened eyes fighting the streaks of sunlight pushing through the window. Manas drew the cover to place it over her but Amala motioned him not to. She sat up and pulled her loose hair into a bun.

'Come, let's go to the balcony,' Manas said to Amala.

'Hey, wait. Don't I need to wash my mouth first?'

Manas didn't remember if she had said 'wait' like that before but now it carried for him the typical intonation Bengali wives used for saying that word to their husbands. He didn't miss the affection in it.

'*Arrey*, I have to wash up, too, but let's see the sun first,' Manas implored.

Amala didn't understand what was so special about looking at the morning sun, but Manas's voice had the urgency of a ten-year-old who had to show a favourite hideout to a new playmate. She put on the slippers he'd lent her in the night.

'*Esho*,' Manas said and when Amala offered to give back his slippers, he said, 'Don't worry about that. Come, come.'

Amala stood with the man in her life watching the rising sun blush through the conical leaves of the betel nut tree, the film of its rays glazing them. She also saw the broad smile that spread across Manas's face, as bright as the sun itself.

'Isn't that beautiful, Amu?' He said, still looking in the sun's direction.

'It is,' she said in a tone so soft, it sounded like a whisper to Manas.

They stood there for another couple of minutes before Manas said, '*Chalo*, let's wash up. I'm sure Sharoda Mashi is making breakfast for us.'

While Manas discovered Amala's *sindoor* on his white vest in the bathroom, Amala busied herself with making the bed and tidying up the room by trying to stuff as many of the bags lying on the floor in the wooden almirah she saw next to the desk. She looked under the bed for a broom but didn't find any, so once done with cleaning up the best she could, she sat at the edge of the bed.

A multitude of aromas—*paanchphoron* five-spice tempering in hot mustard oil, cardamom and cinnamon being roasted in ghee, simmering split yellow lentils—drew Amala as she followed Manas to climb down the stairs. Amala saw a young woman, probably a little older than her, washing utensils in a corner outside the kitchen. The woman mumbled something as she scrubbed the dishes with coconut fibre and soap-mixed ash. She stopped mumbling the moment she caught sight of Manas and Amala. The way she gawked at the two of them made Amala uncomfortable.

Manas turned around to find Amala pausing by the domestic help and said, 'That's Menoka, she has been with us for a few years now. Menoka, this is your Boudi.'

'Oh,' Menoka said, chewing the *paan* in her mouth harder and faking a smile. 'Good, good.'

Amala noticed how quickly Menoka's smile turned back into the previous agape look. She couldn't pay attention to her much longer as Manas called her.

A smoky haze hung over the kitchen, which Sharoda's hands had filled with all those delicious aromas. She had a pot in her hand, containing bubbling hot lentils that she upturned into a large saucepan. Manas and Amala stood at the door until she was done transferring the *daal*.

'Mashi, you have already cooked everything, *haan*?' Manas said, breaking Sharoda's concentration.

Sharoda flashed a jubilant smile at the newlyweds. 'And why wouldn't I? Our Boumoni is here. What will she say if I didn't feed her well on her first day in the house? Besides, aren't Ma and Mashima coming today? Your Dadu has sent Nando to get fish and meat from the market; he should be back soon.'

Sharoda also told them that Manas's grandfather was expecting them for breakfast at the dining table. 'Go there, Baba, Mamoni. I will have tea sent for you,' she said.

Amala tugged at Manas's shirt and whispered she hadn't had her bath yet, how could she join Dadu for breakfast?

Manas relayed her concern to Sharoda who had an instant solution—Amala should still have tea with Haraprasad, then shower. Later, Sharoda could have her breakfast sent upstairs or she could come down to the dining room.

Haraprasad sat at one end of the dining table, absorbed in the day's newspaper spread before him. Lately Manas had seen him using a magnifying glass to read even some of the headlines in smaller type and not just the main content of the story as he did before. Manas wanted to ask if he had seen his ophthalmologist but saved that question for later. He just said, 'Good morning, Dadu.'

'Oh, you are here,' Haraprasad looked up even as Manas bent to touch his feet. His grandfather stood up and held him in a light embrace.

Amala came forward and touched Haraprasad's feet and he blessed her with 'Be happy.'

When Amala bent down again, this time to touch Manas's feet as was the custom, he almost jumped back before controlling himself to steady his feet. He received Amala's reverence awkwardly, stammering '*Bhalo thako*, be well.'

Manas and Amala took their seats on the side chairs; Manas sat closer to his grandfather. Despite his attempts to make small talk, not a lot transpired over tea. Haraprasad remained mostly quiet, responding with 'Hmms' and 'Ohs' and '*O, tai naaki* is that so?' every now and then. Amala had a feeling he wanted to say more to Manas but couldn't in her presence.

When done with her cup of tea, Amala nudged Manas discreetly. Manas edged closer to Haraprasad and said Amala needed to excuse herself to have her bath. As he intended to leave for the station soon, she wanted to receive Dadu's blessings before Manas left.

'*Esho*, Bouma,' Haraprasad said as Amala got up from her chair. She proceeded to touch his feet again but he said it wasn't needed, she need not be so formal with him. Something about his words eased the stiffness that had clasped Amala all this while. As she climbed up the stairs, she realised it wasn't his tone but the fact that he had called her 'Bouma' that reassured her.

After her shower, Amala wore a mustard cotton sari with a red border that Chitra had given her as part of her wedding trousseau, which included three other saris with matching petticoats. Given how little time she had, Chitra couldn't provide blouses for all the saris but made her selection in such a way that Amala could wear any of the saris with a red or white blouse, both of which Amala had.

When she reached the kitchen, Amala found Sharoda removing vegetables from a large tote bag that a man with chalk-charcoal hair held before her. Amala guessed the man was Nando. She was proven right when Sharoda introduced Nando to Maanu Babu's bride. Amala tried to touch Nando's feet but he skidded away, clearly taken aback at the esteem Amala accorded him.

'*Pennam hoi*, Boudimoni, my *pranaams* to you,' he said, folding his hands in a namaskar and bowing before Amala.

'Please, don't say so,' Amala said, still trying to come to terms with the hierarchy of status her marriage had thrust upon her.

Nando merely nodded with a baffled smile. He checked with Sharoda if she needed any other help in the kitchen. When Sharoda confirmed she didn't need his assistance for now, Nando left the kitchen, folding his hands once more to convey a namaskar to Amala. She returned the greeting by joining her palms.

The amount of vegetables, meat, and fish Amala saw Sharoda sorting through boggled her mind. It seemed fit for a feast to her.

'Why don't you go to the dining room, Ma?' Sharoda said. 'You must be hungry. I will have your breakfast sent.'

'Nah, Mashi, I will be here with you. Can I eat here?'

Sharoda didn't say anything but Amala could read the language of the smile that spread across her face, she knew its semantics from similar smiles Malati and Chitra had flashed many a time to indulge her. Amala grabbed a *piri* resting against a wall and sat down next to Sharoda.

'I can help you with the cooking, Mashi,' she said.

'I know, Boumoni. What's the hurry? You will have many opportunities to cook in this house. Take it easy, you have only just arrived.'

Sharoda's warm words almost smothered Amala with happiness. She wondered what her mother-in-law's first impression of her would be like. Amala pushed the thought away, biting into the *luchi* and dry potato dish, along with some split bengal grams cooked with coconut Sharoda gave her. The potatoes tasted different to Amala, a bit sweet. She dipped a piece of *luchi* into the lentils and even that tasted sweet. *The food here is definitely different.*

'Do you like it, Boumoni?' Sharoda asked while peeling *potol* on her *bonthhi* blade.

'It's nice, Mashi. You cook so well. Won't you have some?'

'I don't eat all this, Ma. I had my *doi-chire* early in the morning.' Sharoda told Amala about how she couldn't start her morning without a cup of black tea and some flattened rice with curd. She couldn't eat oily or starchy foods because of digestion problems.

Amala hadn't noticed when Sharoda had put water on the boil, so when the cook placed before her an ornate china cup filled with tea, resting on a matching saucer, her eyes twinkled. She sipped the tea slowly, chatting some more with Sharoda. Once done, she picked up her plate and cup and as she made as if to take them outside to the washing area, Sharoda stopped her. 'Don't worry about those, Ma. Just put them away in the corner. Menoka will take care of it when she comes to wash in the evening.'

Back in her...their room, in the sun-washed clarity of the day,

Amala saw the rows of books resting on the two book racks facing each other on either side of the bed. A pedestal fan stood in a corner. At a short distance from one of the book racks, Manas's clothes hung on an *alnaa*, some piled on top of each other. Amala took down the pile—mostly *kurtas*, a shirt, a couple of *fatuas* and pyjamas and a rumpled *dhuti*—and put them on the bed. Drawing a shirt close to her, she inhaled Manas in a long, greedy breath. She marvelled at how the well-worn clothes had preserved her man's scent, a blend of mild sweat and jasmine soap.

Once the clothes were all folded and arranged back on the rack, Amala stepped out to the balcony. Sunlight had moved over to the southern side. The crowns of the areca nut tree overlooking this part of the house created a near-umbra, keeping the balcony surprisingly cool. Amala rested her arms on the balustrade. She watched a morning similar to what she knew, yet different.

From the luxurious shade of the balcony, the pace of the city seemed like a hot summer's afternoon in Amala's village. She saw a man and a young boy, father and son perhaps, get up from the corner of a footpath where they must have been sleeping all night. Tatty sack cloth, spread over a small area, comprised their bedding and a couple of sacks filled with sand made for their pillows. The man raised one of the pillow sacks against a lamp post and, resting his back against it, took out a *bidi* from behind his ear. Lighting it with a match that he took out from his soiled, half-torn *fatua* pocket, the man started smoking while the boy took an empty canister and went further away, out of Amala's sight. The boy wore a half pant that could be red or orange if it were ever washed but at the moment appeared to be the colour of rust to Amala. He could be ten or eleven. A few minutes later, she saw him return with the canister filled with water.

Amala kept watching them and other morning scenes—a beggar sitting on the other end of the footpath, and two dogs fighting for scraps from a heap of vegetable and other food waste dumped in a corner of the street. Suddenly, a persistent knock on the door startled her. Amala rushed, anticipating Manas, then thought it couldn't be him. She hadn't bolted the door and if it were him, wouldn't he have walked in? She was right; it was Photik, bearing Sharoda's message that 'Boudimoni should come downstairs for lunch.'

'I'm not hungry. Please tell Mashi to eat. And you eat, too, all right?'

Photik mumbled a 'Hmm,' and walked away scratching his head.

Amala let the door remain ajar. Moving over to Manas's desk, she scanned the contents curiously. Unlike the *alnaa*, it was surprisingly tidy. A few fat books stood against the wall; a lime-green table lamp rested on the left-hand side, its arm bent down; a couple of notebooks, one with a pen on top of it. Amala didn't want to intrude yet couldn't help herself from opening the thinner of the two notebooks. It opened to a page that had a pencil tucked in it. The lettering on the page made her face light up, for it was in Bengali.

Clutching the notebook to her chest, Amala ran to the door and bolted it. Spreading herself on the bed, she read the to-do lists Manas had written down. His meticulous organisation had impressed her the day before—the way he remembered to get everything down to the last item, including clothes for Malati, Urmila and Nimai and even her sandals. Now she saw the method behind it all. One thing amused her, though. Manas had written the names for Chitra, Malati, and Nimai in full. For her name, he only wrote 'A'.

Amala returned the notebook to its spot with a smile. She didn't know what time it was. But she could tell it was well past noon. The noise level outside had subsided and the afternoon drooped into a stupor. As a lazy yawn left her mouth, Amala longed for some tea. In her mind, she blamed Chitra and Rani for having turned her into a tea addict. She had never been much of a tea drinker, but in Chitra's house, it was normal for multiple cups of tea to appear within a couple of hours.

Amala realised she had drifted into a nap only when a hard

knock on the door jolted her out of it. She got up with a start and quickly pulling the *anchal* over her head, hastened to open the door.

'Did you fall asleep?' Manas said as he entered the room. 'I knocked a few times already.'

'Didn't realise when I dozed off,' Amala said. 'You got so late. Did they arrive?'

'Oh, yes,' Manas said, narrating how, the train by which his mother and aunt were travelling had been scheduled to arrive at noon but was late by three hours. Taking off his shirt, he reached for a *fatua* and noticed the neatly-arranged *alnaa*.

'So you've been at work already. Did you eat anything?' He asked Amala.

'Don't worry about me, I'm not hungry,' Amala said. Then, almost in a whisper she asked, 'Have you told Ma about us?'

'No, I wanted to surprise her. But I did give her a hint,' Manas said, adding, 'let's go; Ma and Mashi are waiting downstairs.'

Amala straightened her sari's pleats, shoved a few loose strands of hair behind the part of the *anchal* that covered her head and followed Manas to climb down the stairs. He led her down the corridor to a room she hadn't seen yet, the erstwhile *baithakkhana*. The room had little use, save when Mrinmoyee hosted guests on social and religious occasions.

Amala saw the two ladies she had been nervously waiting for talking animatedly with each other. They were sitting on two large, ornamented wooden chairs. Before them, on a table with a marble top were two plates of sweets and two tumblers of water. Amala pulled the sari cover from her head further down to veil part of her face and stood at the room's threshold, behind Manas.

'Ma, Bawromashi, remember I said I had a surprise for you at home?' Manas said. 'Look, here it is.' He gently pulled Amala by the hand.

Even as his aunt adjusted her thick glasses, Manas's mother got up from the chair. 'What's going on here?' Mrinmoyee asked. Her tone sent a shiver down Amala's spine.

'I got married, Ma. This is Amala, your daughter-in-law,' Manas said firmly as he motioned Amala to touch Mrinmoyee's feet. Amala moved forward and bent down but couldn't get much further as Mrinmoyee not only retracted her steps but said in an ice-cold tone, 'Stop right there.'

Manas helped Amala stand back up and put his hand on her shoulder. To his mother he said, 'You seem upset, Ma. And you have every reason to be so. But I can explain it to you. Right now, you and Bawromashi need some rest.'

'Wait,' Mrinmoyee said with a sharpness that reminded Amala of a *bonthhi* slashing fish. 'Is this some kind of a joke, Maanu? Tell me this is one of your pranks.'

'Nah, Ma. Your Maanu has finally grown up. As I said, we'll talk about it. You will understand when you hear it all, trust me.'

'Not sure why I should trust you. But right now, I have a headache coming on and any more nonsense will make me faint,' Mrinmoyee said. Turning to her sister, she said, 'Let's go, Didi. You definitely don't need any of this drama after such an exhausting journey.'

Sreemoyee got up and the sisters left the room without uttering another word. Manas's mother looked back with a gazelle-swift turn, glaring once more at Manas and Amala's hands held together. She muttered something under her breath and although Amala couldn't hear it clearly, she thought she heard a slanderous word. Her feet froze and she couldn't move even when the two ladies were out of sight.

'Come,' Manas said as he drew her away from the spot. 'Don't worry, I am there.' He closed the door of their room behind him silently while still holding on to Amala's hand. Walking over to the bed, he helped her sit down. The veil she created with the sari had moved back and Manas found her face swamped with tears.

'Don't cry, Amu. Ma is a little shocked. See, she had no idea....'

'I knew this would happen. I even asked you.'

'True, but we didn't have any option, did we? Whatever

happens, Amu, know that we have to be together. Nothing else matters.'

'Not even your mother's happiness?'

'I would hate to make her unhappy, but you know what? I've come to realise you can't make everyone happy all the time.' His last sentence came out with a sigh, sounding like a foreboding to Amala.

'I'll be right back,' Manas said. 'Bolt the door, okay? And don't worry.'

He returned in a couple of minutes with two bananas and a glass of milk and found the door open.

'Here, have this now. Sharoda Mashi told me you haven't eaten anything since breakfast.'

'I'm not hungry, I told you,' Amala said, sinking her head into the crook of her arms.

Manas sat down next to her and stroked her hair. 'Be a good girl now and drink this milk. For me, *lokkhi meye*.' Amala didn't budge.

'All right then. If you don't eat, I will have to go hungry, too. All I had since breakfast with Dadu was a cup of tea at the station.'

'That's not fair. Why won't you eat? I'm not hungry, I said.'

'Just have this banana and milk to keep me company. You can do that, can't you?'

Amala relented.

'I can't have all that milk. You have some, I will drink the rest,' she said.

Manas agreed and passed a banana to her, and as she took a bite, Amala remembered the time when Manas had brought her *muri* back in the very first days of her camp life. And how, even then he had managed to coax her into eating without being overbearing.

A sense of fulfillment washed away the sadness that had overcome Amala only moments ago. Manas understood her so well; she didn't even need to utter what troubled her. It was as if the turbid water she was swimming in had been filtered clean, revitalising every clogged pore in her.

~

In her forever-altered reality, Amala would have to cherish every sliver of happiness that came her way. If she thought marriage would make her life steady, she would be quick to correct that perception. And so when Nando came knocking on their door later that evening saying 'Dadababu' had been summoned by his mother in her room, Amala knew she would have to walk over smouldering rocks again.

The noises Amala heard from Mrinmoyee's room, only a couple of rooms away from theirs, sounded more like loud whispers in the beginning. But as the volume of both her mother-in-law's and husband's voice kept rising, she knew they were in a heated argument. Amala felt a cold sweat run through her body. She lay down on the bed, pressing her ears between the pillow and a ball she made with her sari *anchal*. Anything she could do to drown out the conflict. When she removed the pillow, even with numb ears she could hear a faint strain of music playing in the adjoining room. It cut through the conversation between Manas and Mrinmoyee. Amala sat up on the bed; she needed to use the bathroom but felt too scared to step out of the room before Manas returned.

When he returned after what seemed like forever, Manas had a huge bell metal plate heaped with rice and several bowls of dishes in his hands. Amala held the door open for him. 'What happened?' She asked him. 'Ma is still upset, isn't she?'

'I will tell you everything. Let's eat first. I'm starving, as I know you are.'

'Umm, can I go to the bathroom?' Amala asked almost as if she were seeking permission.

'Of course! Why do you ask? Go on, I'll not start until you are back.'

When she returned, Amala pressed Manas again to tell her about the exchange between him and his mother.

'Come here,' he said, extending his hand in her direction. 'I am not going to hide anything from you, good or ugly. But first we must eat this food Sharoda Mashi has made. Deal?'

Manas had cleared some space on his desk to make room for the plate and pulled the desk closer to his bed so they could both sit and eat from it. Even in the midst of the unsettling time she found herself in, her husband's ingenuity brought a flicker of smile on Amala's face. Sitting down next to him for their first meal as a married couple, she watched Manas eat as if he were a child in her care.

Amala started nibbling from the portion Manas had separated for her. She ate a bit of cooked spinach and fried bitter gourd with rice. Since the afternoon's episode, she'd no appetite left. She kept taking small bites so that Manas didn't have to keep prodding her. The sight of him relishing the meal satiated her more than the food itself. She felt an envying sense of admiration for him; all that bitter exchange with his mother hadn't had any effect on his relation to food. She herself could never eat properly, let alone enjoy food, when upset or anxious.

Post dinner, Manas picked up a book from the shelf and lay down on the bed. Amala joined him, and as he read, she listened to the music of the night—the song of crickets, a lone dog breaking into a howl every now and then, the *chowkidaar's* cautionary call of '*Jaagte raho!*'

As Amala closed her eyes, she could even hear the thrum of Manas's heartbeat. Soon, she heard a gentle slush, as if the thirsty street was sipping water dripping off the sky. 'Is it raining?' She asked, opening her eyes.

'It is. You aren't asleep yet?' Manas said.

'I'm waiting for you to tell me what you said you would.'

'Oh that. Yes.' Manas closed the book and put it on the desk. He also turned off the light and slunk under the cover as Amala already had.

'Not happy news, Amala. Ma doesn't want you to eat in

the dining room. So I told her I won't eat there either. We will continue eating here until she changes her mind.' Manas went on to tell Amala that he had told Sharoda to have Amala's lunch sent in the afternoon if he were away.

Wrapping his arm over Amala's shoulder, Manas said, 'I know it's not the best start to your married life, but I promise I will make it better.'

As long as I have you, nothing else matters.

Rain slammed their window and pelted the street outside. Manas's hands moved upwards from Amala's belly. As he began caressing her breasts, Amala flinched. A bad memory, one she thought had been erased from her mind, belched to her consciousness. When she and Kartik were at the border to cross over to India, they had to take a ferry along with others also planning to cross over. Just before they could board the ferry, a group of policemen searched their belongings. They didn't stop there, though. With young women like Amala, they performed a more 'thorough search'. Under the wraps now, Amala shuddered as she remembered shrieking when a policeman fondled her breasts as part of his search mission.

'Am I hurting you, Amu?' Manas asked even as he turned to the other side. 'You need more time to trust me.'

'No. I began trusting you long ago. But this body, do you know how hungry men can be for this?'

Manas turned around and lay his arm softly over Amala again. 'But this one is not greedy; you know that, don't you?'

'I do,' Amala said. She drew his hands and gently moved them over each of her breasts. 'They do, too,' she whispered in his ears.

'I see,' Manas said with a chortle. 'Let me get to know them a bit more while I tell you a story.'

As Manas explored the contours of Amala's body, Amala didn't resent his touch; it exhilarated her. And so while telling her about a childhood incident involving his father, Manas and she entwined in the middle of a wild river. They couldn't tell at what point the mutual discovery paused, lulling them into sleep.

20

I miss Baba. Not his hand on my shoulders but his nod of approval on seeing me take a stand. For myself. For A. We have a battle ahead of us; that I'm sure of. At home. Outside. More for A than me. But I'm ready for it. What is life without a hint of conflict? At least we have each other in all this. Walking the road together will not make it any less weary for us individually, but we'll understand each other's exhaustion. That's what Baba always did, he understood. Even when he couldn't share, much less palliate, another's pain or anguish, he tried to understand. So even if he didn't agree with my union with A, and I strongly feel he would have, he would at least try to look at it from my perspective. Of all the reasons (and there are many) for which I miss Baba, his empathy tops the list.

— MANAS DUTTA, DIARY ENTRY, 27 JULY 1951

Closing his diary, Manas told Amala he would be in the library downstairs after his bath and she could join him if she liked. He showed her how to find the library once she stepped out of her room. Amala nodded. She made the bed after Manas left and stood next to the window overlooking the balcony. The night's downpour had petered down to a drizzle, and the morning breeze carried not only petrichor but also the scent of the *bakul* flowers she could see in their neighbour's front yard. Amala rested her head against the wooden window frame to inhale the rain-washed air and take in the chirps of sparrows. She felt a strong urge to visit Malati and Hablu. It had been only a day but she already missed them. She thought of asking Manas to take her to Bijoy Nagar.

When she stepped out of her room to have a bath, a stern voice stopped her in her tracks. Amala turned around startled in Mrinmoyee's direction, who told her she couldn't use the bathroom upstairs. 'There's a bathroom downstairs that Sharoda, Nando and the other servants use. Go down and someone will show you where it is.'

Amala was taken aback at this sudden call. Maybe Mrinmoyee needed to use the bathroom upstairs? As long as she had a place to bathe, it didn't matter where it was located. When she came to the courtyard, her eyes briefly met Manas's. He pointed out the bathroom to her while walking towards the library. Amala quietly went in the direction of the bathroom. Even without lifting her eyes, she could feel Mrinmoyee's presence near the railing upstairs.

A small toilet was located next to the bathroom. Amala stepped into the bathroom to keep her dry clothes before using the toilet. When she returned for her bath, the bare look of the bathroom, devoid of a mirror or a shelf to keep towels and other accessories, comforted her. As she poured water on herself using an enamel mug, which she dipped inside the lone iron bucket, she remembered how the bathroom upstairs had seemed alien to her, with all those luxury bathing accessories.

Amala picked up a small pink melting bar of soap from a broken saucer where it rested along with an overused blob of washing soap. The bath soap had a faint smell, nothing like the intense jasmine soap upstairs. Once her bath was done, Amala washed her used clothes and came out. She remembered Manas's invitation, but still reeling from the shock of her mother-in-law's eagle gaze only moments ago, headed straight to her room. She closed the door and began clearing some space in the *alnaa* to hang her washed clothes. Snatches of a conversation floated to her ears; she identified the voices as those of her husband's and mother-in-law's. It relieved Amala that it sounded more like a chat than an argument.

'Amala?' Manas knocked on the door barely a minute later.

She held the door open as he walked in with a large bowl.

It had *muri* with milk and mashed banana and some crushed *batasha*.

'So you never came to the library,' Manas said.

'Oh, I forgot. Besides...I had to comb my hair.' Amala said.

'I see. So you need to be properly dolled up to meet me inside the house. Glad you told me because I didn't know that.'

'Don't be angry, *lokkhi shona*,' Amala said. 'Who will I go to if you're upset with me?'

'Don't keep me waiting like that, then,' Manas said with a hint of reconciliation. He invited Amala to join him for breakfast at his desk. She noticed two spoons in the bowl. As they slurped the soggy, sweet cereal, Manas mentioned his plan to visit the Gariahata camp after breakfast.

'Can I come along?' Amala said.

'I would have loved it if you did. But...' Manas suggested it was best for Amala to stay at home. He had asked his mother if she could accompany him, but Mrinmoyee had said no.

'It will get better soon, Amu...' Manas began, but Amala cut him short with a soft, 'no worries, I understand.'

'I will try to be back by lunch,' Manas said apologetically.

'Only if you can. I don't mind the waiting, you know.'

Amala had been in this house for less than forty-eight hours, yet she missed work already. In the inert confinement of the room it occurred to her how much the routine of her work life stimulated her, despite all its stress. Other than during periods of illness, she had never sat idle. She understood that married life meant she probably couldn't venture out to earn a living; she didn't know a lot of married women belonging to Manas's social class who did. But every married woman she knew worked hard, even if only inside the house.

To cope with the monster of a listless day, Amala went to the balcony. She saw two women, not much older than her, talking to each other in the street. They seemed to be domestic helps; both had hitched their saris a little above their ankles and spoke loudly and with animated hand gestures. Amala looked away but kept her ears pressed in their direction. Although she couldn't catch everything they said, she could tell they were discussing the homes where they worked. At one point, she turned her head slightly and found the women looking in her direction. That was when she recognised one of them as Menoka, Dutta mansion's domestic help.

The way Menoka stared at her made Amala uncomfortable; she immediately walked back into the room and shut the balcony door. For an instant, despite everything—the bliss she had felt with Manas, the excess care and affection he showered on her, the happiness she had seen on his face in the time they had been together in this house—Amala wondered if she should have said 'No' to Manas's proposal. The room's walls closed in on her. *I won't be alive for too long here.*

Amala couldn't wrap her head around the fact that the person who was her liberator could also be her captor. At this moment though, Manas appeared to be exactly that. She noticed a window right above Manas's desk; somehow it had escaped her attention all this while. A set of twin drapes, the colour of forest green, hung over the closed window.

Amala walked over to the window and tried to open it. The cleat, rusty with age and disuse, stuck to the window frame stubbornly, and it took Amala quite a bit of effort to undo it. She shoved the window frame just a little while making sure the drapes fully covered the iron grills. Her attempt to take a nap was less successful, though. Sleep evaded her and she got a headache. She wished to distract herself with some sewing but didn't even have a needle and a reel of thread on hand.

The sound of a woman singing reached Amala's ears; she sat up and strained to listen. The music was playing in Dadu's room, she realised. On a radio, she guessed; it sounded different from the kind of songs she knew but wasn't unpleasant.

Amala spent two or maybe three hours, she wasn't sure, tossing and turning in the bed. At one point, the music stopped playing. She could hear Haraprasad and Mrinmoyee talking. Their voices sounded distant, yet she couldn't help but imagine that they were talking about her. A sudden knock on the door startled Amala and she sat up with a start. Her heart pounded but she couldn't muster the temerity to ask who it was as she opened the door. It was Sharoda, holding her plate of lunch.

'May I come in, Boumoni?' Sharoda asked.

Amala nodded yes and closed the door after Sharoda. 'You can keep the plate on that table,' she pointed to Manas's desk.

Sharoda put down the plate and drew closer to Amala. 'I need to tell you something, Ma.'

Mrinmoyee had asked Sharoda to let Amala know that she couldn't stand in the balcony. Amala flinched at the news but stopped herself from asking why. It had become clear to her that questioning Mrinmoyee wasn't just pointless, it could even be dangerous.

'All right, Mashi, I won't. Is there anything else I should know?'

'Na, Ma. Stay happy,' Sharoda said as she put her hand on Amala's shoulder. 'I will go now, still lots to do in the kitchen.'

The look of affection on her face made Amala feel choked with emotion.

Sharoda had covered the lunch with a steel plate that Amala didn't bother to remove. A couple more hours had passed when Amala woke up from the nap she had drifted into. It was past three and Manas still hadn't returned.

Amala's stomach hurt with hunger and her throat with thirst as she got up from the bed to help herself to a glass of water. She dragged herself to the corner where the earthen pitcher rested and had barely taken a sip of water when she heard Manas's voice humming a tune. Amala hastened but she didn't have to open the door to catch a glimpse of Manas; he pulled aside the window curtain and winked at Amala. Once he entered the room, Amala closed the door as well as the window overlooking the inside corridor. She opened the balcony door and kept it ajar. The closed space had almost stifled her.

Manas saw the covered plate on the table and said, 'So you didn't eat, I guess. Just as I had feared. Aren't you hungry?'

'I was waiting for you.'

'You have to eat, Amu. You can't keep starving like this,' Manas said, putting down a tote bag. 'Come now, let's eat.'

'Get me out of here. Please.' Amala said in a muted whisper as she sat beside Manas to eat. The cold, stiff grains of rice staring at them would put anyone off, but Manas gorged on the food. This time, Amala, too, consumed a lot more than mere nibbles.

'I'm going to, Amu, trust me. Your place is not in this room. You are required in Bijoy Nagar, at your workplace, in the world outside. But bear with me awhile. It's only fair that we give Ma a bit more time. If we hurry too much too soon, I fear we'll take a misstep.'

Besides going to the camp, Manas had also visited Chitra. 'Mashi has sent some stitching material that Purnima Mashi brought as gifts for you; she thought it might help you spend time here.'

A pale smile covered Amala's face. *I can always trust my Mashis.*

As they munched on the food, Manas introduced Amala to the various items on the plate: potato and ridge gourd in poppy seed paste, fried bitter gourd, red lentils with onion and garlic, prawn *malaikari*. Amala nodded; despite the generous infusion of sugar in the dishes, she ate heartily today. *Maybe I'll even get used to this.*

'*Shono*,' she said to Manas, 'will you go to our house in Bijoy Nagar tomorrow? Who knows how Mashi, Mesho and Urmi are doing? And Hablu....'

'I was thinking exactly the same thing. I planned to go today itself, then thought you must be waiting for me.'

~

Thanks to the stitching kit Purnima had put together for her, Amala found it a lot easier to bide her time the next day. The bag included several pieces of cotton cloth of different sizes, reels of different colours and types of threads, needles, crocheting equipment, a few printed design samples and even a hoop. Amala picked a design showing a small bird eating berries.

As she had done the day before, Amala closed the balcony window when Manas left in the morning and opened the window overlooking the corridor. She employed a simple back and satin stitch pattern to emulate the design on a parrot-green piece of cloth. She chose blue and red satin threads—red for the bird and blue for the fruits and branches. Working with needle and thread relaxed her in the same way as sitting by a pond or river did back in the village whenever she wrestled with a dilemma.

Sharoda brought lunch at the same time as the day before, and Amala even polished off more than half of the plate's contents without waiting for Manas. She still couldn't enjoy the food. Despite the best of meat and fish, which swam in liberal amounts of oil and ghee, Amala found it almost unpalatable. She longed for the simple food of her mother's, and later, Malati's kitchen— *panta bhaat* with a few fritters or fried small fish, a squirt of lime and raw onion slices. On some days, runny red lentils added to the taste of the cool, watery rice. What could she not do to have a bowl of *panta* instead of this royal feast?

She had finished eating and gone back to her stitching when Amala heard Haraprasad's voice. He seemed to be reasoning with Mrinmoyee to accept Manas's marriage. 'I agree this isn't the best way it could have happened, but we can't reverse it, Bouma.'

Mrinmoyee's tone sounded anything but conciliatory to Amala. 'I have no problem with that *shudra* girl staying in this house. Can't believe I'm being this kind. But Baba, with all due respect to you, I won't have that ugly *Bangaal* girl show up before people as Maanu's wedded wife.'

The needle pierced her finger and Amala smothered a yelp. She put down the needlework and closed the window. Throwing herself on the bed, she let a torrent of tears run loose. For the first time since coming to this city she felt *truly* unwanted. Not even when she and the other camp dwellers had to subsist on government dole and meagre, inedible food grain had she felt like this. She hated the idea of staying in a place where she wasn't even recognised as the wife of the man who had married her.

Amala remembered an episode one of her co-workers had once shared about overhearing two men in the bus who were discussing the problems caused by refugees in Kolkata. One of them said, 'It's not for no reason they say *du-chaar ghaa porle ghaare, Bangal tawbe bujhte paare.*' Amala recalled that she and her friend had laughed hard when they heard that; they had wondered what the man's suggestion of teaching East Bengalis a lesson with a thrashing would actually look like.

Now Amala knew. She felt the whiplash of Mrinmoyee's words even without being physically hit. When he had left in the morning, Manas had indicated he would not be back for lunch. Amala didn't expect him to return until later in the evening. But he was back at around four pm, tired and sweaty. Amala poured him a glass of water and opened the balcony door.

'Why didn't you open the other window like you did yesterday? The room is so stuffy,' Manas asked as he walked in the direction of the indoor window.

'Please!' Amala said, 'leave that one closed. I will tell you why.'

'What happened, Amu?' Manas asked. 'Did anyone trouble you?'

Moving closer to her, Manas gently held her face up. Amala put her head on his shoulder, drenching it with a stream of tears. Manas pressed her face firmly against his shoulder, stroking her head. 'I'm so sorry, Amu. I don't like it one bit to see you like...my dynamite Amu, who didn't shed tears when life put her through one difficult test after the other, is unhappy here. Makes me feel sick. This cannot go on.' Manas moved towards the door as if to exit the room.

'*Ogo*, don't...it will only increase our problems.'

'As if our problems are any less now. Don't stop me. Your tears aren't so cheap.'

'See, you're getting upset. It's nothing. I will get used to it. You talk to Ma when you are calmer. Please.' She added the words '*Lokkhi-ti*' at the end of her request.

The tactic seemed to work, for Manas began changing into his home clothes. He walked over to the desk where the lunch plate rested and lifted its cover.

'You didn't eat again?'

'Look carefully. I ate my portion.'

Manas looked at the plate and breathed a sigh of relief. 'Good girl. Never skip your meals, okay? You need strength to fight, not tears.'

'As you command, my master,' Amala said. She even faked a chuckle.

'It's a joke, is it? I would like to see you give it back to those who trouble you, just the way you did to me whenever you didn't like something I said. Do you hear?'

'Not joking, *goh*,' Amala said, her tone tender yet sincere. 'I mean to follow your advice. Always.'

'Good. Then come and help me out with the treats Malati Mashi sent for you.'

'What?' Amala leapt to the bed with a soft thud. Manas was taking out goodies from a cloth bag Malati had sent with him.

'How are they, Mashi, Mesho, Urmi....Did you meet Hablu Babu?'

'They are all fine. Your Hablu Babu misses you. I told him I will bring Amu Ma to meet him soon.'

A smile as round and big as their bell-metal meal plate lit up Amala's face; that hint of a promise in Manas's statement washed away all the humiliation she felt. What a joy it was to know that someone, especially a little person, loved her enough to miss her presence. Gorging on the puffed rice balls and coconut *narus* that Malati sent only enhanced that sticky, sweet feeling of bonding.

A summon from his mother altered Manas's routine the next morning. Mrinmoyee had planned a visit to Kalighat with her sister but woke up with a massive headache. She asked Manas to take her place in accompanying his aunt to the temple. Manas had been toying with the idea of visiting College Street and later Bijoy Nagar to volunteer at the school. He didn't mind the sudden change to his schedule; if anything, he looked forward to spending some time with Bawromashi. But his mother's headache worried him. She had had migraine attacks before but none in the recent past. Manas knew they were almost always triggered by excessive stress and lasted at least a couple of unrelenting days. At times, the severity of the pain prevented her from eating solid food as the pounding made her throw up. Medicines weren't of much use either; she had to bear it until it abated on its own.

Being an *ekadashi*, it was already a day of fasting for Mrinmoyee. She told Manas she planned to rest and asked him to let Sharoda know she needed nothing other than a jug of water by her bedside. When Manas suggested he stay at home to look after her, Mrinmoyee insisted he and Sreemoyee visit the temple as 'Didi had been looking forward to it all this while'.

Amala was in the shower when Manas left. As she climbed up the stairs and got closer to her mother-in-law's room, she found it closed from the inside. This appeared a bit odd; usually, the door was open with the curtain fully drawn and Amala could hear Mrinmoyee and Sreemoyee chatting as she quickly stepped over to her room, passing by Dadu's room.

Amala combed her hair, put on her *sindoor* and noticed the breakfast on the desk; Manas hadn't even touched it. She put two and two together and decided Manas had gone out along with his mother and aunt. A wave of relief passed through her at the thought of Mrinmoyee's temporary absence. Before sitting down to eat, she opened the corridor-facing window. Then, on an impulse, she also opened the balcony door and stood by its edge, still inside the room, to catch a snapshot of the street.

She couldn't see too much from where she stood but couldn't dare stepping out, not even when Mrinmoyee was away. What if Menoka saw her again? A cat's meowing intruded on her thoughts but she couldn't discern its location. Amala came back to the desk and sat in Manas's chair to eat her breakfast. She missed him yet felt a nourishing sense of wholeness in being able to listen to the mundane sounds of everyday life: the cat's meowing, people chatting, a rickshaw puller's holler. Through it all, she could feel the sound of Manas's voice reverberating with the promise to take her to Hablu and Bijoy Nagar. To the universe that had enabled her to make a living, however small, and even support a family. The universe where she envisioned being reunited with Kartik.

Amala took out her sewing work from a drawer attached to Manas's desk. The desk had three drawers; the bottom one held little but a few boxes of nails, and Manas suggested Amala use it to keep her things.

Amala had stitched out the outline of the bird and the branch on the piece of cloth she had chosen. She decided to leave the berries for the end. As she kept working at it, she remembered a boatman's song her father and Karim Chacha often sang. The song called upon one's spirit to renounce the trance of the world and return home, to the original abode. Amala began humming the tune, mostly in her mind. Tears glided down her cheeks as the memory of her father, enmeshed in that song, clouded her eyes. She always remained his favourite—he would defend her if her mother reproached her for being out too long with her friends. For every fight between Amala and her brother, Subimal invariably determined Kartik to be guilty. The day he caught enough small fish to bring some home, he asked Sumitra to cook it the way Amala liked it. The waves of memories, one cresting another, made it difficult for Amala to continue with the sewing. She put it aside and went to clean the bookshelf.

Amala picked up a duster hanging on the *alnaa* to wipe the books. She also arranged the books neatly, stacking the taller books behind the shorter ones. As she dusted it, one book caught her attention. The cover of the slim book showed the image of a forest path. Amala opened the book with the hope of finding more images but it only contained words, none of which she could read. She was about to place the book back on the shelf when she saw Dadu waving at her from outside the open window. Amala hastily pulled her sari's *anchal* over her head and bent it to convey her respect and greetings.

Haraprasad moved closer to the window and whispered, 'May I come in, Bouma?' Startled, Amala opened the door. He came in and shut the door soundlessly behind him.

'You may want to close the window, too,' he whispered to Amala. She did so even while suppressing her palpitation. Pulling her veil down a notch, she gently pushed Manas's study chair to offer Dadu a seat.

'Why don't you sit down, Bouma? And you don't have to cover your face like that,' Haraprasad said.

Amala sat down by the edge of the bed close to the bookshelf. She moved her *aanchal* back to reveal her face but didn't take it off. Her palms sweated as she tried to infer the cause of Haraprasad's sudden visit. Had someone caught her standing at the edge of the balcony door? Or was it her humming that had somehow flowed outside the room? Maybe he had come to tell her that she wasn't accepted as Manas's wife in the Dutta family. Amala wrung her clammy palms beneath her sari.

Haraprasad cleaned his glasses with the corner of his shawl. 'So, do you like to read, Bouma? Er, you must forgive me for catching you flipping through that book.'

Amala bit her lip to fight her mortification. 'I, I was only looking...I can...not read that.'

'Oh, I see,' Haraprasad said with a chuckle. 'What's wrong with that? Not everyone knows how to read English. Do you read Bengali?'

'*Haan*,' Amala said softly.

'See? There you go. Our Dadubhai reads mostly English books but we have a lot of Bengali books in the library. If you're interested, just let him know and he can fetch them for you.'

Amala didn't say anything but Haraprasad's tone eased her anxiety. 'Would you like to learn English? I can teach you if you want.'

'Me?' Amala couldn't contain her shock.

'It's not that difficult, Bouma. I can't promise you will start reading all those books as soon as you learn the alphabet but you'll be able to read some of them. What do you say?'

'*Aggey*, I don't know what to say. Err, would you like some water?' Amala realised she hadn't offered him any yet.

'Sure. I say you allow me to teach you some English. In return, you can tell me your stories. I know so little about you.'

As Amala took the glass of water to him, he said, 'Of course, you don't have to begin right away, and not at all if you don't want to. But think about it, Bouma. It will keep this old man busy.'

Amala smiled and waited for him to finish drinking the water so she could take the glass back from him.

'*Aaj tawbe ashi*, Bouma,' Haraprasad said, getting up. Amala bent to touch his feet and as he blessed her, he said, 'Thank you for letting me in. Do convey my love and blessings to Maanu, will you?'

'Will do, Dadu,' Amala said. As she closed the door, the fortuitous unfolding of the day made Amala feel like she was dreaming. If this was a dream, she didn't want to wake up from it. She left the dusting and went back to her sewing. Barely twenty minutes later, was it Manas's voice in the corridor she could hear? The other voice didn't sound like Mrinmoyee's so Amala imagined it must be Bawromashi's. She came and stood by the window but the conversation petered down as Manas edged closer to their room.

Manas had arrived close on the heels of lunch, which Amala anticipated Sharoda would bring soon. When she learned where he had been the entire morning and that Mrinmoyee had lain in her room all the while, the colour on her face drained. Manas chirped on about how good it was to spend time with Bawromashi after so long. Before passing a leaf packet of the temple *prasad* to Amala, he dipped his ring finger into the oily *sindoor* stuck on the leaf and put a dot on her forehead, then on her parting and the *loha* on her left wrist. Impressed with his knowledge of applying vermillion to a married woman, Amala bent down to touch his feet.

He pulled her up, holding her in a gentle embrace. 'Never do that, okay? How are you today? You look beautiful.'

'I'm the same I was three days ago,' Amala said, relaxing herself from his grip. '*You* are extra happy today.'

'That's not untrue,' Manas said. Then, drawing closer to Amala, he whispered, 'Maybe our problems with Ma will get sorted out.'

Amala's eyes lit up. 'Tell me more,' she whispered.

Manas winked at her and quickened his pace as he moved to close the window. Then he told Amala that he had had an open, heart-to-heart talk with his aunt. Manas had asked her directly if she thought the same way as his mother did regarding Amala's background. Bawromashi told him she approved; that she remembered what conjugal happiness meant from the two years of married life she'd experienced, before a snake bite had taken her husband's life.

Amala teared up, yet also felt more hopeful than she had in all her days in the Dutta mansion. From what Manas had told her, she knew Mrinmoyee and her sister shared a strong bond.

Manas held open the *prasad* packet before Amala. 'Here, have some. Mashi said that with Ma Kali's blessings, all will be well.'

Amala picked up a piece of banana, and after touching it to her forehead, put it into her mouth.

The tempest she had been hurled into during the past two years, beginning with the death of her parents, the riots, losing Kartik...had made Amala indifferent, if not completely averse, to faith. She still responded to it but only in a secondary capacity, like the time when Chitra took her to Dakshineshwar or now, partaking of the *prasad* Manas brought for her. At this moment, though, she wanted to believe and latch on to every fragment of faith she could find—Dadu's affection, Manas receiving Bawromashi's approval, the *prasad* from Kalighat.

Manas decided to spend the rest of the day at home, which, to Amala tasted like the *nolen gur* rice pudding that came at the end of the scrumptious meal the day had turned out to be for her. She told Manas about Haraprasad's surprise visit. The delight on Amala's face when she heard about Manas's chat with Bawromashi paled in comparison to the way Manas reacted when Amala told him about Dadu's offer to teach her English. He could hardly believe his ears.

Hadn't Dadu told him in a cold voice not too long ago that his match with Amala was unacceptable to him? True, he had invited the two of them for breakfast, but to Manas that was only a gesture of Haraprasad's aristocratic courtesy. For the same man to have come into their room and engaged in a conversation with Amala was no less than a triumph for Manas.

'So, what did you say?' he asked Amala.

'Nothing. I didn't know what to say.'

'Well, you had to say yes, what else? The next time he asks, just say yes, all right?'

Amala couldn't decide what value learning English would add to her life but to keep Manas happy she said she would.

Manas spent part of his evening in the library at home, then went to Bijoy Nagar. He didn't tell Amala but Santu had told him during his visit the day before that the man who had troubled Amala kept coming back to Bijoy Nagar. When Ganesh and a few other men confronted him, he had said he had only stopped by to have tea at Santu's stall.

The man had come alone, Santu said, and left soon after being approached. He also asked Santu if he was interested in a well-paying job at an office. Santu confided in Manas that he told the man, who had identified himself as Noton-da, that he needed some time to think. He asked Manas what he could tell the man if he asked him the question again.

'Tell him, you haven't decided yet,' Manas told him as he sipped his tea. He needed to find out the man's real intentions.

21

The beam of light that had entered Amala's world in the form of Haraprasad continued to warm her days. He dropped by every morning, armed with training material: flashcards of the English alphabet, newspapers, books. On the very first day of the lessons, he gave Amala a new notebook, a pack of pencils, a sharpener and an eraser. He took an easy, unhurried approach but found in Amala a keen student who learned fast and was hungry for more.

Each day, Amala tidied up the room before he came in, folding items of clothing Manas left hanging on his chair or the *alnaa*; putting the books he took off the shelf back on it; and mopping the room. She had seen Menoka clean the other rooms in the house but never hers and Manas's. Amala didn't mind doing the work herself; she preferred it that way.

The lessons had none of the stiffness of a school classroom. Amala shared with Dadu stories from her village days, some of which she carefully censored. He had also become aware of her sewing skills as he caught her embroidering one day. Occasionally, he asked to see her work in progress. She asked him about the music that played in his room and learned it came from a machine called the gramophone, not the radio. By entering into a tacit understanding with Photik, Haraprasad made arrangements for a daily delivery of tea and light snacks during the lessons. This, Amala didn't mind at all.

Amala suspected Sharoda had a hand in the refreshments, at least sometimes. Although Photik mostly brought sugary cream biscuits for Amala and sugarless cream crackers for Dadu, there were days when there would be freshly-fried *beguni* or some *ghugni*, and on one day, delicious *maccher chawp*, fish croquettes wrapped in a crispy potato jacket. Amala couldn't imagine Photik, with his head mostly in the clouds, to be so thoughtful as to bring these special delicacies.

Despite this inlet of light, the cloud of her mother-in-law's fury retained its ironclad grip on Amala. Neither she nor Manas noticed any change in Mrinmoyee's stance following Manas's visit to Kalighat with Sreemoyee. At times Amala felt a desperate need to have a word with Bawromashi. She restrained herself when it occurred to her that little had come out of Manas's chat with Sreemoyee.

One day, while Amala practised writing the letters she had learned thus far, her eyes caught someone's outline outside their room. She couldn't see anyone through the window and brought her attention back to her notebook. Haraprasad remained engrossed in reading the newspaper he'd brought with him. The next instant, Amala's eyes again detected a movement outside the room. She looked up and saw Menoka flitting over to the other side of the corridor, towards Haraprasad's and Mrinmoyee's rooms.

Amala's heart sank. She didn't mean to alarm Haraprasad and pretended to keep her focus on her writing, though she could no longer concentrate. She scribbled something, then kept rubbing it furiously until she gave up and requested Dadu to end the class as she felt like resting. Haraprasad agreed; he could do with a nap, too.

The next day, in the window of time between when Manas left in the morning and Haraprasad came to teach her, someone knocked on Amala's door. '*Ma thakurun* has asked you to go to her room,' Menoka said. She didn't make any eye contact and walked off without waiting for Amala's response.

Amala couldn't help but wonder if the maid had been instructed to come at a time when she would be alone in the room. Before changing, she helped herself to a glass of water and took a deep breath. She opened her purse and checked how much money she had; Manas had left a decent amount with her for emergencies. She could easily take a taxi to Bijoy Nagar....

Amala draped a blue and pink cotton sari, a gift from Snehalata, and made sure to cover her head before approaching Mrinmoyee's room. As usual, the door was open and the curtains fully drawn. Amala knocked on the door softly.

'Come in,' Mrinmoyee's stern voice said.

Amala drew apart the curtain and entered the room. She found Mrinmoyee reclined sideways on the bed, supporting her elbow on a pillow and her raised head on her palm. Amala didn't see Sreemoyee in the room.

'Sit,' Mrinmoyee said as she chewed on the *paan* in her mouth. Amala looked around and saw no chair, stool or any other furniture to sit on.

'What happened?' Mrinmoyee snarled. 'Sit down.'

Amala realised she had been commanded to sit on the floor; this time, Mrinmoyee motioned with her eyes to indicate that.

Amala sat down on the bare floor, her head held down. She put her left palm on the floor beside her and clenched her right fist.

'So, girl, tell me about yourself. What's your name?'

Amala froze. The brusqueness of Mrinmoyee's tone cut through the selfsame air of the morning Amala had started getting used to. The chirp of mynas and sparrows, the clanking of vessels, the bark of a lost mongrel, the chatter of maids, rickshaw pullers, office-goers—the sounds that had become a part of Amala's new mornings were slashed by the razor of Mrinmoyee's words. She couldn't say anything.

'What happened? Cat got your tongue?' Mrinmoyee's tone softened. She turned around to pick up the box of *paan* lying next to her on the bed and plopped a pre-made *paan* into her mouth. 'Want one?' she asked Amala, extending the box towards her. Amala shook her head to say no.

'Don't be afraid; I won't do you any harm,' Mrinmoyee said, clearing her throat emphatically. 'Tell me about yourself. Where are you from?'

The change in her tone made Amala feel better and she opened up, bit by bit. And just like that, she told her entire life story, from her childhood in the village to her parents' death, the riots, the camp, meeting Manas, everything. The only piece she withheld was Kartik. She didn't dare look up at her but from whatever she could read of Mrinmoyee's demeanour, Amala surmised what she really wanted to know was how or rather *why* Manas and Amala were together.

'Look here, girl, I know you've had a hard time. I don't want to make it any harder for you. But you need to understand one thing. This marriage with Maanu that you're talking about, it's nonsense. No one in our society will ever accept you as his wedded wife. You and he simply don't belong in the same place. You see what I mean, don't you?'

Without waiting for a response, Mrinmoyee continued, 'My Maanu is pure gold. But his problem is he's a bit too soft of heart. He sees someone in trouble and runs to save them. Whatever happened was because of his kindness. Nothing more. This will wear off; how can he ever bring you in front of our relatives and friends?

'The best thing for you would be to leave this house, girl. I will make arrangements so you are taken safely to wherever you came from. Don't worry, I will make sure you have enough money for the next little while. You will also get some jewellery, for the money won't last forever. But forget you ever had anything to do with Maanu.'

Amala made every effort to not break down but could do little to stop fat drops of tears from falling to the ground.

'Worry not,' Mrinmoyee said. 'I'm not asking you to leave right now. I will have to consult our family astrologer to decide when it will be. You will be given enough notice. But be prepared.'

Amala got up, wiping her tears from the floor with her sari. As she turned to leave, Mrinmoyee said, 'One more thing. What just happened must not go beyond the walls of this room. You will remember that, won't you?'

Amala felt a noose strangling her throat. She left the room as quietly as she had entered it. Dragging herself to her room, she closed the door, then the open window and flung herself across the bed. There she remained all day, not getting up when Haraprasad came at the appointed hour. She didn't get up when Sharoda brought lunch in the afternoon. The elderly woman kept calling her name, but Amala remained unmoved, as if her limbs were paralysed.

Manas returned late in the afternoon with a packet of roasted chickpeas. 'Here, see, I saved most of the *chhola bhaaja* for you.' He said to Amala, handing her the packet.

Amala put the packet on the desk and turned her head to the side. 'Would you like some water?' she asked him, her voice still dry and choking.

'Not water. I need something to eat, so hungry today.'

Manas went on to tell Amala how his day had been spent visiting the college to meet with a professor, then tagging along with a friend who had to buy some books from College Street.

'Where's your *prasad* from lunch?' Manas asked as he looked at his desk and found the plate of food, usually there every day, missing.

'Oh,' Amala said, still distracted. 'I didn't eat today, wasn't feeling too well. Will you go to the kitchen and get something for yourself?'

'What happened to your voice, do you have a cold?' Manas said, moving closer to her. He saw Amala's face, pale from dried, flaky tears. The part of the bed sheet next to where Amala sat, soggy and rumpled, also caught his attention.

Wrapping his arms around Amala, Manas asked, 'What's wrong? Tell me. You've been crying. Who is it? Dadu? Sharoda Mashi...no, it can't be her. Ma. Ma must have said something.'

'Nobody said anything. I was missing my parents. Now, will you get something for yourself to eat?'

'I will, indeed, for I'm too hungry. But you'll have to tell me what happened,' Manas said, leaving the room in a huff. He returned within minutes, holding the big plate of food Sharoda had prepared for them.

'Come and eat with me. Or I won't touch anything on this plate.'

Amala did as asked, even though she couldn't get too far with the nibbling before yet another sob attack overpowered her. She quickly wiped her tears and took a sip of water.

Manas sat down next to her. Putting his arms around her, he said, 'Ma said something to you today. I know it can't be anything nice. What did she say?'

'I told you nobody said anything.'

'Photik saw you entering Ma's room. And Sharoda Mashi told me you didn't open the door when she brought lunch even though she kept knocking and calling your name. Tell me, what did Ma say?'

Amala didn't respond.

'It's important for me to know, Amu. I'm responsible for your wellbeing. If you don't tell me, how will we resolve this?'

'I don't feel like talking. It's no use. Please don't force me,' Amala said, releasing his arm off her as she lay away from Manas.

'Very well then,' Manas said, taking the plate and storming out of the room. He didn't care to close the door after him; Amala didn't either.

Not too long after he had left, Manas's voice reverberated in Amala's ears. He was talking to his mother. The open door carried the sound of their conversation loud and clear.

'I don't like your tone, Maanu. Have you come here as a police *daroga*?' Mrinmoyee said.

'I am only asking you what you said to her. She won't tell me anything but I know she's been crying.'

'Well, if she hasn't said anything, that's the end of the story. Besides, do I have to report to you everything I say to a stranger?'

'Stranger? Ma! Are you out of your mind? You know that I married her, right? Your not accepting her as your daughter-in-law doesn't change the fact that she's my wife. The sooner you accept *that*, the better it will be for all of us.'

'I ask that you leave my room, Maanu. I won't have you talk to me like that for that clay pot of a girl who's not even fit to clean my toenail.'

'Ma!' Manas shouted. 'Please don't force me to lose all my respect for you.' He left the scene like a sheaf of sheets in a storm's path.

Amala came to the door; she saw Haraprasad standing in the corridor, too. As Manas came out of Mrinmoyee's room, the door was banged shut behind him. Haraprasad put his hand on Manas's shoulder, tapping it a few times. Amala retreated to the bed. She felt more afraid than ever; even Manas, red in the face and flaming, frightened her.

⁓

As they both tossed and turned in the bed that night, Amala said to Manas, 'Take me to Bijoy Nagar tomorrow. I think that's the best thing to do.'

'Hmm,' Manas said in a sleepy voice. Amala couldn't decide if he meant yes, or merely acknowledged hearing her question.

Manas got up before Amala. He couldn't resolve the tangled mess of his thoughts. He considered Amala's request to take her to Bijoy Nagar but felt conflicted about it. Pouring himself a glass of water, he drank it in quick sips while pacing along the small stretch from the balcony door to the inside door. As he pushed back a shock of hair falling on his forehead, he saw something lying at the door. In the soft light of the dawn, he couldn't tell what it was, other than a piece of paper. He bent to pick it up, a letter addressed to him. *Who would drop a letter for me in my room?* The handwriting didn't ring a bell. Manas flipped over the envelope and walked towards the balcony. He didn't want to wake up Amala by switching on the light.

Quietly unlatching the door, Manas stepped out to the balcony. The backside of the envelope had no name or signature. Manas

tore open the envelope. The letter rattled Manas even more and
shook the slumber off every cell in his body.

> *My dear Maanu,*
>
> *By the time you see this letter, I would have left the house, on my*
> *way home. I didn't have a chance to talk to you before leaving, hence*
> *the letter. I know you have a lot going on, I didn't want to burden you*
> *with more.*
>
> *After our visit to Kalighat the other day, I tried my best to make*
> *your mother see your viewpoint. But she didn't think it was a good*
> *idea for me to speak on your behalf. I must respectfully accept that she*
> *is your mother and has a bigger right over you than me.*
>
> *As for your journey ahead, Maanu, all I can say based on my own*
> *life is that in the end, we are all alone. We come alone and we leave*
> *alone, and in the time between our arrival and departure, most of our*
> *life's directions must be determined by our own actions and decisions.*
> *That is how I have known to live this long life of mine, and good or*
> *bad, the path I have travelled on has been one I accepted as mine and*
> *decided to walk on.*
>
> *With all my blessings for the two of you,*
> ***Your Bawromashi.***

Manas felt a stabbing pain as he finished reading the letter. At the
same time, the words from his aunt helped untangle the knot his
mind had been tied up into. He read the letter twice, then once
more. It had no time or date stamp but Manas knew it had been
written in the last day or two. He had a sudden urge to rush to his
mother's room, where he knew Sreemoyee slept. But he stopped
himself from doing so. *If she could meet me, she wouldn't write this*
letter.

His mind made up, Manas went back to the bed and wrapped
his arm around Amala. Happy surprise. She offered little
resistance, as if she were expecting him to embrace her.

'Did you get any sleep?' Amala asked.

'Not much. You?'

'The same.'

'Us owls,' Manas said and recited, to Amala's horror and amusement, Sukumar Roy's limerick on a male owl waxing romantic to his female partner on how lovely her screech sounded.

Amala grinned. 'Will you take me to Bijoy Nagar today?'

'Amu, give me a little more time...just a few days, *lokkhi meye*. I will find a way for us. Did you know my results are out in three days?'

The abruptness of this information puzzled Amala. She didn't know how that was linked to their present crisis but trusted it did.

'You know where to find me if you don't see me here, don't you?' She asked.

'What do you mean? Are you planning to run away?'

'No. Just letting you know that if I'm not in the house, I will be in Bijoy Nagar.'

'You're not going anywhere. Get that out of your head. I know it's tough for you, but if you do something like that, I'd be really hurt.'

'I won't run away. It's still good for you to know where to find me, in case....'

'Can we stop this conversation?' Manas said. 'I'm sad as it is. Bawromashi.... See this,' He handed the letter to Amala.

Amala sighed as she read the letter. 'I didn't even get to know her. See, all this is because of me.'

'Not you alone, it's us. But see, Bawromashi loves you. She blessed both of us.'

'I would love to meet her someday. Who knows...she might like me.'

'I have no doubt that she already likes you, Amu,' Manas said, patting Amala on her shoulder. 'Now let me see if I can get some tea organised for us.'

'I wouldn't mind that,' Amala said. 'Where will you find tea at this early hour, though? Sharoda Mashi isn't there yet, is she?'

'Your useless husband does have a few cooking skills, Madam.'

Manas not only made the drink with minimum fuss, he even smuggled it to their room in a flask. The tea revitalised Amala. Mingled with the first specks of light filtering through the half-open balcony door, it also brought her fresh appreciation for the man she had married. In less than a month of their living together, he had waited for her to open herself up to him, fed her, made her tea, stood up for her. Could it get any better?

Manas decided not to leave during the day. In Sreemoyee's absence, he feared his mother might go after Amala again. He also wanted to find out what prompted his aunt's sudden departure. He would have asked Mrinmoyee but given their argument the previous evening, thought better of it. He spent most of his day in the library, from where he called Proshanto. Their graduation results would be out soon, and Manas told Proshanto he desperately needed a job. Without revealing too many details, Manas gave Proshanto enough indication of how things were at home.

'I understand,' Proshanto said and told Manas he would keep him in mind if he came across any suitable job opening.

The conversation with Proshanto helped Manas find his balance. What a blessing to have friends to lean on at a time like this.

The decision to not get out of the house for two days made Manas restless, especially with the anticipation of university results on his mind. He spent most of his time reading, scouring the newspaper for employment classifieds, and making a to-do list for the coming week.

Haraprasad came to teach Amala at the regular hour. Amala learned to write a new set of letters. Impressed with her progress, Haraprasad began teaching her words with the letters she had already learned. The words he chose were easy enough, and he told her the meaning in Bangla, which she wrote down next to the English word. He made sure they weren't the typical fruit and animal names children were taught but everyday items Amala was more familiar with.

Despite this semblance of normalcy, Amala reeled in fear from her exchange with Mrinmoyee. She felt her days in this house were numbered. Sreemoyee's sudden departure only added to her anxiety.

On the eve of his graduation results, Manas went to his grandfather's room. He hadn't had a chance to talk to Dadu since the breakfast they had eaten together the morning after his wedding. Manas picked a time when Mrinmoyee would be downstairs, first in the puja room for her evening prayers and then the kitchen, to provide instructions to Sharoda and supervise dinner preparations.

'How are you, Dadubhai? Long time, no see,' Haraprasad said as he welcomed Manas in.

'In need of your blessings, Dadu,' Manas said, touching Haraprasad's feet. 'My results are out tomorrow.'

'Is that so? Well, I have no doubt you will come out with flying colours. As for blessings, you have all my *ashirbaad*. Divided by two, ha, ha, ha.'

'That will be more than enough. And thank you on behalf of the recipient of the other half of your ashirbaad.'

'She is my student, and a rather bright one at that.'

'I'm a bit envious, Dadu,' Manas said. 'That she gets to be your student. Without even asking.'

'Keeps me employed, Dadubhai. At my age, that's a blessing.'

In the midst of all this banter, Manas asked Haraprasad the question that had intrigued him since his grandfather's earliest interaction with Amala. 'What made you change your mind about my wife, Dadu? You had said the marriage would be unacceptable to you.'

Manas saw an enigmatic smile on his grandfather's face. Haraprasad remained silent for a few minutes, and then said, 'I gave you my opinion as you asked for it. That was then.' He paused, but a hint of smile still lined his lips. 'When you chose to go your way, my wisdom lay in accepting your choice.'

'Was it just that, Dadu?'

'Well, yes. But that wisdom didn't come to me in a day, Dadubhai. Sometimes when two strangers are forced to live out their lives with each other, the result can be wonderful. But there are also times when it doesn't work that well. In your case, you went against every convention to marry a person of your choice. A person you loved. Something told me there was a seed of happiness in it that could grow into something beautiful if just allowed to nourish. Who am I to stop that from happening?'

The warmth in his words made Manas so giddy that he broke into a wide grin despite himself. He didn't miss Haraprasad's veiled reference to the relationship between his parents. Before leaving the room, Manas made a request. Could Dadu have Photik deliver the newspaper to Manas first thing in the morning? The servant boy usually brought the paper to Haraprasad along with a glass of warm honey-lemon water.

'Sure, I will have it sent to you. But promise you will come and give me the good news?' Haraprasad said.

'If I pass, I surely will, Dadu,' Manas said, taking his leave.

The next morning as he scanned the newspaper's tiny lettering to make sure he looked at his roll number and no one else's, Manas leapt from the bed and lifted Amala, still half asleep, in his arms. He gave her a whirl until she screamed for him to put her down. The result delighted him: first class first.

Running over to Haraprasad, Manas announced the news loudly enough for his mother to hear him in the next room. He sprinted down the stairs to share his joy with Sharoda and requested her to ask Nando to bring three boxes of sweets.

He handed two ten-rupee notes to Sharoda, despite all her protestations and hurried to the library to call Proshanto. Manas waited in the library until Nando returned from the market with the sweets. As soon as he saw him enter through the door, Manas followed him to the kitchen. Opening one of the boxes, he picked up a piece of *chamcham* and put it in a bowl for Amala. He asked Sharoda and Nando to distribute the rest of the box's contents to everyone in the house, while he grabbed the two other boxes.

After a quick shower and breakfast with Amala, Manas headed out for the first time in three days.

While Manas spent the day distributing sweets to Chitra and Malati and gallivanting around the city with Subir to submit applications for jobs, Amala received a notice from Mrinmoyee to leave the house. This time, Mrinmoyee came to Amala's room and asked her to be prepared to be dropped off to where she came from within the next week.

'But I can't leave without letting your son know, Ma. He's my husband,' Amala said. She didn't bother covering her head.

'I see. So you have a tongue, don't you? You can cut out the "Ma", girl. Don't forget it's only because of my son's generosity that you're still in this house. You don't belong here, not even as a servant's servant. Get that? Don't you dare ruin the bright future that's ahead of Maanu. I told you, you will be paid well.' Mrinmoyee left the room reiterating the steely warning that Amala should keep the conversation to herself. Or else.

When Manas returned that day, tired and full of stories and more goodies for Amala, she had only one request for him, to please stay at home for the next few days. Manas figured out his mother had created fresh trouble for Amala but told her he had to go out job-hunting. When he decided to confront his mother, Amala stopped him.

'Just hold your ground, Amu, however difficult it may be. You won't have to bear this nonsense for too long, I promise.'

Manas's frenetic job search over the next four days took him not only to different offices, but also to friends and acquaintances. On the fifth day, a lead came from a person he hadn't approached at all. Manas went to college to view his detailed result and chanced upon Professor Gupta, the teacher who had enthralled Manas and the entire classroom with his impassioned lectures.

The professor asked Manas what his plans were, now that he had performed so well. When he heard about Manas's intention to start working, he wrote down a name and address for him and asked him to go for an interview that very morning. A boy's school in Narendrapur required a history teacher for its senior classes and professor Gupta felt Manas stood a good chance. He even offered to write him a note of recommendation. Manas thanked him but decided to try his luck without the letter first.

Manas returned home after sundown that day, much later than usual. The exhaustion in his body made him want to hit the sack without eating dinner. He yielded to his body's call and landed on the bed next to where Amala sat with her embroidery and alphabet book. Manas lay down, leaning against her waist and said, 'So, how are your lessons going?'

'You look tired,' Amala said. 'What took you so long, Maanu Babu?'

Manas turned his head to meet her face. 'Say that again? Did you just call your husband by his name?'

'*Ei jah!*' Amala said, biting her tongue, alarmed at her transgression.

'You will have to pay for it. Go, bring your husband a nice, hot cup of tea right now.'

'How can I? You know I'm not allowed in the kitchen.'

'I don't know. I need tea, and you're going to get me some. Aren't you obligated to, as a wife?'

'You're making fun of me, are you?'

'No, Ma'am. I am serious. I want you to ask Sharoda Mashi to have a cup of tea sent for me. Why don't you make that two cups of tea and some *muri-makha*? You might even get a prize if you did.'

Amala got up and tiptoed her way out of the room and went downstairs. Pretending to use the bathroom, she first checked if Menoka was around. She wasn't, it was way past her utensil-washing time. Amala then looked up at the balcony in the direction of Mrinmoyee's room. No lady of the house; instead Manas had come and stood outside their room. As their eyes locked for a second, he motioned 'Go on' to her.

Amala repeated a prayer in her mind and moved towards the kitchen. Drawing closer to the entrance, she peeped in to look for Sharoda. Just at that instant, Photik emerged from the kitchen with evening snacks for Haraprasad. Startled by Amala's presence, he nearly tripped before regaining his balance.

Amala stepped back and whispered, 'Please bring some tea and *muri-makha* for your Dadababu,' and dashed to the bathroom without waiting to see if her request had registered with Photik or not.

She took her time in the bathroom even though she didn't need to. Back in their room, she found Manas leaning back against pillows by the headrest of their bed, engrossed in reading something.

'Give that to me!' Amala said when she realised her notebook had his attention.

'Wow—you've made good progress I see,' he said without looking at her. 'And by the way, good job on the tea. Photik said he will bring it soon.'

'Give my notebook back,' Amala said, her face a blushing hibiscus. She had never shown her writing to Manas and felt like a school kid whose errors had landed in the hand of the headmaster.

'*B for boat* and *F for fish*. These are clearly your favourite words; you have written them more than all the other words.'

Amala snatched the notebook from him. 'Where is my reward?' She demanded. 'Your tea will be here as you mentioned.'

'Listen,' Manas said, making Amala sit beside her. 'Your useless man has found himself a job.'

'What?' Amala's face ballooned into a bursting sun that shone through *ashadh's* dark clouds.

22

The week Manas joined work tested him and Amala in more ways than their entire month of marriage had. Manas's first day off work, Sunday, came only two days after he'd started. He went to his mother to give her the news of his employment; enough time had passed since their last interaction. He hoped the news would help her see his seriousness to settle down as a married man. He also meant to ask her about Bawromashi. His optimism would be shortlived.

'It pains me to see that despite such good upbringing and education, this is what has become of you, Maanu,' Mrinmoyee said to Manas. 'I have seen more life than you. I know your relationship with that *chhotolok* girl isn't going to last. I will never accept her as the bride of my only son, the heir of the Dutta family. Not even if my father-in-law or sister asked me to.'

Manas sighed. It was pointless to discuss this anymore with her. If she ever changed her mind, it won't be because of his or anyone else's persuasions; he knew that much about his mother.

And so as Manas kept at his job, leaving early in the morning and returning late in the evening with two hours of commute each way via local buses, Amala shrank. Despite Dadu's daily doses of affection. Despite the snacks Sharoda and Photik smuggled into her room. Despite the needlework that kept her company when Manas couldn't.

Following her latest spat with Manas, Mrinmoyee had had Amala's lunch reduced to a small bowl of rice and some cold lentils. Her threats and curses at Amala became more frequent, direct and audible to all.

Soon it became too much to bear and Amala started skipping lunch. Given how tired Manas would be, she didn't want to nag him. Instead, she poured her sorrow into a diary.

Hunger wasn't new to her but the forced deprivation made her yearn for the dishes her mother cooked. She began to record them, one entry every day. It was as if the food of her memory had become inseparable with the loss of the very things she had once known as her own—village, home, rivers. Freedom.

~

On the Friday of his first full working week, Manas returned early and asked Amala to get ready.

'Where are we going?'

'To be together, that's where. Hurry up, we need to pack our bags; I have the driver waiting downstairs.'

Manas told Amala how lucky he had been to find the very man who had driven them home as a just-married couple at the local taxi stand. He also showed her a stove and a bottle of kerosene, both gifts from Chitra. Manas had gone to share the news of his employment with her, and she forced him to take the stove and fuel. 'You will at least need some tea,' Chitra had said.

Amala probed no further. Something about the waiting taxi and 'being together' took her to a happy place. While stuffing their things into the trunk that had come with her, she asked Manas, 'We'll meet Dadu before...won't we?'

'Of course. Come, let me help you there,' he said, piling the *alnaa* clothes into the trunk.

The packing took no more than twenty minutes. Amala changed her sari and covered her head as she and Manas went to see Haraprasad.

'Dadu, we're moving out,' Manas said.

'Out? Was that necessary, Dadubhai?' Haraprasad asked.

'Yes. At least for now it is. For the sanity and well-being of everyone in this house.'

Haraprasad muffled a sigh and said, looking first at Manas, then at Amala, 'I hope you can return soon.'

Manas clasped his grandfather's hands even as Amala presented to him the finished embroidery she'd been working on. She had signed her name in small letters at the bottom. He held her in a warm embrace.

'This is my most precious gift ever, Didibhai.'

'Your *guru-dakshina*,' Amala said, fighting a sob.

~

Manas and Amala moved into the back of a house in Bidhannagar, close to Amala's workplace. It had a single room, a toilet and a bathroom. The landlord lived in the upper floor of the house while the lower front portion had been rented out to another family. For their kitchen, Manas and Amala had a dank, unventilated corner under the staircase. A passage separated their portion from the front of the house. Though it had only one window, the room looked spacious enough to Amala.

'For now, this is all we can afford, Amu. I know you must feel cheated. I feel a bit like that myself.'

'This is it, you know. This is just *it*.' Amala's voice rose through a whisper as she looked with tears of joy at her new room with its shoebox window opening to the eastern sky. 'This is the dream I never dared to dream since I lost Ma and Baba. And Kartik.'

'Well, I better go out and get us some sheets and pillows. Oh, and a mosquito net, too, or those pesky bugs won't let you have any dreams at all,' Manas quipped.

'Can I start going to work now?' Amala asked.

'You sure can. You will have to agree to save all your money, though. We can manage with my salary. There's also the task of finding Kartik, right? We'd better save some money for him.'

~

When Amala asked to visit Bijoy Nagar that evening, Manas persuaded her to accompany him to the market instead. They needed to buy some household items first. 'You know how good my knowledge is in that department. I need your help,' Manas said.

Amala was glad she agreed. The two hours she spent with Manas at the local market brought her equal amounts of exhaustion and joy. She had shopped many times before, for utility items when she practically ran Malati's household in Bijoy Nagar, and also with Manas at New Market. But this excursion to buy bedding, utensils, bath soaps, a quilt and a mosquito net for her own household gave her a rare thrill, a memory she wanted to preserve like the scent of Manas in his unwashed shirt.

When she and Manas made love that night, Amala felt the very last shred of resistance melting off her body.

~

Despite getting little sleep and waking up with limbs leaden with the fatigue of sleeping on a cold floor, Amala perked up at Manas's suggestion. He wanted her to go with him to his school. Manas had already done his homework. He only had three classes on Saturdays and had asked the principal if he could bring Amala to the school. Mr Dasgupta not only welcomed the idea; he even advised Manas to introduce her to the students. With the school's ongoing volunteering initiatives with refugees involving older boys, the principal thought it would be a good idea to have them interact with Amala and get an overview of Bijoy Nagar.

Manas introduced Amala to the first class on his schedule. Then, while he taught, she waited in the library. When Manas went there some half an hour later, he found Amala sunk in a magazine. He had a break before his next class and spent the time with her in the library. She remained engrossed in the magazine's recipes; he prepared lecture notes.

The next class Manas took Amala to had older boys. Manas began introducing them to her. They conveyed their greetings with namaskars, which Amala returned with an easy smile. As they gently made their way towards the back rows, one of the boys disrupted the ordinariness of the decorum. He dashed to the front and looked straight into Amala's eyes.

'What happened, Nabin?' Manas asked, a little taken aback by the boy's unwarranted leap. 'This is Nabin,' Manas introduced the boy to Amala. 'He likes to give me a hard time with his questions.'

'Nabin? Who's Nabin? This is Kartik, *my* Kartik,' Amala squealed as she grabbed the boy and held him tight, drenching him with a barrel of tears.

When he heard the story of the miraculous sibling reunion, the principal considered Manas's request to let him take Nabin home, who had been living in the school's hostel from the time of his enrolment about a couple of months ago. Mr. Dasgupta said he trusted Manas's word but would need some other proof to establish Amala and Nabin were indeed related. Amala had nothing to show for proof. But when the principal asked Nabin, who had been waiting outside to come in, the boy said he wanted to show him something. He took out a notebook from his bag and opened its pages to several sketches he had made of his sister during the time they had been separated. Astonished at the accuracy with which the boy had drawn Amala's portrait, the principal allowed him to be in Manas and Amala's care.

~

If Amala thought she had been on a rollercoaster all this while, when she heard Kartik's story, she saw her journey as a fairytale. As the three of them returned home in a taxi, Kartik recalled the moment of horror that separated Amala and him. While he waited for her at Sealdah station that sultry April day a year ago, a group of men came and asked Kartik to come with them. When he protested saying he had to wait for his sister, they grabbed and whisked him away to the locality where they lived. He was made to pick rags for no money and barely one meal a day. This went on for three months.

One day, while on the job, Kartik found his way to a refugee camp and never went back. He had been at the camp in Bagjogla for about six months when a group of social workers arrived there. Eventually they had him and a few other boys admitted to the school where he now studied. The school had a basic hostel for orphan boys, and that was where Kartik was placed. Like Amala, Kartik had searched for his sister a lot, and like her, shed rivers of tears.

'How did you become, Nabin?' Manas asked. 'Did the teachers not like your name?'

'No. I changed it. I never told anyone my real name out of fear,' Kartik said, still awkward to admit the fact to his teacher.

'Isn't he a smart one?' Amala said as she ruffled Kartik's hair and gave him a peck while putting down an enamelled plate holding three cups of tea she had just made in her yet-to-be-set-up kitchen.

The three of them sat on a straw mat spread on the floor and for the first time, Amala surprised Manas with her loquacity. She and Kartik didn't seem to tire of sharing their stories.

'Will we keep chatting away into the night, or do we plan to get some sleep, too?' Manas asked the brother-sister duo.

'I don't think I'll get a wink tonight,' Amala said.

23

She slept soundly for a good seven or eight hours, wrapped around Manas and well-guarded by the mosquito net, until Mrinmoyee interrupted her slumber. Annoyed, Amala got up and headed to the bathroom. As she combed her hair before exiting the bathroom, Kartik's face, swimming in innocent sleep, lifted her mood. She woke him up with a gentle nudge.

Manas was still in bed. Amala stirred him too to get up; he demanded a cup of tea.

'No tea without washing your mouth first,' Amala told him.

'What? I always have the first cup of tea in my bed.'

'You used to. Not any longer.'

Manas thought better than to argue. He knew who the boss was in their new house. After a round of tea and biscuits, the three of them took quick showers and got ready.

~

Despite starting early, it took them more than an hour to reach Bijoy Nagar. Just walking to the bus stop from their house and then from the Mandir Tala bus stop where they disembarked to Malati's house in Bijoy Nagar took up a good ten minutes of their commute time.

Even from a distance, Malati's porch announced to Amala a warm welcome. She could see Malati putting *boris* to dry on a large plate while Nimai sat on a *mora* reading the newspaper. Hablu sat next to him on the floor with a bowl in his hands.

When Amala, Kartik and Manas came closer and stood in front of her, Malati looked up and adjusted her glasses. She couldn't help shrieking with joy. Amala sat down next to her and the two of them exchanged a warm embrace. As Malati and Kartik looked at each other with a strange curiosity, Amala tapped Kartik on the head and said, 'What are you looking at, *boka chhele*? Touch Malati Mashi's feet—she's our new Ma.'

~

Manas brought out two stools from inside for himself and Kartik to sit across Nimai even as he took out the box of sweets he and Amala bought the previous evening. He held the box before Nimai and broke a small piece for Hablu. The boy delightedly gobbled it and stood up to grab more from the box that had now travelled to Amala's hand for sharing with Malati. Amala could hardly believe her eyes when she saw Hablu hobbling over to where she was, evidently drawn by the sweets. The last time she saw him, he was still crawling.

'When did this happen, Mashi?' Amala asked Malati pointing at Hablu.

'Ha, ha, just a week ago, Ma. I had to bribe him with *batasha*, though,' Malati said, her chortle bringing on a hearty chuckle from Hablu himself.

'*Tai*? That does make Hablu shona deserving of more sweets,' Amala said as she pulled the toddler towards her and fed him a sandesh, bit by bit. His toothy grin suggested he was thrilled at Amala's return.

Urmila had gone to fetch water with Tara and Moyna, Malati told them. This was another surprise for Amala; she had never seen Moyna as much as step out of her house, let alone go to the pond. Malati finished placing the last of the lentil batter into *boris* and hustled inside. Amala lifted a large bag resting next to Manas and followed Malati inside.

During their shopping the evening before, Amala had picked up a wok and a spatula for Malati. She also brought a bottle of mustard oil and some spices for Malati's kitchen.

In the morning, as they walked to the bus stop, Manas suggested buying some fish from a roadside vendor. When Amala took that out, Malati said, 'So you brought your own food and cooking vessel, *haan?*'

'This is from your *jamai*, Mashi. Who am I to say no?' Amala said, inviting a warm smile from Malati.

As the two of them got busy cooking breakfast, Amala told Malati about the incredible story of finding Kartik, about the rented house they had moved into, about how this strange fairytale story of her life made her afraid sometimes. She played down the events that had led to her and Manas's moving to their own space but failed to keep a look of shock from appearing on Malati's face.

'It's all good, Mashi, trust me,' Amala said, as she peeled potatoes on the *bonthhi*.

'As long as you and Maanu Babu are happy,' Malati said.

'Sitting here with you. Nothing gives me more happiness, Mashi.'

'I know, Ma.'

Malati was rolling out *luchis* and Amala stirred a runny potato curry in the pot on the stove when Urmila came into the kitchen. Hablu had followed her and kept muttering, 'Amu Ma there, Amu Ma....'

Urmila put down the jerry cans and said to Malati, 'You put Amu to work, *haan?* Couldn't you wait for me?'

Taken aback at the accusation, Malati could barely form a response. Amala couldn't be more amused at Urmila's show of affection.

'I will scold you now,' Amala said to Urmila. 'Is this not my house? Why would Mashi put me to work?'

Urmila was about to say something when Manas asked, 'How much longer?' from the porch. She bit her tongue and remained quiet.

Over breakfast, when Amala mentioned to Malati their plan
to visit Chitra, Malati said, 'Oh, you don't need to. Chitra Didi
will be here any time now. I forgot to tell you.' Malati told them
how Chitra had been coming in to train the colony women,
filling in for Amala until she returned. Between Tara and her,
they were holding sewing classes four days a week. Malati said
Chitra had initially been reluctant to take up the responsibility.
She agreed only on the condition that Amala would assume the
role whenever she was able to. Amala's eyes misted up. *Mashi
knew what I was going through, still she honoured me by considering
me a teacher.*

Chitra arrived soon with Minoti and Manik. A furious round
of hugs ensued, following which Chitra, Amala, Minoti, Malati
and Urmila proceeded to the school, the venue of the sewing
class. Manas, Kartik and Manik went to spend some time visiting
Ganesh, Paban and Nitai. They would have their own *adda* at
Santu's tea stall.

Manas didn't forget to ask Santu about Noton-da. Santu said
his visits had become less frequent but hadn't stopped altogether.
Paban felt Noton was part of a larger group. He had information
that a big property dealer had his eyes on Bijoy Nagar. The dealer
apparently had the blessings of the zamindar whose land Bijoy
Nagar was built on.

~

The *khichuri* Amala ate for lunch that afternoon tasted extra
special. As Chitra handed over the class's reins to her, Amala
admired the progress the women of Bijoy Nagar had already
made. A few of them had even started working on small batch
orders and were assisting Tara on bigger projects.

When she went back to *Jogajog* the next day, it was as if Amala
had never left. Her spot betrayed not a speck of dust. Overjoyed
at her return, Purnima got sweets, cooked a special lunch for all
staff members and decided to give them half the day off. That

worked out well for Amala as Manas got done at school by 2:30 in the afternoon. They exchanged ideas for spending the evening, maybe a film or a walk by the lake, Manas suggested.

~

A week later, Manas brought a group of his students to Bijoy Nagar. Manas's idea of field trips for the students to refugee colonies had the support of the principal and other school administrators. The boys went around the colony, talking to the residents, mainly the older folks and children, observing social and infrastructural issues and taking notes with the help of their teacher-cum-field guide. Amala saw them doing their rounds from her place in the school where she sat before *her* students at the sewing class.

At the end of their trip, as Manas walked with the boys to the bus stop, his hand on Kartik's shoulder, Amala thought of the long road the two of them still had to walk—helping Urmila stand on her feet to secure Hablu's future, getting Minoti enrolled at a refugee training centre, dealing with the man who tried to molest her, training Bijoy Nagar women....

For now, she focused her eyes and the dreams they held on the two men walking out of her doorstep. Teacher and student, brothers-in-law, father and son—Amala saw all these in Manas and Kartik as the two of them walked hand in hand towards the rickshaw stand.